Praise for *The Yamhill Barber*

"What a frolic it was to read your manuscript, *The Yamhill Barber*. I really enjoyed the story, the individual characters, and the fast-paced ride. The manuscript is comically fun and poignant, yet subtly deals with social, moral, and racial issues. And of course, it has a happily-ever-after ending."

- Carla Perry, author of *Riva Beside Me, Wanderlust* and others

"When young investigative reporter Barney Starr crashes his car into suspicious circumstances in Sweetbread, Oregon, we expect the standard fare of violence and legal hijinks to follow. *The Yamhill Barber* provides instead light-hearted surprise. Quirky characters transform the story into one of community ties and blossoming love. Beyond the unexpected turns in the narrative is the lovely surprise that Barney's youthful exuberance is matched by the writing style and cover art. Being of a piece, they reinforce each other. Bruce Toien has created a novel that will entertain and hearten you, while perhaps educating you about cosmology and the public costs of a too-close relationship between television programming and sponsorship."

- Susan Carol Stone, author of *The Sati Trilogy* and others

THE YAMHILL BARBER

By Bruce Toien

The Yamhill Barber
copyright © Bruce Toien 2019

First Edition

Paperback ISBN: 978-1-945587-38-2
E-book ISBN: 978-1-945587-36-8
Library of Congress Control Number: 2019904951
Bruce Toien
The Yamhill Barber
1. Fiction; 2. Mystery; 3. Oregon; 4. Willamette Valley; 5. Wine
Book design: Dancing Moon Press
Cover design: Dancing Moon Press
Cover Art: Bruce Toien
Manufactured in the United States of America
Dancing Moon Press
www.dancingmoonpress.com

To my dear wife, my partner in life, Gail.

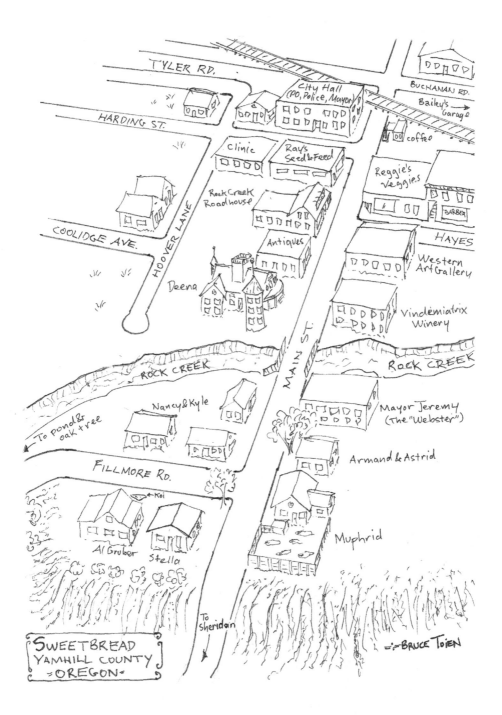

TYLER RD.

City Hall
(PO, Police, Mayor)

BUCHANAN RD.

Bailey's
Garage

HARDING ST.

coffee

Clinic

Ray's
Seed & Feed

Reggie's
Veggies

BARBER

Rock Creek
Roadhouse

HOOVER LANE

COOLIDGE AVE.

Antiques

HAYES

Western
Art Gallery

Deena

Vindémiatrix
Winery

ROCK CREEK

MAIN ST.

ROCK CREEK

Nancy & Kyle

Mayor Jeremy
(The "Webster")

To pond &
oak tree

Armand & Astrid

FILLMORE RD.

Koi

Muphrid

Al Gruber

Stella

To
Sheridan

BRUCE TOIEN

SWEETBREAD
YAMHILL COUNTY
=OREGON=

= CHAPTER 1 =

~ ~ ~

B arney was smiling in spite of himself.

In spite of circumstances, Barney Starr was smiling, smiling broadly and unselfconsciously. Considering the way things went down at the office, the young man should have been angry or, on the other hand, depressed. But no, he was neither angry nor depressed; that simply wasn't possible on this sparkling autumn Saturday, motoring past Oregon farms and vineyards reposing in gin-clear afternoon sunlight, squalls of brilliant fall leaves flying lustily past his windshield. He drew in a deep draft of the clean air rushing past his open window and exhaled with satisfaction.

The cub reporter with shaggy dark hair and a soul patch under his lip looked ahead and saw his destination: a pretty little village coming into view at the top of a rise, a mile distant. The town's vintage white and yellow clapboard houses were nestled snugly under a glorious spread of mature oaks and maples, flaming in oranges, yellows and luminous magentas. Farther away, rising through the background foliage, a slender white church spire pierced the vivid canopy. Somewhere under that same canopy lived a suddenly famous woman who was the subject of his new assignment.

Barney was relieved to be working again, off suspension, back from employment limbo. True, it was not exactly the kind of assignment he wanted, but at least he was back in action. And that was the main reason he was smiling. Smiling even as he gripped the bucking steering wheel of his smoke-belching 1974 Ford Pinto, yanking it this way and that in dubious battle to keep the vehicle tracking straight down the slim country road. Now that he was drawing an income again, maybe he could afford to get that nasty steering problem fixed.

The damaged wheel alignment was his own fault, of course; he couldn't deny that. After a few hard curb-slams rushing to cop an interview with a certain fleeing corporate malefactor, Barney had thoroughly wrecked the little car's steering linkage.

Unfortunately, the one quarry his boss didn't want him pursuing was that particular malefactor: to wit, the daughter of the new CEO.

When Barney first came to the *Portland Mirror* last summer, fresh out of journalism school, the Editor in Chief assigned Barney to the Metro Desk, with the promise of investigative reporting opportunities after he completed his apprenticeship. Consequently, Barney spent the past few months covering dull-as-dishwater city council meetings, budget planning sessions, public works groundbreakings and so forth.

But in his spare time (of which his lack of a personal life afforded him a great deal), he sniffed out a case of embezzlement occurring right under everyone's noses. The trail he bloodhounded led to none other than the new CEO, who had recently acquired the *Portland Mirror* in a hostile takeover, and the man's high-living daughter, who now served as its Chief Financial Officer. As CFO, the young woman lost no time opening a fiscal vein to irrigate her bank accounts and various personal investments. The generous revenue stream afforded her a life of fancy cars, rich men, spendy shoes and high-end designer clothing that she flaunted at lavish parties replete with sex, drugs and rock 'n' roll bands.

When Barney pitched the story to his editor, the reaction was less than enthusiastic: "Are you NUTS!?"

A pause, then, "I'm sorry, let me rephrase that. Are you out of your ever-fucking mind!?" The editor jumped out of his chair and stomped around the office, his eyes bugging out and a fleck of spittle forming in the corner of his mouth. "Maybe you have a death wish, Barney Starr, but I don't! I happen to like my job here at the Mirror and so do the rest of the staff. If you want to do an investigative report on corporate malfeasance involving our CEO's ... *daughter*" (he nearly choked on that word) "you should by all means pursue it—in someone else's employ!"

He stopped and stared at Barney. "I seriously wonder if you don't have a few screws loose in that mop-headed noggin of yours. Jeez-us! I want you to take the rest of the week off while I—no, strike that. You're on suspension until I can figure out what to do with you."

Man, that stung.

After three weeks, his editor offered him a second chance, covering non-controversial human-interest stories. In particular, Barney would be telling the story of the celebrity woman who lived in the charming wine country village up ahead. Harmless fluff, in other words.

Big whoop. So much for support. Especially considering the same editor's original welcome-aboard words, "We consider our staff to be family here at the *Portland Mirror*, Barney. Know that we've got your back at all times." Ha! Some family. And upon readmission to this so-called family, he was now supposed to accept his humiliating demotion with gratitude.

Well, it might have been worse. They could have fired him, right? So, lemons to lemonade, he'd make the best of the situation.

And it was that upbeat attitude that enabled him to so quickly regain his equanimity after the brouhaha. He was the kind of guy who took life's knocks in stride. At least that's what he liked to imagine... Truth be told, exiting the parking structure that unhappy day three weeks ago at thirty-five miles an hour suggested otherwise. A fortuitous bank shot off the concrete island managed to quench his speed before he launched out onto Columbia Street. But the violent blow to the front wheel was the final insult to the car's front-end alignment.

Now, in an altogether fair tit-for-tat, the car was bent on killing him at every opportunity. It insisted on nosing off the road whenever his vigilance flagged.

As if fighting to keep the car on the road were not enough of a challenge, Barney was doing it while holding up at eye level a crumpled scrap of paper with the name of the woman he was to interview and her address scrawled underneath. He squinted to make out the address. It said something about Main Street but he didn't have time to examine the house number, because the grade steepened and he was forced to press the meat of his note-holding hand onto the manual transmission lever to downshift while his feet worked the clutch and gas.

The engine labored as the car climbed the hill. An official green Oregon Department of Transportation sign loomed into view with white block lettering, "Entering Sweetbread, Oregon / Population 1123."

Just beyond the ODOT sign, sitting on a granite plinth, appeared a more stylish greeting, undoubtedly funded by the local chamber of commerce. Within an asymmetric frame of rough-cut wood, in a field of sky blue, these words appeared: "Welcome to Sweetbread! The town that feels like nowhere else!" The word "else" was nearly obliterated by matching sky blue paint, presumably the work of vandals. Barney cracked an appreciative grin at the resulting truncated slogan.

Up ahead, in the drainage ditch that ran adjacent to the road, lay a house painter's brush and an overturned can of—well, what do you know?—sky blue paint!

A speed limit sign came into view. "25 mph." As he slowed, Barney glanced into the rearview mirror. He saw no one behind him, just his own friendly face: smooth pale mocha complexion and endearing dimples, courtesy of his Filipino mother; that indie soul patch under his lip; and a simple silver earring dangling from one pierced earlobe. He winked at himself. "You go, boy!"

Rolling into the hilltop hamlet, the overarching trees showered the windshield with an artist's palette of leaves that his car was too slow now to shed. Instinctively, he hit the windshield wiper wand. *What a great idea! he thought, You rock, dude! Those fools back at the office didn't know what they missed out on when they benched you for three weeks. Well, who knows, this may turn into an unexpected opportunity. Just like what happened with that journalism class you grudgingly took in college when you were a computer science major—the course that of course changed the course of your life.* He savored this cleverly crafted sentence.

After a moment's reflection, he sighed, slumping back into self-pity.

Aw, who am I kidding? This is a crappy assignment for a guy aspiring to be an investigative reporter. My career is veering off the road like my car—keeps— oof!—doing. He yanked the steering wheel and the Pinto wobbled back into line. *One screw-up on the job and now I'm on the human-interest beat, covering a story of some fat lady who's enjoying fifteen minutes of fame for making trendy desserts. It's an insult. That's all there is to it.*

Deena Poole, the "diva of deep-fried desserts," had emerged from the obscurity of this rural Yamhill County town to become the darling of obesity-bound America. A sweet deal for Deena and her sponsors; not so much for public health.

That's it! A fresh angle to the story struck him like a bolt and immediately lifted his spirits again: *Let's see what's really behind this dessert queen's meteoric rise to fame. Yeah! How about an investigative dimension to this story? I mean, the "up close and personal" part will be there, of course, but broader issues*

12

of health can be examined as well, right? At least touched upon. Intimated. What about her sponsors, her corporate connections? That's the ticket! She has no financial connections to the Mirror, so I'm safe on that score.

He thumped the dashboard triumphantly. *Yep, I'll show them what I'm capable of! I'm going to boost the* PM's *readership in spite of my editor's cravenness.* He chuckled, self-satisfied. His roller coaster mood rose giddily.

A couple of houses appeared as he came over the crest of the hill—yellow clapboard on the left, Craftsman on the right.

Meanwhile, his windshield wiper idea was working like a charm. The glass had cleared of leaves almost instantly and stayed clear—except for the annoying pink one that remained stuck under the wiper blade. Looking at the pink leaf sliding left and right, his expression soured. "Oh, that's irritating!" As it turned out, the pink leaf was not a leaf at all; it was a weathered parking ticket. It kept arcing side to side in front of his face like a taunt. Side to side, swish, swish.

Suddenly, an idea occurred to him. Man, he was on fire with great ideas today! He cranked down the window and stretched his hand around the pillar to grab the ticket the moment it reached the limit of its arc. Here it came...

Swish. Slap! Nope.

Swish. Slap! Nope.

Swish. Slap! Got it! "Yes! Woo-hoo!" he bellowed euphorically.

And then all hell broke loose.

~ ~ ~

"Son-of-a-bitch!"

The wayward car nosed off the road and plunged Wover the shoulder into the shallow drainage ditch running alongside. Initially, the front end dove down like a rodeo bronco dropping its head just before violently bucking out of said ditch smack into the cedar plank fence of the first house on the right, bashing open a large breach before coming to rest.

In an instant, everything went quiet except for the creaking sounds emanating from the cooling engine and the wind soughing through the plum tree overhead. Barney hung his head. "Aw shhhhhh...iiitt." He exhaled forlornly, stared at his lap, breathing, just breathing. And thinking. A messy plum pit fell out of the tree, bonked the hood and stuck there in its goo. A crow cawed once and flew away. And of course more of those damned autumn leaves came fluttering down from nearby trees, littering his windshield. He gritted his teeth.

"You OK there, friend?"

"Whoa!" He looked up abruptly and saw, suddenly materialized at his driver side window, a pale man with a goofy lopsided grin and—what the heck was that hanging from his belt?—a child's stuffed animal? That was kind of odd.

Barney cranked the window the rest of the way down and addressed the man. "Huh? Sorry?"

"I said, are you OK there?"

"Yeah, yeah, I'm fine. I suppose I'm fine. Um, is that your fence?"

The man nodded.

"Sorry about that. Really sorry. Hang on a minute, let me see if I can pull this thing back out..." He fired up the engine, threw the gearshift into reverse and tried to back the car up onto the road. He managed to extract the car's crumpled fender from the fence but he didn't get much farther than that. Once the front wheels dropped into the drainage depression, the mid-chassis bottomed out on the lip of the road, lifting the rear wheels uselessly off the pavement like the lighter kid on a teeter totter kicking his legs impotently in the breeze. The engine revved furiously as the rear wheels spun wildly in the air, to no effect. He was stuck.

"Ah, fuck me, I can't catch a break!" Barney clunked his head down on the steering wheel, which honked the horn. Startled, he jerked his head up and found himself staring straight ahead through the splintery gaping hole in the fence at something rather unusual for this time of year when everything else was dead, dying or hibernating: he saw lush green grass growing on large low mounds of earth. He frowned.

"Busted yer buggy pretty good there, dintchya!? What happened?" said the man.

Barney did not answer.

"Listen, friend, that's my pickup there in the carport. I'll grab a tow-strap and getchya hauled outta here in a jiffy."

There was a commotion among a group of onlookers across the street at a lawn party. Someone called out an offer of help, but the pasty-faced man with the goofy grin and ursine plush toy on his belt waved them off, "Got it under control!"

The man disappeared around the left end of the fence, but instead of proceeding to the carport, he entered the yard through a side gate that creaked open and slammed shut with a click of the latch. While the man rummaged around in an unseen shed, Barney got out of the car and peered through the breach. He was alarmed by what he saw. There, before him in the man's yard, was a freshly dug cavity about three feet wide and extending some seven feet away from him. The bottom was too deep to be seen from Barney's vantage point. However, if he had been able to get a little nearer, he would have seen the end of an oblong box. But the fence prevented that observation. Adjacent to the excavation was a large mound of fresh red earth. A shovel stood erect, its blade planted deep into the soft mound.

He swatted a fly and others came. There was a fetid smell. Something was rotting.

Nearby, Barney observed another mound of earth, but that one was low-domed and planted over with new grass. Beyond that, he saw another low-domed mound. It too was covered with grass, albeit taller and more lush and tender green. Across the yard, all the grass was sprinkled with colorful fallen leaves. It was rather pretty. He pushed his head through the hole in the fence to see if there were any more mounds but jumped back when he saw something coming his way.

Shhhrrruffff! Scrrrape!

The man dragged a four-by-eight-foot sheet of plywood up to the edge of the breach.

"Gotta get this hole covered first!" he announced loudly.

The man pushed and kicked the splayed cedar pales back into place then pulled the plywood across, like a sliding door, occluding Barney's view of the yard.

Bang! Bang! Bang!

Hammer blows drove a big galvanized nail into the plywood and violently out through the cedar pale that Barney was standing near. He leapt back and must have yelped because the man called out apologetically, "Sorry, friend, dint mean to startle ya!"

Barney caught his breath and said, "'Sokay. Whew!"

More nails came through, one below the other, down the length of the cedar pale.

"Gotta keep out the vermin."

"Vermin?"

"Yeah, you know: marauding dogs, raccoons...certain chil-dern." The man paused and drove another nail. "Don't want the little thieves snoopin' around."

After a moment's silence, the man began driving nails up and down the cedar pale on the other side of the breach. When he finished, there were five long nails arranged vertically on each side. They looked to Barney like devil's claws reaching through the wood at him.

He involuntarily stepped back and nearly stumbled into the drainage ditch.

~ ~ ~

When the man came around, he commented, "Saw you lookin' through the hole at mah yard..."

"Yeah, well—"

"'Snot what it looks like," the man said without smiling. "'Snot where I keep the bodies." He paused. Then his face brightened. "Ha ha! Naw, jest kiddin' ya. I'm plantin' trees. Two of 'em. Need a big hole for 'em, ya know?"

"Must be big trees. That's a pretty damned deep hole there!"

The man explained that the ground here was full of large rocks. You have to dig deep to get them out.

"Hmmm," Barney hummed. "So what are the other mounds?"

The man seemed discomfited. "Hm?"

"The other mounds, across your yard," Barney said.

The man stared into Barney's eyes, pushed his tongue into his cheek, working his jaw side to side, thinking, then said simply, "Oh, them! Gophers."

"Gophers!?" Barney frowned. "C'mon!"

A shadow crossed the man's countenance. "Yeah, that's what it is, all right. Gophers."

"Pretty big mounds for—"

"GIANT gophers, I'm tellin' ya! Monsters. They come out after dark, ya know. Dangerous to be wandering around here at night!" The man winked admonishingly without smiling.

Barney shuddered. He felt the blood drain from his face. This was getting surreal.

Suddenly, the man's face lit up. He burst out laughing, "Jai-normous gophers! Hahahaha!"

The blood came back to Barney's face. "Oh—ha ha ha."

The man clapped Barney's shoulder. "Hey, ya look like you just seen a ghost! Was just joshin' ya. Flower beds is what they are."

"Don't see many flowers there."

"Cover crop of grass. It's fall ya know. I'll get 'round to plantin' in the spring." The man reflected a moment then added, "Daisies, I figure. Plan to be pushin' up daisies next year! Hahaha!"

Barney forced a grin.

The man said, "Don't go nowhere, friend. I'll go get yer tow strap now. Gonna git you taken care of in a jiffy." He thumped the fence boards twice for emphasis.

Then the man disappeared around the left corner of the high cedar fence again, the side gate squeaked again and there was rummaging in the unseen shed again. Barney walked to the end of the fence to peer around the corner. At that moment, the gate swung open and the man reemerged with the promised tow-strap, that is to say, a length of super-strong yellow nylon webbing with a burly steel buckle on each end. He tossed it in the bed of his pickup and backed the truck onto the street, swinging widely until the two vehicles were positioned rear end to rear end. He fastened one buckle of the tow-strap to the chassis under the Pinto's bumper and the other buckle to his truck. With roaring engine, he eased out the clutch and pulled slowly and gently. The tow strap grew taut and began to strain. The car shuddered, then lurched free, allowing itself to be dragged backwards onto the shoulder of the roadway that, here within the town limits, was officially designated as "Main Street" by the signpost rising out of the laurel hedge at the corner of the man's property.

After unhooking the Pinto, the man drove his truck back under the shelter of the carport while Barney fired up his motor and tried to pull forward. There was a horrible scraping sound from the vicinity of the collapsed fender so he killed the engine and jumped out to investigate. The fender was bent inward so deeply it was scoring the tire. Not good.

By now, the man was back, looking sadly at the stoved-in grille and crushed fender, shaking his head. "There's a feller in town that can fix that for ya. Name's Bailey. Dorgan Bailey. His shop closed up at noon today. I'll call him Monday morning to send a tow truck. So where were you headed today, friend?"

"Here, actually."

"Here?"

"Sweetbread, I mean."

"That right? You visitin' someone?"

"Sort of."

"So ya got a place to stay tonight, then?"

Barney fidgeted. "Well, no. I mean, actually I was going to find a motel..."

"No motels here! Only lodging in Sweetbread is the Rock Creek Inn an' that's all booked up, far as I know. 'No room at the inn' as they say! Goshgolly, I don't know of no motels, hotels, what have you, anywheres near here. Maybe Sheridan."

There was a gaily colored polka dot butterfly bandage on the man's cheek. Must have cut himself shaving. Sure enough, there was a straight razor and pair of scissors in the man's hip pocket. Barney grimaced, *Who walks around with a straight razor in his pocket?*

The man noted Barney's alarm and looked down at the sharp implements sticking out of his pocket. He laughed, "I'm the town barber! Tools of the trade!" He rubbed his soft white face thoughtfully and in so doing felt the little bandage on his cheek. "Ha! An' I cut muh-self shaving this morning! Ain't that a hoot? Me being a barber and all? Never cut nobody else though."

The man cast a look at the young reporter like a collector examining a rare moth he'd like to add to his collection. Barney felt a frisson tingling up and down the back of his neck. "Say, young man, you're a little scruffy around the ears, you could use a shave and a haircut..."

Barney shook his head wildly and jumped back, "I'm fine!"

"Don't worry, friend, I don't bite! Nor cut nobody but muh-self, ha ha!" His eyes drooped and a languid smile crept up one side of his face. "Listen, friend, if you need somewheres to lay your head, you're welcome to stay at my place—"

"No!" Barney exclaimed, startled by his own startling, then quickly backpedaled. "I mean, 'no thank you.'"

"Easy there, young fella! Yer wound pretty tight, ainchya! Guess it's understandable, all things considered, what with yer car an' all. But don't you worry, you're in good hands. Dorgan'll get yer car all fixed up, don't you worry. Now if ya need a place to stay—"

"No, no. I appreciate the kind offer but—I WAS going to stay at a motel but I have uh-uh friend here who'll put me up if I need it," he lied.

18

"Oh! Goshgolly, that's terrific! Who's that? We all know one another 'round here, ya know. Is it, oh, I'll bet it's—"

~ ~ ~

"Hey, Muphrid! Are ya coming to my barbecue party?" The words came from a tawny-blond ponytailed young woman in stretch jeans (stylishly cuffed at mid-calf) standing across the street in her front yard near a portable grill and surrounded by a bustling lawn party. Although the mornings were chilly around here, these recent days had been pleasantly warm, a kind of Indian summer—the perfect last chance to be outside with friends, family and neighbors before winter's cold and rain shut things down. She looked at Barney with an appreciative smile and added quickly to the man she addressed as Muphrid, "Your cute friend's invited too!"

Muphrid shook his head and waved her off. In an aside to Barney he said, "That's Stella. She's the party girl around here. Go ahead if you like. She's got uh extra room too. Say, I didn't catch yer name, friend."

"Oh, I'm sorry! Barnard Starr. I go by Barney."

"Pleased to meet you, Barney!" The man reached out to shake Barney's hand. "My name is Muphrid. Muphrid Thatcher. Heh, your name is Starr and I'm named after a star too! Not that the name ever helped much. Never was a star at nothin'. 'Cept, I guess you could say I'm the star barber in town." He massaged his soft white face and added, "ONLY barber in town, actually! That counts for something, I suppose. Heheh! Barber is as barber does! Heheh!"

Barney wondered if that meant anything at all.

Muphrid pulled a business card out of his pocket, "Here's mah card."

"You're the 'Yamhill Barber', eh?" Barney looked askance. "Does that mean you serve the whole county?"

"Naw. Yamhill town. 'Swhere I started. Moved to Sweetbread fifteen years back, kept the name."

Barney nodded, "Uh-huh. I see."

"So...what brings you to Sweetbread, Barney?"

"Doing a story. I'm a junior reporter with the *Portland Mirror*." He paused when he saw Muphrid furrow his brow. The man looked concerned, so Barney added quickly, "Nothing bad, don't worry! Nothing bad. Human-interest, that's all. I'm here to do a three-part series on your town's resident celebrity, name of—"

"Deena! Gotta be Deena. Am I right?"

"Yep. Deena Poole. Diva of deep-fried desserts."

Muphrid nodded, "Ya got that almost right. It's *'Deena Poole, diva of deep-fried desserts to die for!'* That's the whole thing. How she says it on her TV show every week."

From across the street, the girl called again, "So Muphrid, your friend wanna come or not?" A couple of people near her echoed the question and beckoned to the young man with the silver earring and soul patch standing next to the middle-aged man with the stuffed bear on his belt and straight razor in his hip pocket.

Barney looked up. "Sure! I'll be right over!"

Stella, the young woman with the tawny blond ponytail said, "Right over?"

"Right over."

"OK." She smiled archly. "I hold people to their promises, you know. Just fair warning!" She gave him a comically exaggerated wink and turned back to her guests.

"Duly warned." He wasn't quite done with Muphrid. "So, can I ask you one more thing, Muphrid?"

The man shrugged, "Shoot."

"What's the stuffed animal on your belt for?"

The man lifted it up for inspection as if to confirm that Barney meant this particular stuffed animal and not some other. "This one? This here is a Beanie Baby! Found a bunch of 'em lying around the house when I moved back in last year. My tenant died and left me all his stuff. Had a collection o' these critters. Funny fellow."

Looks who's talking, Barney thought.

"Must've really liked 'em. There was a dozen of 'em stashed here an' there in closets and nooks an' crannies. Me, I got no use for 'em, so I gave 'em all away, 'cept this one. I like to wear it, sorta like a talisman. To ward off evil, ya know?"

"Is there evil around here?"

"No, no! But just in case," he gave Barney a devilish look, "I'm prepared!"

Barney nodded agreeably if a little queasily. Looking at the wrecked fence, he said, "Look, Muphrid, I want cover the damages to your fence. Let me—"

"No need, my little friend. I can take care of it. It's not as bad as it looks."

"Oh, you've got to let me help. I mean, I show up and the first I do is smash your fence, you help me out and I'm such a space cadet I forget to even thank you for that. No, just tell me what the bill is and I'll reimburse you one hundred percent. One hundred percent!" He handed the man his business card, wondering if providing so much information to this strange man was such a good idea. "Just send the bill to my attention at the *Portland Mirror.*"

"I'm tellin' you, don't worry about it, Barney-boy. I can fix that hole in a jiffy. You got a bigger problem than me—the car I mean. You ain't goin' nowhere till you get that fender bent back. Hey, here comes Stella again. She's lookin' at you. Don't make her call you a third time."

There she was, standing at the opposite curb with her arms crossed, glaring across the street at the two of them, tapping her toe impatiently. Barney waved at her and grinned.

"Well, I guess I'd better get going then, Muphrid. And by the way, thank you for your help. Thank you so much!"

"Oh, think nothing of it. All in a day's work!"

Barney started to turn away, then stopped like the TV detective Columbo. He even raised his index finger like the TV detective Columbo always did and said sweetly, "Uh, just one more question..."

The older man said, "Yes?"

"What's the deal with all that healthy green grass? I mean, everything else is brown and dead this time of year, but your grass is vibrant. Like it's springtime or something."

"I'm a good gardener, I guess. Not much to it. Just water, good soil and good... fertilizer. "

"What kind?"

"What kind of what?"

"What kind of fertilizer?"

"Oh," Muphrid winked. "That's a trade secret. Hey, young man, are you going to turn down an invitation from a pretty girl, huh? Stella's waitin' there for ya. You'd better go on over to her party. You'll like her. She's a real live wire!"

"Are you coming too?"

"Naw. Gotta finish fixin' the fence!"

"I'm telling you, Muphrid, I can take care of it."

"And I'm telling you, it's OK. Now, go. Git!"

"OK, OK." Barney felt his pockets. "Hang on a sec." The young man scurried over to his crumpled car and tried to open the trunk (it was jammed). He went around and tried to roll up the driver's side window in case it rained (it didn't budge), grabbed his cell phone (it had flown onto the floor mat), tried to lock the doors (they were jammed too, oh well what did it matter with the window open?) and pulled that scrap of paper from the plush folds of his rumpled velour seat cover. Then he trotted back.

Close but not too close to the man, Barney held up his pencil-scrawled scrap. "This is the address where I'm supposed to go to meet Deena." He reached the scrap to Muphrid who pushed it aside and simply pointed. "She's right there, friend. In the double-wide lawn chair." Sure enough, in Stella's front yard, sitting in a sturdy, oversize lawn chair, was the woman herself, chatting with a group of people gathered around her. The big, vivacious woman broke off her conversation momentarily to wave cheerily to Barney and flash him an expansive smile. He waved back. She beckoned him to come over. "There's your dessert lady. No hurry though, she ain't goin' nowhere. She's what you call anchored to that spot."

"And where is her actual residence? This address?" he held up the scrap again.

Muphrid swept his hand up the street toward a red and pink Victorian house adorned with curlicued bargeboards. "The pink house with the frilly shit. Now go on over an' introduce yerself! You're a nice fella and I appreciate the company, but yer startin' to get a little clingy. You ain't shy, are ya? Naw, yer a reporter, you can't be shy. Go on, now! Git!" He shooed the younger man across the street.

At long last, Barney crossed Main Street. Stepping over the double yellow line at the crown of the road, a strange feeling came over him that he was, in some unforeseeable way, crossing a river, a Rubicon, from which there would be no return to the life he'd known so far.

= CHAPTER 2 =

~ ~ ~

"Well, I thought you'd never leave ol' Muphrid's side!" Stella chided Barney when he arrived.

Barney smiled bashfully.

"I'm Stella," she reached out her hand. "What's your name, cutie?"

"Barney. Barney Starr. I'm a reporter from the *Portland Mirror*. I'm out here to interview Deena Poole." He looked across the lawn to where Deena was sitting. The big lady looked up and beckoned him cheerily to come over. He held up five fingers, winked and turned his attention back to Stella. "Deena's the subject of my human-interest story."

"Oh, we all know that! We heard you were coming."

"Wow, news travels fast."

"Yep, we're a small town. Secrets don't last long here." She suddenly opened her arms, "Welcome to Sweetbread!"

"Thank you."

"So what's your poison, Barney Starr? We got all kindsa beer in the cooler: Bud Light, Natural Light, Miller's Original Lite, Coors Light, Light Light, non-alcoholic Diet Rite, Sprite and of course..." she reached for a bottle lying on the grass next to the cooler, "...tequila!" She jerked it away, shaking a finger at him. "For later!"

Barney looked into her gleaming blue eyes. She was a live wire, all right. He glanced over to the doublewide lawn chair. He needed not hurry. Deena would wait for him; she was indeed anchored to the spot, just like Muphrid said, but due less to gravity than gregariousness, in animated conversation with the half-dozen people circled around her. "The plan is for me to interview her tomorrow, but I was hoping to swing by for a quick

23

hello this afternoon. Instead, I crashed my car."

"Yep, you came in with a real bang! Ha ha!" She pulled out two bottles, extending one to her new friend. "How 'bout a Miller, that OK with you? There you go! That's a twist-off cap, by the way."

They clinked bottles.

"So you're a real big city reporter, huh?"

"Yeah, I suppose you could say that."

"Must be exciting!"

"It's not as glamorous as it sounds."

"Ha! Almost anything is glamorous compared to this town. As we like to say, 'The town that feels like nowhere!'"

Barney chuckled, took a sip of beer and said, "It doesn't seem so bad. Anyway, as you know, I met your neighbor Muphrid..."

"We saw that too. Ol' Muphrid!" She laughed. "Looks like he got you out of that ditch. What'd you think of 'im?"

"Well, he seems a little, um—"

"Odd?"

"Well, yes."

"He's definitely different. Gotta a good heart though. Wouldn't hurt a fly."

"Really. Hm. You know he carries a straight razor and a Beanie Baby on his belt?

She laughed, "I know, he's got his quirks, but that's our Muphrid."

Evening was coming on. Barney looked up at the little white twinkly lights strung overhead along the branches of Stella's sweet gum tree, trying to think of how to phrase his next question—about the mounds—when he spied a Beanie Baby wedged into a crook, peering down at him. He frowned, bemused.

Observing his reaction, she said, "Oh, the guy who use to rent Muphrid's house collected Beanie Babies. Then a neighbor kid broke in and stole a bunch of 'em and handed 'em out, Robin Hood style. They're kinda like our town mascots now—the Beanie Babies, I mean."

Barney shook his head. "Didn't the renter try to get them back?"

"He wanted to, but most of them went to children, so the renter—an Indian, East Indian, guy named PK—was too embarrassed to push the issue." She fell quiet for a moment. "Then PK left town and never came back—'cause he died—so Muphrid moved back into the house."

"From where? Where was he living before?"

"Muphrid? He was living with his mother, in the apartment over the barbershop."

"Hm." It seemed a perfect time for Barney to at last get to his burning question. "All right, since we're on the subject of Muphrid, what's the deal with those mounds in his—?"

Just then a big, friendly looking, pear-shaped man with a goatee and shaved head came over and shook Barney's hand. "I see you've met my little cousin, Stella. Are you the reporter from the *Portland Mirror*?"

"Yep. Barney Starr. I'm here to—" Stella jumped in and gave her cousin the lowdown on the new arrival.

The cousin spoke expansively, as if Barney were a visiting dignitary. "Well, welcome to Sweetbread, Barnaby! We been eagerly anticipating your arrival!"

"Well, thank you. By the way, it's Barney."

"Of course—Barney! My bad! My hearing's not good with background noise these days. Age, you know." The man didn't seem that old—forty, tops—though he was leaning on a cane, probably because of his excess weight. Or maybe he was diabetic. As for background noise, there was music coming out of the portable Bose sound system set up on a shaky card table and there were people talking in their elevated party voices, but as parties go, it was not exceptionally loud. Oh well. The man continued, "Deena's looking forward to talking to you. By the way, my name is Jeremy. Jeremy Gervais." They shook hands. Jeremy revealed himself to be the local web designer and mayor.

Cousin Stella jumped in again. "I do clerical and bookkeeping work for Jeremy on Mondays, Tuesdays and Fridays. Other days, I'm waitressing at the Rock Creek Roadhouse. Best pancakes in Yamhill County! Extra thick! Listen, I'll let you two talk." She winked and went off to attend to the other guests.

Before the two men could utter another word, a sturdily build woman with short cropped hair approached and shook Barney's hand. "So you're the big-town reporter!"

He introduced himself again, concluding with, "And you are?"

"I'm Nancy Lautenberg, Sweetbread's entire police department! You might say I work for Jeremy too—report to him at least."

Jeremy laughed, "It's been a long-term relationship. I can fire her if she gets out of line, but she can arrest me on a whim, so we're kinda even!"

"That's my idea of keeping the peace," she added with a wicked smile. "By the way, I live right over there, across the street. The house with the dead flower garden." She pointed casually to a small wood frame house across the side street, called Fillmore, that led away from its tee intersection with Main. The policewoman's house was fronted with a neatly trimmed "blond" lawn and a berm covered in gone-to-seed petunias.

The berm got Barney to thinking. "OK, if anybody in this town is in the know, you two are. I have to ask you, what's the deal with the mounds in Muphrid's yard?"

Jeremy shrugged, "Mounds? Never been back there myself. Could be some sort of landscaping thing."

Barney looked skeptical and turned to Nancy who ventured an explanation. "I've seen his yard. Yeah, it's a pretty bumpy lawn back there. It's those—whatchyacallit—glacial erratic rocks."

"Huh?"

"Can you explain it, Jeremy? You're the scientist around here."

Jeremy shrugged off the compliment, offered simply, "It's kind of an interesting story, Barnaby. During the last Ice Age, an ice dam up near Missoula backed up a lake half the size of Lake Erie. One day the dam burst and sent a monster flood down into Oregon. I'm talkin' a flood of biblical proportions. Brought along with it a bunch of icebergs full of boulders and dropped 'em all over the Willamette Valley, right up to the four-hundred-foot elevation line in the foothills where we're standing right now. Over time, they got covered with soil. So now we got a bunch of grassy humps. Most of the folks along the edge of this hill have 'em."

"Yep, that's what it is," Nancy confirmed. "See my berm across the street, the one with the dead petunias? There's a glacial rock under that. Soil's super-thin on top, that's why my flowers are so pathetic."

Barney rubbed his chin, "Interesting. But—"

"Hey, you the reporter dude?" This time it was a scrawny guy with a long neck and a peak of curly hair that made his head look like an asparagus tip. Mayor Jeremy and Officer Nancy wandered off, discussing why it took her so long to get around to deadheading her petunias. Asparagus Tip introduced himself, "I'm Reggie. Reggie Reid. I run the grocery store, 'Reggie's Veggies'. Ahaha! Get it? How long you gonna be in Sweetbread? You gonna interview Deena? What're you gonna ask her about? Did she know you're coming?"

From a few feet away, Stella flashed Barney a sympathetic grin.

And so it went, every few minutes another partier would come around and make an introduction, excited to meet the big town reporter. All except for the two teenagers sitting in folding beach chairs near the sidewalk: a young man with a thatch of black hair and his dark-haired girlfriend with creamy complexion. The two of them sat by themselves looking profoundly bored. She had a silver nose ring and wore thick black mascara. So did he. Both were dressed in Goth black. He had sky blue paint on his hands. The girl had a smudge of the same sky blue paint over one of her eyebrows, right where she had another piercing. Both were busily poking at their iPhone screens, completely absorbed.

Stella reappeared at Barney's side, leaned in close and said softly in his ear, "That's Zach and his girlfriend Nadia."

The girl, Nadia, casually looked up at Barney and did something that seemed almost bizarre under the circumstances: she smiled sweetly at him. Then she turned her attention back to her iPhone business.

"Nadia's folks own the winery so they aren't so keen about her dating Zach, 'cause he works at the auto repair shop."

"Old story, huh?" He reflected a moment. "Auto repair shop? Would that be Dorgan Bailey's place?"

"Yeah, that's right. How'd you know that?" She looked across the street at his disabled car, near which Muphrid was wrestling with splayed fence boards in the gloaming. "Oh, duh! Of course! Guess you'll be headin' over to Dorgan's come Monday morning, huh? You got somewhere to stay till then?"

He looked over his shoulder. "I've got a blanket in my car. The seats fold back pretty far. Your neighbor Muphrid offered me his place. But, frankly..." Barney looked down and studied the laces of his square-laced Keen shoes, "...there are things about him that make me kind of uneasy. I think I'd just as soon sleep in my car. He's probably a decent guy and all, but—"

"Yeah, no, he is a little peculiar, no doubt about that. I don't blame you. But he's harmless. Still I don't blame you!"

"It's just that..."

"No, no! That settles it! Mr. Barnard Starr, get ready for your new travel plan. I got a real nice sofa bed in my living room. And it comes with a kitchen and bathroom, car magazines, TV and the most dee-lightful company you'll ever want to know! And I've got extra blankets if you need 'em."

"Really? Are you sure?"

"Of course! I have lots of blankets. I've had 'em for years!" she said with a sly eye.

"No, not the blankets, I mean, I mean...you know what I mean! So...it's OK if I uh—it wouldn't be too much trouble for you to—uh—"

She pinched his dimpled cheek. "You're lousy with the false modesty, Mr. Big Town Reporter. Of course it's OK, that's why I said it! Look, if it makes you feel better, let me double check with the management." She turned sideways and said, "Stella, is it OK if this nice man spends the night on my sofa?" Then she pivoted around and faced the other way, "Why yes, Stella, of course it is!" Then she pivoted back again, "Are you sure?" And turned one more time, "Of course I'm sure!" She looked Barney in the eye, laughed and gave him a squeeze. "So there ya go, Barney. I checked it out with the management and she's OK with it. Case closed. It's settled!"

"OK, then, that's great. That's really nice of you. Thank you!"

Now a bowtied man of patrician aspect, hairline receding at the temples and wire rim spectacles resting on his thin nose came up and shook Barney's hand. His name was Robert Vandershur. He and his wife Callista (who was just now setting out some bottles of wine on the folding buffet table already groaning under the weight of food dishes) owned the local winery, which was called Vindemiatrix. They were the ones Stella mentioned, the parents of the Goth styled teenager, Nadia, texting in her beach chair by the sidewalk. They were the parents who disapproved of her Goth boyfriend, Zach, the teenager sitting sullenly in the beach chair next to hers.

The Vandershurs' Vindemiatrix Winery was a lifeline for this town, for it was the one attraction that reliably drew tourists—and hence business, lots of it—into this otherwise rural backwater burg.

Robert had barely said a word when he was interrupted by a text message. He muttered, "It's my son. Going to be late as usual." Robert excused himself and went over to tell his wife.

Stella explained that the Vandershurs' adolescent son, Aidan—Nadia's fraternal twin brother—was always late, but could be counted on to show up for dessert. From there, Stella launched into a story about how, when she was a similar age to the twins, she was so late to her own sweet six-teen birthday party that the cake was half gone by the time she arrived and her parents were really mad but they forgave her when it turned out she'd been with high school friends driving around Yamhill County's wine country and everybody was drunk but her, and, and, and...

Barney tuned out, but in spite of his lack of interest in her rambling story, he couldn't imagine anything he'd rather do than be here with Stella, hearing about people he'd never met and all manner of details about her personal life he wasn't sure he should be privy to. Well, what the heck! It was pure delight just listening to her voice and drinking in her cowgirl prettiness—from her snug jeans to her fresh-pressed, brown-checked cot-ton blouse and her bouncing ponytail. And the tattoo on her ankle with the curlicue script that said, "Love is a...", followed by a rendering of a lone rose.

After a while, he touched her arm lightly and said, "Listen, Stella, I need to go introduce myself to Deena." Deena was the only member of the party who wasn't likely to get up and come over to Barney, so it was up to him to go to her. The irony occurred to him that Stella was like a dessert he wanted more of and the dessert lady was like a plate of broccoli he had to eat first. "I'll be back in bit..."

"Not a problem, Barn. Anyway, it's time for me to put some fish on the barbie."

"Fish? I thought you were making burgers?"

"Oh those too. But this is a kind of surprise treat."

"Cool! Well, I'm generally a vegetarian these days, but I do eat fish from time to time."

"Well, Barney, you're in luck tonight, 'cause I'm serving up some real special fish."

"What kind?"

She grinned, "High-class fish. Gourmet!"

He was puzzled. "High-class? What kind of fish is that...?"

Smiling slyly, she arched one eyebrow, spun on her heel and headed for her front porch. Barney shrugged, turned to walk across the lawn to Deena and nearly fell on his face. An Irish setter with a black patch over one eye had trotted right in front of his knees. "Ooofff!" he bent over the dog, bracing himself on the dog's spine. Mayor Jeremy leaned back in his folding chair and guffawed, "That's Rogerdog, our pirate canine! Don't mind him, he doesn't navigate so well since he got his eye shot out. No depth perception..."

The moment Barney lifted his hands away, the dog bolted and a moment later there was a noisy crash of utensils onto the lawn, followed by a string of expletives and Rogerdog looking very, very guilty.

"Like I said, no depth perception!"

On her front doorstep, Stella turned and announced that she had to go into the house to get the fish for the main course, but in the meantime, everyone should feel free to munch on the food that others had brought. The affair was the usual potluck potpourri—potato salad, coleslaw, cheese nachos, dips and chips, homemade bread, casseroles, et cetera, all laid out on folding tables. And of course there were stacks of burgers waiting to be barbecued. But no sweets of any kind, for that was Deena's domain!

Barney had just caught Deena's attention when the big woman looked straight past him, covered her mouth and started laughing nervously.

He spun around and could hardly believe his eyes.

~ ~ ~

Stella had reemerged from her house with a scuba diver's spear gun. With her jaw set, she kicked the screen door open and marched across the lawn toward the planted border between her driveway and the neighbor's yard. The spear was three pronged, a trident. A black rubber hose extended from its tail end to a wrist loop. Her hand gripped the shaft to keep the rubber hose stretched deadly taut. It was cocked and ready to fire, in other words. Everyone at the party fell silent and watched, waiting to witness whatever havoc was about to be unleashed. No one made a sound except for one man who chuckled nervously, "What's Stella up to this time?" The determined young woman crossed her grassy dual track driveway and stepped over the planted strip bordering the neighbor's yard. The two yards were similar except the neighbor's had a koi pond rimmed in cobblestones. A humming electric pump kept the water burbling peacefully.

At the edge of the pond, Stella pushed her chin down into her shoulder like a violinist, sighted along her outstretched spear arm with one eye shut and fired it into the water. There was a splash and the black rubber hose flopped around slackly. With a yank, out came a fat, glistening, dappled orange koi fish. The Japanese carp was surely fifteen pounds or more by the way she needed both hands to hoist the squirming fish overhead for a triumphant return to the party. At first, the party goers were slack jawed.

Then they began clapping. Clapping and laughing.

The curtains parted in the neighbor's second floor window and the sash opened roughly. "Hey! What the fuck do you think you're doing, Stella!? Oh, you've gone too far this time. I'm calling the police!" The curtains pulled together angrily and soon he was out on his front stoop shouting at her. "How dare you!"

She turned to face him squarely, holding the squirming fish high, "This is for shooting my dog's eye out, Al!"

"That was an accident! Your damned dog tears up my landscaping, craps on my lawn, barks all night long. You wouldn't lift a finger. I've had it with both of you! Anyway, it was just a BB gun I used. Harmless."

She nodded toward her one-eyed dog. "Tell him that. You call that harmless!?"

"How was I to know I'd hit him in the eye? I can't hit a barn door with a basketball. What are the odds? C'mon, I said I was sorry!"

"Well, now you're even sorrier, aren't you? Apology accepted."

"You'll pay for that fish, Stella."

"Not if Knocker has anything to say about it."

The man went pale. "Knocker? What's he going to do? He's still in the pen." The man rubbed his face nervously. "Isn't he?"

"Not for much longer."

The man retreated into his house, muttering about compensation.

"That shut 'im up, didn't it? Teach him to maim my poor dog!" Rogerdog came up and nuzzled her leg. She stooped down and scruffed him under the chin with her free hand, speaking in baby talk, "Isn't dat right, Rogerdoggie?" The big Irish setter licked her hand. "Taught old Al a lesson didn't we?" She called Zach to come inside and help her with the fish.

Of course, nobody gets "taught a lesson." In a few minutes, her outraged neighbor came back out, stepped over the planted strip into Stella's yard and, not seeing Stella, harangued anybody in sight, impugning their morality for their willingness to eat his prized koi.

"It's already dead, Al," came a rejoinder. "What else d'you want us to do with it, put it in a pine box and deliver a graveside eulogy? Hahaha!"

Al glowered at the remark. This fellow Al was amazed how the clear injustice he'd just suffered was not carrying the day. Then he saw Stella step out onto her porch. Zach was still busy in the kitchen, gutting and filleting the fish. "YOU!" he cried. "You owe me, lady!"

"I owe you nothing, dude!" she retorted.

Some wag in the background said, "Quit yer *'carping'*, Al! Hahahaha!"

"Hey! That fish set me back six hundred and fifty bucks!" At that, he fished a receipt from his pocket and held it up for all to see, pivoting this way and that so no one could say they'd missed it. "Six hundred and fifty bucks! So Stella, you're guilty of property destruction, trespassing and... murd—well, killing a living creature. I'm calling the police!"

"I'm right here," Nancy Lautenberg said. "You don't have to call. But frankly, I'd call it even."

Al waved her off in disgust, addressed Stella again, "I'm calling my lawyer on Monday. I think I have a pretty good case. I got—"

"You got nothin', buddy!" Stella shot back. "How about discharging a firearm into MY property and blinding my dog. I think that puts us about even, just like Nancy said. Hm?" She looked around at her sympathetic jury. "I think I got a pretty strong case here!"

"Well, I'm talking to my lawyers about it anyway. We'll see who has a case!" the man retorted.

"You're threatening me with lawyers!? Seriously!? Listen up, Al: I got at least as many lawyers as you do."

"You got no lawyers whatsoever, Stella!"

"Exactly."

The man's face turned bright red. He kicked the grass, spat and walked back to his house, shaking his head, muttering curses and glancing daggers back at Stella. Stella just waved him off and returned to the kitchen. A few minutes later, she reemerged with a platter piled high with fish steaks and began placing them on the barbeque grill, chuckling to herself.

Jeremy said, "C'mon Stella, this was uncalled for. You're just escalating things."

"Maybe so. But it was worth the look on that man's face!"

"C'mon. I think it's time for an apology."

"You're right, cousin!" she agreed. "I hope he gets to it before I do any more damage." Jeremy rolled his eyes, walked away.

No one said a word for a time. An awkward silence settled over the party. The only sounds were the incongruously upbeat music, the sizzling burgers and koi steaks.

Finally, Deena broke the spell with a rousing reminder that after the main course she'd be serving a sinfully delicious deep-fried dessert from the cooler. "Woo-hoo! Can't wait!" people exclaimed.

All at once, there was an upwelling of renewed good cheer.

~ ~ ~

People lined up with plates when the fish was ready, though the burgers had a ways to go. Despite the impression their eagerness gave, not everyone was comfortable eating the koi—Barney among them—and opted for other fare instead. For those without such qualms, however, the koi was surprisingly tasty with the olive oil and pepper rub Stella had applied. In any case, virtually everyone was inclined to rush through the main course to get to Deena's surprise dessert.

When the time came, Deena bent forward on her double-wide lawn chair and pulled the lid off of the cooler before her. A terrycloth towel lay over her frozen confections.

"Is this your mystery dessert, Deena?" Reggie the grocer asked. "The one you said you'd unveil this week on your show?"

"Oh no, not that. That's the one Mr. Starr came here to interview me about. That is what the interview is about, isn't it, Barney?"

He rocked his head, "Sure, if that's what you want to talk about."

She seemed puzzled by his response. "In any case, I'm not going to unveil my mystery creation till I tape my next show on Thursday." She looked at Barney. "If you're nice and no hardball questions, I'll give you a few hints about it, but I'm not divulging any secrets, so just be forewarned!"

"So warned. So what are you unveiling tonight, then, Deena?" Barney asked.

With the grand gesture of a master magician, she whipped the towel away and revealed dozens of cinnamon-tempura-battered spheres stacked like miniature cannonballs. "Voila!" She lifted one that had a wedge cut out to display the concentric inner layers of caramel, chocolate chip studded brownies, ground walnuts and gelato. Near her, within reach, a portable deep fryer rested on the yielding grass in dangerous proximity to the klutzy half-blind Rogerdog. Almost on cue, Rogerdog jumped up and hurtled past the deep fryer already so hot the oil was starting to smoke. There were gasps but no mishaps—yet.

"Get that goddamn dog outta here!" someone yelled.

Meanwhile, Deena dropped the battered balls into the fryer for a quick searing. The climax of the evening did not disappoint; it was indeed a deep-fried dessert truly to die for. En route to their eager recipients, the aromatic balls of fried batter each received a sprinkling of powdered sugar and bacon bits from the hand of the Diva herself.

"Enjoy!" Deena said. And oh did they!

~ ~ ~

Under a canopy of stars, the air began to chill and people put their jackets on and sat close together, chatting in close proximity to the residual warmth of the Weber grill and the portable deep fryer. To cap off an evening of excess, Stella broke out the promised bottle of Cuervo tequila and a tray arrayed with shot glasses, a bowl of cut limes and a salt shaker.

For novices, she demonstrated the technique: First she filled a shot glass with the agave spirit. Then she licked the crotch between her left thumb and forefinger, looking around suggestively at the onlookers. The saliva held the salt she poured onto it (over a napkin so as not to kill the grass). Then, in rapid succession, she licked the salt off her skin, downed the shot glass and bit into a lime wedge—to a chorus of enthusiastic hoots.

She let out a triumphant exhalation, then, "And that's how it's done!" She hugged herself, "Mmm...makes you feel warm all over!"

One by one, they took turns, cheering each other on. The *joie de vivre* burned brightly a while longer, but the food, dessert and alcohol eventually took their toll. Half an hour and three empty tequila bottles later, people began filtering home with the food containers they'd brought. The neighbor boys carried Deena's deep fryer home for her.

Jeremy and another man helped the big woman out of her lawn chair and once she was properly upright, she took up her cane with the orange gumdrop knob. She walked ever so gingerly back home, her elephantine gait rocking from side to side. Jeremy picked up his own cane and walked home, waving good night to whomever might be behind him.

Barney and young Zach helped Stella haul the tables and grill inside. Zach's girlfriend Nadia made herself useful by tweeting on her cell phone about the lame party. When Zach finished up, the teen couple went home too.

"Good night, Stella."

"Good night, Zach."

Barney looked over at the four divots in the lawn where Deena's chair had rested before she weighed anchor and set sail for home. As it turned out, he'd gotten to talk to her just long enough this evening to nail down a time for their interview tomorrow. He would come by her place late morning. That would afford him a leisurely breakfast and time to review his interview questions before visiting this self-styled doyenne of deep-fried desserts. He pulled out his cell phone and texted a message informing his editor of the plan. A text came right back with a little emoji giving him the thumbs-up.

Stella motioned for Barney to come inside.

~ ~ ~

Leading the way into the house, she paused to flip on the light. Sure enough, there was a well-worn chintz sofa bed with threadbare armrests and a tattered throw over the back. On the coffee table Barney scanned a scattered pile of automotive magazines. The cover of one of them featured a big-breasted babe stretched sensually over a blown-fuel dragster, displaying her cleavage in all its glory and licking a socket wrench like it was an ice cream cone or...something else. "You—uh—into cars, Stella?"

She laughed. No, not her! Those mags belonged to her estranged auto-mechanic boyfriend Joe, known around town as Knocker. Knocker! That was the name that threw her irate neighbor Al back onto his heels earlier this evening. Hmm. She explained that the sofa bed was where he slept after any of their innumerable arguments. No worries about him coming around; he had his own cot at the state penitentiary down in Sheridan. "Three hots and a cot," she said. "Good riddance to him, I say."

While she went to get a pillow and blankets, Barney surveyed the room and imagined the rough scenes that must have unfolded in this house. He swallowed uneasily: there was a fist-hole in the wall. The young reporter felt a little queasy about this arrangement though he wasn't sure there was any objective reason to feel that way—her perp boyfriend was safely locked up after all. He decided the queasiness was just the ultra-rich dessert and tequila.

"Here you go!" she came in and lobbed a fluffy pillow at him and laid a neatly folded green army blanket on the coffee table. There was a stain on the blanket.

Stella leaned unsteadily against the wood veneered wall on which hung a portrait of a young woman in military fatigues. The portrait had a yellow ribbon pasted on it. It said, "Support Our Troops". Noticing from the corner of her eye that the portrait was askew, she reached over languidly with both hands to straighten it; the tequila had slowed her dynamo down a few notches. When she finished, it was crooked in the other direction. Then she addressed her new friend, "Listen, Barn, I'd love to hang with you some more but the room's spinning 'round and 'round so I'm gonna crash. You know how to pull the sofa bed open, right?" She waited for him to nod. "Cool. My bedroom's right there. If you need anything during the night...just knock. See ya in the morning."

"Thanks, Stella. Good night."

"Night."

He stood there alone, quietly contemplating the stained blanket, the sofa, the living room and Knocker's car magazines, and wondered what he was getting himself into. *"Just knock," she says.* He blew through his lips. Eyed the fist hole in the wall. *Just knock. Knock, knock, KNOCKER. Knock, knock, HELP!*

= CHAPTER 3 =

~ ~ ~

The next morning, Barney Starr awoke to sunlight pouring through the slit between the curtains behind the sofa bed. There was something on his forehead. He pulled it off. It was a Post-It. "Good morning sleepy-head! Sunday mornings I waitress at the Rock Creek Roadhouse just up the street. It's a few blocks north on Main where Hayes Street comes in. Come find me!"

He massaged his eyes and blinked twice, wondering how she managed to recover so fast. Lots of practice, he supposed.

When he came to town yesterday, he hadn't reckoned on spending more than one or two nights. He planned to conduct a quick interview or two with Deena and hightail it back home. Consequently, he'd not packed anything but a toiletry kit and laptop (both of which were currently trapped in the trunk of his car). This morning's preparations would therefore be brief: his shirt and trousers were on the arm of the sofa—er, on the floor now—and as he had no toiletries with him, a swizzle of water would have to do. His mouth tasted like a used insole. Swinging his legs to the floor, he sat up and looked around, blinking. On the table lay a brand-new toothbrush and a travel size tube of Colgate toothpaste rolled up partway with another Post-It: "Use this!"

There was also a pre-owned Gillette safety razor. It was not pink; it was dark colored—a man's. There was whisker debris lodged between the blades. He picked the thing up daintily between thumb and forefinger as if they were a pair of hazmat tongs and transported it into a nearby waste basket.

~ ~ ~

The Rock Creek Roadhouse was exactly where she'd indicated; he could see its sandwich board out on the sidewalk a few short blocks north along Main Street at the point where Hayes Street teed in from the right. As leaves fell through the crisp morning breeze, Barney walked in that direction. He passed a couple of residences and came to the Rock Creek Bridge. Merely laying his hand on the railing caused the end of it to swing out over the rocks below. It creaked and swung back into place, ready to freak out the next pedestrian. At his feet something blue caught his attention. Kicking leaves away, he discovered a crudely painted skull and cross bones with an arrow pointing to the rail and the words, "Fix or Die!" He took note of the sky blue grafitto and continued across the bridge to where Deena Poole's pink and red Victorian home overlooked the creek. Pausing at its waist high white picket gate, he whispered to the manse, "I'll be back," and resumed walking.

Next came a small shop, "ANY OLD THING Antiques & Collectibles" and then came his destination, the Rock Creek Roadhouse. The sandwich board on the sidewalk announced the morning's specials.

Pulling the brass door handle and entering the roadhouse was like being drawn into a warm embrace. The place was aromatic with comforting breakfast smells. The soft sounds of conversations and clinking forks filled the high-ceilinged room. There were all kinds of people here this Sunday morning—some familiar to Barney from last night (whom he waved to), others who apparently were unmet locals and, to fill out the roster, a few tourist families from the lodgings upstairs. All sat in wooden captain's chairs at the rustic tables and talked between bites while working their way through stacks of maple syrup-soaked pancakes (extra thick, you know!), Denver omelets, smoky link sausages, ham and hash browns chased with orange juice, tomato juice, coffee or, in one case, a beer.

"You made it!" It was Stella, flying a tray of loaded breakfast plates over the heads of the patrons, en route to a table where a mom and dad and three eager kids locked sights on the approaching food, as if able to reel it in with their eyes. Setting the tray down she turned and called over to her new friend from Portland, "Sit anywhere you like, Barney. I'll be right with you!"

He sat down at a vacant window table in the corner and waited. To pass the time, he surveyed the Western-themed decor then casually looked outside to take in Sweetbread's Sunday morning street scene. He saw Reggie's grocery store, where the screen door swung out at just that moment. There was Reggie, with his brushy asparagus-tip hair-do, holding his door open for a woman with an armload of groceries.

Then Barney looked down Hayes Street where he spotted a barber-shop, presumably Muphrid's. A sign in the door said "Closed." Across from the barbershop he saw an art gallery specializing in Western art. It was also closed. A car drove by. High above the street, a squirrel ran along a power line and scared off a bird. Barney yawned, pulled out his cell phone and jotted a few notes with a stylus, then scanned the dining room for Stella but she was running for another order. The other waiter, a pillowy twenty-something fellow, rushed up to the chef's counter and clipped a ticket onto the rotary order holder. Directly below it was another one of those Beanie Babies. This one was a rabbit. Barney shook his head, amused. He yawned again. There was no menu on his table, so he occupied himself with pushing the paper place mat around with his stylus.

He looked out the window again and saw Muphrid come out of the grocery store with a single carton of milk. The young reporter began ruminating about what—or whom—that man had buried under those mounds. Something nourishing to the grass, that much was clear.

"Ready to order?"

Barney startled. He hadn't noticed the pillowy waiter approach his table. "Sorry to scare you, sir!" The young man looked down at the table-top and said, "Oops, let me get you a menu!"

"'Sokay, how about pancakes with maple syrup?"

"Want hash browns with that?"

"Sure."

"Ham or sausage?"

"Hm. Can you substitute a fruit bowl?"

"You got it!"

Now Muphrid was moving toward his shop. Maybe the milk was for his mother upstairs.

"Anything to drink?

"Huh?"

"Something to drink?"

"Oh! How 'bout, um, a glass of orange juice? And a coffee."

Muphrid disappeared into the stairwell adjacent to his shop. Must be an errand for his mother.

"Room for cream?"

"Um. Naw. Just black, thanks."

Muphrid did not reappear, so Barney turned his attention to Stella waitressing around the room, gliding and pirouetting among the tables like a figure skater. Soon, his coffee and orange juice arrived. Sipping a little of each, he sat back and looked across the cavernous room past the wagon wheel chandeliers to the far wall, adorned from floor to coffer ceiling with horseshoes, worn harnesses, a steer's head with some of the fur rubbed off and several cheesy cowboy-themed paintings. There was even a portrait of a weeping rodeo clown. Barney bet himself a hundred bucks the paintings came from the art gallery across the street. On the same wall near the window hung a poster of the American flag with a caption that asserted, "These colors don't run!" It was sun-faded nearly to monochrome.

He yawned again and fell to examining a portly man a few tables away wearing a green and yellow sports cap. Barney watched the way the folds in the back of the man's shaved neck moved as he chatted with the other people at his table.

Then the big front door swung open and some familiar faces from last night's party appeared. They sat down at the table next to the one the portly man was sitting at. The new arrivals were so busy exchanging greetings they didn't see Barney sitting at his corner window table. Stella and the pillowy waiter shoved several more tables together to accommodate the newcomers.

Stella whispered something to the portly man and he twisted around in his chair, "Hey, Barnaby! I didn't see you sitting over there! Come on over and join us. You're not a stranger here anymore, you know!"

It was Stella's cousin, Jeremy, the webmaster cum mayor, wearing his green and yellow University of Oregon Ducks cap to cover his naked pate. As Barney picked up his drinks and came over, his attention fixed on a square-built stone-faced fellow in workman's overalls situated opposite Jeremy. There was a finished plate in front of the man and a travel size bottle of pink Pepto-Bismol at hand. His eyes were rheumy and his tired face was framed in a Brigham Young chinstrap beard. Near the corner of his unsmiling mouth a toothpick bobbed up and down as he quietly observed the goings-on around him.

A sturdy woman came up behind the man, settled her hand on his shoulder and gave it a squeeze. "Hi Dad." He looked over his shoulder and smiled thinly at his policewoman daughter, Nancy, whom Barney recognized from last night's party. She glanced up and said, "Hi Barney!

Have a seat. This is my dad, Tom." She looked down at her father's graying crew-cut. "Dad, this is Barney Starr, the reporter I told you about." Like a weary chieftain, Tom Lautenberg lifted a silent, mirthless palm of greeting to Barney. In overall aspect, he seemed a man resigned to the fact that he'd given the world plenty of opportunities to come through, and each time it had come up short.

As Barney would learn in time, Nancy had gone into police work partly in hopes of keeping the world from disappointing her father any further than it already had. And in that regard, as Sweetbread's sole peace officer, she'd accomplished that goal fairly well. She'd even gotten that bad apple, Knocker, Dorgan Bailey's son, run out of town and locked up at Sheridan. Alas, that was not soon enough to shield her ten-year-old son, Kyle, from that renegade's bad influence. Kyle's first escapade was burgling Muphrid's house (when Muphrid was renting it out to the Indian fellow) and "liberating" a cache of Beanie Babies from the front hall closet. Nowadays the boy was leading a band of kiddie delinquents under his nom-de-gang, "Chinstrap." The reason for that name would become apparent to Barney soon enough.

Sitting next to old Tom was an oddly familiar fellow, forty-ish, scrawny and pale with tall sprigs of kinky beige hair shaped liked an arborvitae—or even an asparagus tip. He was as outgoing as Tom was taciturn. He immediately reached over the table settings and shook Barney's hand. "Name's Ray! I'm Reggie's twin brother. I own the store next store, Feed & Seed and More. Heh! I'm the bore from the store next door!" He flashed a jazzy grin out of one side of his mouth, impressed with himself, and exclaimed, "Listen to me! Hey, I coulda been in show business!"

"Or in a circus act," Tom said sourly and went back to chewing on his toothpick.

Undeterred, Ray went on, "So you're the reporter, Barney Starr, we been hearing about, eh? The guy that knocked down Muphrid's fence!"

"Yeahhh, well yeah. That would be me," Barney admitted mournfully, heaved a sigh and laughed. "That would be me, all right. Nice to meet you Ray. I promise not to drive too close to your storefront window!"

Conversation paused until Ray stopped guffawing.

A woman in a fuchsia warm-up suit leaned her arm across the table and her bracelet tinkled against the tabletop, "Callista Vandershur—and this is my husband, Robert. We met you last night." Robert had dispensed with his bow tie since then. But his wire rim spectacles remained perched on his thin nose and they glinted when he reached a hand to Barney.

"The Vindemiatrix winery, right?"

"Yes, you have a good memory for details! No surprise, I suppose; you're a reporter after all. And quite the party crasher I must say!"

He heaved another sigh, "Yeah, that was quite an entrance wasn't it? I am really sorry about that! Muphrid turned down my offer to pay for the damages, said he'd fix it himself, but I'm determined to compensate him for it. By the way, I sure was surprised to see those big mounds in his yard—"

"Mounds? What kind of mounds?" Callista said. All around, there were looks of incomprehension; he wasn't going to get far with this crowd.

"It's where the chopped-up bodies are buried," said the girl with heavy mascara who raised her head from the crook of her arm just long enough to make her statement. Callista and Robert blanched at their daughter's macabre joke.

Callista apologized on the girl's behalf. "My daughter is a bit of a drama queen."

"How do you know it's not true, Mom? Chinstrap and his creepy little friends snuck into Muphrid's yard a few nights ago and saw him digging up something." Barney recognized the teen: she was Zach's Goth girlfriend Nadia from last night. The one preoccupied with her cell phone the whole time until she looked up and smiled at him. The one with a smudge of sky-blue paint over her eye. That was gone now—but not the mascara.

"My son Kyle—his name is not Chinstrap by the way—has what you could call an overactive imagination," Nancy said flatly. "I'm the police department around here. If anything remotely illegal was going on, I think I'd know about it. Like I said, it's glacial rocks. There's nothing more to say."

"But the big hole—"

"Trees. Nothing more to say."

Case closed apparently.

"Hm—well, here comes the man himself!" Indeed, the barber was at that very moment walking up Hayes street from his shop. The milk carton was gone.

"Why don't you just ask Muphrid himself?" Robert suggested to his daughter.

"Are you kidding, Dad? The guy creeps me out."

"I asked," Barney interjected. "He just laughed and said 'gophers.'"

"Musta been big gophers!" Ray said, guffawing.

"That's exactly what he said."

Robert laughed, "Yeah, that sounds like Muphrid! He's a character."

"All right, speaking of barbers!" Jeremy announced, slapping both hands down on the table and looking from eye to eye, "Here's a little brain teaser...ready? It's a philosopher's riddle." Stella showed up with Barney's breakfast and listened in on her cousin's story as she unloaded her tray.

~ ~ ~

"OK, there's a town—not this one—with only one barber. In this town there is a law that all men must be clean-shaven. Every day, every man either shaves himself or gets a shave from the barber. Now, the barber has an ironclad rule: he is the only one allowed to shave another man and he never shaves a man who shaves himself." He paused to let that thought sink in. "So the question, the riddle to solve, is this: Does the barber shave himself?"

"Sure, why not?" rheumy-eyed Tom volunteered, then put the toothpick back in his mouth.

"Why not? Because he's not allowed—by his own rule—to shave himself. Remember the rule? He is not allowed to shave any man who shaves himself."

Tom waved his hand dismissively, "That's a stupid rule. They should get a new barber." He resumed looking at the mangled remains of his hash browns and worked the toothpick up and down vigorously.

"Well," Callista said, "Then maybe someone else shaves him."

"Nope. Every man either shaves himself or gets shaved by the barber. Only the barber can shave someone else."

Ray said, "So what's the answer?"

"There is no possible answer. It's self-contradicting. He can't shave himself because, as barber, he may not shave a man who shaves himself. But if he doesn't shave himself, he's in trouble again because then he's *required* to be clean-shaven. But as soon as he shaves himself, he has broken the rule. It's no-win. A catch-22. There's no possible solution—":

"Sure there is, Jeremy," Stella averred.

"Hmm?"

"HE'S A BOY," she said emphatically. "The barber's not a man, he's a boy. So his rule doesn't apply."

Jeremy looked stunned. Barney couldn't help but grin. He winked at Stella and whispered, "Nice job!"

"But. Hm. Right. You're right, little cousin!" Jeremy whistled softly to himself. "I can't believe it. You solved the riddle!"

"So what do I get?"

Jeremy laughed. "How 'bout a really big tip!"

She was about to say something to that when the big front door creaked and in came Muphrid.

~ ~ ~

Ray, the scrawny "Feed & Seed and More" proprietor, called to Muphrid as he entered: "Hey, lookit who the cat drug in!"

"Grammar, Ray, grammar!" Jeremy commented.

"Sorry, Mister Mayor!" Ray responded, "Let me rephrase that: 'Lookit WHOM the cat drug in!' Ahohohoho!" Then he started tapping the ends of his silverware, bleeding off nervous energy. He addressed Muphrid again. "Hey Myoofee, you had any close shaves lately? Ahohohoho!"

Without removing the toothpick from his mouth, Tom muttered, "Why don't ya just shut the fuck up, Ray?"

Ray looked stung. Nancy laid a hand on her father's arm, "Leave him alone, Dad. Why are you always so mean to Ray? He never did anything to hurt you."

Tom cast his eyes down at his plate. "Aw, he just gets on my nerves after a while."

Ray said, "It must be tough being you, Tom. But I know someday you'll find yourself on the sunny side of the street and you'll turn that frown upside down!"

Tom squeezed the following words through his clenched teeth: "I'm gonna kill him, Nancy. Sweartogod I'm gonna kill that fuzzy headed freak!"

Ray pursed his lips.

Nancy interceded, "You know he says those things just to piss you off don't you, Dad? Just let it go." She looked across the table at Barney. "Don't mind these two. Ray and my dad've been going at it like this for years."

Muphrid the town barber seated himself a couple of tables down, waved at Barney and flashed his trademark lopsided smile. "Hiya, Barney!" Barney could swear Muphrid's eyes crossed ever so slightly during that facial maneuver.

Nadia looked up and stuck her tongue out at the window. Standing on the other side was a boy who bore a striking resemblance to her. He was looking in, making goofy faces at her.

"Who's that?" Barney inquired.

"That's my useless twin brother, Aidan."

Her mother explained, "Nadia's grounded for a little sign painting incident the other day. That's why she's here with us this morning and Aidan's free to go where he wants."

Nadia flipped her brother the bird. That got the boy laughing wildly. Satisfied he'd gotten her goat, he skipped away, waving sarcastically at her.

Returning to the business of eating his breakfast, the young reporter continued doing what reporters are good at: saying little and listening a lot. He tossed out an occasional question, but mostly he just listened. Conversation turned to the struggles of the small businesses in town, Ray's desire to expand his hardware store, the prospects for repairing the bridge's railing before someone fell into the creek and broke their neck, matters of people's personal problems, the need to drain pipes before the first freeze and who's going to help so-and-so with canning her last boxes of apples gathered from her prolific backyard trees. Eventually, the conversation wandered back to Barney and his reason for coming to Sweetbread, "So Mr. Reporter, did you get to talk to Deena last night? Are you going to ask her about her mystery dessert?"

Barney explained that he hardly got five words with her, what with all the goings-on. They talked just enough to schedule an interview at her home this morning after breakfast. He snapped his wristwatch into view and abruptly cut the conversation short. "The time's gotten away from me! I'd better get going!"

He was already on his feet when Jeremy called after him, "Hey Barnaby, we gonna see you back here tomorrow?"

"Yep. Looks like it. Same time, same place. I'll be here!"

After paying the bill at the counter—where a Beanie Baby plush toy frog reposed against the register—he said "see ya" to a busy Stella and left the warm embrace of the Rock Creek Roadhouse for the pink and red Victorian mansion two doors down Main Street at the creek crossing.

~ ~ ~

On the way, Barney decided to take a side tour to better examine Muphrid's place of business. The shop was self-consciously old-fashioned.

Outside in front stood a red, white and blue striped barber pole topped with a white knob. Stenciled on the plate glass window were these advertisements: "Yamhill Barbershop" in fancy script and below that, "For Evening Appointments Call/Text (541) 020-3579." Through the glass one could see a single barber chair with a folded apron draped over it, and a big broom leaning against the stainless steel shelf below a wall length mirror. Containers of talcum powder, after shave, Barbasol, hair oil and mousse were arrayed along the length of the shelf. At the end of the shelf was a container with scissors and a straight razor. Electric shears dangled from a black cord hanging over a hook. Against the wall opposite the mirror were a few Naugahyde waiting chairs, above which hung a wide poster showing various men's hair styles—from the 1950s—including the "Flat Top" and "Flat Top with Fenders." Finally, on the back wall, over a doorway, was a fancy sign: "Home of the World Famous Late Night Razor Cut!" A sign hung inside the glass door showing a white clock face and adjustable red clock hands. It said, "Back at:" and the hands indicated noon. Below, it said "Hours: Mon-Sat 10-6, Sun 12-5."

Walking back toward the roadhouse, he immediately passed a flight of stairs leading up from the sidewalk to a worn door with a push button doorbell affixed to the adjacent wall. *That must be the second-floor apartment where Muphrid keeps his mother*, he thought. Any doubt about that conclusion was dispelled by the stair lift chair waiting at the top of the staircase.

= CHAPTER 4 =

~ ~ ~

Barney slowed as he walked past "ANY OLD THING Antiques & Collectibles." He peered through the big storefront window and saw a heavyset gray-haired woman wandering the aisles dusting a clutter of wood furniture and porcelain knickknacks. An old TV monitor mounted on the back wall was showing a news program. The woman kept stealing glances at the TV as she carried out her chores. Eventually, she saw Barney standing outside the window and smiled. He smiled back and resumed walking.

The sudden roar of a leaf blower across the street diverted Barney's attention. Except it wasn't a leaf blower. It was a yard vacuum, its distended canvas bag hanging off the back like an inflated bagpipe. Furthermore, the man employing it was eight feet off the ground, standing on an A-frame ladder. He was vacuuming his maple tree.

Sensing Barney's eyes upon him, the man turned and yelled, "Preemptive gardening! Clean up the dead leaves before they hit the ground. This is the lawn that won the Lawn Beautiful Award two years ago. I'm hoping for a second award next year!" It made some kind of sense, Barney figured. If nothing else, one could not dispute the fact that the man's perfectly manicured lawn was completely free of the autumn leaves littering all the other yards up and down the street.

Barney jotted down a couple of notes and continued to Deena's place. There, he pulled open the little white picket entry gate and beheld the woman's Victorian home. Although hidden somewhat within the gloom of several large Douglas firs, it was an imposing manse, its stateliness only slightly diminished by the satellite dish, the freshly painted pink exterior and the dessert themed topiary scattered throughout the front yard: cylindrical privet shrubs truncated in steps to mimic giant wedding cakes. The flagstone walkway leading up to the front veranda ran between a dozen boxwoods shaped like oversized bonbons. And everywhere the eye landed, there was some kind of colorful plastic garden art: gum drops, candy canes, chocolate kisses and jelly beans. *Willy Wonka landscaping,* Barney whispered to himself, shaking his head at the silliness, wondering why he ever agreed to come here.

He took a breath and stepped heavily through the gate like a child resigned to eating his broccoli.

A short flight of wooden steps brought him to the veranda and the ornate front door.

He poked the doorbell button and heard chimes inside. He was secretly hoping no one would answer.

The light dimmed briefly in the front door's leaded glass window and an instant later the door pulled open. A corpulent though attractive woman greeted him cheerily and bade him come in. "Welcome to my humble abode, Barney Starr!" Deena said.

Inside, it was all red velvet upholstery and crystal chandeliers, ceramic sconces, violet crown molding at the edges of the ceilings and fine wood scrollwork everywhere. The atmospheric music of Yanni set the mood. A tiny dog-like creature known as a Shih Tzu went scampering over the Persian carpet, yipping excitedly. Barney chewed his lip.

She told him to make himself comfortable; she'd be back in a moment. Presently, she waddled back with a walking cane dangling from one arm, carrying a silver tray generously laden with tea cookies, bonbons, truffles, and some eye-catchingly elaborate confections arranged around an antique silver coffee pot, porcelain cups and saucers and creamer, and of course a heaping bowl of white sugar and another of brown.

Barney fidgeted and a little voice inside was groaning, *What am I doing here!?*

She recommended the brown sugar "because it's both flavorful and full of healthful natural ingredients." Pushing another ceramic bowl toward him, she added, "And if you're in for an adventure, this is a healthy Indian sugar substitute called jaggery."

He tasted it, hesitantly. "Mmmhm. Nice. I've heard of jaggery. As I understand it, though, jaggery comes from sugar cane too, doesn't it?"

"Yes, but it's expressed from the cane in a very different way that pre-serves the nutrients!"

After pouring a full cup of steaming hot coffee for each of them, she settled into her wingback chair, hooked the cane over the armrest ("Poor circulation in my feet") and took a sip of her coffee. With eyes half closed with pleasure she said, "Ahh, delicious! I hope you enjoy Sumatra as much as I do."

Then she said, "I noticed you looking around, Barney. May I call you Barney?" She saw him nod. "My decorator and I have tried to stay true to the character of this house. This house has an interesting history."

"Tell me." He pulled out his notepad.

"Well, it was originally commissioned in the late eighteen hundreds by a railroad baron by the name of Alexander Sweetbread. Colonel Alexander Sweetbread. As you might guess, he's the one that founded this town. He founded it as an agricultural rail hub. Made a fortune transporting farmers' crops to market and you'd think that would've been enough. But apparently it was not.

"Early into 20th century, he decided he could multiply his wealth by investing in the speculative booms of the 1920s. First, it was the Florida land boom bubble that burst during the Coolidge administration. That was a setback for him. But he had deep pockets, so he was able to weather through that experience. Then it was on to Wall Street. Well you know what happened to that! The Stock Market Crash of 1929 during the Hoover administration ruined him, finished him off. He lost everything, including his wife and this great house. According to legend he took a hatchet to the street sign at the corner of Coolidge and Hoover, chopped it down and spat on both names as they laid there in the gutter. Then he packed up a carpet bag and made his way out of town, never to return.

"Well the house fell into decay, got passed from owner to owner and was on the verge of being torn down when my husband and I arrived here and bought it for a song. The place was pretty scary, like the Addams Family mansion, dust and water damage everywhere, but we pumped our life savings into restoring it."

"It shows," Barney said.

"Thank you. It's on the Historic Registry now, by the way, so I have to keep it up to snuff. It was my cable TV show that made it all possible. And the show is what you came here to interview me about, isn't it?"

"Yep. And about your mystery dessert."

"Which I'm going to unveil on Thursday and not before. But that's the big scoop you're after, isn't it?"

"Of course," he replied, then added, "Is that what it is?"

She looked puzzled, "I don't follow."

"A big scoop? Is that what the dessert is?"

"Oh! Ha ha! Of ice cream? Ha ha! That's cute. Well, that's for me to know and you to find out, as they say!" She leaned forward, took a bonbon and chased it with a sip of coffee. She offered him one. His eyebrow arched with delight. It was delicious. "Well, let's begin at the beginning, shall we?"

"Let's." He took another bonbon and readied his notepad.

She sat back and began her story.

~ ~ ~

Twenty years ago she and her husband, who sold farm equipment, moved here from their hometown of Moorehead, Minnesota. "That's just across the river from Fargo, North Dakota. Ever since they made that movie, people chuckle when they hear the name Fargo. Kind gives me goosebumps to think that scary stuff was going on when I lived there."

After her husband ran off with a Louisiana belle he met on one of their vacations, she went catatonic for a long time. The only thing that kept her going was baking and dessert making. That's when she first packed on the pounds. But she couldn't eat everything, so she shared her wares with friends and neighbors. Eventually, when she was ready to hear it, they suggested she think about peddling her amazing dessert creations. "I thought about it long and hard. You know, Barney, I'm the daughter of a long line of German and Swedish confectioners. My mother's family in particular were famous for generations for their konditorei pastry shops in Bavaria. So it was inevitable that I would eventually open a shop of my own here in town. My claim to fame was my line of deep-fried desserts. I got the idea when my ex-husband—the unfaithful rat bastard, pardon my French—and I were staying in New Orleans for one of the trade shows, John Deere I think it was, at that big Ernest Morial Convention Hall.

"While he was busy inside that big convention hall or sneaking off to pork that bitch girlfriend of his—don't put that language in your article please!—I roamed the city, exploring the cuisine of the Big Easy. If you can say anything about Southern cuisine, it's this: they deep fry everything—

and I mean EVERYTHING. And why not? It makes everything delicious! They deep fry chicken of course—that's where Popeye's started—and they deep fry alligator and they deep fry ice cream, they deep fry Oreo Cookies. They even deep fry sticks of butter! Talk about mouth-watering! Mmmm! I thought, why not deep fry all the pastries I'd been making, all the French confections? Deep fried gelato! How about deep-fried pies! Chalu-pies, I call 'em! You know, like chalupas? Get it? Anyway, I took the notion of deep-fried desserts back with me to Oregon, experimented on my neighbors and after a while got the whole town hooked."

Barney thought about how many supersized people he'd seen in this town already.

"Then, as I said, George took a powder. And I took a dive. Checked out mentally for a couple of years. But, with a little encouragement from my friends—when I was ready to hear it of course—I went entrepreneurial and shipped my desserts all over the world. Even the Sultan of Brunei put in an order! He paid for trans-Pacific refrigeration and everything. But the turning point was when I did that YouTube video that went viral. That led to my e-books, apps, my online university of dessertology and before you can say Jack Robinson, I got my own TV show on cable. The rest is history, as they say!"

"And that's your workshop?" Barney pointed to an archway at the back of the room that opened onto what looked like an industrial kitchen. There were spoons hanging from rails, huge stainless steel mixing bowls and wide ovens.

"Yep. That's where the magic happens! I'm always coming up with new delights, trying them out on the Sweetbreadians. Just like last night— how'd you like my latest?"

"That was...amazing. I think my blood sugar has tripled, but it was so good I'm still thinking about it."

"'Tastes like some more,' as they say, doesn't it?"

"Oh yeah!"

There came a clang from the kitchen. Deena called over her shoulder, "Is that you, Juanita?"

Unseen, a Latina woman's voice, 'Jeys, Meesus Poole!'

Deena explained. "Juanita comes in on weekdays to clean up after me! I make such a mess. I don't know what I'd do without her!" She assumed a pensive look. "Ran away with her family from Guatemala or Columbia

51

or one of those places. I mix 'em up, they're all kind of the same—violence and brown people."

Barney frowned.

"Oh, not you! You're light. More mocha, I'd say. Very attractive I might add. Where are you from?"

"I was born in San Diego, if that's what you mean," Barney said flatly.

"Oh, Mexican?"

"No, American. My mother came from the Phillipines. So I'm half Filipino."

"Oh, I love Filipinos! That's such a wonderful country, so I've heard! The people are very kind and generous, so I've heard." She shifted nervously on her ample buttocks.

"Yes, many of them are," he replied with an indulgent smile. "So I've heard."

"Well then!" she exhaled. "Shall we continue the interview?"

"Yes, let's."

So they talked a while longer, then she said she had some other business to attend to and they should continue the interview tomorrow, so Barney quickly cut to the chase: "I know it's a secret, but is there anything you're willing to share about this upcoming mystery dessert?"

She fumbled around for her walking cane and awkwardly leveraged herself vertical using both hands. "Ah, that will have to wait till tomorrow's interview!"

"So you're willing to talk about it, then?"

"Come back tomorrow and find out!"

He smiled indulgently, "Sure."

On the way out, he half turned back and said, "Just one other thing."

"Yes?"

"Do you know anything about the mounds in Muphrid Thatcher's yard?"

Deena got a twinkle in her eye, "You mean his garden plots?"

"Yeah, I guess you could call them that."

She clasped her hands together, paused, then said, "Muphrid's taken up gardening. Grass, flowers, trees. Uses my discard water for fertilizer. Really makes thing grow. But mounds? Can't help you there. I haven't seen his yard, so I don't know anything about any mounds. He probably turned up the earth to mix in amendments. Sort of fluffs up the soil, you know. Just a guess. All I know is he loves working his plots."

"He's dug some pretty deep holes."

She shrugged, "Don't know anything about that. Must be one of his crazy projects." Before Barney could ask her what kind of projects, she put a firm hand on his shoulder and smiled, "See you tomorrow at ten."

"Right. Tomorrow at ten." And with that he was out the door.

~ ~ ~

He had all the material he needed for his first dispatch. He would hammer it out later—after he liberated his laptop from his car's trunk. But for the moment, Barney was most eager to tell someone about how well it went, and he knew exactly who that someone was. He crossed the Rock Creek Bridge with the creaky loose railing lolling in the breeze and the sky-blue graffito warning to passersby. A moment later he found himself threading through a swarm of oncoming children. The red-haired boy in the lead, who couldn't have been more than ten years old, appeared to be sporting a chinstrap beard. Barney stared in disbelief, pivoting around as the boy flew past, trying to make sense of what he'd just seen.

Chipstrap! Officer Nancy's renegade rug rat son Kyle. The very same Kyle corrupted by Knocker. The same Kyle who'd burgled the Beanie Babies.

He abruptly stopped to jot down more notes. Shoving his notepad into his hip pocket, he resumed his journey to the little yellow clapboard house on Fillmore Road. Stepping up onto Stella's creaky front porch, he banged on the screen door frame. He hoped she would be back from her roadhouse shift by now.

She was.

= CHAPTER 5 =

~ ~ ~

Stella was over-the-top excited to see Barney. She grabbed him by both shoulders and roughly pulled him inside, "Come here, you!" and kissed him big on the mouth. He was stunned, amazed and delighted.

They tumbled onto the still-open, still-rumpled sofa bed, madly throwing their clothes all over the living room. His shirt landed on the car magazines, her blouse landed on his shirt. He kicked the door closed with his foot, thinking all the while, *Ohmygodohmygod what am I doing!?*

To which he replied, *IdontcareIdontcareIdontcare!*

Breathing heavily, she said, "Do you have protection?" He fumbled for his wallet. Its smooth leather had a telltale raised condom ring and he deftly took care of business without missing a beat.

Mattress springs and sofa hinges squeaked and she looked so beautiful, more beautiful than any of the fantasies of her he'd been entertaining since meeting her last night. She rapturously caressed his body up and down and savored the novelty of his hairless body.

He kissed her all over, up and down. His fingers slid over her belly and continued down into her lush marshy cleft. She moaned and turned and he ran his tongue over her left breast as it rose to him. Upon it he saw another tattoo which gave him momentary pause: a cherry red heart on a satin pillow captioned with these words, "Handle with Care."

He didn't pause long for she was already shimmying down to tickle his belly with the tip of her tongue. From there, she worked her way south. "Mmm."

She came back up, looked straight at him and pulled him into her. For a time the moans and cries could be heard all the way across the street. The sounds scared the birds away outside. A startled cat jumped out of Stella's sweet gum tree and hightailed it across Main Street where it nearly got run over by a passing car. A sidewalk passerby slowed and looked and smiled.

The sofa bed squeaked and bumped against the wall, the windows rattled for quite some time until climax and denouement. Things quieted down and they cradled each other tenderly.

After a while, they went at it again.

The sun crept down the western sky and poured golden yellow light into the room. Curled up against his body, her head in the curve of his armpit and his arm draped limply across her smooth waist, the two of them fell into a sweet sleep.

As dusk approached Stella awoke and gently kissed Barney on the cheek and on the neck and on the ear until he opened his eyes. She murmured, "Wake up, my sweet Barney, I want to take you someplace special."

"Oh, babe, I think you already have."

She smiled, "Well, this place requires clothing. Put your pants on, we're going for a little walk."

"Oh, but it's so nice lying here with you!" he protested, but she persisted...and prevailed.

She opened the guest closet and put on a denim jacket. She pulled a sweater off the shelf and tossed it to him. "Let's go!"

~ ~ ~

Stella led Barney by the hand along Fillmore Road, away from where it teed into Main at Muphrid's house and toward its west end where the asphalt turned to gravel and dropped off the shoulder of the hill into the forested Rock Creek ravine. Descending, the road headed downstream a ways then doubled back and bottomed out in a big round cul-de-sac near the creek. The cul-de-sac was ringed by concrete parking bumpers secured with rusty rebar spiked through at each end.

They stepped over a bumper onto the bare dirt picnic area under towering alders and one enormous eastern white oak overhanging a large pond on the creek. Barney paused to admire it. The tree must have been a century old or more.

"Come on!" She pulled him to a smooth flat boulder that edged the pond. They sat beside each other, laid back and looked up. Autumn leaves flittered down in the mellow sunlight.

"It's so pretty and peaceful here," Barney remarked.

"It is, isn't it? I used to come here when I needed to recharge or just get away."

Barney considered her words, "Get away from what?"

"Oh...everything. My family. This town. A lot of people here call it 'Autumn Town.'"

"That's rather poetic."

"Means it's dying," she said. "Been dying for years. Anybody who has any sense gets outta here. Or dies trying." She laughed, "One day when I was about fourteen, when it was springtime and there was lots of water in the creek, I ditched school and came down here to, you know, just hang out. I saw an empty Pepsi bottle wash down into the pond. I watched it bobbing around, working its way to the place over there where the water spills out and goes on downstream. I thought about where that bottle would end up."

"Well, somewhere downstream, right?"

"Right. But I tried to imagine it, visualize the whole thing. I thought to myself, OK, Rock Creek dumps into the South Yamhill River down by, ya know, just past Highway 18. Near Sheridan? From there, the Yamhill takes over and works its way down to the Willamette, right?"

"Uh-huh, yeah, I guess so."

"The bottle would go down the Willamette to Willamette Falls, then downstream from there past downtown Portland into the Columbia River, right? And the Columbia goes into the ocean. From there, it's all winds and currents, so who knows what beach it would finally wash up on? So I fished the Pepsi bottle out of the pond and guess what I did?"

"You put a note in it," he said.

"Yep, that's right! I took a sheet of paper from my school notebook and wrote a note to the world that said—" she gazed at him silently.

"That said...?"

"That said, 'Get me out of here! Stella Gervais, 439 Fillmore Drive, Sweetbread, Oregon.' I'd decided this town was the most pathetic place on earth. Even the streets are named after loser presidents. You know, Fillmore, Hayes, Coolidge, Hoover, Buchanan. Pathetic. I mean who names a street after Millard Fillmore!? We had a Washington Street once, but this guy Sweetbread—the rich dude that founded the town back in the 20s—thought Warren G. Harding was more presidential looking. So he changed the name to Harding Avenue. What a fuckin' moron! But hey, who's gonna argue with the founder of the town? So we got no Washington Street, no Lincoln, no Kennedy, not even a Reagan."

"Reagan?"

"Yeah, none of the greats."

He chewed his lip. *Reagan?* Ah well, he figured he could live with Reagan if that meant he got to be with Stella. Oh, this was not a good road he was barreling down. But come on, who was he kidding? He'd already swerved off anything resembling a road since he came to this town. He sensed a pattern.

She was still talking. "...or even a Jackson. I guess he was pretty great too."

"Don't forget Madison, Monroe, Jefferson. Or Roosevelt."

"I'd vote for them too. Wait—the Mt. Rushmore Roosevelt, not the socialist one. But Fillmore, give me a break! What'd he do? Nothing! And that's the street I have to live on!" She looked at him. "Why are you laughing?" Then she started laughing too.

"I don't know, I'm just enjoying being with you."

"I am a bit of wonderful, aren't I?" She winked.

"Yeah, I guess so. So did your family find out about your escape plan?"

"No, never!"

"Hm." He found a pebble and tossed it into the pond. "Where are they now? Are they still living in Sweetbread?"

"Nope." She chuckled, "Turns out, my *family* escaped this town instead of me! Ironic, huh? Ma and Pop moved to a retirement 'villa' in King City, up your way. They're lovin' it there. I go visit once in a while. And do some shopping while I'm there."

"What about sibs? Brothers? Sisters?"

"Just a sister. Older. She escaped to the military. Died in Iraq. Anbar Province. There's a picture of her on my wall."

"Yeah, I saw it."

Stella looked away, suddenly somber. "She was one of the good ones."

The creek gurgled and robins were taking turns fluffing themselves up against the chill then flying up into the branches and then back down to ground. The water rolled a smooth stone into the pond and the ploop! brought Stella back.

"I'm so glad I met you, Barney." She reached her arm around him and they shared a deep soul kiss. Then she pointed to an old rope dangling above the stream bank from a lofty bough. The monumental oak that it belonged to sprang from the hillside and extended its extraordinarily long arms, kinked arthritically from bough to branchlet, out over the pond. "The boys used to swing out over the pool on that rope," she explained. "In the early summer, when it was warmer and the water was deeper, they'd let go and jump in."

"What about you?"

"I was a girl." She paused for effect. "A tomboy girl. Naturally I had to outdo 'em!"

He raised an eyebrow.

"I climbed out to where the rope is tied to the branch—see it up there?" Barney gulped. "—and kept going. I shinnied out as far as I could..." she swept her pointing finger out along the length of the bough, past the rope to the successively slimmer branches beyond. At a certain point, she stopped. "That's as far out as I figured I could go and still have it hold my weight."

Meanwhile, in a thicket nearby, a pair of girlish eyes had followed Stella's sweeping gesture. Stella concluded her story with a whoop, "...and then I leapt off! Hoo-yaaa!"

She looked around as if addressing a large audience. In the thicket behind them, a boy's hand yanked a little girl's head down out of sight and caused the leaves to rustle.

Stella abruptly looked over her shoulder and studied the thicket. Seeing nothing, she supposed it to be robins or some other kind of birds moving around in there and turned her attention back to Barney, who was still gawking at the sickeningly high branch she'd jumped from.

"Jeez..." Barney muttered.

"The boys drug me out of the pond with a broken arm. But I was grinning from ear to ear! Pissed 'em off!"

"I can imagine."

"They treated me as an equal after that."

"So you've always been kind of a risk taker..."

She nodded and sighed.

~ ~ ~

"That's how come I hooked up with Knocker, I suppose..."

As she explained, Knocker was the *nom de guerre* for Dorgan Bailey's son, whose real name was Joe. Dorgan Bailey was a rough man who owned the auto repair shop over on Buchanan, the one Muphrid referred Barney to. Dorgan and his little woman had two sons, Jimmy and Joe. The younger brother Joe became an auto mechanic like his dad and, like his dad, had a nasty temper. Hence the moniker, Knocker. His brother Jimmy was somewhat more even tempered. Jimmy eventually left town—with his Vietnamese wife, Nga Phan—to get away from his father and his brother.

Eventually Knocker got away too, in a manner of speaking, if you consider the state penitentiary in nearby Sheridan to be a get-away.

"Living with Knocker was like a roller coaster. When we were up, it was good times. The best. But when we were down, it was fucked up. Knocker an' me used to have crazy bad arguments, knock-down drag-out. Finally gave me a black eye one night. I gave him one back, matching colors, kicked him in the nuts, then kicked him out of my house. I told him it was over. As in 'OVER', ya know?"

She thought a bit and a wry smile crept over her face, "But he kept comin' around, ya know what I mean? I said 'Knocker, I'm a zero-tolerance gal. You punch me once and you're out.' He kept comin' around though, apologizing and whining pitifully like a cat stuck out in the rain, so in a weak moment I let him come back." She sighed. "Big mistake! A smart guy like you woulda put some sense into my head. But you weren't around yet, were ya? Knocker, he knew he was on thin ice with me, so he stayed on guard all the time we were together and had to fling his shit elsewhere— that guy he banged up at the Lost Weekend bar is on disability now."

"Banged up" slightly understated the case. As she told it, the altercation started when some crosstown yokel sitting at the end of the bar wondered aloud how he got the nickname Knocker, "since knockers means boobs, am I right? Huh? Hahahaha! So you're like a big boob, huh? I am right? Hahahaha!" So addressed, Joe Knocker Bailey leaned over, grabbed the guy by the hair and with a swift arcing motion whipped the smartass's forehead directly onto the beer-splattered countertop as a hands-on demonstration of the proper meaning of the word "Knocker." Just to reinforce the lesson, he did it again. And a few more times again for good measure.

"Everybody has their own learning style," he said afterward during the court hearing, "but in my opinion, everybody understands the school of hard knocks. I guess you'd say I'm a teacher. A, wutcha-callit, educator."

The judge was not impressed.

As Stella explained, Knocker was at this moment nearing the end of his two-year sentence for aggravated assault. The legal modifier "aggravated" was based on the testimony of witnesses who said he delivered his concluding remarks by swinging a brass barstool down on the man's head. Those witnesses got beaten up pretty badly by Knocker's dad, Dorgan, for flapping their lips about something that was none of their goddamn business.

Strangely no witnesses came forth regarding those beatings and the charges against the senior Bailey were dropped.

"Me? I think Knocker got a bum rap. Not that he didn't deserve to be punished, but people were so fast to judge him. They didn't know his good side." Lying on her back next to Barney on the smooth rock, listening to the stream gurgling into the pond, Stella explained, "Knocker was rough sometimes, no doubt about that, but he could also be very sweet. He was so protective of me! Nobody else knew that side of him, that's all I'm saying. It's his asshole father—the guy who's gonna fix your car tomorrow?—he's the guy I blame. He used to beat Joey—Knocker—regularly. His own son! Imagine that! He's the one belongs in prison. Everybody says Knocker's a bad apple, but no one knows what he's gone through, how much he hurts inside. I mean, that loudmouth little jerk at the bar had it coming, right? Knocker says the guy shoulda seen he was in a bad mood that night. Only had himself to blame for what happened to him." She stopped and thought about it. "I also blame Nancy."

"Nancy? The policewoman here?"

"Yeah, her."

Stella propped herself back up on one elbow. "Nancy's the one that arrested Knocker, you know. So she and me we don't talk much anymore."

Barney countered, "She was just doing her job."

Stella waved off the notion, "Look, there's doing your job and there's doing your job. She was there at the bar. Saw the whole thing. She coulda just talked those two guys down and sent 'em home. Some people say she stood there waiting till the damage was done so she could have Knocker put away. She hated Knocker, hated the way her little boy idolized him."

"Chinstrap, you mean?"

"Yeah, that's right. Kyle. And if it wasn't about her boy, it was about proving herself to her daddy, old Tom. Arresting Knocker was her little trophy to get his approval."

"Did she get it?"

"His approval?"

"Yeah, did she get her dad Tom's approval?"

"Hard to say," she mused. "Tom's kinda hard to read. Doesn't talk much. You saw him this morning at the Roadhouse. Just sits there, never smiles, just watches. Didn't hear him say much, did you?"

Barney shook his head. "Nope, pretty taciturn guy."

"What's that...taciturn?"

"Means he doesn't say much."

"So just say it that way! Plain English. You college boys kill me!"

He laughed.

They fell quiet for a while, then Barney asked, "Are you going to get back together with Knocker when he gets out?" Barney noticed a sudden tightness in his throat.

She sprawled herself out backwards on the rock, laughing, "Ohmygod no! I'm so over him. I mean, I can't be his mother and I'm not about to put my face in the way of his fist again. It's just that people need to know that he's not a monster. He's more like a wounded animal, that's all. You feel pity, but no way are you going to put yourself in a cage with him, right?"

"I'm just glad I was using protection. If I'd had a kid with Knocker..." she shook her head like someone who'd just sailed through a red light without getting hit. "That woulda been the end of any chance of gettin' outta this place. I still hold to that hope. Of gettin' outta here someday."

She looked far away, straight up through the leafy canopy to the darkening indigo sky. In the west, Venus shone brightly through the branches. She closed her eyes and shook her head slowly, "No, no, we're not gettin' back together, not in a million years. I learned my lesson. We're over."

"Does Knocker know that?"

She didn't say anything.

"Do you talk to him?"

She said nothing, then finally, "I'll let 'im know when the time is right."

There was more rustling in the nearby thicket and a little boy's chipmunk voice, "Cut it out, man!" Another boy's voice chastised his friend, "Shhhhh! Nice going, dumbass, they heard you! Let's get outta here!" Suddenly, four little children burst out of the bushes like a startled covey of quail and ran up the Fillmore Road switchbacks as fast as their short little legs could carry them. But one of the foursome hung back, the one with straight hair, black as jet. The girl with Asian eyes. She hung back to study the long branch of the overarching oak, as if memorizing its every detail for later reference.

"C'mon Twee!" the boys yelled, "Why're you just standing there!? C'mon, let's go!"

Twee broke out of her trance and ran.

Stella rolled her eyes.

"Who was that?"

"The 'Chinstrap gang.' Bunch of delinquent grade schoolers."

"Chinstrap?"

"Yep, Kyle Lautenberg. He's their leader. The kid with the tattoo under his jaw."

Barney exclaimed, "Oh, is THAT what I saw!? It's a tattoo! I thought he was a little young to be growing a chinstrap beard!"

"Yeah. Knocker was involved in that too. Always the bad influence, that man. It's a long story, I'll tell you about it sometime."

Barney frowned, but decided he had plenty of time to learn more about that. The subject he wanted to get to before the conversation ended was Muphrid's mounds. "On another subject, Stella?"

"Yeah?"

"I've been wanting to ask you about your neighbor Muphrid and his—"

"Oh Muphrid again! He really fascinates you, doesn't he! Hey what's this?" She reached out and ran her fingers over a scar above Barney's left eye. "How'd this happen, babe?"

He shrugged. "My older brother. The usual. We were horsing around when we were kids and usually I was the one who got hurt. He grabbed my Gameboy and I chased him for it. We were running full tilt, he saw an open casement window and ducked but I couldn't react fast enough, so I caught it right over the eye. He felt pretty bad about it, really guilty, especially when I started wailing and blood was streaming down my face."

"No fighting?"

"Oh, scuffles yeah, but no fists. Compared to your life, my life sounds pretty tame."

She chuckled, "I'm jealous actually. My sister could throw a punch too. Fighting is no fun. Where's your brother now?"

~ ~ ~

Up on Fillmore, the kids slowed down and began exchanging impressions.

"Looks like Stella and Barney are getting lovey-dovey!" Peewee said, giggling.

"Sure looked like it," said Chinstrap. "I wonder if they're gonna do the you-know-what!"

"What?"

The pint-sized gang leader tried to explain, "Didn't you see 'em suckin' face? That's what a man and a lady do right before they do the you-know-what."

"What's that?"

"Oh man, Peewee, you don't know about the-you-know-what!? Jeez, where've you been livin', in some kinda cave?" Chinstrap rolled his eyes. "Twee can tell y—" He looked for the girl, but she was lagging behind, lost in thought. "Hm, well ask Dingo, he kin tellya. Tell 'im, Dingo!"

Dingo said, "Arf!"

"Oh man, you guys are such morons! Forget about it!"

"No, tell us. What's the you-know-what?"

"Forget about it!"

"C'mon! Tell! What is it?"

Chinstrap thwacked Peewee's cowlick. "I said, forget about it! Don't make me say that again!"

They walked in silence for a time, then Peewee called back to Twee, "C'mon, Twee! Hurry up! Whatchya doin'?"

Twee caught up with the boys. "I'm going to do what Stella did!"

Peewee's eyes opened wide. "You mean suck face!?"

"No!! The other thing I was talking about."

"Oh! You mean climb out on that branch?"

"Yeah. I mean, no. I'm gonna go out on an even higher branch."

Chinstrap threw his hands up and huffed. "You can't do that!"

"Why not?"

"'Cause yer a girl! You'd be too scared. Girls aren't strong enough anyway or brave enough t'do dangerous deeds like that."

"I'm gonna do it someday, you'll see!"

"Sure thing, Twee. Even if you got up there, you'd probably fall off an' get yerself killed." He reflected, "Then we'd have to mop up the bloody mess."

"Anh-ah!" she said, shaking her head. "You'll see."

Chinstrap started to scoff again, but as they came around the corner onto Main Street, the boy nearly ran into a skinny man with beige Brillo Pad hair shaped like an asparagus tip. "Hey, watch where you're sashaying!" the man said.

"Oh, sorry Ray!"

"Hi Ray!" Twee said.

"I'm not Ray. That's my brother. Don't get edgy, you're talking to Reggie!" he said. "Ha ha! Get it? Don't get edgy, you're talking to Reggie!"

"Oh, sorry, Reggie," Chinstrap said, in revision. "How was I spost t'know?"

"No problem-o, so no blame-o. What're you kids up to?"

"Just hangin' out at the pond where Barney an' Stella are suckin' face!"

Reggie frowned, "Sucking face? You mean, kissing?"

"Yeah, that's what I mean."

Reggie rocked his head from side to side. "Hm! Those two are getting little lovey-dovey, eh?"

Twee looked surprised, "That's what Peewee said! Lovey-dovey!"

"Well, you kids should leave them alone. They deserve a little privacy."

Peewee responded, "But they're doin' it out in the open!"

"Yeah, well you should still not bother them, OK?" Reggie looked from face to face. Each of them looked down penitently.

Peewee scuffed his shoe on the pavement. "OK."

Dingo did a dog-whine followed by a contrite "woof".

~ ~ ~

"My brother?" Barney said. "My brother's in Portland, works for some little start-up firm as a software developer. He went the I.T. route."

"I.T.?"

"Information technology. And I went for journalism. Sort of self-protective divergence among siblings—lessens the internecine competition."

"You and your twenty-dollar words! So you became a newspaper reporter, huh?"

"Yeah..." He looked around, unfocused.

"What?" she asked softly. "Whaddya mean 'yeah'? What's that about?"

"Oh, nothing. It's just, my brother was the star and I was always trying to get out of his shadow. My parents sort of overlooked me when I was growing up. Mostly my father, not so much my mom. My mom was a good Filipino mother—warm, loving no matter what—but my father was more distant and critical. Detached, you might say. I mean think about it, she wanted to name me Bernardo but he insisted on Barnard—as in Barnard's Star—for his...amusement. A real prince. That's probably why my mom and dad fought so much."

"Divorced?"

"No, Catholics aren't supposed to do that. They should have though. It would have been better for everybody. I always had the feeling I was a disappointment to my father; he would say, 'You're going to end up a bum, a schlub. Why can't you be like your brother?' My mother defended me."

"That must have been a comfort to you."

"Yes and no. It meant so much to have her love, but in a paradoxical way it undermined my confidence that I fell so short that I had to have a defender. And he was intimidating, especially when he was drunk. Socially, I felt like a loner. Although I had friends, I preferred to go my own way, alone. I nosed around the periphery, looking in. I imagined I was scouting around just outside the circle of a campfire, looking in at the people who seemed to know how to be happy together in this world."

"You were like a wolf?"

"Mm, no, not a wolf exactly. I thought of myself more as a coyote—unable to compete head to head, but clever and able to evade and outrun those who came after me. I knew all the escape routes. Like a coyote, I stayed aloof, turning my nose up at the comfortable people in the campfire circle and at those in authority who would try to steer my life. I wanted to be in that circle, and yet I didn't. I wanted to understand what everyone else seemed understand, but not be of them. I was, a, a—"

"A misfit," she offered.

"Yeah. A misfit."

"It's misfits that fix the world you know. 'Cause they can stand outside and see what others don't...or won't. When you got nothing to lose, you can afford to be honest."

"Huh. Yeah. Funny how that works, isn't it?

"I guess we have to live by our own lights. And that's what you're doing, Barney."

"Yep, that has been my calling. I couldn't compete with my techie brother, so I became a journalist, someone who noses around the periphery and discovers the dark corners just beyond the light of that campfire, in the shadows where injustice is committed. Well that's my idealistic idea. And that's how I came to this profession, to the *Portland Mirror*."

He looked glum.

"Something wrong?" she asked.

"Oh, big talk. I've dreamt of becoming a famous investigative reporter, but here I am, covering desserts. Human-interest crap."

"Oh Deena! That's important too, I suppose. Human-interest. You're gonna put our town on the map. That's good for business right?"

"Well, her cable TV show's already done that. I'm not adding anything of value."

"Well, aren't you a barrel of cheer? At least you got a good job, what's so bad about that?"

"Fact is, I kind of shot myself in the foot."

"How's that?"

He found a pebble and lobbed it into the pond. Gloop! "When I came on as a cub reporter, I told them about my ambitions to be an investigative reporter so they said I should start with the police blotter. I'd report on petty and not-so petty crimes around town. But I didn't need the police to tell me about one case of larceny. It was happening right under our noses at the City Desk. On my own time I followed the trail. It led to the daughter of someone very important, a bigwig, a honcho."

"Yeah? Who?"

He looked at his shoes, "The daughter of the CEO, the same CEO who acquired our *Portland Mirror* in a hostile takeover."

"Phwew! So the CEO's kind of a thief too?"

He was impressed. "Yes, that's true. Astute observation. So his daughter came by that trait naturally. Anyway, I decided to look into what she was up to. It turned out she was, as CFO, embezzling from the *Portland Mirror*, her own father's company! I decided I was gonna nail her."

"Even though you were biting the hand that feeds you. That's pretty ballsy!"

"There's a fine line between ballsy and stupid," he said. "In this case, though, it was pretty stupid. They put the kibosh on the story and told me to cease and desist."

"And, let me guess, you didn't?"

"Right on. My editor was furious that I'd defied explicit directions. I had thought that if I told the story, they'd be so impressed, they couldn't say no. I thought wrong. They put me on probation and reassigned me to fluff stories—like Deena. I mean, nothing against her, I should be thankful I still have a job, I suppose. But that's not the kind of career I'm after. Anyhow, that's what I'm doing here in your town of Sweetbread."

"Well, if it's any consolation I'm glad you came." She stroked his cheek with her fingertips.

He smiled. "Thanks."

"And so you're on probation for doing what they hired you to do, eh?"

"Ironic, isn't it? Everybody likes to air somebody else's dirty laundry, but not their own."

She chuckled, "So true!"

He scrutinized her face, "So what's that over your lip?"

She touched the little scar that intersected her upper lip. "Oh, that's where Knocker hit me before I kicked him out. I guess we all have scars of one kind or another. Part of living. Anybody makes out to have no scars, watch out, they're liars."

"Amen. Watch out for anyone who pretends to be perfect."

"Yay for the oddballs and misfits."

A breeze came through and Barney hugged himself, "Hey, it's getting a little chilly, don't you think?"

"Woosy city boy!"

~ ~ ~

As the October darkness fell, they chased each other this way and that all the way up Fillmore hill back to her yellow clapboard house. Giggling like children, they caught each other at each turn for a full mouth kiss, then ran off again till the gravel incline ended and the level asphalt began, the exact place where her neighbor Al's house stood—Al Gruber, the one with the koi pond. She thumbed her nose at his house, blew a big raspberry and pointed at his koi pond, "Anything else happens to my dog, Gruber, another one o' your fish is goin' on my grill!" Almost on cue, Rogerdog the eye-patched Irish setter came loping out of nowhere toward Stella and Barney, tongue lolling, right through Mr. Gruber's flowerbed. Stella thought that was hilarious, but Barney just closed his eyes and shook his head.

"Come on, Stella, let's go."

Moments later, they stepped onto Stella's porch. While she opened the front door for him, he paused to look across Main to where his Pinto sat at the roadside. There was Muphrid's pickup too, parked right in front of his car. The carport itself was vacant. He stood there, trying to imagine why Muphrid would do that. Not park his truck in the carport, that is.

"C'mon in, don't be shy!" Stella dragged Barney in by the shirtsleeve.

~ ~ ~

"Koi stew work for you?" Stella said, pulling open the fridge door. "Lots of koi leftovers. Won't last forever."

Barney blew through his lips. He had eschewed the koi last night, but tonight maybe he'd ease off on his moral compunction a bit. Hunger will do that to you. "Sure."

"Change of heart?"

"I suppose...."

"You're not sure?" she insisted, holding the fridge door open just far enough so the light stayed on inside.

"No, I'm sure. I'm sure, my 'Koi Mistress'!"

"Mistress!? Hey pal, I'm not your mistress!"

"No no! It's a poem. *To His Coy Mistress*." He threw his head back and recited, "'Had we but world enough and time / This coyness lady were no crime / We would sit down and think which way to walk / And pass our long love's day ...' You know, the one by Andrew Marvell?"

"Who's that, a magician?"

"No, no!" He laughed. "He was a poet, lived just after Shakespeare."

"Well, I'm nobody's mistress, just remember that." She looked askance at him, still holding the door of the Amana fridge open.

"No, I didn't mean that! I was just free associating. You know, 'coy' like demure and 'koi' like the fish and thought—"

"All right, shut up, college boy. Are you in with the stew or no? It's me and the stew or neither nothin'!" She winked.

"I'm in!"

"OK, then. Man, you think too much! No wonder you drove off the road!" Chuckling, she pulled a foil covered platter out of the refrigerator and placed it on the counter. She went back to the fridge. Out came veggies. From a cabinet drawer, with a clatter, out came knives, forks and other utensils. "I gotta keep an eye on you. Keep you from getting into trouble."

Barney sat down on one of the cheap vinyl kitchen chairs while Stella chopped the veggies and threw them into a stainless steel bowl. Soon after, onions were sauteing in a saucepan. Barney rose to help, but she pushed him back down into his chair, "Hey, this in my domain. Take a load off your feet and talk to me. How did the interview go?"

"Oh, it went fine. She seems like a nice lady."

"She is. Deena's sort of like everyone's favorite aunt around here." Stella poured a carton of broth into the pot and turned on the flame. "So what're you gonna write?"

He leaned back into his chair, "Well, so far I've got a mini biography on her—sort of a rags-to-riches, small town girl makes it to the big time kind of story—which will comprise my first installment."

"So, a series, huh?" She ground black pepper over the sizzling, now-translucent onions. Then she picked up a spatula and began pushing them around in the saucepan. The aroma made Barney's mouth water.

"Yeah, a short series. I figure maybe a three-parter."

"Well you can work on Part One after dinner. I'll clear a space on the coffee table for you."

That sounded fine to him. "Meanwhile, Stella, tell me about this Muphrid guy. I'm trying to figure out what the deal is with the mounds in his yard. I just can't let it go."

She sprinkled salt into the pot as the broth came to a boil. "Boy you're obsessed with this guy. What kinda mounds are we talkin' about? Whaddya think's under 'em, bodies?"

He just looked her.

"Oh get real! Sweet simple Muphrid? You gotta be kidding!" She turned the burner down. "Tell me about these mounds, then. Never been back there myself. What did you see?"

He told her about what he saw through the hole in the fence before Muphrid hastily slapped up the sheet of plywood: mounds, the lush grass and raw earth spilling from a gaping hole.

She looked straight at him. "You're not making this up, are you? Are you trying gin up a story for your paper? Squirm outta this Deena assignment?"

No, he wasn't.

As if to reinforce that point, he offered a possible explanation. "Muphrid says the hole is for planting a tree and Nancy says the mounds are just glacial erratic rocks," he said. "Like the one under her garden berm. Maybe that's all it is."

"I don't buy that." Stella set the spatula down and looked straight at him. "I don't trust that bit—that woman. You said there was thick grass growing on top of the mounds. That doesn't sound like glacials. Not much grows on top of those rocks, soil's too thin. Look at Nancy's petunias. They're pathetic. Something's feeding that grass."

"Maybe it's not rocks under the mounds? Is that what you're saying?" Barney sat up straight.

"That's what I'm thinking. And what's all that digging he's always doing there? I've heard digging over there for a long time. Sometimes in the day, sometimes at night. I figured he had some garden project going. But for months? Listen—you swear you're not making this up?"

Absolutely, he assured her. They were both thinking the same unspoken thought.

"Bodies?"

She shrugged. "Don't get too excited. Probably a simple explanation." She picked up the spatula again and pushed the sizzling onions around in the saucepan, then dumped the chopped veggies in, sprinkled them with sage and stirred some more. The ensemble smelled good, the fragrance was comforting. "But I have been wondering about the things going on since he moved back in after his renter died."

"The renter being PK?"

"Yep, that'd be he." She amplified, "PK Sharma."

"Sharma, huh? What kind of things were you wondering about? About Muphrid, I mean."

"Well, for starters, I can see straight across Main to Muphrid's house from this kitchen window. See?" She pulled apart the curtains above the dinette table. "Every so often, always on a Sunday, always kinda late at night, this guy in a pinstripe suit shows up in a big SUV—one of those high-end luxury jobs with tinted windows, you know, like a Lexus or Cadillac Escalade? One of those sissy city SUVs that oughta have a license plate that says, 'POSER!'" She shook her head, smiling sardonically. "ANYWAY, I always know when this dude is coming, 'cause Muphrid pulls his truck out of the carport during the day and parks it on the street."

"Like he did today," Barney said. "I saw his truck at the curb when we came back from pond."

"I saw it too."

"So you think the suit is going to show up tonight?"

70

"Yep."

"What time?"

"Oh, around ten. We got time." She went back to the fridge, hiding her grin. "Hey, you wanna beer?" He did.

She pulled out a church key and popped the tops off two beer bottles and clunked one down in front of him, clinked it with hers. "Cheers, Barn. I think you got yourself your investigative story after all—and I'm gonna help you!"

~ ~ ~

"Sh-sure." He took the beer bottle uneasily to his lips. Then he pressed on. "Tell me what happens after this guy shows up. The suit, I mean."

She dumped the fish into a hot saucepan and the moisture popped and sizzled noisily until she covered it with a lid. Then she lowered the flame, grabbed the handle and shuffled the contents. She poured ready-made broth into the pot, turned on the fire under it and finally sat down opposite him, beer in hand, "OK, here's where it gets weird." She leaned in close. "There's lights flickering behind the fence, digging sounds, like I told you. Sometimes, the shovel rings, like it's hitting rock or cement—you know what I'm talkin' about?"

Barney's expression did not change. "Uh-huh."

"There's another guy too. Big guy with a shaved head. Comes along with the suit. Anyway, I've seen that big guy loading something into the SUV...and money changing hands afterward. Muphrid says it's just one of his regulars coming in for one of his famous late-night razor cuts."

"What the hell is a 'late night razor cut'!?"

She laughed, "Who the hell knows!? Muphrid says the suit is a favorite client, some McMinnville lawyer type who lives in a fancy estate back in the hills. Apparently, he really likes Muphrid's razor cut hair styling, but it has to be after hours, way after hours. On Sundays before the work week starts. So Muphrid put up a sign on his barbershop, 'Businessman's special: Late night razor cut. By appointment only.' So far, he's only got the one client, far as I know." She reflected for a moment. "Well, maybe Big Baldy gets his head shaved too."

"So let me get this straight, the suit who comes around Sunday nights is a lawyer needing a haircut and a shave?"

"According to Muphrid, yeah. But..." She got up, dumped the fish and veggies into the pot and stirred it, laid the lid on and turned down the flame. "Ready in a little while!" she announced. "But there's also the digging and loading something into the SUV. And the money changing hands. Maybe it's money for the haircut but it all seems pretty...fishy.'"

Stella didn't notice when the spiral bound notepad had come out, but Barney had it in hand and was scribbling little notes into it. Barney thought about Stella's observant reporting, figured she might be an asset to him in this case. But he wanted to keep her out of the action; she had to live here with her neighbors long after he'd gone, after all. But as an anonymous source, she was, well...stellar. "So how did Muphrid meet this guy?"

"Used to be the attorney for his renter, that Indian guy, PK Sharma. The one that died."

"Tell me about Sharma."

"Oh, he was a retired Intel engineer. Jeez, half this town is retirees! Gets pretty dull around here!"

Barney was thinking Stella more than made up for the town's reputed dullness.

The aroma of fish and onions and pepper filled the kitchen. The stew was ready.

She ladled the stew into bowls and sat down. "Yeah, old PK. He was a nice man. Quiet though. Not a big talker."

"Taciturn guy, eh?"

"Yeah," she laughed. "Taciturn."

She related how PK had been looking for a quiet town to retire to in anonymity. Muphrid offered to lease his house out to Sharma. Muphrid moved back into his elderly mother's apartment over his barbershop on Hayes Street where he could take care of her. Sharma kept mostly to himself. The only thing people knew was he had a predilection for collecting Beanie Babies and gardening. And sweets. In time, he got so addicted to Deena's desserts he became morbidly obese and eventually developed type two diabetes, which was not only rampant in the nation, but seemed especially so in this town. Ailing, he went back to India and died soon afterward. The attorney, name of Fliess, handled his estate and in so doing became acquainted with Muphrid—and his excellent razor cuts.

"Speaking of razors, you didn't use the one I left for you this morning, did you? Now you got that stylish stubble going. Kinda faint so far, but it shows promise!"

"Ah, I'm not a hairy guy. But no, that razor you left me was used."

"Just once! Picky picky! Well, we'll go get you a new one tomorrow. Unless you wanna go for one of Muphrid's famous late-night shaves to-night!"

"NO THANKS."

~ ~ ~

They ate, talked and speculated more about the mystery of Muphrid's late night visitors.

Afterward, Barney asked Stella if she had a screwdriver to pry open his car's trunk. He needed it to extract his laptop and file his report.

"How about a crowbar?"

"Even better!"

It worked like a charm and within minutes he was back in the warmth of her home with his laptop, power supply and toiletry kit. She told him to make himself comfortable in the easy chair at the end of the magazine-strewn coffee table. She cleared a space for his laptop and went back to the kitchen area.

"I'll help you with the dishes, Stella—"

"Forget it, you've got work to do. I'll race you to the finish!"

While dishes and silverware clinked in the kitchen sink and the water turned on and off, he retrieved his notepad and hammered out his first dispatch:

~ ~ ~

Sweet Dreams of an Avid Diva
By Barnard Starr

Sweetbread, Oregon—*Growing up in Moorehead, Minnesota, heir to a long line of German and Swedish pastry shop owners, young Deena Joy Olson dreamed of becoming a famous dessert chef. But reality outstripped that girl's wildest dreams as she became the Dessert Channel's "diva of deep-fried desserts to die for." Deena Poole broadcasts her wildly popular cooking show from her grand pink and red Victorian home in the quaint little town of Sweetbread in Oregon's Yamhill wine country. Her rise to wealth and fame has been so rapid, her celebrity so widespread, her sense of success seems not to have completely sunk in. She leans back in her regal red velvet wingback chair and surveys her grand Victorian home, with awards vying with paintings for space on the dark wood wall, and her face glows with girlish wonderment at how far she has come, so fast. Sweeping her arm like a proud magician, she discloses breathlessly how "it never fails to amaze me that I've come to this grand place in my life's journey. But it's the joy I bring to everyday people that really makes me tear up."*

Asked about the secret of her technique—aside from her well-known penchant for deep-frying everything—she says she strives to bring together radically different flavors, dissimilar taste modalities like salt and sweet and bitter and sour, to make for gustatory excitement. "It's like a town full of conflicting personalities—their interactions make life interesting!" she exults.

~ ~ ~

The dispatch went on to describe her road to success and conclude with a teaser: *In my next installment, I hope to prise out a few clues about her upcoming Mystery Dessert!*

~ ~ ~

"Done!" he announced, closing the lid of his laptop just as Stella hung up her dishtowel.

"Cool! Let's hear it!"

He read the dispatch to her and she approved, not without a little awe. "You really are a reporter! Your thing sounds just like something I'd read in the paper!"

"Well, um, thank you," he said, somewhat unsure how to respond. "I guess that's because I really *am* a reporter, ha ha!" He immediately changed the subject: "So now that that's done, let's get back to Muphrid's nighttime visitors. You said this pinstripe lawyer guy Fliess shows up around what time did you say, ten?"

"Yep."

He snapped his wristwatch into view. It was 9:30. "OK, this is probably another one of my bad ideas, but I'm going on a reconnaissance mission tonight."

"Awesome!" she pumped her fist. "Hey, I'll help you, Barn. Let's do this as a team. I can stand guard. What's your cell phone number? I can call you if things heat up over there and you need to high-tail it outta there."

He gave her his number, and she gave him hers. But he expressed his reservations about getting her involved in something that might make life hard for her in this town.

"I don't give crap about that, Barn. If things turn sour for me here, it'd be just the excuse I been looking for to blow outta this place. Naw, don't worry about me!"

They talked a while longer, then Barney said, "Look, Stella, that may

be fine, but there's other factors I have to consider, like your physical safety."

"I'm not scared." She looked at the portrait of her sister on the wall.
"Us Gervais's, we don't scare easy."

"Well, that's for sure. But there are still other things I have to consider."

"Like what?"

"I don't know, professional, I guess. This little escapade is tangential
to my assignment."

"English please?"

"It's verboten."

"That's not English, Barney, but I get the idea. You're afraid of violat-
ing your probation."

"Yeah."

"And you're afraid I'm going to mess things up for you."

"No, no, no, that's not it at all!" Now he was squirming. "I just am
worried about you. You know, having to live with the consequences here."

"I told you, I don't care. Hey, if I'm not scared, you can't be either!
Sheesh!" she protested. "This is too important! This might be a case of
murder. You can't run away from that! You DON'T want to run away from
that! Don't be a dope, this might be your big break!"

"I know. I just gotta think this all out before we go off half-cocked.
By myself, no offense. I'm going for a walk to think all this through. Ten
o'clock, right?"

He saw the frustration on her face as he looked back at her through the
screen door as it hissed shut. The cool night air felt good. Cool and fresh
as freedom.

= CHAPTER 6 =

~ ~ ~

Barney began walking west on Fillmore Road, toward the pond, watching furtively over his shoulder. A sliver of door light suggested Stella had left her front door cracked open to furtively watch him as well. He looked straight ahead now and continued past Al Gruber's down the dark switchbacks to the Rock Creek pond. He waited a minute or two then doubled back. When he saw that the sliver of door light had vanished, he sprinted past Stella's doorstep to the intersection with Main, scooted around the corner, ducking low like a commando past her kitchen window. On he ran, down the hill he'd driven up only yesterday. Only yesterday! Could it be? It seemed months had passed since then.

Once he was sure he hadn't been seen—or followed—he stood erect and resumed an easy walking pace down the rural road. He had some time to kill. His Keens crunched on the gravel shoulder. The cold night air was sweet. In the distance, he could see the lights of Sheridan. Knocker was down there somewhere. After a while, Barney checked his watch. It was ten minutes before 10:00 pm, so he crossed the quiet road and walked briskly back toward town, staying on the shoulder along the drainage ditch that edged the farm fields. The air was still and clear and the stars were strewn out across the black sky like spilled sugar. Gradually, as his eyes adapted to the dark, he was surprised how the sky no longer looked black at all, but seemed to glow softly, illuminated as it was so many pinpoint lights, each a little world with its own stories to tell. *You peer into the dark long enough,* he thought, *and gradually unsuspected things will come into view. Patterns emerge.* There was the big W of Cassiopeia. Or an M if you look at from a different orientation. And there, rising triumphantly in the east, was Orion. The Hunter.

Looking up the road, he saw the big sign again, "Welcome to Sweet-bread! Living here is like living nowhere—!" It occurred to him it would be a good idea to look down once in a while. He was walking along the edge of a drainage ditch, after all. It would be good not to tumble into it. Ten yards on, his foot struck the can of blue paint. Clunk! It rolled noisily down into the ditch. Oops.

Suddenly, the ground ahead grew bright, his shadow elongated weirdly out in front of him, bisecting the brightness. Then the shadow began to shrink back toward his feet. A car was approaching from behind! He checked his watch again: a couple minutes before ten. The Suit and Big Baldy, right on time! Lest they spot him, Barney reflexively dove out of sight into the ditch. There, he experienced an unintended reunion with the paint can. He pushed it aside and, keeping low, watched as the big SUV swept by. He felt the whoosh of air on the back of his head. That was it, the Escalade! The instant after it passed, he exploded out of the ditch, running after the receding taillights like a maniac. Charging up the hill to Muphrid's house, gasping for air, his lungs and limbs screamed for relief. But he kept running as hard as he could till he reached his idled Pinto, where he hid behind the rear bumper. There he remained until he could breathe normally again. Through the rear window he could see the suit and the brawny bald man climb out of the SUV and saunter out of sight around the far corner of the fence, presumably to Muphrid's porch. A doorbell rang.

This was his chance. He bounded to the fence-hugging plum tree whose sticky pits had so recently heaped insult upon his poor car. He tested the first branch and it felt sturdy, so he hauled himself up into its dark foliage. Leaves and sticky pits fell to the ground. Then he carefully climbed a bit higher till he could see over the fence into the yard. There he could discern mounds cast in dark relief by the house lights. In particular, there was the one with a cavernous hole beside it.

And there was that fetid smell again.

Across the street, Stella doused her kitchen lights and looked out her kitchen window. She saw the black Escalade in the driveway. With tinted windows concealing its interior, it resembled nothing so much as a hearse. She saw the men talking to Muphrid on his front porch. She saw the plum tree against the fence, but she did not see Barney in it.

"Pick up, Barney!" she said to her cell phone as it rang his number. "C'mon!" She held it up to her ear, but it just kept ringing.

Immediately, Tchaikovsky's 1812 Overture began playing in Barney's pocket. "Jeezusfuckinchrist!" He nearly fell out of the tree trying to muffle the sound. He fumbled in his pocket, frantically trying to silence the infernal noisemaker. Fortunately, the volume was low, but now the display lit up brightly as he pressed the side button to turn off the ring tone. When all was back in order, he looked toward the porch, but none of the three men seemed to have noticed. He blew through his lips, relieved.

Stella texted him: *They r here. Where r u? Come back now!*

Now Barney felt the phone vibrate, but there was no ring tone, thankfully. "Cut it out, Stella," he hissed through his teeth. "You trying to get me killed?"

The men switched on flashlights and came into the yard, so he crouched involuntarily. They were talking and pointing.

~ ~ ~

What happened next confirmed Barney's darkest suspicions.

The large sleek headed man donned a camper's headlamp, went into the yard and climbed down into the Stygian pit. Down in the hole, the man wrestled with and pulled back a lid of some sort. A minute later, the searching beam of the headlamp announced his reemergence. Out he came, elbowing his way out of the pit while dragging a big black body bag up to the rim. Muphrid and the suit observed the bag from the porch, then went inside the house. Baldy climbed out, then squatted down for leverage to pull the heavy bag all the way out onto the grass. He studied it for a while, occasionally pressing on it to feel the contours of what was inside. The man's toothy grin sent a chill down the back of Barney's neck. Barney looked around through his leafy blind across the street to Stella's kitchen window. The lights were off. The phone vibrated again. The caller ID said Stella Gervais. If he had picked up the call he would have learned that she was down at the pond, looking for him.

Meanwhile, Baldy resumed his work. He dragged the body bag to the Escalade, hit the foot pedal under the rear bumper and the trunk lid opened automatically to receive its dark cargo. The man hefted the bag into the trunk, pulled out a hankie and wiped his brow. Then he sat on the bumper under the yawning trunk lid and waited.

After a while, Muphrid's front door opened again, pouring light across the porch. He and the other man came out. The man in the pinstripe suit was patting his cheeks and caressing his freshly styled hair, smiling with satisfaction. Baldy hopped off the bumper, said something to Mr. Suit who nodded and pulled the trunk lid down. But the lid hung up so Baldy shoved the black bag deeper into the trunk till the lid closed cleanly.

"Good job, Milo," said Mr. Suit who then turned to Muphrid and handed him an envelope. "And this is for you, buddy." Muphrid opened it, thumb-counted the bills inside then tucked it into his pocket—alongside the Beanie Baby and the razor.

A bright light shone on Barney. Maybe it was headlights or maybe it was Stella, shining a flashlight to see him from across the street. *Dammit, Stella, you're going to give away my position! Just turn off—*

~ ~ ~

"SIR, I NEED YOU TO COME DOWN OUT OF THAT TREE." It was a husky, somehow familiar, woman's voice. "RIGHT NOW!"

Startled, he looked down and saw that the uniformed woman was Officer Nancy Lautenberg. She aimed her service flashlight directly into his eyes and the whole world went blindingly white. He froze.

"I mean NOW!"

"OK, OK!" In his haste, his foot slipped and he fell out of the tree. On the way down, his outstretched arm caught one of the protruding fence nails. With all the adrenaline, he hardly felt it. But lying there on the ground, he noticed the blood.

"Would you mind telling me what you were doing there...Barney?"

"Uh, uh, uh." Then came the lamest and most ancient of prevarications. "Uh, I can explain!"

"Then why don't you just do that?"

"I'm bleeding."

"All right, let's get you bandaged up and you can 'explain' at the station." She found a rag in the car to wrap around his arm. She called over to Muphrid and Mr. Suit, told them not to worry, she had everything under control. She led Barney to the back seat of the patrol car, pushed his head down so it would clear the door frame and shut the door after him.

Just for the heck of it, she turned on her flashers for the quarter mile trip back to the "police station," which was in fact merely her office in the City Hall building. Separated from Officer Nancy by a steel mesh, Barney noticed there were no inside door handles for the backseat passengers.

Interesting! He supposed she was aware of that and would get that fixed sooner or later.

Meanwhile, Barney's cell phone lay on the ground under the plum tree. It illuminated again and began vibrating.

~ ~ ~

Officer Nancy's office was down a short hallway from Mayor Jeremy's office. The room contained a dismal gray steel desk, some informational posters on the wall and a water cooler. The fluorescent lights imparted a pallid bluish cast to human flesh. The "jail cell" consisted of a keyed shackle connected by a short chain to a ring that slid along a cable running from a simple cot with an army blanket lying square folded on it to a scarred wooden chair and thence to a tiny bathroom. The idea was to let the prisoner travel from cot to chair to bathroom and back—a jail cell minus the cell.

"If you don't mind, just place your foot on the footprint painted on the floor and we'll get you hooked up here."

Barney demurred. "Wait a second. Maybe I was snooping. OK, I'll concede that. But I saw a man dragging a body bag out of a hole in the ground. I think there's a crime you need to investigate."

Nancy looked at him without expression, then burst into laughter.

"What?" he uttered in disbelief.

"It's potting soil!"

"Huh?"

"Was it a big black bag you saw?"

"Yes!"

She laughed again. "Muphrid's renter—name of PK Sharma—ordered a bunch of industrial size bags of potting soil. Had some crazy gardening project in mind. After PK died, Muphrid had all these bags of soil to get rid of. His attorney, Jason Fliess, who lives up in the hills, is doing some landscaping so he comes by Sunday evenings for a haircut and to pick up a bag or two of soil."

"Doesn't that seem a little suspicious to you?"

"How should I know? I'm a police officer, not a gardener. If you think it's foul play, I can tell you this: there hasn't been a murder in Sweetbread since 1927. So enough with the questions. I need you to put your foot right here, on—"

"All right, forget the hole, who's the big bald guy that carried the bag to the car?"

"That's Fliess' nephew. Big strong guy. Living with his uncle till he can find a place of his own." She looked at Barney, "Satisfied?"

"Not really."

"Well, tough beans, the conversation's over." She pointed to the painted footprint on the floor, "Now put your foot there or I'll charge you for resisting arrest."

He complied and allowed himself to be thusly "incarcerated" with a shackle on his ankle.

She went over and laid the shackle key on her desk. Out came a sheaf of forms from the drawer, which she flopped down onto her blotter. She sat down in her chair, filled in some information then swiveled to address the journalistic renegade. "Overstepped your assignment there dintchya, Mr. Starr? You were supposed to be interviewing Deena Poole, wasn't that the plan?"

"Well, uh, yeah but—"

"'Well, uh, yeah but now you're dealing with the consequences of sticking your nose where you have no business sticking it," she said.

"May I ask, what I'm being charged with?"

"Trespassing. Stalking. Property damage—you broke the limb off Muphrid's plum tree. Reckless endangerment."

"Endangerment? Whom did I endanger?"

Nancy pointed at his bleeding arm, "Yourself."

"I don't think there's a law against that."

"There is around here."

Barney frowned.

Nancy pointed to his arm. "Here, let me take care of that." She got up, went to the wall mounted first aid kit and pulled out a roll of gauze, some alcohol wipes, antibiotic ointment, adhesive tape and a pair of scissors. Then she pulled her swivel chair up to Barney and proceeded to dress his wound.

"So how long am I going to be in custody? I have the right to contact a lawyer and go before a judge."

"Do you have a lawyer?"

"Well no," he said. "But I'll sure as hell find one!"

"You can cool your jets," she said as she put the finishing touches on the dressing. "It may all be moot. Depends on whether Muphrid decides to press charges."

As if on cue, her cell phone came to life with its ring tone, Wagner's rousing "Ride of the Valkyries."

"Yeah? Uh-huh. OK. Come on over." After a quick chat, she terminated the call. "Muphrid's coming over soon as his business associates are ready to leave. Wants to talk to you."

"Is he angry?"

"No. In fact he said he understood why you might have been curious and so he's going explain everything. After that, as a peace offering, he's going to give you one of his 'late night razor cuts'. For free. That's a fifty-dollar value right there. Just to show you there's no hard feelings."

Barney gulped. "Um, I don't need a haircut."

"I would beg to differ. You're lookin' pretty scruffy there, fella. He'll clean you right up!" She laughed. "Now here's how to navigate with that shackle on..."

Barney found it hard to focus on her subsequent instructions or anything else she had to say.

Finally, she declared, "Look, this is between the two of you, so after I process your paperwork, I'm going home for a while. I need to put my son Kyle to bed. I'll leave the office door unlocked for Muphrid to come in."

Barney pulled at his shackle. "Are you sure that's a good idea?"

Nancy said nothing, just scribbled information in one of the forms she plucked from the sheaf. Then she checked her wristwatch and wrote down the time in one of the little boxes on the form. She looked up. "What's all the blue paint on your trousers?" Before he could answer she said, "Never mind, I don't care to know. I'm outta here. Want me to bring you something to eat when I come back?"

"N-no." He shook his head and tried to convince her it was not a good idea to leave him alone with Muphrid.

She shrugged, "I think you're letting your imagination get the better of you again."

"But—"

"Muphrid's harmless! Not too swift, a little odd, but he's a gentle and kind man."

"But—"

"Wow, you look like a scared puppy! I'm telling you, he's not gonna bite you."

"But if—"

"No more buts! No more ifs. As my mom used to say, 'If ifs and ands were pots and pans, there'd be no need for tinners.'"

"Huh?" he felt like he couldn't breathe.

"Here, if you need anything..." She scribbled her cell phone number on a scrap of paper and handed it to him.

He took it and reached into his pocket for the cell phone that was not there. He groaned. "Lost my cell phone when I fell out of the tree, so I can't call anyone."

Nancy shrugged, "Oh well."

"What if I try to make a break for it?"

She laughed and patted his thigh, "I'm not concerned. I don't think you got the cojones—or the stupidity—to try to make a break for it."

"Will you lock the door at least?"

She shook her head, "No."

"Why not?"

Her eyes darted around at first then she fixed her gaze on Barney and explained, "I told Muphrid I'd leave it unlocked in case he gets here before I get back."

Barney fidgeted. "What if somebody else wanders in? I'm helpless here."

"No one's going to bother you, no one even knows you're here except Muphrid. Now calm down, Mama'll be back soon." And she was gone.

~ ~ ~

It was pitch black around the pond, so Stella had to step carefully.

"Barney?...Barney!?...Barney!?" No answer. "Barney!" Nothing.

She sighed, looked around in the darkness. It was time to take desperate measures. She punched 911 on her cell phone. The dispatcher routed her to the local police.

Nancy was just getting into her cruiser when her cell phone began playing "Ride of the Valkyries."

"This is Officer Lautenberg."

"Something's happened to Barney!"

"Who is this?"

"Stella Gervais. Barney's disappeared."

"Yeah, I arrested him. Caught him snooping in Muphrid's yard."

Stella puckered her lips. "So that's where he was. Where is he now?"

"I put him in the pokey for the night. He was—" Nancy paused to weigh her next statement.

"He was what? Hello?"

Nancy sighed, "He was ranting about a body bag he thought he saw."

"Body bag! Ohmygod..."

"It wasn't a body bag. I wasn't gonna say anything but he's gonna try to scare you with that story, so I want you to know the truth."

"Which is what?"

"It was just a bag of potting soil."

"I think Barney knows the difference between potting soil and body bags."

Stella couldn't see Nancy smiling indulgently at the other end of the line. "Muphrid has a bunch of industrial size bags of potting soil, so they could be confused with body bags I suppose. Especially by a hot-headed reporter scrounging for a sensational story."

"Piss on you, Lautenberg."

"Easy there, Gervais, settle down. You know it's true."

"No, I don't know it's true. But in any case, you have no right to lock him up for doing his job, he's an investigative reporter you know—"

"He's supposed to be interviewing Deena Poole, not snooping around neighbors' yards. And yes I can lock him up—for trespassing, property damage and peeping tom-ism."

"You've got a pretty thin case there. Listen, I'm coming over to see him."

"Sorry, jail's off limits right now. Visiting hours start at nine, so come back in the morning. I'll let him go if Muphrid doesn't press charges. Figure he'll learn his lesson either way."

Nancy couldn't see her, but she knew Stella was fuming.

"Just cool down, Stella. Get some sleep and you can see your—boy-friend—" she chuckled, "in the morning."

"Oh gotohell, you smug bitch."

"Whatever."

Nancy ended the call just as the black Escalade pulled up alongside her cruiser.

Jason's shave-headed goon of a nephew stuck his head out the passenger window. "Is he in there?"

"Yep. Door's unlocked."

~ ~ ~

After Nancy left, Barney just sat there in the sickly light, wondering what was going to happen to him. Every time he heard a creak, he jumped. As a distraction, he studied the phone number she'd given him. He thought about his lost cell phone. *Must be lying there in the weeds right now.* He exhaled with heavy resignation and let the scrap flutter to the floor.

Now there was nothing but time for reflection and self-pity. He saw himself shackled and alone with that murderous, razor brandishing barber. Contemplating his untimely end, he went into mourning over his short dance with Stella. Tears welled up at the thought of never seeing her again. No! He would not let this happen!

The shackle key sat in plain sight on Nancy's desk, taunting him, daring him to take a chance. He walked toward it as far as the cable allowed, then hopped a couple of feet farther on his free foot with his rear leg extended backwards so he looked like a track athletic clearing a hurdle. He stretched his swiping hand towards the desk. But the desk was still a few inches away from his fingertips. It was futile. Nevertheless, desperate circumstances call for mindless actions. So he took a breath, lunged for the key and fell flat on his face.

"Shit."

He looked around and saw his wooden chair near the cable. He could use that to extend his reach!

Moments later, he was flat on his face again, the chair lay on its side and the key had flown under a bookcase in a far corner of the office. He dragged the chair back to the stenciled shoe outlines, sat down, hung his head and sighed.

Eventually, he got restless. To keep himself occupied, he practiced moving his shackle from one end of the cable to the other. First he worked his way to the cot, where he attempted to lie down with one leg on the floor. With a little finessing, there was just enough slack to get the fettered ankle up onto the bed. Scooting the bed frame closer to the cable relieved the tension. Yeah, that would work. If he inadvertently rolled over in his sleep, the cable might just drag him to the floor. But sleep was not a top priority for him right now. It was the possibility of the Big Sleep being visited upon him that preoccupied him at this particular moment. He wondered what it would be like lying under one of those grassy mounds, 'pushing up daisies', to echo Muphrid's words. Or petunias.

He noticed his ankle was giving him pain, so he put his feet back on the floor and decided to leave behind morbid thoughts and see if he could slide his shackle over to the bathroom. It was critical to practice this before his time of need. That expression "time of need" sent a chill creeping down the back of his neck. Focus! Sliding himself sideways into the john did the trick. Boy that was a tight squeeze in there! The room was the size of a broom closet. But there was a new roll of toilet paper within reach and a free-standing sink. And withal, it was surprisingly clean for jail accommodations.

He went back and sat on the wooden chair. He idly examined the words carved into it. Beside the usual obscenities (some actually misspelled, if that could be believed), there were also people's names. One of them appeared more frequently than any other: Knocker. Ugh. At that point, he looked away and scanned Nancy's desk again.

There were the usual framed photos: On vacation with her son Kyle, minus his milk teeth; another one of just Kyle with a phantom hand on his shoulder. It took a moment for Barney to realize that the disembodied hand belonged to Dad, now airbrushed out of the picture.

Beyond the desk, by the "waiting area" appointed with metal chairs near the door, were the *de rigeur* cork bulletin board and wall posters. The first poster was McGruff, the crime fighting dog detective, the collar of his trench coat turned up around his floppy ears, advising you to be alert to suspicious activities. Apparently, this town had not seen the poster, else Muphrid would be shackled here instead. Wherever he went, there was an inexplicable obliviousness to Muphrid's suspicious backyard excavations. To the contrary, to the extreme contrary, it was Barney's own eminently explicable behavior that was regarded with suspicion.

Life is strange.

~ ~ ~

Stella fidgeted and paced around the house. Finally she decided to get some sleep. She would come for Barney in the morning. She got into bed and clicked on her TV and checked Netflix for a movie to watch. Scrolling through the comedy section:

"Spring Break."

"Sweeney Todd, The Demon Barber of Fleet Street."

She recoiled at that one, scrolled back to "Spring Break" and clicked SELECT.

~ ~ ~

Barney jumped when he heard the door latch squeak. The latch handle rotated and the door opened slowly. Had Nancy returned this quickly? No. It was not Nancy. It was Muphrid. There was that freaky little plush toy on his belt. And beside it, in its sheath, the same straight razor Barney had seen yesterday.

The polka dot butterfly bandage was still on his cheek. And there was that weird, lopsided smile.

Reaching for the razor, he said those two, simple, now blood-curdling words:

"Hello, friend..."

Barney couldn't breathe.

"Just want to let you know there's no hard feelings."

Fliess and his nephew Milo came into the office. Milo came around and stood behind Barney's chair, saying, "Lucky you, you're gonna get one o' Muphrid's famous razor cuts."

Muphrid said, "Don't worry, my razor cuts are quick and painless."

Everything went black.

= CHAPTER 7 =

~ ~ ~

Next morning, the usual locals came tumbling into the Rock Creek Roadhouse. The tourists were gone, as it was Monday, the start of the work week. The proprietor, Mel Bernstein, a middle-aged man with thinning black hair, black pencil mustache and skinny black bolo tie with a turquoise slider, was wandering around the floor making sure his regulars were being well served. Among the regulars were Mayor Jeremy, a few store owners and a couple of local farmers. The farmers were large, barrel shaped men clad in overalls, work boots and John Deere caps (bills turned forward like normal folk, forgodsake). They bantered jovially and dug into their Hungry Farmer combo plates with gusto, praising the extra thickness of the griddle cakes.

Feed & Seed store owner Ray commented that he had a new trick to show everybody: "Saw this on YouTube."

"Yeah? What kinda trick ya got, Ray?" one of the farmers said. He and the other farmers were doubtless customers of Ray's farm supply business.

"Put a placemat over a full glass of water, turn it upside down on the table. Then you pull the placemat away. The water stays inside."

"Yeah? And that's it? I done that b'fore. Big whoop."

"No, no, my fine friend!" Ray said. "There's more. Next you lift away the glass, twisting it gently so the water stays there, in the shape of the upside-down glass."

"No way, man!" The farmer blew through his lips.

"Way, man. Way!"

"You're crazy. Let's see it, then."

"You gotta wait."

88

"Wait for what?"

"Wait till Barney comes in. I want Barney to see it too."

The farmer threw down his wadded-up napkin, "Aw, you're full of it."

"You'll see. All things come to those that wait."

The proprietor had been eyeing Ray for a while. "If you dump water on my table, you're mopping it up."

"Don't worry, Mel, I saw this on YouTube. I know just how to do it."

"I doubt it."

Jeremy was observing from the next table, chuckling quietly to himself.

Ray changed the subject. "So where's our new pal Barney?"

The others shrugged. "Dunno."

"How 'bout Stella?"

The mayor explained, "It's her day to work for me instead of Mel. Billing and bookkeeping. For my website business, you know."

"Oh yeah."

The cowbell over the door clanged and in came Callista with her scowling daughter Nadia in tow.

Ray looked up. "Hey! Nice to see a young face at the breakfast table. What do we owe the honor to?"

Nadia narrowed her eyes. She didn't speak, so her mom spoke for her: "Same as yesterday. She's still grounded for that little stunt she pulled with Zach."

"Revising our city motto," Jeremy said. "We're getting that taken care of real soon."

"And for painting a skull-and-crossbones on the bridge."

"Wasn't aware of that," Jeremy said.

Nadia broke her silence and spoke directly to the mayor: "Yeah, we did that one too. On our way to the sign. Zach and I are trying to save lives. So when are you going to fix it, Mr. Mayor?"

"Fix what?"

"The railing. The railing on the Rock Creek Bridge. It's a deathtrap."

"Oh that. Well, we're short on funds..."

"What if someone falls in the creek and dies?"

"We're working on it, Nadia. It's a priority but there's no budget. If you wanna pay for it, hand me the cash and we'll get started today."

Nadia rolled her eyes. "I'm just a kid, how am I supposed to come up with that kind of money?"

"So you got budget problems too."

She showed him her middle finger.

Callista swatted her daughter on the back of the head. "Tsk! Mind your manners, young lady!"

And so it went.

~ ~ ~

Half an hour passed. As the customers thinned out, Muphrid wandered in, self-consciously wiping his hands on his dungarees to get the red clay soil off.

The pillowy waiter was cleaning a table with a damp white cloth. Mel nudged him so he looked up. "Hey, Muphrid! You're in late this morning. You're usually the first one in. Oversleep?"

"Naw, just workin' in the garden."

"Kinda early for that, ain't it?"

"Naw, I'm a mornin' person. There was hole to fill in."

"Huh. Well, whaddya want for breakfast?"

Muphrid said, "Oh a cuppa coffee to start with, I suppose..."

"Food?" the waiter said. "Something to eat?"

"I'll take the Hungry Farmer. Cuz I'm pretty hungry this mornin'. All that shovelin'."

"Yard work, that'll do it!"

The waiter went over to the air pot on the counter and filled a cup for the tardy barber. Bringing it over, he said, "Grubby hands! Didn't your mother make you wash up before breakfast?"

Muphrid tilted his head sideways and looked almost lovingly at the waiter, a big loopy smile growing on just one side of his face as if the other side wasn't so sure there was anything to smile about. "Noooo..." he said in a singsong, then spun out a fanciful story. "When I stopped by, she was sleeping. Like an angel. I couldn't bear to disturb 'er so I tiptoed away an' came here. Huh-huh-huh!"

"You're a real weirdo, you know, Muphrid. Not many grown men spend half their time with their mothers and the other half walking around with a stuffed animal on their belt—" He was surprised to see there were now two Beanie Babies on Muphrid's belt. "Say, when did you get number two?" Number two was a floppy-eared doggie.

Muphrid's tone became more matter-of-fact. "I found it while I was, uh, digging in the garden."

The waiter shrugged, "So ol' PK left some of his whatchya call 'em, Beanie Babies, lying around the acreage, huh?"

"No!" Muphrid reined himself in. "I mean, no, I found this little feller in the garden shed." The stuffed animal certainly looked too clean to have been left out exposed to the elements. "He definitely didn't bury them in the yard or nothin'."

"Bury them?"

"Or leave them around, I mean."

The waiter took his hands off the table and stretched erect. "Whatever. The longer I talk to you, Muphrid, the more I feel like I'm losing my grip on reality. Listen, you want a muffin while you're waiting?"

"Oh sure, that would be nice. A muffin...and do you have any of that marionberry jam?"

"Sure do. And I'll freshen up that coffee for you."

"Thank you. You're a very nice man, Frankie."

~ ~ ~

Twenty minutes later, Stella came briskly walking up the street, on time for her eight o'clock shift at Jeremy's. But she was distracted this morning, looking nervously left and right, scanning up and down the street. She nearly fell over the Chinstrap kids as they came running past her with backpacks to catch the small rural school bus waiting by the broken railing at the south end of the bridge. The little girl Twee had a Beanie Baby bear hanging off the back of her pack.

~ ~ ~

When Stella got to Jeremy's home-cum-office, the glass front door was locked so she rummaged in her purse for the key. Once found, she pushed it into the lock. At that moment, she saw another woman's reflection in the glass. She spun around, smack face to face with officer Nancy Lautenberg.

"You!" Stella screamed, "What're you doin' sneaking up on me! Never mind that, is Barney okay!?"

Nancy put her hand on Stella's, shoulder but Stella pulled it off.

"Easy there, Gervais," Nancy said. "He's fine."

"When're you going to release him?"

"Already did. Muphrid came by the station late last night and asked me to drop the charges I booked him on—"

"So where's Barney now?"

"At Muphrid's. Muphrid said there were no hard feelings and let Barney spend the rest of the night at his place."

"Barney spent the night at Muphrid's?"

"Yeah." Nancy looked down the street at the yellow clapboard house under the sweet gum tree. "Your bed feeling a little empty already?"

"Shut up," Stella said.

"Everybody knows about you two, you know," Nancy said, sour as vinegar.

"Piss off!"

"Anyway, you might not recognize your boyfriend—Muphrid promised to give him one of his late-night razor cuts."

"What!?"

"Said he wouldn't press charges, was gonna take him home for a special razor cut."

"Special razor cut?"

"An olive branch."

Stella pushed Nancy aside when she saw Muphrid come out of the Rock Creek Roadhouse and start to cross Main. "Hey Muphrid! Hey! Hold it right there!"

The barber looked up, bemused.

Stella ran right up the middle of Main Street and, in the crosswalk, grabbed Muphrid by the lapels, "Where's Barney!? Is he in the roadhouse?"

"In the roadhouse? Nooooo...not there..." That weird singsong again.

"Where is he then? What've you done with him!?" Tears welled up in her eyes.

"Why're you yelling, Stella? I didn't do nothin' wrong. I let him spend the night on my guest cot. He was so awfully tired. He went to jail, you know."

"I know that!"

"Yeah? Well, he's not there anymore. I brung 'im home and took care of him."

"Took care of him *how!*?" she nearly screamed.

"Ohh, I gave him nice razor cut an' cleaned him up an' put him down—"

"'Put him down'? Ohmygod. Where is he now?"

"Ohhhh, I dunno." He sighed. "Still sleeping, I suppose." Muphrid's eyes wandered over to a squirrel running up a tree and he laughed,

"Look at that crazy squirrel!"

Stella pulled Muphrid's face around. "Whaddya mean, you 'suppose'?"

He gently removed her hand. "Ohhh, when I left, I tried to wake him up but he was...dead to the world. He looked so peaceful lying there."

She saw the red earth under his fingernails.

"What's that about?"

"Ohhh, digging. I went diggin' in the garden."

"At this time of the morning?"

"Sure Stella. Why not? There was a hole to fill. Why are you so upset? Is there somethin' wrong?"

"You bet your ass there's something wrong! What've you done with Barney!?"

"I told you, he's sleeping. Dead to the world. He'll—"

Stella's eyes grew large, "You murderous freak!" She shoved him backwards, jumped on him, began beating him around the face.

Muphrid fended off her blows, starting to weep. "Why're you hitting me Stella? What's gotten into you? Please! Stop hitting!"

"You killed him! You twisted freak, you killed my sweet Barney and buried him in your yard!"

"No! No no no! Why are you saying that, Stella?" He looked at her as if she were crazy. "I wouldn't do nothin' like that. I like Barney. Anyway, I wouldn't kill nobody."

Just then a car swerved around them—they were still in the crosswalk—and that distraction was enough for Muphrid to disengage himself from the enraged Stella. He backed away, holding up his hands defensively.

"Come see for yourself, Stella. I'll take you to see 'im."

The young woman backed away. "Whoa, no. You're not gonna off me too?"

"I don't know what's got into you, Stella. Jest come with me and I'll show 'im to ya. But you have to be quiet cuz—"

"I know, cuz he's 'sleeping'!"

"Yeah. Sleeping."

She shivered. "All right. Take me to him."

The two walked back to Muphrid's house. Nancy was still hanging around the glass door, barely concealing a smirk. As they passed Jeremy's window, the mayor/webmaster stood in the window and gave Stella a questioning look. She just waved him off. He frowned and looked at Nancy standing nearby. She smiled wryly and mouthed the words, "Who knows what her problem is?"

Coming into Muphrid's living room, Stella observed that the cot was empty. On the cot lay a neatly folded blanket. There was a big blood stain on it. Next to the blanket was a neatly folded sheet. It too was soaked in blood.

Stella gasped. She called out, "Barney?" but there was no answer from anywhere in the house. "Barney!"

"He's gone," Muphrid stated.

"Ohmygod." She ran to the window and looked out into the yard. There was a mound of fresh red earth where the rectangular hole used to be. She nearly passed out. "Ohmygod. Ohmygod!" She stared at Muphrid with blazing eyes, trembling. Abruptly, she pivoted and ran to the front door, breaking into tears because she couldn't get it open fast enough. An instant later, she was running up Main Street in full panic.

She ducked into Jeremy's home office, shoving Nancy aside, and locked the door behind her and pulled down the shades.

"What's going on, Stella?" Jeremy said, emerging into the front office.

She grabbed his arm and pulled him into a back room and told him everything.

Neither of them heard the tow truck drive by outside.

~ ~ ~

Barney heard the truck though.

He was at Stella's house. Fifteen minutes ago, after waking up on Muphrid's cot and finding himself alone, he had neatly folded up his blanket and sheet, embarrassed about the blood that leaked from his arm during the night. He was surprised to see Muphrid's handiwork out in the garden. The dirt pile was gone and the hole was completely filled. There was a mound of red clay soil in its place. He shook his head, marveling what an industrious early bird Muphrid was!

Suddenly, like an electric bolt, he realized that Stella had no idea where he was. He quickly dressed and ran across the street to her house. The front door was locked but she'd given him her extra key.

Inside, it was dead quiet. No Stella.

He remembered that she worked for Jeremy on Mondays, so she most likely was over there. Just in case, he sat at the kitchen table and wrote a note:

> Hi Stella,
>
> I hope you're not too worried about me. I spent the night at Muphrid's. I would have called you this morning but I lost my cell phone when I fell out of the tree last night. I'll see if I can find it now that there's daylight. Meanwhile, I figure you're at Jeremy's, so I'll look for you there. Anyway, I am fine.
>
> Barney

That's when he heard the tow truck. He looked out the kitchen window and saw a "Bailey's Garage" truck pulling up across the street from Muphrid's house. The truck eased over to Muphrid's side of the street, facing in the wrong direction, backed up until it was rear-end to rear-end with the Pinto. Barney ran out to greet the driver.

= CHAPTER 8 =

~ ~ ~

The diesel tow truck was large and loud; it seemed as wide as it was long as it was high, with a short crane rearing up from the bed like an erection. The flat steel fenders, running boards and every other walkable metal surface were embossed with a non-skid pattern. The kid driving it sported a mop of soft black hair that fell across his forehead and nearly obscured his gimlet eyes. A sprig of black whiskers sprouted under his chin.

The young man rolled down the passenger window, leaned out and pointed to the damaged Pinto idled at the road's edge. "This the car you wanted towed back to the shop?"

The answer seemed so self-evident, Barney had to restrain himself from any number of deliciously sarcastic jokes. Instead, he just nodded.

Something was puzzling him, though. The young man seemed somehow familiar. Suddenly he blurted out, "Zach?"

"Yes, Mr. Starr. I and my girlfriend met you at Stella's party. Remember?"

Sure enough, it was Zach. Of Zach and Nadia, the Goth couple. No mascara for Zach today though, he was on the job.

The young man lowered a hook from the hoist and attached it under the Pinto's rear bumper. The T-bar went under the wheels.

Meanwhile, Chinstrap Kyle and his entourage—scrawny Peewee with freckles and cowlick, the little Eurasian girl Twee and stocky Dingo— erupted from the school bus that sat waiting near the bridge. The bus wouldn't depart for another few minutes so the kids had time to hustle over to see what was going on with the tow truck. They swarmed around, peering inquisitively at the damaged fender.

"What happened to your car, mister?"

While Zach ran the winch to lift the Pinto's rear wheels off the ground, Barney replied simply, "Smashed up the fender." Saying that reminded him to tell Zach about the trapped front wheel that wasn't going to turn during the towing process. Zach thanked him for mentioning it. He lifted each front wheel onto its own tow dolly, stared at his work for a moment then climbed into the truck cab.

He motioned to Barney that he was ready to go, so the cub reporter stepped up onto the running board and pulled the passenger door open. Before getting in, he squinted and scanned the ground under the plum tree, hoping to spot his lost cell phone. Just then he heard Peewee call out, "How'd it happen?"

Hanging out the still-open door as the truck began inching forward, Barney looked down at the kids and uttered two words, "Pilot error."

Suddenly, Chinstrap produced a cell phone from his back pocket, "Hey mister! Look what I found under the tree! Is this yours?"

"Ohmygod! You found it. Hold on, Zach!" Zach hit the brakes.

Barney jumped out and studied the boy with the reddish chinstrap beard. The beard made him seem sagacious, pious even, like a solid little Amish farmer. "Here you go," the boy said.

Barney smiled warmly and reached out to take the phone but the boy jerked it away. "Ten bucks!"

Barney recoiled, "What the—?"

He looked over at Zach. Zach shrugged and smiled sympathetically.

"Ten bucks for the phone, Mister. Goin' up to eleven." The other children looked on admiringly.

"I'm not giving you anything, you little—"

The boy shrugged and turned away.

"OK! I'll give you a dollar."

"Five or I walk."

"Four."

The boy mulled it over. "OK, deal."

Chinstrap handed over the phone with one hand and took the cash with the other.

"Thanks, I think," Barney said, watching the boy divvying up the spoils equally among his eager mates.

Peewee looked up, exclaimed, "Hey the school bus is leaving, let's go!"

So the four took flight.

"That little extortionist!" Barney pulled his door shut, saw the black-haired youth grinning.

"Y'gotta watch that kid." Zach stared at Barney then handed him a clipboard. "Might as well take care of paperwork before we go."

While Barney filled out the form and signed on the dotted line, Zach watched the gang of four scurrying across the street to reach the school bus before it left them behind.

~ ~ ~

The bus driver, a large, oddly shaped woman with jowls and dark bags under her eyes, pulled the brake lever, reopened the door and activated the red flashing warning lights. She smiled indulgently as the four ten-year olds exchanged leads in their race to be first through the bus door before the driver closed it. The children already in the bus were jumping out of their seats, screaming and yelling for the four to get aboard before the lady drove off without them. Of course she wasn't about to leave these rag-amuffins behind, though the thought crossed her mind. It certainly would make for a quieter thirty-minute ride to the school in Sheridan, but...naw. She grasped the silver door control knob and waited till the last child was safely inside.

"Safely inside" is a relative term. In fact, all the seats were taken so the Chinstrap Gang had to stand in the entry well. A series of budget cuts meant the school district couldn't afford a bigger bus. The situation violated safety regulations, but what else was there to do? At least they weren't standing outside on the running board. In contrast, the Vandershurs personally drove their twins to the school in Sheridan. Alas, for most of the low-income working families around here, that was not feasible.

The driver pulled the shiny chrome knob and the door closed. With a hiss of releasing pneumatic brakes and growl of diesel acceleration, off they went!

~ ~ ~

"All done?" Zach took the clipboard, set it on the seat. He released the parking brake, hit the accelerator while man-hauling the steering wheel for a U turn with the Pinto trailing after. They roared up Main Street en route to Bailey's Garage, as stenciled so elegantly on the both doors of the truck.

"What happened to your arm, Mr. Starr?"

Barney looked down at his bandaged left arm, those butterfly bandages, brown with dried blood but still leaking. "Oh this? Yeah, I snagged it on a nail. Muphrid's fence."

"Ow. Musta hurt!"

They passed Deena's pink mansion on the left, Mr. Armand Ordonne's assiduously vacuumed maple tree on the right.

"Honestly, I don't remember it hurting at all," Barney said, "Adrenaline. Best pain killer in the world."

Jeremy's home cum web studio went by on the right. Barney was puzzled that the shades were pulled. He thought of Stella. *I'd better call Stella and tell her I'm all right.* But his cell phone was dead after lying in the weeds all night.

"You can use my cell phone, Mr. Starr."

"Thanks, but her number's in my dead cell phone."

"No problem. I got Stella's number in my contact list."

"Great! Thanks."

When Stella picked up, she was confused.

~ ~ ~

This is what Zach overhead:

"Stella? No this isn't Zach. It's me, Barney."
Pause.
"Yeah, it's me. I'm using Zach's phone. My phone's dead."
Pause.
"I'm fine! Really! Muphrid took good care of me."
Pause.
"Hunh? You saw blood on the blanket?" He looked at his arm. "Oh! Caught a nail with my arm. Muphrid cleaned it up and bandaged it for me. Woulda been hard for me to do with one hand."
Pause.
"No, I'm telling you, I am absolutely fine."
Pause.
"Where am I? I'm on my way to Dorgan Bailey's Garage. Get my car fixed."
Pause.
"The mounds? The body bag and the other stuff? No, it's not at all what we thought."

99

Pause.

"No. It wasn't that. It was—well, don't tell Muphrid I know, but—it's something entirely different. Even weirder than I thought. But it's not bodies. What was in the body bag will blow your mind. I'll tell you later. Anyway, I'm fine, don't worry!"

Pause.

"What's that? Yeah, I guess you might want to offer Muphrid an apology."

Pause.

"Look, I'll tell you the whole story when I get back. Yeah. Me too. Bye bye!"

~ ~ ~

Zach looked at Barney, "Got things straightened out with Stella?"

"Yeah."

"Cool." The young man added, "Nice haircut, by the way!"

"Thanks."

"Muphrid?"

"Yep."

= CHAPTER 9 =

~ ~ ~

The tow truck crossed the railroad tracks and turned right onto Buchanan Road. Buchanan paralleled the railroad, so it was lined with warehouses, a smattering of light industry and artisanal workshops with folksy names like "The Joinery" and "Abracadabra Candelabras" and "The Glassworks." There was also a sprawling, impersonal personal storage facility followed by a welding shop. Finally came a large white roof-mounted plastic sign dulled and cracked by years of exposure to the elements. It sported faded red lettering that said, "Bailey's Garage." Below it, the main entrance opened like the maw of a whale. Zach turned into the driveway and drove straight into the gaping maw.

The walls inside Bailey's Garage were so grimy Barney imagined a Brobdingnagian mechanic had used them to wipe the grease off his hands before clocking out. As his eyes adjusted to the low light, a hulking form loomed into view.

For a late-middle aged man, Dorgan Bailey was an imposing figure, not simply for his physical enormity but his intimidating presence. Whether his rust red complexion was due to alcohol or sun exposure or a lifetime of simmering anger, his face looked like it had been hacked from a slab of roast beef. Thin black hair combed straight back accentuated the rest of his face that swept forward, led by a challenging jaw and two rows of well-formed teeth that seemed ready, willing and able to rip into flesh on a whim.

Zach and Barney disembarked.

"You the fella that trashed his car?" the big man said.

"Yeah, really stupid of me. Muphrid said you could fix it up."

101

"Muphrid, eh?" The man took the clipboard from Zach. He eyed the car then looked at Barney. "Insurance?"

"Yeah...here's my card."

The man wiped his hands on his overalls, took the card. He glanced at Barney's wounded arm. "What happened there? Looks like between the car an' you, you got the worse end of the deal!"

Barney shrugged and smiled amiably.

There was a whirring as Zach unspooled the winch and the Pinto came down to the grimy concrete floor and bounced once on its suspension. Zach unhooked the car while Bailey scanned the insurance card in the Xerox copier. From the copier, Bailey looked back at Barney with one eye closed. "Mexican?"

"Hunh?"

"What are you, Mexican or somethin'?"

"Uh-I'm actually Filip—*half* Filipino." As if that would dilute the charge of Hispanicism.

"Hmph! All the same in my book. Takin' good American jobs. What kind of work you do? You do work don't ya?"

"I work for a newspaper. The *Portland Mirror*."

"Delivery boy, eh?"

Barney bit his tongue, said nothing. He needed this man's services. "I'm a reporter," he said flatly.

"Reporter?" The man looked skeptical. "Well you talk good English, so I guess I kin see 'em lettin' you do some easy stuff. Affirmative action 'n' all that crap."

Returning the card, Bailey drew up close and personal to deliver the blast, his eyes narrowed like a snake's: "I know who you are. Hear you been spendin' time with my boy Joe's fiancé. That right?" Barney started to shrug. "Cut the crap! Let's get somethin' straight right here and now: you fuckin' better knock it off! Stay away from that girl. Comprendo!?"

Barney sighed. "We're just friends."

"That ain't what I hear. You gonna lie to my face, you little—"

Barney backed away. "She's been been helping me with my story."

Suddenly Dorgan Bailey stiffened up and shot a withering bear-like glower at Barney. "'*Story*' hunh? What the hell kind of 'story' are you workin' on with her? Hunh? HUNH!? Hey, look at me—eyes up here!" Bailey advanced on Barney and Barney involuntarily shrank back. Those big teeth! Barney's mouth dried up instantly; his throat tightened and his words stuck on the way out.

"Just a h-human-interest st-story. Ab—about Deena Poole. That's all."

The mountainous man's neck veins were bulging, but he just grunted. "Yeah, well, you kin do it without Stella's help. Understand!? I said, do you understand, you little jerk-ass spic!?"

"Yes sir."

Bailey eyed him for a moment, then said, "Good."

The eruption was over. "Leave Stella alone and I'll take good care of your car. But you cross me, and I'll take good care of YOU. Are we clear on that?"

Barney swallowed to lubricate the pipes. "Yes. Totally clear."

"Clear?" the man demanded again.

"Yes sir!"

"Good. Now let's take care of yer jalopy."

Bailey examined the damage. He walked around the car, examining it from all sides, tried to close the trunk lid but it refused to seat. After a while, Barney ventured, "Um, any idea how long you think it'll take to fix my car?" He grimaced, anticipating another blast from Bailey. But there was no blast. Dorgan Bailey considered the question, looked at the fender, ran his hand over it like a vet would an injured colt and shook his head. He called to Zach who was standing by, "Toss me that crowbar, Zach." The big man caught the airborne crowbar with the easy grace of Fred Astaire catching a cane tossed to him from the wings. There any resemblance to the dancer ended. For instance, no one would have worried that Fred Astaire might use his cane to murder someone.

Bailey pried the edge of the fender away from the tire but it snapped back as soon as he eased off. He exhaled heavily, squatted down and opened the tire valve. With his finger stuck in the end of the valve stem to keep it open, air hissed out. The tire collapsed away from the fender. "That'll save the tire from further damage." Putting one hand on his knee to help him rise out of his crouch, he announced glumly, "The frame's most likely tweaked too. That's why the trunk lid won't seat. That'll cost ya and I ain't equipped t'handle that kind work anyways. I can bend the fender off the wheel and see what I can do with the alignment, which looks pretty bad. It'll at least let you limp back to—where'd you say you're from?"

"Portland."

"Yeah, as I figgered. Five hunderd bucks?"

"Sure. That's under the deductible so State Farm won't care."

After signing some more papers, Barney dutifully thanked Dorgan Bailey and headed out. Suddenly, from the cavernous work area, Bailey's gruff voice echoed after him, "Hey Mex! Don't forget yer insurance card!"

~ ~ ~

Barney retrieved his card and angrily stomped out to Buchanan Road without looking back. Zach briefly tagged after him. "Wanna ride back, Mr. Starr?"

Barney shook his head.

"You gonna go see Stella?"

Barney charged onward without acknowledging the inquisitive young man's query. He pulled up his collar against a sudden chill autumn gust and continued westward along Buchanan back to Main Street.

~ ~ ~

Thinking of all the ways he'd like to get back at that beef-faced bully, Barney's walking pace accelerated to a furious pitch. So engrossed was he in revenge fantasies, he nearly fell flat on his face when he rounded the corner onto Main and his toe caught one of Alexander Sweetbread's railroad tracks. Upon recovering his footing, he looked across the street and beheld City Hall, at the corner of Main and Harding, the very place where mere hours ago he'd been ingloriously shackled and ultimately emancipated. An ordeal to be sure, but upon reflection, he reckoned he'd gladly take that experience over dealing with Dorgan Bailey.

Barney looked around. On this side of Main, all boarded up, reposed a forlorn coffee stand, formerly a service station. Faded coffee-related signs still remained: "The Espresso Station" and a menu board with pricing for strengths:

Unleaded
Leaded
High Octane

and sizes:

Regular
Super
Premium

Now grass sprouted through cracks in the asphalt around the concrete gas pump island. At each end of the island, white painted steel poles held up the canopy roof. Colorful graffiti, along with water stains and peeling paint, decorated the exterior stucco wall that contained the drive-up window. At the edge of the parking lot, near the railroad tracks, an empty Doritos bag snagged on a tuft of grass.

But there was one ray of hope. A hand lettered sign said, "The Espresso Station has moved into Vindemiatrix Winery at 145 Main St." There was a red arrow pointing in that direction. It was just a few doors down.

He continued walking in that direction and shortly came to Reggie's grocery store, "Reggie's Veggies." It occurred to him this would be a good time to pop in and buy a few necessities. Reggie greeted him enthusiastically. "Heya, Mr. Reporter! You gonna write about my store? That'll be your first story about my first-story grocery store-ee here! Ahahaha!" He even joked like his brother. It was amazing Tom Lautenberg hadn't killed them both by now.

"Naw, just need to pick up some gauze and tape and a box of Band-Aids," Barney said, holding up his wounded arm.

"Ouch!" Reggie sympathetically grabbed his own arm. He pointed to where the first aid supplies were. "Right over there, down the far aisle. There's disinfectant there too if you need it."

En route, Barney scanned the aisles and was amazed. Deena's wares were everywhere: cakes, candies, ready-to-deep-fry treats, cake mixes, refrigerated cookie dough. Her big smiling face beamed from every package and cannister. There was even a special Deena Poole section of the store with forms you could fill out to enter a "Guess the Mystery Dessert" contest. In contrast to the expansiveness of Deena's presence, the toiletries section was tucked into an obscure little corner of the store. At the far end of the shelf a rack of condoms caught Barney's eye. Reaching for a box, Barney was relieved he hadn't needed to ask Reggie for help finding them.

At the cash register, Reggie rang up the merchandise and bagged it. The last item was the box of condoms. He held it up and squinted at the label. "Ooo, the glow-in-the-dark ones! These are my favorites!"

Barney averted his eyes and busied himself with pulling cash from his wallet.

When everything was settled up, Reggie dropped a large carrot into the grocery bag before handing it over to his customer. "On the house. It'll neutralize anything Deena feeds you next time you interview her."

~ ~ ~

Back out on Main, Barney trotted across the street to the Rock Creek Roadhouse. He pulled the big door open and went inside. Before he could say a word, the pillowy waiter announced from behind the counter, "She works over at Jeremy's on Mondays."

"Oh yeah, that's right. I knew that. Thanks!"

So he trotted back across the street again and briefly peered through the window of the winery. Inside, Robert Vandershur was pouring a sample of his two-year old Pinot Noir for a customer. The customer wore an expression of serious anticipation as the red liquid streamed into her glass. The other customer, possibly her husband, was at that moment spitting the same wine into a spittoon, ready to sample another vintage.

Barney went on. He crossed the Rock Creek Bridge and came to Mayor Jeremy's street-side web design firm. Through the window, Barney saw Stella at a keyboard, navigating her mouse around, completely focused on her work. Every so often, she plucked a sheet from a stack of papers and typed while she read whatever was on the sheet. Barney came in and she turned to see who had rattled the cowbell hanging from the top of the door. When she saw the him standing shyly at the entrance, she leapt out of her chair and flung her arms around him, delirious with joy. "Ohthankgod you're OK, Barney! Oh, Barney! I thought—oh I'm so stupid for thinking it—I mean worrying that—I thought, oh you know, I thought—"

"What, that Muphrid had cut my throat?"

"Ahgh! Yes!" Stella began crying, sobbing.

"I'm OK."

She held him away from herself to gaze upon his face. Then she got mad, mad as a mother who finds her wandering child. "Why didn't you CALL me!? I was worried sick!"

"I couldn't. I lost my phone when I fell out of the tree."

"But you stayed with Muphrid. Doesn't he have a phone?"

"It was late, I didn't want to disturb you."

She threw her hands up into the air, exasperated.

They looked at each other for a time.

"He didn't hurt you?"

"No, he's as harmless and simple as you said." He wiped her tears away. "I'm to blame for all this, Stella. I got everybody thinking Muphrid was some kind of fiend. It was all my wild imaginings about his straight razor and those mounds."

"So what are they then? Rocks, like Nancy said?"

"No, not rocks. Bunkers."

"Bunkers?"

"Bunkers full of Beanie Babies."

"Whaaat!?" She pulled back to look Barney in the eye. Tears still rolled down her cheeks. "Are you pulling my leg?"

"Nope. It's the truth."

A man's voice echoed from another room. "Is everything OK out there? Hey, is that you Barnaby?"

Stella looked up. "Yeah, we're fine. It's just Barney, back from dead. That's 'Barney' by the way. As in B-A-R-N-E-Y. Got it?"

"Oh, OK. Well, hi there, Mr. B!" Jeremy said from the other side of the wall.

"Hi Jeremy."

She whispered to Barney that they should get out of there and called to her cousin through the wall. "We're going over to the Espresso Station." She looked at Barney, "Is that OK with you?" He nodded. She raised her voice again, "Can I get you anything while we're there, Jeremy?" His answer was negative.

~ ~ ~

They walked across the bridge to "Vindemiatrix Winery (and Espresso Station)." Entering, Barney tugged at Stella's arm. "I'll buy you a glass of wine."

There were cafe tables along the window. Barney gestured to Stella to have a seat. Walking up to the counter, he noticed a dusty bottle of Bordeaux in a glass case. The winery owner Robert came over and explained that the bottle was over 150 years old and valued at many tens of thousands of dollars.

"Wow! I'll bet the wine is unbelievably good!"

"No. In fact, it's probably terrible by now. But it's a novelty, a collector's item. If someone will pay that much for its rarity, then that's how it's valued. The quality of wine itself has essentially nothing to do with it." He said that opening it would in fact instantly destroy its stratospheric value.

"So it's worth something only so long as it remains useless?"

"That's right. Once it's opened for tasting, its exorbitant 'exchange value' collapses down to its nearly worthless 'use value,' to use Karl Marx's terminology. I'm a retired professor of economics so I find these things interesting." He adjusted his spectacles and they glinted as they must have once upon a time in the glare of lecture hall lights.

"Interesting. Well, I know that stamp collectors put great value on defective misprint stamps that have no 'use value' either, right? I guess that's the same kind of thing, huh?"

"True. We're funny creatures, we humans. We'll work ourselves to death so we can afford to spend a fortune for things that have no use. On the other hand, there's things that have inherent value, like food and good wine. Tangible, tasteable value! In fact, if you enjoy something, there's value right there. And especially if you enjoy it with someone you care about."

He looked at Stella and winked. "Now there's the greatest value anyone can have in life." He smiled a benign smile and his specs glinted one more time.

"I'm sold!" Barney said, "May we have a couple of glasses of your Pinot?"

Robert laughed. "No, I'm not allowed by the liquor licensing board to serve alcoholic beverages by the glass like a bar would. You can buy a bottle or case, though!"

Stella's ring tone sounded. It was Sarah McLachlan's "In the Arms of the Angel." The caller was her cousin cum boss calling her back to the office. "Fifteen minutes, OK Jeremy? We're at Vindy. What's that? Can it wait? I need to talk to Barney. Yeah. Thanks. Bye."

Robert said, "It's a bit early for wine anyway. How about I get you two some complimentary coffee?" He went over to the scaled down Espresso Station along the far wall, whispered something to the woman there and brought back two steaming mugs glazed with the Vindemiatrix logo—namely, images of the "female grape gatherer" and her namesake star in Virgo.

"Cream and sugar?"

Both shook their heads. They thanked him and he retired to behind the counter to offer a tasting to a new arrival.

Stella leaned in and whispered vehemently. "So tell me, Barney: what the hell *happened* last night!?" She saw the blood-caked butterfly bandages holding the skin together on his forearm. "And what's *that* about?"

Barney looked around to make sure no one was eavesdropping and began.

~ ~ ~

He recounted seeing the body bag—yes, it was a body bag—and slipping and falling out of the tree when Officer Nancy showed up and arrested him. And how he lost his cell phone. He described his incarceration and the arrival of Muphrid. He sheepishly admitted to fainting dead away when Muphrid pulled out the straight razor for a "late night razor cut."

This is what happened after that.

~ ~ ~

When Barney came to, Muphrid was holding a mirror in front of his face.

"Howdya like your new look, my friend?" Muphrid said.

Indeed, Barney's face was clean shaven (except for the soul patch, which was spared the blade) and his hair was stylishly trimmed. Out with the scruffies, in with the GQ look. He looked like a million dollars. His cheeks dimpled with an involuntary grin.

However, the buzz got killed off moments later when Nancy came in, fists on hips. "I want to introduce you to someone," she said grimly then stepped aside to reveal a vaguely familiar man. "This is Jason Fliess, attorney at law and the executor of PK Sharma's estate. He's also a good friend of Muphrid's."

Barney now remembered where he'd seen this guy. He was the same man who had handed Muphrid the envelope of cash earlier. Barney timorously shook the attorney's hand "Uh, hi."

But Fliess had no time for small talk. "I'm going to cut to chase, dude. You told everyone you were writing an article about Deena Poole for the *Portland Mirror*. Well that's bullshit isn't it?" The man's eyes narrowed menacingly. "You want to tell us the real reason you're here? What were you doing up in that tree? Spying? What did you see? I want the straight truth or I'm going to rake you over the coals."

Muphrid interjected. "Don't be mean to Barney. He's a very nice feller. He was jest curious. That's his job. He's a reporter, you know?"

"Cram it, Muphrid!" The attorney barked. "This isn't any of your business."

"Well I think it is," Barney countered nervously. "I saw the body bag and I saw the money you put into Muphrid's hand. And I saw the bald guy helping you." It pleased him to watch the attorney blanch. Then it frightened him to see the man's face turn red and the veins in his neck bulge. Barney quickly fortified his assertion with a fabrication. "By the way, if you're thinking of killing me too, you should know that I—I already submitted my observations to my editor at the *Portland Mirror*. Did it when I—I was,uh, sitting here waiting to be released."

Nancy regarded him suspiciously. "How?"

"How what?"

"How did you submit your—observations—to your editor?"

"With my cell phone."

"Oh yeah? Show it to me."

Barney froze.

"I patted you down. You had no such thing on you. You're just plain lying, aren't you? In fact nobody in the world knows where you are right now, do they?"

There was a long silence. Barney began to feel faint again.

Finally Fliess spoke. He was suddenly conciliatory. "Look, I don't know what you imagine is going on, but I can assure you it's not what you think." He whistled at the office door where Big Baldy was standing guard.

"Yeah, boss?"

"Milo, bring the bag in."

"Are you sure you wanna do that, boss?"

"Yeah. I'm sure."

Milo raised his eyebrows and sighed, "OK."

A few minutes later, the big man returned, dragging a heavy black body bag behind him.

Barney grimaced, but when Milo unzipped it, a dozen Beanie Babies spilled out and the quailing reporter began laughing. There must have been a hundred of those plush toys in the bag. Barney laughed harder and harder, almost hysterically. He laughed so hard he began hyperventilating, so he closed his eyes and took a few calming breaths. Then he opened his eyes again and looked around the room and sputtered, "You're all crazy! You're all...batshit crazy!"

Fliess pulled up a chair and explained the whole story.

Back in the mid 1990s, an Intel test engineer named Prashant Kumar

Sharma (or PK as he was known) began collecting a wildly popular new line of plush toys called Beanie Babies. He anticipated that one day these stuffed animals would become collector's items and he could sell them a few at a time to provide himself with a small retirement annuity. When he finally did retire, he sought out a rural home where he could live quietly and anonymously. As it turned out, Muphrid Thatcher had just placed an ad in the *Portland Mirror* to rent out his house with an option to buy. PK was the first caller and he snatched it up. And so it was that the Indian test engineer came to live out his retirement in Sweetbread. Over the years, he puttered in the garden and collected more Beanie Babies. His collection burgeoned. And, according to plan, he was able to supplement his pension with revenues earned through the sale on HotAuctions of the clamored-after Beanie Babies. But his cruise down Easy Street came to a rough patch when he lost a batch of Babies to theft. Although he was a private, secretive fellow, word had somehow got out about his collection and it wasn't long before little Kyle Lautenberg, Nancy's delinquent grade school son, broke in one night and made off with a satchel full of them, distributing his booty to children who would pledge loyalty to him and his gang.

Fliess perambulated the room while he talked. "Paranoid fellow that he was, PK hired a contractor to build five grass-covered bunkers in the yard and a tall cedar plank fence to conceal them from view. He went down to the local morgue and got hold of a dozen 'pre-owned' body bags—"

"Eueww!" Barney grimaced.

"—and filled them with Beanie Babies, 100 to the bag, and hid the bags in the locked bunkers. As a final measure, he covered the bunker hatches with soil so a minor excavation was necessary to get to the hatches to get to the bags to get to the Beanie Babies. There were no further break-ins.

"Sadly, PK became addicted to Deena's desserts and over time, he grew morbidly obese and very ill. One day, he packed his bags—clothes, toiletries and insulin—and left for India, never to return. In his will, executed by me, he deeded everything to Muphrid. Muphrid didn't know what to do with the bunkers or the body bags full of Beanie Babies, so I offered to buy the Babies one a bag at a time for a handsome compensation."

"$1000 a bag!" Muphrid blurted out and Fliess frowned disapprovingly.

"I generously donated them to a McMinnville children's charity, for which I got a nice tax write off and the satisfaction of bringing joy to underprivileged children."

"Yeah and don't forget the $250 contributions to the policeman's fund!" Muphrid blurted out again.

Fliess responded, "Muphrid, those numbers are confidential."

Muphrid apologized.

"So you're a benefactor to lots of charities!" Barney chuckled archly, "And one of your donations is a payoff to the lone officer in town as a *quid pro quo* for guarding your late-night secret business dealings, in other words?"

"No, no! You're way off base there, buddy!" was Nancy's retort.

The attorney fidgeted, then clarified. "It goes for police office supplies and so forth. This town's budget is bare bones so the police department can use all the help it can get. And yeah, it's also kind of a quid pro quo for Nancy guarding us from prying eyes during the visits. We don't want to attract treasure hunters and thieving riffraff, you know."

Nancy glared at Fliess. "That's my son you're talking about, you ass."

Fliess wilted. "Oops. Sorry, you know what I mean."

Yeah, she knew exactly what he meant. That was the problem.

In the end, the story was strange, convoluted but not utterly implausible. Still, in Barney's opinion, something didn't add up. But he wasn't sure specifically how. The story was like a cloth bag that holds water for a while because it has no big holes, just hundreds of tiny leaks.

"Look, this can't get out," Fliess implored. The initial threats seemed to have evaporated. The man was worried about exposure. Barney wondered why. What was he hiding? Somehow the key to this whole weird escapade lay in the answer to that question.

"Keeping this private among the concerned parties is what PK expressed in his will." The attorney picked up the photograph of Nancy and her son from the desk and examined it. Holding it up for Barney to see, "Look, you don't want to jeopardize them, do you? A single mother trying to make ends meet and raise a delinq—uh, troubled—son? Think of the children in McMinnville, think of your friend Muphrid. I'm asking you to please keep all this to yourself and stick with your Deena Poole story."

Barney drummed his fingers, thinking. "I'm sorry, but I can't comply. I'm a journalist. If I smell something I'm going to investigate and might well report on it. That is my job."

Fliess twisted his lips around, "This is...awkward."

112

The four of them conferred.

Fliess said, "All right, Barney, you want a cut?"

Barney glanced at the razor in Muphrid's pocket. "A cut?" the word caught in his throat.

"Of the proceeds!"

"Oh," he exhaled. "No. Absolutely not! Are you trying to buy my silence?"

"No, no, no, of course not. Just want to take the sting out of not getting to investigate what you'd ultimately discover is a dead-end story. Look, I've tried to be frank and open with you," the attorney said with a comforting smile. "If you have any further questions, do not hesitate to ask. Here's my card and you can text me anytime of day or night. I'll try to answer all your questions as best as I can, but in exchange for that courtesy, you need to promise to be discrete about all this. We're asking you not to mention this to anyone else, understand? Not even Stella."

Barney raised an eyebrow. Even Fliess knew about him and Stella! Maybe they should be quieter during their love making. He said, "I just can't promise that."

"Well, OK, I understand that this is your job but just know that a lot of good could be undone if word gets out."

"I'll keep that in mind." Barney started to get up but the shackle grabbed at his ankle.

Nancy stooped down and unlocked it. "Guess I can't hold you here any longer. Muphrid, can you put him up tonight?"

"Sure thing, Nancy."

"'Sokay, I have a place to stay—"

Nancy shot back, "Not at Stella's, you hear!?"

"But—"

"No 'buts'! We're decent folk here in Sweetbread. You're staying with Muphrid tonight, got that?" She turned to the barber. "Keep an eye on him, huh?"

"Sure, Nancy. You kin depend on me," the man said with a big pasty-faced grin.

Once freed from her charge, Fliess grasped the reporter's wounded forearm, causing him to squirm in teeth-gritting pain. "Listen to me, Mr. Big Time Reporter: Stick to the Deena story. Got that? I have no compunction about calling your boss if you stray from your assignment. There's no good that'll come of you nosing around in our business here."

With his face contorted in rictus of pain, Barney nodded compliantly. "Good."

~ ~ ~

Barney sipped his coffee and looked Stella in the eye. "So I spent the night on Muphrid's cot. I woke up and he was already out in the garden, filling in that hole. After that, Muphrid left, went to the roadhouse apparently. So I walked over to your house to find you and tell you I was all right, but you weren't there. Zach showed up with the tow truck. Before we left for the auto shop, that Chinstrap kid came running up with my phone. He demanded payment for it. What a little operator! Anyway, riding out to Bailey's shop, my phone was dead so I used Zach's phone to call you—"

She was hardly listening anymore. "Oh Barney, I really thought Muphrid had killed you! When you disappeared, I thought that's what happened." She sniffled and wept. "I thought he'd buried you in his garden! Along with the others!"

Tears puddled in his eyes when he saw her distress. "I thought I was goner too, at first." He reflected for a moment. "I thought I was a dead man—till I woke up with a nice haircut and a fresh shave. And a dash of aftershave lotion!" He flashed her a big toothy grin.

She laughed through her tears and clasped his hands across the cafe table. "I'm so glad you're all right."

He smiled gently. "I'm fine. Even after dealing with Dorgan Bailey himself. That guy's bad news!"

Stella nodded sympathetically. "So you got Dorgan-ized, huh! Welcome to the club." She shifted gears. "Back to your fun at Nancy's jailhouse, whaddya think's up with her and that attorney and Muphrid?"

Barney shook his head. "Not sure. It's all fishy as hell."

"I oughta known Nancy was up to no good—"

"Yeah, sure seems that way, Stella, but I don't know what to make of it. I mean, bags of Beanie Babies!? There's something else going on. It's just fishy business, that's all I can say right now."

She looked straight at him. "Well there's one thing for sure, now that you've told me about all this, you're in deep doo-doo with those goons. *If* they find out you spilled the beans to me, that is. *If.*"

"Well, that comes with being an investigative reporter. Don't worry, I can handle 'em." Barney pronounced this with paper thin bravado.

Stella started to speak just as her cell phone sounded again. She read the screen. "Ugh, Jeremy's gettin' antsy. I gotta get back and put out one of his brushfires. An irate customer. You know the drill." She got up, regarded her unfinished coffee and apologized for leaving so abruptly.

"It's OK. I've got my second interview with Deena coming up in a short while. See you tonight?"

"Absolutely, Barney baby. I'll be expecting you." She started to blow him a kiss, looked around and saw that Robert and the customer were not paying attention so she bent down and gave her new boyfriend a deep languid kiss. "Don't be late."

Then she was gone.

= CHAPTER 10 =

~ ~ ~

After Barney finished his coffee, he grabbed the grocery bag and thanked Robert on his way out. He checked his watch and, seeing he still had some time to kill before he was due at Deena's, stopped in at the antique shop to inquire into the valuation of Beanie Babies.

He could not have imagined at that moment the unexpected direction the answers to that inquiry would take him and indeed the whole town.

The antique shop's entry door set off an electronic chime as Barney came in. Once inside, he became aware of a certain mustiness. He scanned the room. There were the *de rigeur* rocking chairs and wall-mounted banjo clocks ticking away the minutes. Here and there were pale porcelain Hummelware figurines holding up dusty lampshades. Arrayed along a nearby shelf, a row of Toby mugs faced outward, all except the one with Falstaff's lusty face on it, turned askew so the rascal was staring straight at him. He looked away and saw the gray lady emerge from behind a teak armoire.

"Hello there." She asked him if he needed help with anything.

"Yes, I do. What do you know about, uh..." he glanced down, examined the old walnut credenza next to him, ran his hand over its marred surface while framing his query. He looked up at her again. "Are you familiar with, uh, you know, collector's items?"

She pressed her hands together solicitously. "A little. What kind of collector's items do you have in mind?"

"Oh, you know, things like coins or stamps or, I don't know, say... Beanie Babies?" There! He got it out!

A wan smile came to her featureless face. "Stamps I know something about. Coins not at all. But Beanie Babies I am quite familiar with. What do you want to know about them?"

He brightened. "Are they considered collector's items? Beanie Babies, I mean?"

"Oh yes, without question."

"Really! Can you give me an idea how much they might be worth? The collectible ones, I mean."

She said it depended on the age and type. "There are scads of different types of Beanie Babies. Some are commonplace and not worth much, just a few dollars apiece. But other models are rare or in great demand. The most sought after are the early originals going back to 1993. Those can fetch a pretty penny. Do you have any specific ones in mind that you're wondering about?"

Barney felt he had to be coy. "A friend of mine...has one that's a bear. How much would that be worth, for example?"

Her smile blossomed into a full grin. "Would that friend be a fellow by the name of Muphrid Thatcher?"

Well that subterfuge was short-lived! Barney exhaled. The veil had parted, the cards were face-up on the table, there was no need for pretense. Well, maybe a little; it might be prudent to keep one or two cards out of sight until he knew whether it was prudent to be prudent. "Yep, it's Muphrid all right. He's got all kinds of Beanie Babies. I want to know if he's getting a good price for them."

"Oh, is he selling them?"

Oops.

"No, no. I mean, not necessarily. But someone suggested he could sell them, so I figured I'd inquire whether it would be worth it for him. I had a little time to kill before my interview with Deena Poole, so I took this opportunity to stop in and talk to an authority!"

"Well, I don't know if I'm a true authority, but I do have some knowledge in this realm. Helping Muphrid is very thoughtful of you. He's a bit naive about financial matters, so it's kind of you to look after him." She led him to her vintage oak roll-top desk under the muted TV monitor.

"He can't be completely financially naïve—he owns a house and has a renter."

"His mother owns the house, not him. She moved out because the house was too big—and anyway she couldn't manage the stairs after a while. The infirmity of old age you know. It gets us all in the end. So she took up residence with Muphrid in an apartment over his barbershop. She owns that building too."

"But she still has stairs to climb, doesn't she? I saw them."

"She uses them once in a blue moon. And she has an electric lift for those rare occasions. She mostly stays home and Muphrid brings in groceries and anything else she needs. That man dotes on her, I tell you. He takes good care of her—and her properties." She hefted a fat catalog out of her desk drawer and split it open. "Here we are! Let's take a look-see, shall we?"

"You actually own a catalog devoted specifically to Beanie Babies?"

"Yes, of course. PK—Muphrid's old renter—was a serious collector of those little plush toys and he plagued me with all kinds of questions about them. He had hundreds of them, many of them first run originals. So I finally broke down and got this catalog and we spent many hours poring over these pages. This was before the days of Google, so the prices in the catalog are somewhat lower than today's."

She leafed through the dog-eared pages and colored Post-Its. Putting both hands flat across the book, she looked straight at Barney. "In the end, he sold off a few of his Babies on HotAuctions, but sadly he died before he could realize anywhere near the full value of his collection." She gazed briefly out the window, as if hoping to see the departed PK out there somehow. "In his will, he left all his property—including the Beanie Babies—to Muphrid. But Muphrid seems not so very curious about them. He carries one around on his belt and he's given a few away. But that's about it."

"He seems to like his little Beanie Baby bear. Calls it a talisman to ward off evil."

"That sounds like Muphrid. Peculiar fellow. But he's never once asked about the price. Completely uninterested. But now here you are, curious as PK was, curious on Muphrid's behalf, carrying the torch for PK. May it stay lit longer for you than it did for him," she concluded darkly. "But what am I saying? You're young and healthy. Just stay away from Deena's treats." She thumbed through the catalog. "Look at all these!"

There was an astonishing number of varieties of these plush toys. Some were valued at a few dollars, some at fifty or a hundred and a few rare ones commanded thousands of dollars. Almost all the first run Babies were in the last category. Barney's eyes popped open. "Why would anyone spend so much money on these things?"

"Why does anyone spend money for any collector's item? Because it's rare or special or old. It's like the old bottle of wine across the street at Vindy. People collect all kinds of things—old books or glass insulators. Even lint."

"Lint I can't speak to. But old books I can understand because you can read them. Insulators, on the other hand? I never understood collecting things like that."

"How about carnival glass?" she picked up a green glass ashtray.

"Carnival glass?"

"Yes, that's what this is. It's also called 'pressed glass'." The woman explained that carnival glass refers to cheap extruded glasswares like ash trays that were given away at carnivals in the 1920s. "Junk, in other words."

"So what makes it valuable?"

"Age. Antiquity. Relics of a bygone era." She swept her arm across the room. "Antiques! I've made a living off the human fascination with the old and the rare. We're all collectors, one way or another."

Barney listened thoughtfully.

"For example, take my husband, Armand. You may have seen him out vacuuming our tree?"

"That's your husband!? Yes, I have seen him. Quite the neat freak! I beg your pardon, that's not nice for me to say—"

"No apologies necessary. He is a neat freak. In the extreme. He's always been quite anal about keeping things just-so." She revealed that his surname, Ordonné, was quite apropos because it means in French, literally, "orderly".

"Armand is retired now—he was accountant, no surprise there—so when he's not tidying up the landscaping or when the weather turns wet, he stays inside with his stamp collection."

"Your husband is a philatelist, then?"

"Ohmygoodness no! He's always been faithful to me!" she exclaimed.

"No, no, what I meant was—"

She stopped him mid-sentence with a barely detectable wry smile and a tiny wink.

"Ha! You got me!" Barney absolutely did not see that coming from this stolid gray lady. People can surprise you!

"That's his joke he likes to pull on people. Anyway, back to the subject at hand, some of his most highly prized stamps are the defective ones:

119

misprints, offset registration, upside-down images and so forth. Useless, but highly prized—and priced."

"There's one more ingredient, Ms—um, Ordonne?"

"Astrid Ordonne. You can call me Astrid, of course. And what is that missing ingredient, Mr. uh—?"

"Starr. Barney Starr. You can call me Barney!" He smiled as they shook hands. "What is the missing ingredient? The missing ingredient is a buyer! Someone willing to pay a high price for your useless possession."

"Yes, what the market will bear, in other words. Speaking of bears, let's get back to your Beanie Baby." She hummed softly while she flipped through the pages till she found one that seemed pertinent. "Now here's a Brownie the Bear that's $30 but here's an original for $125. And, oh, here's another rare one for $200 and my goodness, here's a super rare first generation one for $500!"

Barney rubbed his chin, "So a bag full—er, collection of—one hundred could range from $3000 to $50,000 depending on the styles and ages?"

"As I said."

So Muphrid is grateful for attorney-out-law Fliess' "generous" payments of $1000 per hundred, Barney thought. *There's that fishy smell again.*

"All these plush toys started off originally at a few dollars per?"

"Yes. Just like coins or stamps. Or cheaply made glass ash trays. Then the price goes up over time. The highest prices go to defective merchandise, as I said. Any oddity that makes them rare and unusual makes them desirable." She pointed to a photo in the catalog. "Here's a good example." It was a magnified view of a Beanie Baby label. It said, "SUFACE WASH." She cracked another wry smile. "Now this misprint, a typo really, renders this plush toy extremely valuable."

"Amazing. Absolutely amazing. This is a pyramid scheme, isn't it? The price climbs up and up and up, just as long as everyone agrees to pretend there's value there." He thought about Wall Street, the dot-com bubble, real estate speculation. "In the end, someone refuses to pay the high prices and sells low. That starts a panic, a stampede of selling off at lower and lower prices. In the end someone is left holding the bag when it all collapses."

"In the end, yes." Barney thought for a moment, then offered, "Someone like Alexander Sweetbread, yeah?"

She nodded approvingly. "You know the story!"

"Yep. I'm a reporter you know."

"Well, you've done your homework." Then she brought them back to the topic, "In any case, for now the Beanie Baby prices are still climbing. But who knows for how long? If you want to help Muphrid, you ought to encourage him to sell sooner than later." She winked conspiratorially.

"So you think the bubble will burst?"

"Not immediately. Prices might subside, but not collapse. It's been slow growing and so it's not really a bubble. Not like the stock market crash of '29 or the Wall Street shenanigans a few years back or Tulip Mania."

"Tulip Mania?"

"Yes, PK was obsessed with it."

"What's Tulip Mania?"

"Speculative madness that swept a whole nation. Not ours. Holland. In the 1630s." She took Barney's arm. "Honestly, Barney, I think that man was up to something and it wasn't just the Beanie Babies. But I could never figure out just what it was. Now he's gone, so I guess I'll never find out."

"Tulip Mania, eh?"

"Look it up. I think it's the key. You're a reporter. Maybe you can figure out PK's secret."

"But—"

~ ~ ~

The rear door flung open and Astrid's shop partner, an Asian woman, came gusting in. The instant she laid eyes on Barney, she announced exuberantly, "Hey mistah! I see you at Stare-ah's big potty Satta-day night! You remembah me?"

"I'm sorry, your name was?"

"Nga. Nga Bailey, but now just back to origin-ah name, Nga Phan."

"Are you from Vietnam?"

"Bone there, but Taipei. Den come here, stott family." She looked at the Beanie Baby catalog splayed open on Astrid's desk. "You like Beanie Babies? My doddah have one of dem Beanie Babies too. Ha! She love it. You meet my doddah, Twee?"

Barney shrugged uncertainly. "I think so..."

"You seen huh. She hang out wid dat no-good-foe-nudding Chinstrap gang."

"Oh yeah, the little girl!"

"Yeah, I thought you see huh. Anyway, I teh huh stay way from doze boys. Day no good a-tah. Bad infoo-ence on my dodduh, you know." She sighed. "But she know evvey-thing doan she? So she no listen huh mud-dah. Ah-ways duh case! Since dawn of time, huh? Ha ha! I hate speshee dat Chinstrap boy wid tattoo make him look like granddad, Tom. Vay-ee pecue-yuh. He whatchya caw bad seed, dat boy. But back to my dod-dah, Twee. She need fadduh. But fadduh gone. Poof! Gone. Jim, he coulda hepped Twee, but he gone now. Gone, gone...dead." She paused and took a slow breath while Astrid nodded affirmation. "Bad foe us. He was good man, Jim. Not like brudduh Joe. You know, Joe? Doe-gun Bailey's boy day caw Knockah. He—"

Barney halted her non-stop information dump with a raised palm. "Wait, wait. Stop!" She stopped. "Let me get this straight, uh, Nga. You're saying Knocker is your brother-in-law? Twee's uncle?"

"Yeah, I marry his ode-ah brudduh Jim. Duh good one. But 'long wid Jim, come Knockah and Doe-gun as pot of package. Lousy package, huh!?" She started laughing and held her arms up in a gesture of weary resigna-tion. "What can you do? Life dat way sometime, huh?"

Barney checked his watch. "Oh boy, I'd better get going. Gotta prep for my date with Deena!"

On his way out, Astrid called after him. "Tulip Mania! Remember, it's the key to it all."

~ ~ ~

Barney went back to Stella's house, had a bite to eat and got himself set up with his laptop to do some preparatory research. One article about the deleterious effects of sugar and fat led to another. He got deeper insights into the corporate world of Fast Food, Big Food, industrial farming, agri-cultural chemicals, genetic engineering and more.

Before he knew it, it was nearly 3:30 pm, the time Deena agreed to meet with him at her home.

He closed up his laptop, grabbed his notepad and flew out of the house.

~ ~ ~

While on his way to Deena's, the half size school bus rumbled up to the stop near the bridge where the loose railing creaked in the breeze and swung in and out over Rock Creek. With a hiss, the school bus door opened and disgorged a dozen schoolchildren. They came pouring out, chattering and laughing and boy-yelling and girl-shrieking. Among them were the four members of the Chinstrap gang.

The instant they saw Barney, the foursome ran over and swarmed around him.

"I know what your name is, mister!" Chinstrap announced proudly. "It's BARNEY!"

"That's right," he said. "What's yours?"

"Kyle, but everybody calls me Chinstrap. Cuzza my beard!" The boy looked around at his mates. First was the skinny one with freckles and cowlick. "This is Peewee." Then came the chubby kid with the quasi-canine muzzle. "That's Dingo."

Dingo woofed like a dog. "Arf!"

Finally, Chinstrap introduced the girl with the Asian face: "And this is Twee."

"Right! I just met your mom."

"At the antique shop?" she asked.

"Yep."

Chinstrap pointed to girl. "We call her Twee Fwog."

"Twee Fwog?" Barney was grinning.

The girl explained, "My name is Twee Phan, but—"

Chinstrap Kyle interrupted, "But my Grampy Tom calls her Twee Fwog, cuz she's always climbin' in the tweez! Hee hee hee!" He proceeded to make suction sounds as his cupped hands climbed an imaginary tree trunk. The other kids giggled wildly.

"I see!"

~ ~ ~

Walking along, Barney noticed little Twee had come up alongside him, trotting to keep pace.

"Hi Barney!"

"Hi Twee!"

"So, you met my mom, huh?"

"Yes, she's very nice."

"I know! She's the best mom in the world!" Twee reached around behind her and pulled her Beanie Baby bear loose from the Velcro strip her mother Nga had sewn onto her backpack. She pushed the plush toy up to his face. "Wanna hold my bear?"

"Uh, sure." He took it and dutifully examined all sides of the bear. He noticed something hard inside the bear's posterior but decided it was nothing. He nodded approvingly before returning it to the girl.

"His name is Berry. Berry the Bear!"

"Barry the Bear, huh?" He looked across into the Vindemiatrix window as they passed and saw Callista inside pouring a Pinot for a customer. "Barry's a good name. I have a friend named Barry."

"Not Barry—BERRY!"

"Right, Barry."

"Yeah, Berry. Cuz bears like to eat berries, right?"

"Oh...BERRY!" he said. "I get it!"

"That's what I said, Berry the Bear! Don't ya get it? BERRY!" She rolled her eyes and exhaled impatiently. "I thought you were a reporter!?"

He chuckled, "I am. Just not a very good one, apparently!"

= CHAPTER 11 =

~ ~ ~

"What happened to you, Barney?" Deena exclaimed as she opened her front door.

"Am I late?"

"No, I mean, what HAPPENED to you?" Deena made a sweeping gesture toward the butterfly bandages peeking through his ripped shirt sleeve and pointed to his torn trousers smeared with sky blue paint. "You look like you were on the losing end of a particularly vicious paintball fight!"

He grinned self-consciously. "Fell out of a tree. It's a long story. Let's get to *your* story, shall we?"

She acceded to his suggestion, making sure to thank him for the first installment, which she read with delight, especially the palindromic moniker he used in the title, "The Avid Diva".

"Did you notice it's a palindrome? I got the idea from Nadia and Aidan, the Vandershur's fraternal twins."

She admitted she'd never thought of their names that way. "Well, ya learn something new every day!"

Settling into the cushions of her wingback sofa, she declared herself ready to begin. "Let's begin!" she said.

Unfortunately, her continuing account of how she rose to fame failed to hold Barney's attention. His thoughts kept wandering off to Beanie Babies, speculation, something called Tulip Mania and, of course, his unpleasant encounter at the auto shop.

Deena fidgeted and finally asked him with not a little irritation if he was really listening, was she boring him?

"Of course not! I'm sorry, it's just that I had a rough time with that guy

125

Dorgan Bailey at his auto shop and I guess I'm having trouble putting it behind me."

The woman immediately softened. "Oh, why didn't you tell me, you poor thing! That man is just terrible." She looked at his ruined clothes. "Did he do that to you?"

"No, no, not at all!"

"Are you sure about that?"

"I'm sure. It was all verbal."

"Well, sticks and stones may break my bones, but words leave scars that can't be seen. Don't I know that!" She offered him a consolation truffle. "I hope you don't judge all us Sweetbreadians based on him."

"No, don't worry. The way I look at it, he makes everybody else shine!"

She laughed appreciatively. "I like that! I like you! Shall we continue then?"

"Sure. How about some tidbits about your mystery dessert?"

"I did promise to share a hint or two, didn't I?" And with that she began the most recent chapter of her career story. She explained how Agri-Corp had "incentivized" her to showcase their new super-crystalline GMO sugar. The crystals were dense-packed, tripling the sweetness and calories per gram. The nouveau sugar was designed to literally explode when it hit the moisture on the tongue. "It's good for gardening too. Muphrid's been using my waste water to fertilize his grass. Uh—please don't put that part in, okay?"

Like a bolt, it hit Barney: That's why the grass on Muphrid's mounds was so lush! That's why the flies and fetid smell of fermentation!

"That's all I'll tell you, Barney. The mystery dessert shall remain a mystery till my Thursday show airs!"

The interview focused on some of her pivotal dessert creations, how she came to the notice of the Food Network and the travails of getting her own cable TV show produced. In the early days, she used to drive out to the studio in Portland but as diabetes diminished her mobility and her show skyrocketed in ratings, the TV crew started coming out to her home here in Sweetbread every Thursday to tape her show. In two ways, that turned out to be fortuitous: First, it provided a homey setting that appealed to the focus groups. And second, her biggest sponsor, AgriCorp, paid to upgrade her kitchen to full professional level.

Part way through the session, Barney excused himself. The coffee was begging to exit. While he stood at the toilet in the guest bathroom, he passed the time looking around. The wallpaper was a bas relief of dark red velvet curlicue patterns. There was a stack of napkins by the wash basin, suggesting that the designer hand towels on the rack were for decoration only and off limits for anything as radical as actual hand-drying. Finally, he noticed a bread box size container in one corner that said "Sharps" and had a corresponding biohazard warning symbol. After he was done with his business, he went over and lifted the lid of the box and saw a small pile of hypodermic syringes and spent insulin vials. This sharps container was for guests, so Deena likely had another one in her own bathroom.

For the second half of the interview, they continued to talk about the ups and downs of the show and again how much she appreciated the support she got from the network and from her sponsors, especially AgriCorp. She pulled out her cell phone and showed him pictures of her crew, of the old studio, of her friends and family. She shared a montage from an award ceremony and showed him all the supportive emails thanking her for her recipes and the enjoyment her desserts brought to the American public.

There was an email folder entitled, "Grumpies." That's where she shuttled the negative emails off to.

"What kind of emails are those?"

"Oh complaints. All variety of complaints."

"About?"

"About health and such. There's a lot of people calling me a health menace."

"What do you say to that?"

She shook her head dismissively. "The studies are inconclusive. Personally, I think those people hate me for my success. They're just jealous. All I know is, I make people happy. All except for the grumpies, of course. They'll never be happy. The way I look at it, we all die eventually, right? Might as well die happy!" She offered him another truffle. He declined. "A wise friend of mine once said, 'It's not the length of your life, but the breadth that matters.' So that's my response to the killjoys."

She certainly has achieved a considerable breadth, he thought, suppressing a smile.

Deena resumed talking about the early days and how much fun and hard work it was getting a cable TV show off the ground. Eventually, almost simultaneously, she and Barney both looked at their watches. It was time to wrap up the interview for today.

On the way out, Barney saw a Beanie Baby sitting on an antique table by the door. He picked it up and examined it. "Tell me about this guy. Did you get it from—"

"Kyle Lautenberg, our resident Robin Hood. 'Hood' as in 'hoodlum'. Stole it from that strange Indian man, PK, Muphrid's renter." She got no response from Barney; he was busy feeling the plush toy's rear end. "Hello? Earth to Barney!"

He suddenly snapped to. "Oh, sorry! What's this hard thing inside?"

"Oh I don't know. Maybe a rock. These things are made in China, not much quality control you know."

"Hmm."

Suddenly he put his hand out. "Well, thank you for the interview, Deena. Let's do another interview on Wednesday and then a final one on Friday, after your show airs?"

"Sounds good."

She pulled out her cell phone, he pulled out his and they worked out a specific time.

"Thanks Deena!"

"My pleasure."

= CHAPTER 12 =

~ ~ ~

The interview had run longer than expected. It was late afternoon already and the sunlight was beginning to fail. Cold autumn gusts sent Armand Ordonne scurrying for his leaf vacuumer before more falling leaves littered his immaculate front lawn. The four members of the Chinstrap gang came running down the other side of the street.

Their red bearded leader pointed toward the unsuspecting Armand and the A-frame ladder he'd erected into the understory of his maple tree. Of special interest to Chinstrap was the gasoline powered leaf vacuuming machine lying on the sidewalk. By the giggles and the buoyant excitement of the kids, it was evident that Chinstrap had alerted them to a source of potentially hilarious amusement: flipping the reverse lever on the leaf vacuumer that shifted the airflow from sucking to blowing.

Chinstrap and Twee created a diversion, running across their victim's lawn to pluck flowers from his winter camellia bush while the other two casually drifted over to the leaf vacuumer. While Armand scolded off the flower pickers, Dingo blocked Armand's view of the machine while Peewee squatted down and flipped the lever. Then they all scampered away, ducking behind Muphrid's hedge and peering back around it with their cell phones at the ready in video mode.

Sure enough, once Armand had examined his molested winter camellias and decided no serious damage had been done, he came back to the sidewalk, scooped up his leaf machine and climbed to the top of the twelve-foot ladder. The four children hiding behind the hedge could hardly contain their gleeful anticipation.

Armand Ordonne adjusted his horn-rimmed glasses and then

placed his thumb on the ON switch.

But he didn't press it. There was a commotion near Muphrid's hedge. Rogerdog had escaped from Stella's back yard, dodged a car to get across Main to where the children were hiding. With uncontainable exuberance, the Irish setter snatched the Beanie Baby bear off Twee's backpack and headed straight for Armand's ladder. Twee and the other Chinstrappers, Dingo and Peewee, lit out after the dog, grabbing for his leash but missing it each time it bounced away. Chinstrap himself did not participate, choosing instead to trot slowly behind, video recording the pandemonium.

The fastest runner, Peewee, managed to finally catch the leash ("Gotcha!") just as he and Rogerdog reached Armand's ladder. The man looked down in horror as Peewee and Rogerdog ran past on opposite sides of the ladder. The ladder toppled, with Armand screaming his head off as he fell onto the neatly trimmed lawn and tumbled into his rose bushes. Scratched and bleeding, the man screamed and cursed loudly. Meanwhile, Peewee gripped Rogerdog's leash, struggling with all his might and what little body weight he possessed to hold the dog in check while Twee tugged on the hapless Beanie Baby in the dog's teeth. Of course, Rogerdog thought this was the greatest fun of his life. He growled and tossed his head from side to side, gripping the plush toy in his bared canines. Each time Twee yanked on the toy, Rogerdog bit harder, growling fiercely, then waited for the girl to struggle some more, triggering the next cycle of canine entertainment. In the end, the Beanie Baby ripped in two. Falling backwards with their prised-off prizes, the two—Twee and the dog—each found themselves with half a toy.

But there was a surprise bonus.

Chinstrap pointed at a gray square object lying on the sidewalk between girl and dog. "What's that?"

Attracted by the noise next door, Stella came out of the web design office, with Jeremy close behind. Surveying the disaster zone, she noticed Armand brushing himself off and still bleeding and scolded the Chinstrappers, "Look what you kids did to poor Mr. Ordonne! You should all be ashamed of yourselves! I'm telling your par—"

"Wait a second, look at this, Stella!" Jeremy picked up the little dark square object that fallen from the late Beanie Baby's guts.

She held it up between her fingertips and examined it, front and back. "What the hell is this?"

Armand came over to examine it. "Looks like a computer chip, Stella."

Jeremy confirmed the injured man's supposition.

"Probably for the voice synthesizer," Armand suggested, re-leveling his glasses.

Stella shook her head. "No this was a Beanie Baby, Armand, not a Furby."

The three looked at each other. Suddenly a car screeched its brakes and blared its horn at a man running toward them across Main from Deena's house.

It was Barney.

~ ~ ~

"What's going on?" Barney said, out of breath.

Stella held up the computer chip. "Look what fell out of Twee's Beanie Baby."

"A computer chip? That's weird. Is it for a voice thing?"

"No, you're thinking of a Furby," she clarified for the second time. "Beanie Babies don't talk."

Jeremy took it from her and studied it. He whipped out a pair of bifocals and peered at the cryptic numbers and letters embossed into its surface. "Hmm. It's an 8088 chip. Look, right here." The others came close and saw those four numbers too.

"So? What's that mean?"

"It's the Intel chip that powered the first ever IBM PC's. It's an antique."

"An antique," Barney echoed. "An antique computer chip in a plush toy?" The young reporter tried to make sense of this. He asked, "How antique is it?"

"Oh, thirty, forty years. A few decades ago," Jeremy said. "They were manufactured in the mid to late 80s."

Barney did a quick calculation. "So they could have been floating around when the first Beanie Babies came out in the early 90s, no?"

Jeremy shrugged, "Yeah, I suppose so."

"Why would there be a PC computer chip in a stuffed animal?" He looked around at seven uniformly vacant expressions.

"Maybe it fell into the stuffing at the factory. You know, by accident?" Stella offered.

"I'm not so sure about that that." Impulsively, Barney snatched the chip back and pocketed it. "Come on Stella, we're going to do a little re-search!"

With the Chinstrap kids tagging after (Twee snatched the halves of her bear so her mother could sew them back together), Barney led Stella across the street to Deena's mansion. More screeching brakes and a blaring horn. They were already out of earshot on the far sidewalk when Jeremy called after his cousin, "Don't worry about finishing your work, Stella. Why don't you just go ahead and take the rest of the afternoon off? Yeah, you're welcome. Think nothing of it." He stood there for a while, watching her and Barney open Deena's knee-high white picket gate. He shook his head and went back into his office.

Suddenly Armand was alone again. But not for long. Muphrid came up to him ever so silently, like a ghost. Startled, he exclaimed, "Godblessa-merica! Stop sneaking up on people, Muphrid!"

"Sorry, Armand." The barber looked at Armand and saw that he was bleeding. "Ohmygoodness, you're injured!" Muphrid unhooked the Bean-ie Baby doggie from his belt and reached deeply into its butt crack, pulled out a packet of butterfly bandages and alcohol wipes. Lemme clean you up, my friend."

~ ~ ~

Before she entered Deena's Willy Wonka gumdrop garden, Stella whipped around and glowered at the tag-along kids, "Shoo!" and sent them scurrying away.

Barney trotted up to the porch and rang the doorbell insistently. Final-ly the light in the leaded glass dimmed and a moment later Deena pulled the door open, clearly irritated. "What's the emergency? Oh, it's you, Bar-ney! What's wrong?"

Barney pulled out his pocket knife. "May I?" He picked up the Beanie Baby on the small antique table by the door...and plunged his knife into the stuffed animal.

"Good heavens! What on earth are you doing? Are you crazy!?"

Barney pushed his fingers into the stuffing and pulled out a dark, square, flat computer chip. He handed it to her. "Can you read the letter-ing on this?"

With a look one might have in the presence of an unstable madman, Deena nervously complied. She donned the reading glasses hanging from a chain around her neck. "Hmm. It says all kinds of gibberish."

Stella urged her, "Tell me if you see numbers. Like 'eighty eighty-eight'."

Deena adjusted her bifocals and scrutinized it. "Here it is, yes. Eight. Zero. Eight. Eight. What does that mean?"

Barney said, "I don't know yet. Mind if I hold on to the chip? Sorry about your Beanie Baby. I never learned how to sew but I have some duct tape in the car—"

"No! Give that back to me. I can sew it up myself. What in the Sam Hill is going on?"

"Don't know. We're gonna find out."

"Well you just go and do that. Now, if you don't mind, I'm preparing dinner for a small party."

Out on the street, Stella and Barney fairly bounced down Main Street back to her place, chattering as ebulliently as children on their way to the circus. With a rumble, Dorgan Bailey drove by in his big F-350 diesel truck. It was getting dark and hard to tell if the man saw them, but both fell silent for a moment. Once he passed out of sight, they tentatively resumed their chatter.

The two crossed the Rock Creek Bridge, stepped over the sky-blue skull and crossbones where the damaged railing was. "Drunk driver did that," Stella remarked. "Early one Monday morning."

Barney gave her a questioning look. "Don't tell me."

"Yeah, it was Knocker," she sighed.

"Huh. A real prince. So how come they can't fix it?"

"Look at the posts," she pointed to the rail supports knocked free of the bridge's support pillars. "It's more major than it looks. Town's short on cash so we...wait."

"Hmm." He thought a while then said, "So the drunk driver was Knocker?"

"Yep."

"The Bailey family's been kind of a curse on this town."

"Hey!" she said. "You know why he hit the railing?"

"Because he was drunk!"

"Well that. But he swerved to avoid the children waiting for the school bus."

"So, in other words, it was early morning. He was drunk at break-fast time?"

Stella grew impatient. "You're missing the point, Barney!"

"The point being?"

"That he cares. Under all that rough exterior, he cares. Deeply. People around here consistently—I'd say conveniently—ignore that part of Joe."

Barney rubbed his face. "But it wouldn't have happened if—I mean—the fact is that—"

"He's been hurt too, Barney. You of all people should understand that."

"I know, I realize that but...never mind. No further questions. The prosecution rests."

"Good. 'Cause I didn't like the tack the prosecution was taking." Stella said. "So let's get back to—hey look who's coming our way!" Ahead, coming around the corner from Nancy's house on Fillmore, appeared a square built man with a no-nonsense gray crew cut, a Mormon beard and the toughened hands of a retired lumber mill machinist. It was Nancy's father, Tom Lautenberg. Stella greeted him cheerily as he approached. He nodded with a polite smile, but no more than that. He immediately refocused his gaze past them both and fixed it on his grandson who, in the company of his co-conspirators, had been stealthily tailing Barney and Stella since they reemerged through Deena's picket gate.

"Hi Grandpa!" Chinstrap Kyle called when he saw Tom coming his way.

But Tom did not acknowledge his renegade scion in any discernible way; he simply walked past without so much as a sideward glance. Kyle turned and watched his grandfather's back for a while then hung his head, whereupon he saw a soda can and kicked it into the street and laughed hard when a car drove by and flattened it. Then he up and punched Dingo in the gut.

"Ow!" Dingo cried.

Twee scolded Kyle. "What'd you do that for? Poor Dingo! He didn't do anything to you!"

Kyle turned his back on them, 'dropped trou' and exclaimed, "Kiss my ass! Ha ha ha ha!"

Twee set her jaw angrily and Dingo expressed himself as he usually did when facing adversity: by barking like a dog.

A cold wind came up and Kyle launched into a full sprint home, yelling back as he rounded the corner at Fillmore, "So long losers! I'm goin' home! It's freezing out here!"

The other three took the cue and scattered like the leaves blowing across the streets of Sweetbread.

= CHAPTER 13 =

~ ~ ~

It was hard to close Stella's front door, for it had caught the cold wind that was blowing the rest of autumn's glory off the trees. Up the street, Armand was thinking about re-erecting his A-frame ladder, but darkness was falling fast so he finally capitulated and went inside.

On Stella's porch, hugging each other for warmth, kissing and caressing, she and Barney pulled open the door and stumbled into the living room. Stella abruptly pushed Barney away. "Later babe, we got a mystery to solve!" She went to the kitchen and got a pot of coffee going.

While she was working, Barney said, "What've we got so far?"

She looked over her shoulder. "Beanie Babies and computer chips."

"And Tulip Mania."

"Tulip Mania? What's that?"

"That's what you're going to find out about while I research Beanie Babies—trading, prices and maybe find out why they'd put old computer chips in them."

She got irritated. "Keep the little girl busy with tulips while you do the man's work, eh?"

"Oh right—like Beanie Babies are a man's domain! Listen, after Astrid told me about the Beanie Babies she said PK was up to something and it had to do with Tulip Mania. Said it was the key to everything."

That mollified her. "The key to everything, huh?"

"You know what I think the bottom line is?" he added.

"Hmm?" she brought two mugs over on a thick tray.

Barney winced when he realized the tray was her Android tablet. "I'm not sure that's such a good idea there, Stella."

136

"Do it all the time, never spilled once. Hey, I'm a professional waitress. I know how to handle a tray!"

Barney cleared the coffee table of her ex-boyfriend's piles of car magazines so she had a place to set the "tray." He wondered why she left those magazines there if they had really broken up.

To his dismay, Stella handed him the mug with the "Pennzoil" logo on it. It seemed nearly impossible to escape Knocker's ubiquitous presence around here.

"So what's the bottom line, Mr. Starr?"

"I think that attorney—Jason Fliess—is ripping Muphrid off."

"Me too," she concurred. "Poor Muphrid's getting fleeced. Get it? Fleeced?"

"Yes, I get it. Fliess. Fleece. Cute."

She sat down next to him on the sofa and stroked his face. "I love seeing you smile." She kissed him and he kissed her and as it became more serious, suddenly she sat back. "Let's not get carried away. We're on a mission. Save this for, you know, 'dessert', eh?"

He nodded and sighed. "Stella, I think I have a mania for your 'two lips'." That set them both to giggling. "I love your smile too. All right," he finally said, "Let's do some sleuthing!"

And so, the two of them opened their respective laptops and set to work. With fingers flying and mice jiggling and faces lit up in the glow of their LCD screens, amid self-addressed mutters and humming and so forth, it was Stella who spoke first.

"Check this out, Barn. Tulip Mania was a financial thing back in the Middle Ages."

Barney craned his neck to see her screen. "1630s in Holland. That's not quite the Middle Ages, but anyway, what does it say?"

She read the Wikipedia article:

Tulip mania was a period in the Dutch Golden Age during which contract prices for bulbs of the recently introduced tulip reached extraordinarily high levels and then suddenly collapsed. At the peak of tulip mania, in March 1637, some single tulip bulbs sold for more than 10 times the annual income of a skilled craftsman. It is generally considered the first recorded speculative bubble. The term "tulip mania" is now often used metaphorically to refer to any large economic bubble (when asset prices deviate from intrinsic values). The 1637 event was popularized in 1841 by the book Extraordinary Popular Delusions and the Madness of Crowds, *written by British journalist Charles Mackay. According to Mackay, at one point 12 acres of land were offered for a Semper Augustus bulb. Mackay claims that many such investors were ruined by the fall in prices, and Dutch commerce suffered a severe shock.*

"Here's a quote from this guy Mackay," she said.

People were purchasing bulbs at higher and higher prices, intending to re-sell them for a profit. However, such a scheme could not last unless someone was ultimately willing to pay such high prices and take possession of the bulbs. In February 1637, tulip traders could no longer find new buyers willing to pay increasingly inflated prices for their bulbs. As this realization set in, the demand for tulips collapsed, and prices plummeted—the speculative bubble burst. Some were left holding contracts to purchase tulips at prices now ten times greater than those on the open market, while others found themselves in possession of bulbs now worth a fraction of the price they had paid.

"Those were the suckers left holding the bag," she clarified.

"Well, that's what Robert over at Vindemiatrix winery was talking to me about this afternoon. Astrid at the antique store too. Exchange value can be different than inherent usefulness."

"I guess I know what you mean. Or not." She could not summon anything of inherent value to say so she shifted the subject. "Look, why's Tulip Mania the key to all this? Is Astrid saying these Beanie Babies are like a tulip bloom—ha ha! Oops! I mean—I mean tulip BOOM?"

Barney shifted his weight to the other butt cheek. "I don't know. She says no, the Beanie Babies are not a bubble. She says PK was super interested in Beanie Baby prices. But she also said she thinks PK was up to something besides just the Beanie Babies."

"Computer chips?"

"Beats the heck out of me. I could not find anything about a connection between Beanie Babies and computer chips." He groaned. "Absolutely nothing. But I did find that prices are even higher than ever for original issue Beanie Babies, which I think Muphrid has a boatload of."

"Boatload! Ha! I always thought it was 'butt load'!" Stella laughed. Suddenly her expression changed. "Wait a second, Barney."

"What?"

"PK," she said.

"Yeah?"

"He worked at Intel."

"Intel...computer chips...whoa!"

"Ohmygod," she said. "PK was hiding computer chips in those Beanie Babies!"

"I wonder why?"

"Were they valuable?"

"Not especially. Anyway, they're antiques now. Worthless."

"Worthless antiques? Astrid makes a living off of 'worthless antiques'," Stella averred.

"You're right. I think we should go over and tell Muphrid to stop selling his babies to that attorney until we can get a proper appraisal of his collection. He's getting shafted," Barney said.

"Right on. Let's go! Wait till he hears about the chips—"

"Don't say anything about the chips, OK?"

"Why not?" Stella cocked her head.

"We hardly know anything about the chips yet. It'll just confuse Muphrid and muddy the waters. Let's just stick with what we know so far."

"So far we know the Beanie Babies are worth way more than Fliess is paying Muphrid for them," Stella said.

"And that's what we'll tell Muphrid tonight. OK?"

"OK."

~ ~ ~

Muphrid recoiled when he opened the door and saw Stella standing there with Barney.

"I come in peace, Myoofee," she assured him. "You and I are cool now."

"Sure?"

"Sure."

"OK. Good. I'm glad." At that, Muphrid welcomed the pair warmly into his home, "Would you two like some soup? I'm making it for Mama and me, but there's plenty for friends too."

"What kind is it?"

"Gopher."

Barney gasped. Muphrid laughed and laughed.

"Come on Muphrid, quit freakin' Barney out. What is it really?"

Muphrid dipped a ladle into the kettle, filled a bowl and offered it to Stella. "It's barley soup. Careful, it's real hot."

She approved.

At this, the decision was made to stay for dinner and talk. During the meal, Barney explained that Jason Fliess was shortchanging Muphrid, but the barber placidly dismissed his concerns. "It's money ain't really mine anyway, so any amount helps."

"Helps with what?"

"Payin' the mortgage. Mama 'n' me don't need a renter long as Jason keeps givin' me money. He's a nice man. He was PK's friend, ya know, not jest a lawyer to him."

"Well you could get more money for those things. A lot more. Let's find out how much more. Could we see your collection?"

Muphrid explained that they'd have to pull out a bag from a buried backyard bunker, though he had a few Babies in the house.

"Well, what're ya waitin' for, Myoofee, go get 'em!" Stella said.

The barber drew a napkin across his mouth, got up and motioned for Barney and Stella to follow him down a hall toward a small room in back. Flipping on the light revealed a table with a sewing machine on it, a dressmaker's mannequin and a steam iron on an ironing board. Evidently this had once been his mother's sewing room. Along the far wall was a glass-doored cabinet containing skeins of colored yarn and colorful Beanie Babies packed behind the glass like jelly beans in a jar. Muphrid gathered up an armload of the plush toys and dumped them on the sewing table.

Barney meanwhile had pulled up the HotAuctions website on his cell phone. "Muphrid, get a pencil and write these numbers down."

Sixteen times, Stella picked up a Beanie Baby, fed its information to Barney, then Barney called out the going price and Muphrid wrote it down.

"Now, let's total these up." It came to about $1100. "If this is a representative sample, you're looking at six or seven thousand dollars for each of your, uh...body bags. Six or seven thousand dollars for each visit from your so-called friend, Jason Fliess. Instead of one thousand. He's ripping you off."

Stella implored Muphrid to demand a higher price.

Muphrid squirmed. "But I don't want to make him mad at me. Maybe he'll stop buyin' them altogether. Then I'll have nothin'." He seemed on the verge of tears. "I wouldn't know how to sell 'em muh-self."

Stella touched his shoulder tenderly. "Don't worry. Fliess—Jason, I mean—he's not going to abandon you. There's no one else he can buy from. He needs you more than you need him. Be brave, OK?"

"OK." Muphrid reflected a while, then said, "But wuddoo I say to 'im?"

Barney offered. "I'll talk to him. Give me his number. I'll call him right now."

Muphrid had Fliess' number posted on his refrigerator, so they trooped out of the sewing room. The light from the sewing room illuminated a squat bookcase in the hallway. "Wait, Muphrid. Can you leave the light on?"

Muphrid and Barney squatted down and looked at the books. Muphrid said, "These were PK's. He was some kinda genius I think. I can't make no sense of mosta the names o' these books."

Barney surveyed the titles. Many were technical books, dealing with computer architecture and integrated circuits. There were quite a number of mystery novels, a couple of books on mathematics and some puzzle books. And there was one that was quite old, an antique. He pulled it out. *Memoirs of Popular Delusions and the Madness of Crowds*. Barney nearly gasped. "Stella, come here! Muphrid, was this PK's book?"

"Yep. Sure wasn't no book o' mine!" The barber took the book and gently opened it, to reveal the "Ex Libris" stamp and PK's name on the inside. It read, "Prashant Kumar Sharma" with an apartment address on Cornell Boulevard in Hillsboro, Oregon.

Barney flipped forward to the table of contents. "Tulip Mania" was one of the entries.

It was highlighted in yellow.

The chapter itself was easy to find: PK had bookmarked it with an old envelope addressed to his Cornell apartment. Barney set the bookmark aside and splayed the book open on the hallway floor to study the story that Astrid foretold would explain everything.

Soon, the three of them were sprawled out on the hallway floor while Barney read aloud Charles Mackay's account of the financial feeding frenzy that drove prices for simple tulip bulbs into the stratosphere until the last buyer declined to buy and the whole castle in the sky came crashing back down to earth.

They were just about to get up when Barney stopped them. "Whoa, wait a sec'!"

Scribbled into the margin at the end of the chapter were these words:

A most marvelous scheme for acquiring immense wealth has occurred to me. Sadly, there is very less room in this margin to describe it. I shall keep the full description in a safe place where you will come to know my plan.

"That bastard! That clever, devious bastard!" Barney exclaimed. "He's pulling a Fermat's Last Theorem maneuver on us!"

"What're you talking about, Barney? Who's Fair-MAH?" Stella squinted one eye.

"Pierre de Fermat, the French mathematician who lived around the time of Tulip Mania. His theorem is one of the most important in all of mathematics. It deals with the Pythagorean equation—"

"Pythag—get to point, Starr!"

"Yeah, yeah, sure. So this brilliant dude, Fermat, wrote a tantalizing little note in the margin of a book stating that he had discovered the most marvelous proof of one of the most important theorems in mathematics but alas the margin was too small to describe it! Or so he said. If he ever wrote down this marvelous proof, it was never found. Over the next four centuries, the best mathematicians in history busted their brains trying to prove his theorem themselves, but with no success until just a few years ago."

Stella said, "So what are you saying? It's hopeless to figure out PK's scheme?"

"Maybe. But there is one difference. Unlike Fermat, he said he wrote down the description and it's 'in a safe place'."

"Like, what, a safe deposit box?"

"That's a good possibility."

Muphrid said, "But PK died an' only he had the key."

"Yes, that's true, Muphrid, his executor—his lawyer—would get the key and so he would know where the contents went." Barney got up. "It's time for a little courtesy call to Jason Fliess, attorney at law."

They hastened to the kitchen where Barney dialed the number on the fridge. Fliess answered, but when Barney identified himself, he got an abrupt dial tone. Further calls went to voice mail. They tried email too ("Just want to ask you some questions about your client PK") and waited. No reply. Same with text messages.

There was nothing further to do, so Barney and Stella thanked Muphrid for the soup and went across Main back to her house to consider what to do next.

~ ~ ~

An arctic wind was blowing and the two held each other close as they crossed the street. The evening had gone completely black, save for a faint line of orange on the western horizon. The light of the street lamp in front of Stella's house rhythmically dimmed every time her sweet gum's branches swung past it in the wind. Up the street, in front of Armand and Astrid Ordonne's house, near the spot where Armand's ladder had been, little phosphorescent green blobs danced gaily in the air.

Barney halted.

"What?" Stella asked.

"Do you guys have fireflies around here?"

"No. Never seen one, at least." She turned to see what he saw.

Barney suddenly released her and clapped his hand over his mouth, mortified. "Ohmygod! Ohmygod!"

"What is it!?"

"It's—it's...ohmygod, it's my new condoms!" He looked down sheepishly. "Glow in the dark." Indeed, the Chinstrap kids had found the grocery bag he'd left on Armand's sidewalk when they discovered the chip inside the Beanie Baby.

"Hey, you kids!" He ran across the street and they all scattered—except Chinstrap himself who grabbed up the bag, held it hostage.

"Hi Barney! Want this bag back?"

"Yes, give it here!"

Chinstrap put it behind his back and held out his other hand. "Ten bucks."

"Oh fuck! You little swindler!"

"Goin' up to fifteen!"

Barney pulled out his wallet. "Only got...eight." He held the empty wallet open.

"Close enough, dude!" Chinstrap grabbed the cash and dropped the bag. He ran off, jubilantly holding his fistful of bills high for the others to see.

"Damned urchin." Barney picked up the bag and looked inside, worried they'd taken all the condoms. They had not. There remained an ample supply.

He walked back to where Stella stood. She was laughing hysterically. "Come on, you," she said, taking his arm. The two came into her darkened home, flipped on the lights and tumbled onto the sofa where they warmed each other up.

Barney pulled away.

"What's the matter, babe?"

"I hate to say it, but before I do anything else, I absolutely have to get today's interview with Deena out to my editor," Barney asserted. "I'm on a timetable." His articles were meant to create hype about Deena's upcoming TV show on Thursday.

"But," he added, "there are more important things on my mind."

"Like what?"

"Like you." He pulled her close again and she complied gladly and fully. Soon they were entwined, breathily caressing and nearly knocking the coffee table over with swinging feet. She reached down between his legs and began massaging his man-parts when—bang! A loud noise outside. They both jumped and Barney ran to the door. He paused to ready himself for whatever he was about to encounter and pulled the door open forcefully. There was nothing out there under the twinkling stars. Then came a creaking sound followed by another bang and he saw what it was. It was a rogue gust strong enough to whack the loose railing hard against the side of the Rock Creek Bridge. Barney breathed relief, his tense muscles relaxed. But not for long, for just as he was about to close the door against the wind, a black Escalade came up Main Street. At the corner of Fillmore, the SUV slowed and its amber left turn signal began blinking. But when Barney stuck his head out farther to get a better view, the signal went dark and the car continued up Main and disappeared into the night.

Barney pulled the door closed, turned and walked smack into Stella. "Jeez Stella! What're you doing there!?"

"It's my home, you know," she said dryly. "What did you see?"

"Fliess. He just drove by."

"Relax, he's just a lawyer, not a killer. You're gettin' paranoid there, ol' Barney."

Bang! Stella was suddenly in his arms.

"Who's paranoid now?" he said.

"Cram it." She stuck her tongue out at him.

"Ha ha! By the way, Jeremy really needs to get that railing fixed." He nuzzled her ear. The two kissed and caressed until she abruptly pushed him away. "All right, I don't want to be responsible for you missing your deadline. I'll make another pot of coffee so you can get that article banged out and we can have the rest of the evening without...interruption. Sound like a plan?"

He gave her a thumbs up.

He got to work while Stella surfed the Web on her coffee-stained Android tablet.

~ ~ ~

The Bitter Side of Sweet
By Barnard Starr

Deena Poole is ever the gracious hostess. She delights in bringing delight to the world. But there is a dark side, not entirely of her making, for a large industrial complex known as AgriCorp has co-opted her good intentions and muddied the boundary between good and ill.

We humans are not good at assessing risk. We pay attention to sensational but rare things. We worry about shark attacks and terrorist bombs even though far more of us die from auto accidents, smoking and sugar. These are so commonplace and familiar to us there is a perception of control and correspondingly less anxiety. But the excessive amounts of sugar we eat are as deadly as smoking. It's not an issue of moral weakness. The desire for sweetness served us well when we were hunter gatherers and sources of concentrated calories were scarce. The only really sweet thing was honey and that was difficult and often dangerous to obtain. Nature endowed us with a strong drive to get it despite the risks in obtaining it. But now we can provide ourselves with as much as we want, despite that fact that our sedentary lifestyles require less, not more, calories. Even in farming days, sweets, cakes and so forth, were quickly burned off. But for a society of office workers and machine operators, it's turning us into diabetic lardballs. This is called the "mismatch hypothesis" and leads to many so-called diseases of civilization such as diabetes, cancer and cardiovascular disease, a constellation known as metabolic disorder.

In the town of Sweetbread, as across America, public places such as the Rock

145

Creek Roadhouse have insulin needle disposal bins in the restroom. One third of Americans are obese and another third overweight. Sugar is such a public health problem that there is a movement afoot to label it as a toxin.

An even greater concentration of calories is found in fat, more than twice the calories of sugar. Again, we crave fat for the same reasons as we do sugar.

Yet marketeers find they can sell products by exploiting these urges. And so it is not surprising that agricultural giant AgriCorp generously bankrolls Deena Poole's wildly popular show on the Dessert Channel to promote sugar and fat.

Although a good-hearted woman, Deena Poole has been prodded by AgriCorp to produce ever richer, ever sweeter deep-fried confections. As a consumer of her own wares, she too is a victim...

= CHAPTER 14 =

~ ~ ~

"Done! Whew!" He heaved a weary sigh. "Yay!" Stella tossed her
tablet aside and nearly pounced on Barney.

Kissing passionately and caressing madly, she led him away from
the living room sofa bed, leaving the lights burning, and drew the two of
them stumbling through her bedroom door and tumbling into her cannily
turned-down bed. After removing the gingham ribbon from her ponytail,
Barney proceeded to remove her blouse and bra and then his own shirt
and trousers. Soon they were both completely nude and he went down
between her thighs.

"Ohhh, mmm, ohhh!" She heaved and moaned.

By and by, the room grew strangely quiet and she heard a peculiar
sound emanating from her loins. It was the sound of...snoring.

"Wake up!"

"Oh, sorry. I—"

She sighed sympathetically. "It's OK, babe. You've had a long, long
couple of days." She pulled him up alongside her and the two fell into a
deep sleep.

= CHAPTER 15 =

~ ~ ~

Barney awoke briefly, just long enough to see Stella dressed and ready for work at Jeremy's office and bending over to kiss him on the forehead.

He roused himself to alertness and sat up. "I must have dozed off last night!"

"Oh, you did that all right, big time! You're quite the romantic."

He rubbed his eyes, "Oh yeah. Oh man. Nothing personal."

"Nothing personal taken. Go back to sleep, babe—you need it."

"Did I finish my dispatch?"

"Yep. You're off the hook. I'm going to Jeremy's again—it's my day to balance his books. But call me when you're among the living and I'll come back an' rustle up some breakfast for you."

"Oh, thanks, Stella, but I'll be fine."

"Not an option, mister." She mimed a telephone with her outstretched thumb and pinkie and singsonged, "Call me!"

"Yes ma'am. Sure thing."

"See you later alligator!" she said.

"In a while, crocodile," he said.

"I'll hurry back, Cadillac!" she said.

"Heh heh! Hm, let's see...I'll be sure to call-ya, my little dahlia!" he said.

She laughed. "Wait, wait, oooh, I got it! My sweet ear of corn, I wanna make a meal o'you when I retorn! Ahaha!"

"Ohhhh-kay then, my dear, I think it's time to wrap this up."

"That was pretty good, huh? You're my sweet ear of corn and I'm gonna gobble you up when I reTORN! You bring out the best in me, Barney!" She blew him a kiss on the way out and he retorned it.

At the door she paused. "Not to spoil the mood, but you're starting to look kinda shabby in those pants. You're better'n that. I left a pair of Joe's jeans over the back of the chair there. You two are pretty close in size, I think they'll fit you."

"Mm-hmm." Barney nodded agreeably and flopped his head back down on the pillow, waved goodbye with his fingertips. The last thing he heard before the front door banged shut was Stella's sing-song, "My sweet ear o' corn, gonna gobble you up when I retorn. Hee hee! My sweet ear o' corn..."

~ ~ ~

Barney woke up from the middle of a dream about a tow truck chasing him when a song started playing on the nightstand. Fumbling around in a fog, not exactly sure where he was, he found Stella's alarm clock. He hit the snooze button but nothing happened. He pushed the "Off" button but that didn't silence the infernal thing. When he finally came to, he realized the sound was emanating from his cell phone. He managed to pick up the call just before it went to voice mail.

"Hello, this is Barney Starr," he drawled. He looked at the alarm clock. It said 10 a.m.

He listened to the voice at the other end. It was the City Desk editor.

Deena was very upset about the article he'd submitted.

"The—article?"

Pause.

"Oh that one!" He propped himself up on one elbow and switched the phone to his other ear.

"How upset is she?" Barney frowned. "Wait! What!? You vetted my article with her?"

Pause.

"Why would you do that? You're breaking the cardinal rule of journalism. The one you inculcated in me from my first day on the job: never let the subject of your story vet your story."

Pause.

"No! It's about journalistic independence. Otherwise, it's just a promotional for her and—"

Pause.

149

He sat all the way up. "Oh, I see, this is SUPPOSED to be a promotional piece? I can't do that!"

He sighed.

"No, I'm not going to shill for—"

Pause.

"Yeah, yeah. All right. Sure. Yeah, I know I don't have a leg to stand on. Yeah, skating on thin ice. Yeah, yeah, I get your point. OK. I'll tone it down."

Pause.

"Right. Waaay down. Got it. Yes, I know you're serious. Yes sir. OK. Bye."

Barney touched the red hang-up icon, threw himself bodily around on the bed, yelling and shaking his fists in impotent frustration.

He dressed (eschewing Joe's jeans for his own), put the cell phone in vibrate mode, stuck it in his hip pocket, shuffled into Stella's little kitchen, filled a bowl with sugar-charged Froot Loops and, choosing to ignore the manifest irony of that choice, filled the bowl with milk and set to work revising his article. The cell phone was uncomfortable in his pocket so he laid it on the table.

~ ~ ~

The Sweet Taste of Success
By Barnard Starr

The doyenne of American dessert, Deena Poole, is going to unveil a deep-fried confection on Thursday that has the nation holding its breath and drooling for details. She remains secretive except to say that her sponsor, AgriCorp, is letting her debut its latest patented GMO product, a super-dense ("super-crystalline") form of sugar that packs three times the sweetness punch of normal sugar and virtually explodes on the tongue. It will add a new dimension to her usual confectionery artistry, a tower of pleasing power that she will share with the Dessert Channel public on Thursday night. GMO means never going back, as she puts it.

~ ~ ~

Barney's cell phone buzzed and the vibration caused it to drift around on the kitchen table. He picked it up, "This is Barnard Starr."

He smiled broadly. "That was fast!"

His car was fixed and ready to be picked up.

Barney finished the new version of his second installment about the Diva and submitted it. In moments, he was fairly cantering up Main Street, en route to Bailey's Garage, the shop on the wrong side of the tracks. The day had dawned overcast and chilly and now a dreary mist was coming down.

He called Stella and told her he was taking a rain check on breakfast, he had a car to fetch.

Passing Deena's on the left, he saw that the Deep-Fried Dessert queen was out on her porch, refilling a bird feeder. When she saw him, she screamed at him, "You! You snake! You treacherous snake in the grass!"

He held up his arms defensively.

She was in tears. "You betrayed me! How could you!?"

He approached the white picket gate. "I'm a journalist, Deena. My first duty is to my readers, to inform them."

She set her teeth and rocked her weight onto her cane. "You can inform them without defaming my reputation. I trusted you! I thought,"—she fought back her tears—"I thought you were my friend!" She began sobbing, turned and headed back in through the open leaded glass door. "No more interviews."

He protested, "I portrayed you as a big hearted, generous person, Deena."

"Oh don't patronize me! To hell with you!"

"Didn't you see my revised article?"

She stopped, "No. What revised article?"

He told her about it, said he'd cc'd her. She had not seen it.

"I'll look at it. But no more interviews. We're over. Tell your editor to send someone else next time."

She went in and rattled the leaded glass when she slammed the door.

Barney walked a few feet and the phone buzzed again.

"Hello. This is Barney Starr," he said flatly.

Pause.

"You're firing me!!?" He held the phone away and looked at it like it was an alien entity. "I completely toned down the article about Deena Poole. She just hasn't seen it yet—what? It's not about that?"

Pause.

"Holy shit! Jason Fliess called you!!?" Barney stumbled over a sidewalk crack and nearly fell. He stopped in place and listened to the editor's voice for a long while. The long and short of it was this: he had brazenly broken the terms of his probation. It was over.

The line went dead and the dial tone came on.

Barney staggered on as if he'd been hit by a truck.

Ray walked past. "Top of the morning to you, Barney!"

Barney walked on, zombie-like.

"Are you OK, buddy? Is it something I said?" Ray watched Barney's form shrink as he got farther and farther away. "'Cause if you're unhappy, maybe a 20% discount on any item in my shop'll cheer you up!" Barney kept walking. "No? Tell ya what, I'll keep the offer open so you can think about it, OK?" Barney kept walking. Past the roadhouse, past the City Hall. On to Bailey's garage.

~ ~ ~

"I don't think you should be smoking next to that gasoline container, Mr. Bailey," Barney opined with not a little trepidation.

"You gonna tell me what to do in my shop? Huh?" Dorgan spat a dollop of saliva on the fender of Barney's newly repaired Pinto and stubbed his cigarette out in it. "There ya go. Happy now?"

"Hey!" Barney grimaced. "What'd you do that for?"

"You got a problem with that?" Dorgan loomed threateningly over the ex-reporter, then withdrew, grabbed a rag off a workbench and wiped the mess off. "There. Jest like new."

Barney was angry with himself for automatically catching the disgusting rag Dorgan abruptly tossed to him. He set in on a counter. Then he decided that this was no time for politeness. He slid it off the counter onto the floor.

"Pick that up!"

He meekly obeyed, hating himself for his timidity.

Barney chose his words carefully when he asked about the repairs. Dorgan led him over to the desk in the corner of the shop. The large man snatched Barney's car keys off a peg, pulled out a billing sheet and went over the repairs. The bill was for the full estimate plus more, no surprise.

He drew up a wooden chair. "Here, sit down."

Putting on a pair of bifocals, Dorgan drew his finger down the itemized list: "Straightened out yer fender, corrected yer alignment, replaced one headlight, patch welded the radiator and refilled it. Antifreeze and miscellaneous consumables. Ya got your insurance card with you? I need to see it again."

While the man examined Barney's insurance card the missus came in from the side door. She was slender and mousy. And she had a black eye. Dorgan looked up "Whaddya want now, Dorothy? Can't you see I'm busy?" He leaned over and confided to Barney as if they had suddenly become drinking buddies. "The wife. She can't see I'm busy, the dimwit. We all got our burdens t'bear, don't we?"

Dorothy Bailey said, in a thin, quavering voice, "There's a delivery truck out back, Dorgan. He needs your signature."

Dorgan didn't even look up, just waved her off. "Yeah, yeah, tell 'im he can wait. I got a customer." Just then, an elderly man came in. "Make that two customers."

Barney looked at the timorous little slip of a woman and the shiner under her left eye. He empathetically pointed to his own eye, "Does that hurt?"

She shook her head and looked down at her feet, then looked shyly back up at Barney. She glanced back anxiously to see if the delivery man was still there, waiting.

Barney looked at Dorgan who was now hunched over the copying machine and then looked at the woman again. "Don't tell me, you took a bad fall?"

Dorgan looked over his shoulder and squinted at the reporter suspiciously, "Yeah, smartass, she took a fall. Clumsy as hell."

The woman looked down again apologetically and said, "Yes, I'm such a stumblebum."

"Now, ya better quit talkin' to my wife if you know what's good for you." Dorgan came back from the copier, pulled off his bifocals. "I got a delivery waitin'. You wanna wrap this up or not?" The big man stared silently, then continued. "Credit card?"

Barney gave Dorgan his MasterCard in exchange for the insurance card. Dorgan ran the credit card. Finally Barney signed the credit receipt and billing sheet and got his copies.

Then he waited while Dorgan put his bifocals on again and opened a file drawer. Dorgan looked up acidly. "You gonna just stand there like goddamn fool?"

"Wasn't sure if we were done."

"What else would there be? Is there a problem?"

Barney shook his head, "No," and got into his car. It started up fine and the steering worked compliantly for the first time in months. It felt good. What a relief!

As he backed out of the garage, Dorgan looked up and said, "I know what you been up to, Mex."

Barney was afraid to ask what that was supposed to mean, though he knew Dorgan had seen him and Stella together.

Driving back to town, he tested the brakes well before each intersection.

~ ~ ~

The fuel gauge needle was touching empty, so Barney pulled into the service station wedged between the Lost Weekend bar and The DTs Saloon. Nice locales.

By the time he'd killed the engine and set the parking brake, a friendly looking man sporting a walrus mustache and clad in a grimy jacket and woolen watch cap tapped on the window.

Barney cranked it down and the man said, "Fillawih regglur?"

"Huh?"

"Fillawih regglur?" the man clarified.

"Yes! Yes please!" and Barney handed the man his credit card. This was Oregon, after all, where the few remaining non-outsourceable jobs like service station attendant were preserved by law.

While he waited, Barney opened the door and hung upside down from his seatbelt harness so he could peer at the undercarriage. The pavement was well-soaked with petroleum-derived fluids but there were no shiny fresh pools. Then he felt something brush the back of his head. He pulled up and saw two grease stained boots. The man indulged his customer by squatting down to hand back the card.

"Yer card," he said. "Lose sumpin?"

"Oh, just checking for oil leaks."

"Hm." Walrus mustache got onto his knees and looked around under the car. "Nuthun downear!" He rose up with a hand braced on one knee. "Yubin havin' probums?"

"Problems?" there came that involuntarily dimple as he mentally ran through the list. He just shook his head. "Naw. No problems. Just being proactive."

The man's eyes crinkled. "Ah-weeze a good idear."

The nozzle clinked to "off." Soon the man was back with the receipt.

"Hava goodun," the man waved as Barney drove away. At the driveway apron, he hit the brakes hard and the tires screeched and the car stopped smartly; the brakes had held. He sheepishly looked back and saw the man grinning with a puzzled look on his face. Then he plunged onto Buchanan Road and drove on.

~ ~ ~

On Main Street, Barney executed a U-turn and pulled up in front of Jeremy's office, where Stella sat in the window. She waved him in, cheerily.

A minute later Barney was standing before her. She swiveled around in her chair and heard the whole sorry saga of the morning. She placed a hand on his arm, the one without the bandages. "I'm so sorry, Barney."

The two leaned their foreheads till they touched. She said, "You've got a greater calling. You're like me, you don't fit in someone else's mold. You gotta stay true to what you believe in. You'll end up pissing people off sometimes, but that's their problem. If the *Portland Mirror* doesn't understand what you're trying to do, then that's not the place for you."

Barney sat back. "I never thought of it that way."

She held out her open palm. "Ten bucks for the counseling session!"

"You and Chinstrap. Extortionists! I gotta keep an eye on you both!"

She said, "Jeremy's gone through this kind of thing, feeling like a failure 'cause he couldn't please everybody all the time." She described how, as mayor, he had a lot of power to do things, but only within the limits of an austere budget. So in other words, not that much real power. The town's tax base was so poor, he had to make painful budgetary trade-offs. In this case, it was a choice between continuing school bus service or fixing the Rock Creek Bridge railing. He chose the former, hoping the warning placards mounted on traffic horses near the railing would offer a word to the wise. But a couple of juvenile wise guys stole the placards and the horses. And stole the second set that were chained down—along with the chains and locks. If only that energy could be harnessed into fixing the railing! Bottom line, a lot of folks in town accused him of leaving their children exposed to danger.

"But I think he did the right thing. The kids can be careful on the bridge but they can't get themselves all the way to Sheridan every day and give themselves a proper education. That's how I see it, anyway."

Barney smiled lovingly. "You're something else."

She slapped his torn, paint splattered pant leg. "And you're starting to look like a bum. You're not a bum, so you shouldn't look like a bum. I told you to put on Joe's pants. I laid 'em on the chair for you. Go home and change. Then come back and I'm gonna put you to work on your true calling: investigative reporting. I mean the story you're dying to tell, about shady lawyers, body bags full of Beanie Babies and computer chips—and assorted dirty dealings in Sweetbread. And godknows what else you dig up in the process. Honestly? I think you've only scratched the surface."

He nodded and got up.

"Oh, one other thing?"

"Hmm?"

"I love you, Barney Starr."

He blushed and left.

~ ~ ~

Stella pushed aside her work when Barney "retorned" with his laptop, wearing a clean pair of (Joe's) blue jeans. With his stylish haircut, shave and new pants, he was cleaning up nicely. All he needed was a fresh shirt and he'd be ready to go out on the town!

She set him up with his own desk and resumed her bookkeeping work. For the next couple of hours, the two worked silently.

The weather was thickening outside and the office grew dark. Stella got up to turn on more lights, then came around and stood behind Barney, peering over his shoulder at his laptop. "Whatchya workin' on pookie?"

He explained that he was fleshing out copy.

"Huh?"

"Writing my article about the Beanie Babies, my arrest, and so on. Also some research into those computer chips."

"Whaddya find out about—?"

His phone started singing to him. "Hold on, I gotta take this—it's a text from Deena."

Deena wanted to let him know she approved of the new version of the article.

"I don't know if I should be happy that she likes it—or self-loathing because I sold out."

"You think too much, my dear," she said, kissing the back of his head. "I say, be happy." She lit up. "Hey, does that mean you got your job back?"

"I doubt it. She still doesn't want me doing any more interviews."

"So you're still a noble outcast. You should be glad!"

"Heh heh, thanks coach!"

She looked over his shoulder again. "And what's this? You sellin' something on HotAuctions?"

"Research." He described the frenzied trading in obsolete Intel 8088 chips on HotAuctions. Crazy inflated prices. "Pristine, never used chips. That's typical of collectors of anything. They even like things in the original sealed box, if that's possible."

"But look—the highest priced ones are all advertised as defective. That's weird, don't you think?"

"Nope, not according to your local experts, Astrid and Armand. Defective is more desirable. Pristine and defective is the most sought after."

She wrinkled her brow. "What kind of sense does that make?"

"Think about it. From misprinted postage stamps to puppies with mismatched eyes or the runt of the litter, we seem to have the greatest love for the odd ones, outcasts, the misfits."

"Like you and me, huh babe? Like you and me." Her ponytail bobbed when she reached around and gave him a smooch on the cheek.

She ran to the corner of the office and pulled up a portable whiteboard. "Let's map out what we know so far. First..." she uncapped a Dry Erase marker pen and sniffed it. "Mmm, I love the smell of these things!" She sniffed it again.

"Ahem!"

"Right! OK, the first thing is Beanie Babies." She wrote that down in the middle and drew a circle around it.

Barney said, "Put into—eeyeuch!—used body bags, a dozen at a time by an Indian Intel engineer named PK Sharma."

"Prashant Kumar Sharma." She wrote his name, circled it and drew a connector line.

After a while, the list went like this:

Valuable Beanie Baby plush toys:
Collected by Indian Intel engineer Prashant Kumar ("PK") Sharma during 1990s
Buried by the 100 in crypts in Muphrid's yard
Purchased from Muphrid @ 12.5% of $8000 market value per 100 by

PK's attorney Jason Fliess every few weeks
 Officer Nancy gets kick back for guarding the transactions
 Fliess donates the Beanie Babies to children's charity (and gets a write-off?)

 Computer chips
 Useless and defective antique computer chips shoved up the plush toys' "poopers"
 Chips are traded at ridiculously high prices at HotAuctions
 PK worked at chip maker Intel
 Fliess is smuggling?

 <u>Jason Fliess</u>
 Atty at law, lives in hills, office in McMinnville—not to be trusted

"Hard at work on billing, I see!" Jeremy emerged from the back office with Tom Lautenberg.

Stella started to explain, but everyone's attention went to the arriving school bus across the street. With a hiss of brakes and opening door, the children came running out. Tom suddenly grew agitated. "Gotta run, Jeremy. Thanks for the help." The elder Lautenberg hurried out to his Toyota pickup truck and was in the act of opening the cab door when the yellow school bus across the street pulled away from the curb to reveal his grandson Kyle staring his way. Tom averted his eyes, got into the truck, fired up the engine and drove off.

Kyle watched forlornly as his grandfather's veteran's license plate grew smaller and smaller until it was unreadable. He spat into the gutter and marched toward his freckled playmate Peewee.

"I wonder why Tom was suddenly in such a hurry?" Jeremy wondered.

Stella explained that he'd as much as disowned his delinquent grandson.

Jeremy broke off the conversation and swore a blue streak. Across the street, scrawny Peewee was clinging to the railing and screaming in terror as Chinstrap swung it out over the sharp rocks of the creek far below. Dingo stood aside laughing and making barking noises, glad it was Peewee this time and not him. But Twee was yelling for Chinstrap to stop.

The three in Jeremy's front office ran out onto the sidewalk and yelled at Chinstrap to stop. He at first stared back defiantly, but when the three adults came running, he reluctantly pulled Peewee back to safety. At that, the four children went running around the corner of Fillmore, past Stella's house and the house where Chinstrap Kyle and his mom Nancy lived. Out of sight of the adults, they continued past the end of the asphalt and descended the gravel switchbacks to the pond.

Shaking his head mournfully, Jeremy said, "It's bad enough I couldn't get that railing repaired, but Nancy's criminal son—she'd never admit to that but it's true—insists on making a bad situation worse. It just takes money—lots of it. You know how much it costs to repair one lousy railing? You could buy a couple of brand-new Porsches!"

"Really!?" Barney was amazed.

"Really. It's not just the railing, there's structural damage. The supports." He sighed wistfully. "This town just can't raise that kind of money."

Stella touched her cousin's arm. "You can't do everything, Jeremy. Even Superman had his kryptonite."

"I'm not sure what that means, Stella."

"I'm not sure either, but...you know what I mean."

"No, but thank you anyway."

The three of them stood in the drizzle for a while.

Then Stella blurted out, "Barney got fired from his job."

"How come?"

"Trying to tell the truth about Deena and GMO super-crystalline sugar. Trying to investigate the Tulip Mania chips shoved up the butts of Muphrid's Beanie Babies."

Jeremy rubbed his face. "I'm sorry, but I am just not tracking this conversation at all. Did I just have a stroke or something?"

She laughed. "No, it'll all make sense when Barney publishes his findings on his blog—or maybe with a different newspaper. You can do that, right Barn?"

"Yeah, I suppose so. The *Willamette Week* and the *Portland Tribune* and the *Portland Mercury* are still in business."

Jeremy scratched his head, "Well, I'll leave you two lovebirds to whatever save-the-world quest you're on."

They started to go back inside when Barney halted them. "Listen," he said. It was the sound of children again. The members of the Chinstrap gang minus Twee were coming back, full tilt.

"Twee's in trouble! Help us, PLEASE!" Chinstrap shouted.

Across the bridge, somehow Nga knew to poke her head out the door of the antique shop. "Whatsa madduh!? Twee in trubbah?" Peewee and Dingo waved frantically for her to come with them.

= CHAPTER 16 =

~ ~ ~

Led by the scruffy threesome, Stella and Barney ran west on Fillmore Road and descended its gravel switchbacks to the creekside cul de sac. They leapt over the concrete bumper blocks and rushed to the rocky creek bank. There the three children pointed straight up into the huge old eastern white oak growing out of the hillside whose exceedingly long branches arched high over the pond. Still working his way down the switchbacks, cane in hand, stepping gingerly on his neuropathic feet, portly Jeremy came huffing after them as quickly as he could.

Looking up, Barney and Stella simultaneously gasped at what they saw hanging from a broken limb far overhead. It was the gang's fourth member, Twee, Nga Phan's little girl. Inverted, head below her feet, the child clutched a slender branch that had snapped at its junction with the main bough. She looked like a huge chrysalis hanging there. Still attached, albeit by mere splinters, the branch held her swinging in the breeze.

The boys frenetically recounted how they were loitering at the pond when they started talking about emulating Stella's epic dive from a high limb of the big oak. Twee boasted that she could do that too. The boys laughed at her, told her a girl like her couldn't carry out such a dangerous endeavor. At the receiving end of such a goad, Twee declared right then and there her intention to not only match but to exceed Stella's feat. She would climb out on an even higher limb than Stella had.

The boys hardly got a deprecating word out before the girl was up the tree, climbing like a motivated squirrel. She soon got herself onto a limb that was several feet higher than the one Stella had used. She shinnied out on her belly as far as she could go. In time, she realized her dilemma. She had gone higher than Stella, but the branches up there didn't reach as far as the lower ones, so to get over the pond she needed to leave the stout main limb for a slender offshoot that angled away from it. Halfway along the offshoot, barely past the edge of the pond below, her weight torqued the branch so that it snapped at its junction with the main limb, dropping her in an arc until she was swinging six feet under the main limb from a tentative hinge of tenacious splinters. And there she hung, upside down, thirty-five feet above the rocky ground, the lifeline branch clenched between her knees and gripped in her desperate hands. Her straight black hair hung earthward. Whimpering with terror, all she could do was call for her mother.

Sprinting past Jeremy, mother Nga arrived on the scene, looked up and screamed hysterically. She ran to a location directly below her daughter. Craning her neck, squinting unblinkingly upwards, sobbing uncontrollably, Nga caught droplets of fear urine on her face. By those droplets, she knew that she was exactly where she needed to be to catch her daughter should she fall. Nga opened outstretched arms. She moved this way and that, jockeying around as the droplets fell first here and then there, hoping to be in position and ready for the girl when she fell. Between plaintive sobs, Nga called to the others to please oh please do something to save her little girl.

Soon half the town was here—word spreads fast in a small town—and the other half was on the way.

Mayor Jeremy mobilized the burgeoning group to gather close and create a human safety net below the girl.

~ ~ ~

Immediately, Barney had an idea.

"Muphrid, go get your tow strap. Everyone else, give me your belts!" In an instant, he had a pile of donated belts at his feet. Some were leather, some were woven fabric, some wide, some thin. He buckled the belts head to tail, coiled them around his waist and readied himself at the base of the oak tree when there came the sound of a rumbling diesel engine followed by a loud thunk and squealing tires. It was Dorgan Bailey's Dodge RAM 3500 Crew Cab truck humping over a concrete bumper block.

The big man's mouth was already disgorging a torrent of obscenities when he threw the cab door open and leapt out, leaving the engine running. "Who the hell's responsible for this!? Who told my granddaughter to climb up there!?" He swung his accusatory gaze across the group as if strafing them with machine gun fire. The adults shrank back and the boys scattered up the hillside like birds flushed from a dovecote. Slowly the boys crept back, protesting timidly, "We told her not to do it! Honest!"

"You should have stopped her! You boys deserve to be horsewhipped for this and so help me—" He saw Chinstrap standing there and the veins nearly popped out of his head. "YOU! You're the one behind this! Whatingodsname have you done to my little—"

"Shut up, Dorgan!" Stella had had enough. "Just SHUT THE FUCK UP! We're trying to save your precious little granddaughter. What's wrong with you!?"

Jeremy took the opportunity. "Come help us, Dorgan. Look, you're not doing any good yelling. Give Barney your belt."

"What the hell's he think he's gonna do with my belt?" he spat out the words as he handed over his belt.

Behind Dorgan's back, there was a noise. It was the sound of his truck shifting into gear. The big man whipped around. "Hey! What the hell you think you're doing, Stella!!? Goddammit!" Stella had commandeered his F-350. Before Dorgan could utter another word, she was already speeding up the Fillmore switchbacks, slowing only long enough to pick up Muphrid, who was running back to his house to get the tow strap.

While all this was going on, Barney found a foothold on the knobby tree trunk, reached up and grabbed a knothole and began hauling himself up the massive oak. The soles of his Keen shoes gripped the rough bark and there were plenty of hand-holds so he was able to ascend rather quickly to a height that made him queasy when he dared to look down. The sight of the townspeople watching him from below spurred him to defy his fear and continue climbing. In the back of his mind, he wondered if he would ever be able to climb back down. No time to think about that; the perilous ascent demanded his full attention.

Soon, he reached the first limb, which was the one Stella had climbed out on years ago as a feisty young girl. It was fairly high above the hillside, so the horizontal platform it provided afforded him some sense of safety. But Twee was dangling from the next limb up, so he took a deep breath and resumed his climb. By now he knew better than to look down.

When he got to it, Barney carefully maneuvered himself onto Twee's limb, straddling it with his legs as if on horseback. Out at the distal end of the limb, he could see the inverted child hanging on for dear life from the swinging branch, which itself was hanging on for dear life to its mother limb.

"I can't hold on, my hands are getting tired! Mama!"

"Hode on baby!" Nga called up.

"Just hang on, Twee. Barney is going to help you," someone said. It sounded like Callista.

Barney laid forward and hugged the limb like a bareback rider hugs a horse's neck. Now it was time to shinny his way out on his belly to the end of the limb. People below were dead silent.

As he worked his way toward Twee, the hillside below dropped away. Further out, the ground below leveled somewhat until it came to the creek bank. Now he was directly over the little girl.

"I'm here baby. Just hold tight and we'll get you down," he said, trying to sound confident. He looked down at the ground far below, imagined the sickening fall and the sudden hard impact of his body on the hard, rocky ground. He felt like he was going to faint again. Instead, he focused on the task at hand and said, "Just hold tight there." He set to work while Nga and the others echoed his words. "Just hold tight Twee. Stay as still as possible, OK? Keep yourself still."

Even so, the occasional breeze did its work and you could hear fibers popping with every small swing. *Mrrn...mrn...creeeek...pop!* Barney wondered how much time he had.

He heard a noise and briefly looked over his shoulder to see the F-350 returning over the crest of the hill. It struck him that he was almost as high as the top of the Fillmore switchbacks. The people gathered below looked disturbingly small. A wave of queasy dizziness swept over him. He quickly averted his eyes and retrained them on Twee, hanging under him, six feet under.

~ ~ ~

He took an end of the belt "rope" and wrapped it around the limb, using a clove hitch he still remembered from scouting days. He took a couple more wraps for good measure and tucked in the bitter end. Of the other end, he made a slip knot loop and lowered it to the girl.

"If she dies it's on your head, Mex!" Dorgan shouted.

Barney gritted his teeth. "For sure she'll die if I don't try," he responded angrily then shut his ears to any further bloviation from that ass of asses, but was unable to restrain himself from adding, "I don't see you up here, Dorgan!" Considering how much Bailey outweighed him, it briefly occurred to him that this high branch might the one place he was safe from that animal.

He called down to the girl, "Twee, can you hear me? Can you listen to me?" She turned her head ever so slightly, beseechingly, as tears streamed downward over her eyebrows and forehead into her hair that was already damp with urine.

"Can you listen to what I say?"

She nodded meekly and her hanging black hair shook a little.

Barney dropped the makeshift belt rope until the loop end reached Twee. "Try to put one arm through the loop, but keep holding the branch."

"OK."

The loop came down, but it encircled her head instead of her arm.

"Shit," he muttered.

"If you kill my granddaughter, it's on you!" Dorgan bellowed.

"Forget it, Twee, keep holding on with both hands." Shaking, Barney splayed out over the tree limb, panting, thinking, thinking. He wasn't sure he was strong enough to haul her up anyway and even if he was, he wasn't sure all the belts were strong enough to support her forty or fifty pounds. Just one weak link and...disaster.

"Now what're you gonna do!?" Dorgan shouted.

A couple of people told the man to shut up. Dorgan turned on them with withering ferocity. "That's my fuckin' granddaughter up there! You shush me one more time—any of you—an' I'll rip your fuckin' head off!"

They stopped shushing Dorgan.

Barney tried to marshal his thoughts. He looked around for ideas. People shouted suggestions but none seemed practical and all sounded even more dangerous than his belt scheme.

Finally there was a familiar rumbling noise and here came Dorgan's commandeered truck—with Stella at the wheel. Muphrid was riding shotgun with his yellow tow strap on his lap. In the bed sat Ray with a coil of rope and Armand with a steadying hand on his twelve-foot A-frame ladder. The truck bumped to a stop and everybody jumped out.

Ray ran ahead, carrying the coil of braided orange Dacron rope. Holding the bitter end in his left hand and the coil in his right, he explained while winding up for the pitch, "This is our Rope-of-Hope everybody! It's strong as heck and smooth as a baby's behind. Will never snag." Then FLING! All eyes followed the ascending, unfurling coil as it flew heavenward, up and over...a lower branch.

"Darn darn ding dang drat!" Ray swore, loud and salty.

The hardware store owner pulled it back down for a mulligan. He coiled it, flung it and it fell short again, draping itself over the lower limb.

Then Muphrid tried and the coil arced a bit higher, high enough for Barney to swat at it, but not high enough for him to catch it. The barber pulled it down off the lower limb and tried a couple more times. Then, one by one, people tried their hand at the rope toss but each time it came to rest over the lower limb.

All were surprised to hear an offer of assistance from a squeaky little boy's voice. It was Chinstrap. "Leave it hanging there, I'll get it to Barney!" Before anyone could stop him, the boy clambered up the trunk, foothold by foothold, crawled on hands and knees out the stout lower limb—Stella's limb—seized the Dacron rope and made his way back to the trunk, clenching the rope in his teeth like a pirate. From there, he climbed up to Twee's bough, shinnied out and handed the rope off to Barney.

"Good boy, Kyle." The boy smiled proudly. Barney added, "What do I owe you?"

"Free of charge!"

While Barney took the rope and shook out the loopy tangles, the boy watched the people down on the ground. He saw Muphrid starting to attach the tow strap to one end of the rope. But the open hooks kept falling off. He saw Armand at the truck lifting his aluminum ladder from the bed. Chinstrap touched Barney's sleeve and pointed at the man, "Look at Armand. What an idiot!"

Barney shook his head. "No, Armand's going to save the day."

"But the ladder won't reach!"

"Don't worry, I have an idea." He called down, "Bring your ladder over, Armand." He described for Kyle his unusual plan for the ladder. The boy was surprised but emphatically approved. "Cool!"

Meanwhile, down on the ground, Dorgan weighed in, yelling up into the tree, "You dipshit. That ladder's not gonna reach. What're you thinkin'!?"

Kyle flipped Dorgan the bird. "Kiss our asses, old man!"

Dorgan responded with his own obscenities against which Kyle readied a return volley. Barney put his hand on the boy's forearm. "Cut it out, Kyle. We need to focus on Twee."

The boy nodded seriously. "Right." Barney gave Kyle the job of lowering the end of the rope currently in their possession down the other side of the limb. When it touched and coiled on the ground, Barney instructed Armand to thread the rope under the apex of the A-frame ladder, running it transversely under the red plastic top step. Armand drew the free end up and joined it to the main line with a deftly tied Boy Scout bowline knot.

Barney looked down to Twee. "How're you doing there, Twee? We're gonna get you down real soon."

"My hands are tired. I can't hold on!"

"Just hang on. It won't be long." Then the branch popped, Twee shrieked, Nga screamed, Barney gasped, but thankfully nothing happened. Barney exhaled. Twee's movement made the branch creak a little but still nothing happened. Barney breathed slowly for a moment then called down to the group to grab the rope and haul the ladder up.

Ray was right, the Dacron rope traveled smoothly over the limb without snagging on the furrowed bark. In a moment, the red plastic top step of the ladder came up and nestled under the bough Barney and Kyle were splayed over. The ladder was so close to Twee, it brushed against her denim blouse. He shouted down, "Hold the rope tight, I'm getting on board." Barney felt around with his left foot for the top rung of the ladder. When he found it, he planted his shoe firmly on the middle of the treadle and tested its support with a tentative application of weight. It held. Now he prepared to make a full commitment.

Red, white and blue flashing lights caught the corner of his eye. It was Nancy Lautenberg arriving in her patrol car.

"That's my mom!" Kyle said.

Nancy jumped out and her first words were to a bystander. "Ohmygod! Did Kyle goad her into doing this?"

The answer was, probably not. Well, hopefully not. Anyway, he's up there helping.

"Good boy," his mom said.

~ ~ ~

Now the time had come to act, the moment of truth. Barney took a breath and swung himself off the main limb onto the ladder. The townspeople holding the rope strained as his weight put tension on it. While the ladder twisted around, Barney carefully climbed down its rungs till he was adjacent to the inverted girl. To his dismay, his center of gravity caused his feet to push the lower part of the ladder away, so he ended up hanging somewhat away from the ladder. It was unnerving. With one arm crooked around a leg of the ladder, he reached around the waist of the upside-down girl who looked at him with big dark imploring eyes. He took another deep breath and…

"Oh doan let my dodduh die, please mistah be keh-foh!"

"You drop her, Mex, and I will crucify you!"

No sooner had he drawn his arm around her waist but suddenly the girl started squirming. She let go of the branch and lunged for the ladder and his pant leg, but she couldn't get a grip and her hand slipped off. Now he had the upside-down child by the clothing around her waist and she was slipping from his grasp. As they struggled the ladder swung around crazily.

"Grab the ladder, Twee!" Kyle yelled from the limb above, instinctively reaching down and swiping air to get hold of her, though she was well out of reach.

"Hode on to huh, Bah-nee!" Nga screamed again. "Doan let huh go! Doan let huh go!"

During the struggle, Twee's lifeline branch broke free and fell twirling to the ground.

In that instant, somehow the girl hooked her arm around the leg of the ladder and she got another hand on a rung and, with Barney holding her by the waist, she managed to pull herself upright, rung by rung, till she was next to Barney, fully upright. Once she got a foot on the lowest step she stood up. She smiled at him. He put an arm around her for protection, puffed out his cheeks and blew a big sigh of relief. It was only after a while that he became aware of the cheering below.

"Watch out everybody, I'm comin' down!" It was Kyle. He swung himself off the limb onto the ladder.

"Wait!" Kyle yelled. He stretched his reach toward the limb and grabbed the linked belts. "OK, you can let us down now." The folks down below played out the line and the ladder, laden with Barney and the two youngsters, descended slowly to the rocky ground.

Barney was trembling when he stepped off the ladder and lifted Twee into her mother's arms. A round of applause rose into the treetops. With her free arm, Nga wrapped a thankful hug around Barney's waist, sobbing. She rose on tiptoes and kissed his cheek. Kyle clambered past and jumped to the ground, holding up his arms triumphantly.

People came up to congratulate Barney, but he was too emotionally spent to take in much of anything, least of all jubilant approbation. He smiled politely, but hung by one hand from the ladder, staring at the ground, panting softly. Finally, when he saw Stella beaming, he stood up walked toward her. There was a divot and he tripped, felt himself falling but miraculously someone caught him before he planted his face on the sharp rocks. *Who caught me?* It was Muphrid.

"Be careful there, friend."

Barney looked up into the man's kindly eyes and thanked him, abashed for this and any number of other reasons.

People continued to come around and give their new hero high fives and thanks.

Ray clapped him on the shoulder and winked. "Rope of hope!"

Nancy was next. With Kyle proudly at her side, she shook Barney's hand. "Thank you, Barney. That was very courageous." Her walkie talkie came to life and she excused herself. Kyle ran a few feet after her and watched her drive off in her patrol car, lights flashing.

~ ~ ~

Even Dorgan saw fit to put his beefy hand on Barney's shoulder. "I guess I underestimated you, Mex." He fished for more words. "Didn't know you had it in you."

Then Dorgan noticed someone taking pictures of Twee reunited with her mother. He went over to get into the shot, but when Twee saw him coming, she moved around so her mother could shield her from the hulking man with teeth as big as piano keys. "Who is that man, Mama?" she asked.

"That yo granfadduh. Last time he come roun, you wuh lidduh baby."

Every time Dorgan, smiling like a crocodile, tried to address Twee, the girl scooted around behind her mother. Nga finally snapped at the man. "Go way Doe-gun! Leave huh alone! You nevah come roun no more since she was lidduh baby. She doan know you! Why you come now? Yoh wife Doe-a-thee, she come all duh time. Come see huh gran-dodduh, Twee. You? Nevah!"

Dorgan squinted angrily, "Dorothy's been goin' over to your place behind my back!?" He spat. "Well that's what I get for trusting that woman. I let her out to go shopping, and she sneaks over to your place! I need to keep a tighter leash on her."

"What? You think she yoh dog? You ah sonofabitch, no offense to your mudduh. I fee sah-ee foh huh racing son like you!"

The man looked at Twee and guffawed. "I feel sorry for my grand-daughter having a mother like you, you shrill little gook!"

"Why is he saying all those mean things, Mama?" Twee cradled her head against her mother's bosom.

"Look, you make huh cry now!" Nga screamed, "Go way! You ah vey bad man!" She pushed Twee aside and marched angrily toward Dorgan who quailed before the diminutive woman's fury. He took a single step backwards, turned and walked away, muttering, "Shrew."

"What you caw me!? Huh!?"

He just waved his arm dismissively, said to Barney as he passed, "Women! Can't live with 'em, can't shoot 'em!"

Barney frowned.

Dorgan sneered. "Aw, don't go lookin' down yer snot nose at me, you know I'm right, dontcha, Mex?"

He got into his truck and yelled through the open window, "No wonder Jimmy killed himself, you squinty eyed little gook shrew!" He roared away in his behemoth truck. A squirrel ran from Dorgan's ferociously advancing wheels, then inexplicably darted back in front of the truck and froze there, as if in defiance. An instant later, the truck lurched over the furry obstacle, then bumped one more time over it before coming to the switchbacks.

Nga watched the truck blast up the hill. "Hope you crash yoh truck! Good riddance!" She spat in his direction.

Barney came and put an arm around poor Nga. "Don't let him get to you, Nga. He's poison." Stella put an arm around both of them. Astrid came and wrapped her arms around them. Armand put his arms around, followed by Callista. Soon a good many Sweetbreadians had come around to enclose Nga and little Twee in a protective cocoon of arms.

Slowly, the arms fell away and the cluster of friends escorted mother and daughter up the Fillmore switchbacks, while others carried away ropes and ladders and retrieved their belts. The walkers weren't far up the switchbacks before one could hear Nga berating her daughter for her foolish escapade, the immemorial mix of anger and thankfulness a parent feels for a reckless child who has just survived a brush with death.

Walking along with the others, Barney felt a hand on his shoulder and flinched. It was Stella, come up behind him. "You're a good man, Barney," she said. "You're our hero."

He just shrugged. "Oh, I don't know about that. I didn't really think about it. If I had realized how dangerous it was, I probably would have talked somebody else into doing it!"

"Well, you did it though, didn't you?"

~ ~ ~

Up on Fillmore, Twee grew alarmed. "Where's my backpack!?"

Someone handed it to her.

She grabbed the pack and quickly turned it over. The Beanie Baby bear was gone. "Where's Berry? Berry the Bear is gone!" she exclaimed frantically, starting to cry. "Berry's gone!"

"Don't worry, Twee, we'll find him."

Muphrid overheard and ran back down to the pond.

"Muphrid's going back to look for him, sweetie. OK?"

"OK," she sniffled.

They waited until Muphrid returned, holding the toy bear up for all to see. The stitches from her mother's repair job last night were barely visible. Twee's face illuminated through the tears like the sun breaking through a rain shower. Once she had the soft little bear in hand, she cradled it and began talking to it. "I was so worried about you, Berry! I thought you were lost! Well, let me tell you all about what just happened. I almost fell out of a tree!" She continued with a high-speed line of chatter as the caravan resumed its progress toward home.

~ ~ ~

After the crowd had departed and the lengthening afternoon shadows reached across the pond, the place grew quiet save for the sound of the gurgling creek and one chirping robin...and one hyperactive boy with a red beard tattoo named Kyle Lautenberg. The square-built boy went whooping and hollering and making Tarzan sounds as he ran around the creek bank, jumping up on the oak trunk and flinging himself off again, swaggering around with his arms raised triumphantly. "I am mighty! I am invincible!"

Unseen by the boy, a square-built man with granitic face, gray no-nonsense crew cut, chinstrap beard and toothpick bobbing between in his teeth stood beside a pillow of prickly blackberry bushes near the cul de sac, watching the boy's antics with barely concealed amusement. Only the merest smile showed on the man's face, but his eyes gleamed.

When Kyle finally stopped to recharge for his next run-amok, he caught sight of the man and exploded with joy, "Grampy!"

Tom Lautenberg did not turn away and leave this time, but instead merely stood in place as the boy bounded full tilt toward him. The boy flung his arms around his grandfather's thigh and pressed his cheek against his waist. Looking up, "I helped Barney save Twee! Did you see me!?"

Tom looked down at the boy, beaming, "Yes I did. I did indeed."

Tom laid a thick but gentle hand on his grandson's shoulder and the two began walking up the gravel switchbacks together. Old Tom listened with grave attention while the boy skipped along beside him, relating with relish all the details of his great adventure. At the first switchback, Tom touched a finger to his lips and pointed toward the western sky. For the first time in anyone's memory the boy stopped talking and stood quietly for a moment. He followed his grandfather's pointing finger to the wedge of cackling Canada geese flying across the indigo sky. Venus beamed like a brilliant, unblinking eye as the birds passed in front of her.

"That's Venus, Kyle. The 'evening star.' But it's not a star, it's another planet."

"Wow," Kyle murmured softly. They both fell silent.

Soon, though, the boy resumed his animated chatter and the two of them continued on their way home.

= CHAPTER 17 =

~ ~ ~

Up on Fillmore, the group walked down the middle of the road. Suddenly, rounding the corner at Main, came the flashing lights, blaring siren and intermittent guttural honks of an oncoming paramedic fire truck. The truck in turn was followed closely by a big hook and ladder. The group parted for the vehicles, but Nga Phan placed herself square in their path and waved at the driver of the paramedic truck. "We OK now! Thank you anyway! You can go home!" The truck slowed to a halt and Twee ran around to the driver's door, climbed onto the running board and hooked her hands over the open window shouting to the men in the cab using her outside voice, "I'm OK now!" She jumped off and ran back to her mother. "I told them I'm OK now!"

"We heard," someone said.

Nga went to the driver and confirmed her daughter's statement.

While the truck made a U-turn and the hook and ladder backed up onto Main, Al Gruber waved goodbye to the others and trotted up his front walk past his koi pond. Standing on the porch, between two slim faux-Doric columns supporting a small peak-roofed portico, he fumbled in his pocket. Out came his cell phone. He held up his hand for the others to wait. "Hold on everybody!" He studied the little screen. "Hold on. Looks like a bunch of us are inviting Barney—where's Barney? Oh there you are!—a bunch of us are inviting you to the roadhouse for a thank you dinner."

The cell phone vibrated again, he studied it again, then clicked off a quick message. "Mel Bernstein, Mr. Roadhouse himself, says dinner for all is on him and the Vandershurs are providing libations."

173

Barney looked uncomfortable, abashed. "Oh gosh, this is not necessary."

"Come on Barney, just say yes."

"Well, hm, OK! What time?"

"Six o'clock."

Stella grinned and squeezed Barney's arm.

Al said, "So, you're coming?"

"Uh, yeah I guess, but..."

"No buts, just come!"

"Don't be embarrassed, Barn. It's as much for us as it is for you. It would hurt people to keep all that gratitude bottled up. You know what I mean?"

"I think so." He called back to Al, "All right. I'll come."

"Great!"

~ ~ ~

After folks went home and got washed up they came back out to the roadhouse at the appointed hour. The dining room there began filling up. Proprietor Mel Bernstein, sporting a skinny black bolo tie to match his black pencil mustache and his dyed-black thinning hair, stood in back watching with great pleasure as the community assembled in his western-style dining hall. He played with the turquoise slider on his bolo tie, smiling broadly.

Wearing a clean shirt and denim jacket from Knocker's abandoned wardrobe, Barney was among the last to arrive, Stella on his arm. People at the table held up their glasses and cheered him.

Notably missing was one well-known disgruntled diva.

With their son Aidan, Robert and Callista Vandershur came from across the street with two cases of wine. "We have a nice vintage of our Cabernet, and for our bold honoree, a full-bodied Syrah!" Mel and the pillowy waiter brought out a couple of trays of wine glasses. Robert produced a fancy double-action corkscrew from his belt-pouch and opened a bottle of the Syrah. Rree-Rree-DLOOP! The cork came out cleanly and everyone cheered. They were in a cheery mood!

He poured a little in a glass and offered it to Barney. Barney swirled it, viewed the "legs," brought it to his lips for a taste and immediately approved. Robert poured more into the glass.

Callista began pouring and passing out the wine glasses while Robert opened the next bottle.

Aidan leaned close to his mother, "Where's my sister?"

"No idea, honey. I haven't seen her all afternoon."

~ ~ ~

In the thickening dusk, down by the pond, there was a rustling in a copse of willows. Two heads popped up and looked around. "The coast is clear. Let's go!" The pair high tailed it up the switchbacks, smoothing their clothes and brushing leaves out of their hair as they ran.

"Hold on Zach, your shirt's not tucked in."

While he fixed his shirt, Nadia checked her cell phone. "It's Mom, she wants to know where I am, she's worried. Says to come to the Roadhouse."

"How come?"

"A free dinner or something. Who knows?"

~ ~ ~

A few minutes later, the two adolescents came in through the back entrance of the Roadhouse and tried to look casual.

Callista plucked a willow leaf from her daughter's hair. "Busy studying?"

Nadia turned to Zach and mouthed, "I'm busted."

"Yeah. Again."

She scowled. "How come I'm always the one that takes heat?"

Zach whispered to his busted girlfriend, "Hey, don't complain. Dorgan's gonna kill me—literally—for playing hooky from work. I'm scared to go back."

Nadia adjusted his collar. "Well don't, then."

Now Robert got up and made the first toast, thanking Barney for saving the life of a beloved daughter of Sweetbread. Others followed suit. The last was Nga, suddenly shy. With her hand on her daughter's shoulder, she uttered a simple thanks to Barney, choking back her tears.

Finally, with a little prodding, Barney stood up and thanked everyone for coming together and making his efforts successful. "Everyone was a star in this episode." He made a special point of toasting Stella for commandeering Dorgan's truck, Armand for his ladder, Muphrid for his tow strap and Ray for, "that rope."

"I'm Reggie. Ray's over there."

"Oh, sorry." Barney turned to the other twin. "Ray! Without your rope I couldn't have done it. Thanks to you, my Ray of Hope!" He continued, "And especially young Chinst—er, Kyle, who risked his own life and limb—out on a limb!—to aid in the rescue." Kyle stood up on his chair and bowed in four directions.

Everyone clapped enthusiastically and raised another toast to Barney, and Barney raised a final toast, "To all of us."

The dinner was, in honor of Barney's dietary preferences, lentil loaf. It was quite tasty for a first-ever attempt.

As the meal wound down, Mel stood up and announced dessert. It would be Deena's ready-to-heat, ready-to-eat, deep-fried tiramisu. "Sadly, Deena couldn't be here to make it fresh for us this evening. Apparently, she was not feeling well."

Barney leaned in to Stella, "It's a urinary tract thing."

"Huh?"

"She's still pissed off at me."

Stella chuckled and nodded knowingly.

While people were enjoying their tiramisu, Jeremy ceremoniously presented a Beanie Baby lion to Barney, who received it politely. "This lion represents the bravery of our young friend, Barney Starr." There was a round of applause as Barney took it in hand. The applause ceased the instant he began palpating its leonine buttocks, lifting its tail for a better feel.

"Barney? What're you doing? Is something wrong?"

He grinned, "Yep, found it!"

"Found what?"

Stella took him by the arm. "Come on, let's go. We've got some detective work to finish!"

"Thanks everybody! We gotta go!"

People started whispering, "Where are they going?"

The instant the pair walked out, the roadhouse transformed into a petri dish for incubating new rumors.

~ ~ ~

Back at her place, while Stella heated a mug of coffee, Barney pulled out a pocket knife and extracted the chip from the lion's derriere, holding it up to the light. "Yep," he said, "it's an 8088."

She flipped on some lights. "Wow. Another one."

His dimples deepened as he got ready to lay a new piece of information on her. He slowly brought the Pennzoil mug to his lips, then set it down. "I didn't mention this yet, but Astrid said that PK was interested not only in Beanie Babies, but in the computer chip trading bubble. He frequently urged her to invest in it while prices were still going up."

"So what was this guy PK up to? What was his 'marvelous scheme'?"

Barney shook his head. "Dunno. We keep getting little tidbits."

"He used to work at Intel. That's where he got the chips, I guess?"

"Right." Barney scrunched up his face. "Hold that thought." He plinked the keys on this laptop. His face lit up. He was smiling. "Whoa! Bingo! Listen to this..."

She sidled up to him, nuzzled his ear. "This is so fun! I love you Barney Starr!"

He blushed, but kept his focus and directed her attention to his screen: "Here's a little news blurb on *Fortune Magazine's* website from a few months ago. They trace the HotAuctions bidding transactions back to 2002 when two members called MiddleMonths and Ashram Papakilo put in successively higher bids for a special kind of computer chip, an 8088—"

"Hm. Tell me again, what's the deal with this 8088 chip, anyway?"

"The Intel 8088 was the processor chip they used in the very first IBM Personal Computers back in the eighties. As I recall, the first IBM PC debuted in 1981—"

"Before I was born, in other words."

"Uh-yeah." He studied her face. "Before either of us was born, in fact. Long before." He touched his laptop. "In any event, the IBM PC along with the original Apple computer were the two progenitors of my laptop, your laptop, our cell phones, our tablets and all the billions of computing devices we use around the world today."

"Sort of like the Adam and Eve of personal computing, huh!"

"Yeah!"

She smiled, "And these 8088 chips are what the IBM PC used?"

"Yep."

"And they're not used anymore?"

"Nope, they're way obsolete by now."

"Well I guess I can see why people'd want to collect those chips," she said. "Kind of historical antiques, huh?"

"Yeah," he said, adding, "And, apparently, the most prized ones are the ones that were rejected during testing as defective."

"That's what you said before and I still don't get it. You're not shittin' me, are you?"

He loved her earthiness, so different than any of the other girls he'd been with.

"I shit you not!" He laughed and his sweet dimples aroused in her an unexpected wave of desire; in turn he drank in her blue eyes shining brightly and he wanted her so badly he could hardly bear it. But their quest could not be abandoned at this critical moment. He sighed in frustration as she snuggled in close to him. "Let me continue..." He could feel his arousal growing, tried to continue, but her tongue playing on his earlobe put him over the edge.

~ ~ ~

Their passionate lovemaking went on for some time, scaring the squirrels out of her yard and the birds off her roof.

~ ~ ~

Stella sat up and stroked Barney's cheek. "You can continue now."

"Already? What's the hurry to...continue with...where was I, anyway—?"

"Not sure anymore. Defective chips?"

"Right!" He rubbed his face and sat up, back against the headboard. "So these two—MiddleMonths and, um, Ashram Papakilo—took advantage of the rising prices of these defective chips."

"I wonder how they knew these things would be a hot item."

"Dunno. But they sure came in at the right time. Pretty soon a growing community joined in, bidding prices higher and higher."

"Like the tulips!"

"Yep. Like the tulips." He pointed to his two lips and she leaned in and kissed them.

She reflected for a moment. "But there's no crash yet?"

"Nope. Apparently, the Chip Mania bubble is still inflating. Else Fliess wouldn't keep buying those bags of Beanie Babies from Muphrid."

She countered, "You're assuming he knows about the chips. Maybe he's just selling off the Beanie Babies and doesn't know about the chips?"

"That's true. In that case, he's missing out on a bonanza! Hmmm."

Stella reclined into a throw pillow in the corner of the sofa. "So these two guys—"

"Or gals."

"Or gals—were makin' out like bandits!"

Barney shook his head. "They got in on the ground floor. How did

178

they know?"

"Smart guys, I guess. What were the names again?"

"MiddleMonths and—"

"Weird name, MiddleMonths," she said. "And, I'm sorry, what was the other?"

"Ashram, um, Papakilo. Ashram Papakilo. Equally weird name."

Stella got up and paced. "Not weird. And that's what's weird about it. There's something about that name that rings a bell. Why?" She enunciated the binomial moniker again and again, turning the sound of it over in her mind. "Ashram Papakilo. Ashram Papakilo. Ashra—"

Barney started to say something when Stella nearly exploded, "Sharma!" She jumped up and danced around the room. "Ashram is Sharma! PK Sharma!"

"But what's Papaki—oh, of course!—PK! Papa Kilo!" Barney grinned. "You are the clever one, aren't you!"

"I'm goddamn brilliant, that's what!" Stella strutted around. "And there's the connection with the chips—he worked at Intel as a whatchyacallit—test engineer. At least that's what he told me."

Barney's eyes opened wide again. "Oh, he was a TEST engineer! So he had access to hundreds, maybe thousands of rejected defective chips. And he needed a market for his bad chips!"

"They weren't his chips though, right?"

Barney got a strange look on his face. "No...no, they weren't." He picked up his Beanie Baby lion and the chip lying on the table. Moving to insert the chip back into the lion's buttocks, he said, "What a great way to smuggle the chips out of the lab!"

She lit up. "Sure! Of course! People at the lab probably thought he was just another quirky nerd who liked carrying a Beanie Baby around with him."

"Beanie BABIES, plural. They probably didn't notice that it was a different one each time."

"Sure. And he left the chips in the Beanie Babies for storage, nice and soft and fluffy, so they wouldn't get damaged?"

"Right—damaging a defective chip would reduce its value...!" He rolled his eyes at the absurdity. Stella laughed and swirled her finger around the side of her head in the universal "crazy" gesture. "And now we know why PK wanted Astrid to invest in the chip bubble."

"The little con man!" she exclaimed. "He was trying to drive up the value of his—ohmygod, he had a racket going! And we all thought he was just a quiet retiree." She shook her head.

"A quiet retiree selling off the buried treasure in his yard."

"Why would he bury them in the first place?" she wondered.

"I guess to keep them hidden so nobody would know what a big supply he had. And doling them out just a few at a time."

"To keep the demand high, right?"

"Yep." Barney nodded with a faraway look in his eyes.

"He really wanted to keep them away from prying eyes," she said.

"By burying them in crypts in his yard, wow."

"Kind of over the top, huh?"

Barney agreed. The two of them fell silent and mulled over their conclusions. Meanwhile, the wind outside was making a din, swooshing trees and rubbing branches against the house. An empty can could be heard scuttling down the gutter. It made Stella's dingy bedroom feel warm, protected and cozy.

"So the other person, MiddleMonths, I wonder who that was?" Barney said.

Stella rose to the challenge. "OK. Let's figure this out. What are the middle months?"

"June, July?" he offered.

"Hm. June's a woman's name, but July—"

"July could be a woman's name too, if her parents were counterculture hippies or New Age types."

Stella averred that she knew of no humans with that name, woman or man. Julie maybe, but not "July."

He said, "But MiddleMonths is plural, so it's got to be both names."

"True." She furrowed her brow. "So June the first name, July the last name?" She Googled that and turned up nothing human. "Hm."

"Any other ideas?"

"No, not yet," he sighed.

~ ~ ~

They sat there for a while, pondering, blurting out dead-end theories. Finally Barney changed the subject. He put his hand on her leg. "You're a smart cookie, you know that, Stella? Did you ever go to college?"

She removed his hand, "No. Didn't want to clutter up my mind with useless facts and figures. I prefer the school of hard knocks, the university of life."

"You should consider it. It could be your ticket out of here."

"Oh, so I can come back and lord it over my former friends, no thank you."

He frowned. "That's not the purpose of education. Listen, you have native intelligence. You surprise me—and, to tell you the truth—turn me on with your cleverness."

For the first time he saw Stella Gervais blush.

"You're blushing!"

"Am not, you shameless liar!"

"Are too!" He cuddled and kissed her.

"You're just trying to lure me back to into your lair with your sweet words!" she winked.

"That's not out of the question. But seriously, you ought to consider going to college."

"I already know what I need to know."

"Wrong! You don't know what you need to know. How is it you're doing clerical work for Jeremy instead of programming websites alongside him? Waiting tables instead of running a business?"

She said nothing.

"Education would leverage your smarts."

She looked at him lovingly. "You really want to help me, don't you? I've never known a man like you, Barney. I so love you."

He looked down.

"No?"

He shook his head. "I'm not good with compliments I guess."

"Why not? I can take compliments all day long and not get tired!"

"Or blush?" he suggested.

"Well, there's that."

He pulled back. "Let's get back to the chips."

"We will. Right now though, I want to know about you. Don't you feel like you deserve to be complimented, to be loved?"

"You sure know how to go straight to the heart of the matter, don't you?"

She smiled. "That's what I'm good at. Now spit it out and no pussy-footing around."

He shook his head. "It's embarrassing, stupid."

She grabbed his chin, "No...pussyfooting. Tell me straight. I won't say anything bad."

He sighed, "OK. The thing is I don't trust compliments. Love is a shaky proposition too." After some amount of pussyfooting he finally worked his way back into early childhood when his father worked for a defense contractor, so no one knew what he actually did there. It probably fell short of expectations he had for himself, so he made his three children proxies for his own ambition. He set high expectations that the daughter and older son seemed to meet but not him. A frustrated, unhappy man, Starr *pater* was also prone to fits of anger, especially after drinking. There were terrible fights with Mom (he called it "working out differences of opinion") but it always seemed to fall to Barney to be the peacemaker. At his own expense if need be. Swallow any kind of humiliation to keep his father's anger down to a simmer. Curled up in the corner pleading, "Please, I'll be a good boy, do better in school, won't let you down if you just be nice to each other!" Barney wept as he talked.

"What about your mother? You said she was warm and loving."

"My mother, bless her Filipino heart, was just that—warm and loving. I always knew she loved me. But not so my father. I suppose he loved me too, somewhere deep inside, but it came out in mixed signals."

"How so?"

"He would turn compliments upside down, inside out. Like, if I did well in school or in sports, he'd say, 'Well that's great to hear, you're finally honoring the family name!'"

"Ouch."

"It's obvious to you, but to me, as a boy, it confused me."

She stroked his cheek, "I'm sorry, that must have been hard."

"Still is, it's still echoing in here," he said, pointing to his head. "The other thing he would do is diminish things that weren't his idea. When I got my degree in Journalism, he declared it to be second only to basket weaving in uselessness."

She frowned. "What a jerk."

"He was. But I could never get that perspective on him that way when I was growing up. No one gets a detached perspective on their parents. Anyway, he had a third way of deflating his children—and in this I was not alone. He would appropriate anything good and take ownership.

When I got an award for a piece I did for the *Portland Mirror*, he called me to congratulate me and said he was glad to know that I had some of his own drive for excellence."

Stella shook her head. "You weren't tempted even once to bash him on the nose?"

"That's the problem, when you let a bully take away your self-esteem, you let him take away your rationale for defending yourself. Perversely, his intermittent glints of praise led me to excel but always feel like I'd fallen short no matter how well I did."

"Wow. Did your mother protect you?"

"She tried, but having my mother as protector felt unmanly. And anyway, my mother was no match for him either. My name, for instance?"

"Barney?"

"Bernardo."

"Oh right. That's what she wanted to call you. And Barnard was your father's idea, right?"

"Right! Barnard—as in Barnard's Star—that's what my father made of Bernardo. It was his private joke, shared only by those as interested in astronomy as he was. He was a smart and interesting guy. And that was the problem. I never knew which side of him I was dealing with. My mother wanted to name my oldest sib Andrea. But my dad had to own that idea too, so my he declared her name would be Andromeda."

"From Greek mythology?"

"Yes. Very good. Also the name of our nearest galaxy. He said, 'The Aquino family could use some stars.' Aquino was my mom's maiden name. What an arrogant shit he was!"

"What happened to Andromeda?"

"Andie, as we called her, went on to get a degree in chemistry then became a Wall Street trader. Then came my brother Aldo. That got reworked into Aldo Baron."

"Aldo Baron. That's a nice name. Kinda like European royalty or something."

"That's not why he picked it. He chose it because it sounds like Aldebaran, the bright red giant star in Taurus."

"No bull!"

He looked at her askance, wondering if she knew what she'd just said. She laughed, "I know a few things."

183

"Stella, you never cease to surprise me!"

"Naturally!" She concluded, "And then came baby Barney, right?"

"Yeah, Bernardo got vetoed in favor of Barnard. So, it's Barnard Starr." He pursed his lips and shook his head slowly.

"Tell me again, what's so special about Barnard's Star?"

"Barnard's Star is a red dwarf star, the third closest star to Earth. So he'd say I was the red dwarf of the family."

"The shilpit one?"

"Huh?"

"Farm talk. Means 'sickly.' Like the small, sickly one of the litter."

"Oh great, well thanks for enhancing my vocabulary! Now I have a name for what I was," he said.

"You weren't shilpit. Such a lousy father! Was he ever nice to you?"

"Oh yeah, of course! That's strangely the hardest part because I never knew if he was a good man or bad. He was well respected in the community. And a good family man—at times. For example, he would take us out star gazing and point to the heavens." Barney pointed to the ceiling. "There's Andromeda, an island universe of a hundred billion stars, he'd say. Over there is red giant Aldebaran in the eye of the bull. An out there somewhere, is a very special star called Barnard. You need a powerful telescope to see it but that doesn't make it any less special. It's special and wonderful in many ways. It's our third closest companion star. Like other red dwarfs, it will outlive all the other visible stars because it is even-tempered. And like other red dwarfs, it is also very likely to have a planet or two with life. And Barnard's star has a special talent. Every so often it flares and shines ever so brightly!"

Stella now had stars in her own eyes. "And what a beautiful thing to say! That's so interesting."

"That's how I knew he loved me. But that's also what turned my brain inside out when he'd offhand refer to me as his red dwarf. Did he mean to say I was the favored one or the...shilpit?"

"Wow. He is—"

"Was."

"Oh. I'm sorry. He was difficult, huh?"

They sat in silence for awhile, hand in hand.

Finally he said, "So I guess that's where I got the urge to tweak the nose of authority, of bullies, of the arrogant and powerful elite. To expose people doing harm behind the mask of respectability. An urge that got me canned."

She smiled. "It's what makes you a good and honorable man. You are a decent, caring man. Fighting battles that need to be fought. You should never apologize for that. You're charting your own course and not following someone else's lead. You're not takin' the easy route, the high road never is. You're one of the truth tellers that suffer so others don't have to. You just need the courage of your convictions. I've seen your courage, so I know it's there."

He blinked a few times, trying to process this.

"Don't wimp out when you know you're right. You gotta get this chip trading story out to the public. And the rest of the story about Deena. Getting the truth out to the public is your quest. I wanna to help you, but it's just fun for me, it's everything for you. You can do it...if you don't wimp out!"

"Thank you, I think," he said.

"Oh I forgot, sorry about the compliment!"

"No, no, it's OK! Compliment me whenever you want. I need the practice!" He winked and his dimples showed. "You're really something, Stella. You're my guiding star."

"I love you more and more, the more I know you, my darling Barney. Barney Bernardo!"

He looked at her. "I—I—"

"Go on, say it! Don't wimp out."

Barney chuckled nervously. She kept staring at him, not offering assistance. "I love you too, Stella. I really do. You thrill me and amaze me and everything about you delights me." He reflected a moment. "Saying 'I love you' feels awkward, I don't know why."

"But you said it."

"Yes. And I meant it. I love you, Stella. Love you so much."

They caressed and found their way to her bed, she singing the Cowboy Junkies' song,

Won't you come with me? she said
There's plenty of room in my bed.
You're looking cold and tired
and more than a little human...

Then Barney joined in with her,

I know I'm not part of the life you had planned,
but I think once your body feels my hand
your mind will change
and your heart will lose its pain...

~ ~ ~

They tumbled together into Stella's bed and in the midst of their tender and breathless lovemaking, all at once Stella sat bolt upright, "Jason!"

Barney pulled away, startled, discomfited, "What!"

"It's Jason!"

"Where!? Here?" Barney was already halfway out of bed, braced for an assault.

"No, no, relax! There's no one here. Jason—he's the other one!"

"Other who?"

"The other speculator. *MiddleMonths.*"

She jumped to the floor and brought her laptop back to the bed. He climbed back under the covers. They both shimmied themselves backwards up against the headboard. He peered over her breasts at the device on her lap then returned his gaze to her ample breasts. She lifted his chin and pointed her veed fingers first at his eyes and then at her laptop monitor. "Ahem! Eyes forward!"

"Sure," he said glumly.

"What are the initials of the months? In order, I mean, from January."

"Um, let's see. J-F-M-A-M-J-J-A-S-O-N-D." He watched her type these characters into a Word document as he called them out.

"Do you see a name in there?"

"Of course!" Barney could not stop laughing, "The MiddleMonths! It's JASON! Ohmygod, it's gotta be..."

In unison, they enunciated the man's name, "Jason Fliess!"

"Gotta be," she affirmed. "That sneaky rat."

"Jason Fliess must have been PK's confederate."

"A Southerner?"

"No, no! An accomplice. PK's co-conspirator."

"Ohhh."

"What a name, 'Jason Fliess'," Barney murmured.

"Whaddyoo mean?"

186

"Did you ever read the stories about Jason, the legendary Greek seafarer?"

She touched her chin. "Hmm, I did...Jason and the Astronauts!"

Silence.

"I mean Argonauts! Oh I can't believe I said that! What a dingbat! Haha! What the hell are Argonauts, anyway?"

"The sailors on his ship, the Argo. So: Argo plus nautical equals...Argonauts!"

"Oh."

"But it's the other Jason story I'm thinking of..."

She scrunched her nose, "Oh, yeah, Jason and the, and the, uh, Golden Fleece—oh sure, I get it. Jason Fliess!" That really tickled her. "Jason Fliess. Jason and the Golden Fleece. Oh, that's bad!"

Barney conceded ruefully, "I guess I'm not the only kid whose name was meant for his parent's entertainment."

"Guess not. You got nothing to whine about now! So what's the deal about a Golden Fleece?"

"It was the fleece of the golden ram that Jason sought."

"Aha. So our Jason's been fleecing a golden sheep, so to speak?" she said.

"Yep, and the sheep's name is Muphrid."

They decided that the missing pieces of the story must surely reside with Jason Fliess. Perhaps the attorney was even safekeeping a writeup of PK's "marvelous scheme".

Stella nodded thoughtfully then suggested, "Let's check out Fliess' website."

With a few keystrokes and a tap on the touchpad, she brought it up on the screen. There it was, a surprisingly humdrum homepage titled simply: "Jason Goldman Fliess, Attorney at Law."

Barney mused, "Wow, his parents really had a field day with his name."

Below Fliess' name was a photo of a storefront law firm in McMinnville with address, phone and email. Alongside the photo, there was a sidebar of testimonials from satisfied clients.

Adjacent to a smiling portrait of the man himself was a box listing his areas of expertise:

Personal Injury
Real Estate
Wills, Trusts and Estate Planning
Probate
Business and Financial

They agreed that a morning visit to the law offices of Jason Fliess, Attorney at Law was in order. The game was afoot!

"We're on the case, oh yeah baby we're on the case!" she crowed. "Gonna nail that snooty suit! We're good, we're the A-team." She bounced around on her butt, arms upraised victoriously. Barney drank in that heavenly sight, admiring her smooth skin and absolutely loving being with her. Presently, a wave of desire swept over him and he began kissing her all over. She rolled over to set the laptop on the nightstand then came back into his embrace. She reached down and pulled him into her, moaning with pleasure.

The sounds of passion and squeaking bedsprings sent a raccoon scurrying off the roof.

= CHAPTER 18 =

~ ~ ~

Barney pulled the blanket away from his chin and turned to the girl sleeping beside him. "Good morning sunshine!"

Stella groaned.

"Rise and shine! We've got big day ahead!"

She rolled away from him. "Uck, what's got you so revved up? You're supposed to be the late sleeper."

"Can't sleep anymore. I'm on a quest!"

"A quest, huh? For what? The golden fleece?"

"Yep!" He sat up, looked around and stroked her honey hair. She rolled over to face him as he laid out his plan of action. "After breakfast I'm going to pay our fine friend Fliess a visit at his office in McMinnville."

"Yeah?" She brightened a bit. "Cool! It's about time. I'll go with you."

He squinted. "Aren't you supposed to go to work?"

"Naw. Not today. Wednesdays and Thursdays I'm off duty," she said. "Weekends at the Roadhouse, Mondays, Tuesdays and Fridays at Jeremy's. Wednesdays and Thursdays I'm free as a bird."

"All right, then, my little birdie. Let's have breakfast and then we're going on a road trip!" He looked her in the eye. "You're sure you wanna go?"

"Absolutely. With you, Bernardo, I'll go anywhere!"

Outside, the day was blowing clear and cold, evident through the drawn drapes even from the warm confines of Stella's bedroom. There was a filigree of frost in the corners of the window. The two tumbled out of bed and got dressed. Overriding his protests, Stella made Barney put on Knocker's denim jacket against the chilly morning. He looked himself up

189

and down in the mirror, coming to realize that he was dressed in Knocker's clothes from shoulders to socks. Except for underwear. That's where he drew the line. He'd rather go "commando" than wear Knocker's briefs!

When Barney came into the kitchen, Stella pointed to his sky-blue paint-dribbled Keen shoes. "Take those things off. There's a pair of Joe's boots in the closet that'll fit ya." Barney relented. When he came back to the breakfast table, Stella looked at him and pronounced him fit to go out in public. "You clean up real nice, Mr. Starr!"

Breakfast was scrambled eggs and toast and kibbles—the last item destined for the dog. Stella let Rogerdog in the back door and the mutt nearly knocked her over en route to the doggie dish. Lacking depth perception, he accidentally plunged his paw into his water bowl while positioning himself for his meal. Stella went back to the table and sat down. They ate their breakfast to the noisy accompaniment of kibble munching and water slurping. Yum.

~ ~ ~

Meanwhile, on the other side of town, Dorgan Bailey's wife looked up from breakfast to see her husband grab the truck keys off a wall hook and head out to the garage.

"Where are you going, Dorgan? You didn't finish your breakfast."

"Not hungry."

"Where're you going?"

"What difference would it make if I told you? Huh?" He grabbed the edge of the table, lifted it slightly and dropped it. Dishware rattled.

His wife pursed her lips, looked down at her plate diffidently. "No difference, Dorgan. I'm sorry, I was out of line."

"Damn right you were, woman."

He jerked a victorious nod and went out. She heard the truck roar to life and screech away. When all was quiet again, the poor woman could barely feed herself, her hands were trembling so.

~ ~ ~

After putting Rogerdog out again, Stella and Barney cleared the dishes and downed the last of their coffees. Then out the door the two of them went.

Wham! The screen door slapped loudly behind them. The autumn breeze chilled their nostrils. Barney shivered briefly and hugged Stella against the cold as they walked. Nearing the Pinto parked in Stella's driveway, he started to comment on the weather but was interrupted by the sudden noisy appearance of the Chinstrap kids running from the waiting school bus. The couple walked past the Pinto out to the sidewalk to receive the oncoming ragamuffins.

"Hi Stella! Hi Barney!"

He checked his watch. The school bus wasn't due to leave for a few minutes so the kids had some time for a "meet 'n' greet". They swarmed around the couple like a pack of happy puppies, each vying for attention. As alpha dog, Chinstrap jumped in closer than the others, "Hey Barney, how come yer wearin' Knocker's stuff?"

"Stella lent them to me till I can get my regular clothes cleaned."

"Oh." Kyle looked momentarily pensive, then pulled a figurine from his pocket, "Hey! Check out my favorite action figure—Wolverine! See his claws? They're lethal weapons! Here—you can have 'im!" He shoved the fearsome X-man up to Barney's face. "Take 'im!"

Barney shook his head no.

"'Sokay, dude, I got another one at home." So Barney took his prize in hand, examined it approvingly while Kyle meanwhile continued his chatter in a different vein, "Ya know, Barney, I thought we were goners up there, up in the tree, ya know? I mean we were miles above the ground an' coulda fallen down and died. Splat! Argh!" He put himself into a dramatic contortion, replete with gruesome sound effects. "But we survived! An' we saved Twee, cause you an' me, we're like super heroes!"

Not to be overlooked, Peewee pushed the others aside. "Yeah an' I helped too an' bruised my tooth when the branch came down an' hit me in the face!" He lifted his lip to display his allegedly injured tooth. Kyle rolled his eyes.

Nor was Dingo to be denied the celebrity reporter's notice: "Yeah, me too! Arf! Arf! Arf! Arf!"

Kyle slapped the top of Dingo's hair. "'Me too'? What's that supposed to mean? You didn't bruise your tooth. Peewee did. That doesn't make any sense anyway. What a couple of dopes!"

Dingo retorted by barking fiercely into Kyle's face.

Kyle looked at Barney. "Dingo's such a dawg!"

Barney shook his head disapprovingly. "That's not a nice thing to call your friend."

"But he IS a dawg! He's got a tiny brain, doesn't talk, just barks. That's why we call him Dingo!"

"Well, it's still not a nice thing to call your friend a dog. Say you're sorry."

Kyle said nothing.

Barney narrowed his eyes. "I said, say you're sorry!"

Kyle looked down, rolled his eyes, and in a nearly inaudible whisper, said to the ground near Dingo's feet, "I'm sorry."

Dingo grinned triumphantly and said, "Arf!"

Then Twee said softly, "Are you and Stella gonna get married?"

Barney looked at Stella and Stella looked at Barney. Barney looked at Twee, "Um..."

Just then a shiny sedan slowed and the windows rolled down. It was Callista Vandershur driving her twins to school. Nadia hung out the window and addressed Chinstrap Kyle and his friends, "Hello, my little monsters!"

~ ~ ~

The four children jumped up and down and yelled greetings back at the chauffeured girl. During their raucous response, no one noticed a hulking gun metal gray pickup truck quietly pulling to the curb a few cars up the street, just in front of the school bus. The truck's driver just sat there with the engine idling.

~ ~ ~

The school bus horn honked twice to summon the kids loitering in front of Stella's house.

Stella exclaimed with exaggerated consternation, "Ohmygoodness children! You're going to be late for the school bus. You'd better get going before it leaves without you!"

The pair watched the foursome run up Main Street to the bus stop, waving their arms importunately for the driver to pleeeease wait.

At the school bus, Chinstrap started pushing Peewee toward the broken railing. Barney saw this and yelled, "Hey Kyle! Cut it out!" and cast him a baleful look that even two blocks away stopped the boy in his tracks.

Barney couldn't hear Chinstrap's words, but they went like this: "Uh, sorry Peewee, I was just kiddin' around."

"'Sokay, Chinstrap, not-a-problem," came Peewee's high-pitched reply.

Twee noticed the gun metal gray truck parked in front of the school bus and tapped Kyle on the shoulder. "Hey Kyle, look who's here!"

But there was no time to talk because the school bus driver was hollering at them to get in or she really would leave them behind.

Soon after the kids were on board, the school bus squeaked its tires away from the curb and headed out of town, bound for the elementary school in Sheridan.

~ ~ ~

Stella watched the departing bus and said, "Those kids really admire you."

"Hmm."

"Kyle thinks the world of you."

Barney put Wolverine into his breast pocket. "Hmm."

"And seems more assertive today. Did you notice how he curbed his inner bully when you scolded him?"

"I didn't scold him. I just pointed out that he was not being very nice to his friend."

Stella took him by the arm. "Well, regardless, he listened to you. That's big."

He shrugged. "If you say so. I guess that's encouraging, huh? Well, I hope it helps."

"I think it will. You know what else I think?"

"Mm?"

"I think you're swell!"

He blushed. And there they were again, as if on cue: those cute dimples. As the two turned to the Pinto in the driveway, Stella could take it no longer; she impulsively grabbed Barney and kissed him big and wet on the mouth. "Oh, I love you Barney!" She shook her head. "Wow, I just love saying that! I love you, Barney! I love you! I love you! I love you!"

He smiled sweetly and said softly, "I love you too, Stella."

They embraced and kissed again. And then the unexpected happened.

~ ~ ~

Without warning, with a screeching of tires, there came the menacing roar of a 6.7-liter diesel engine in full rev. It was Dorgan, flaming mad, driving his big gun-metal gray F-350 pickup straight for them.

Barney turned around with alarmed celerity, faced the oncoming truck, and realizing he was the intended target, shoved Stella into her yard and ran off toward Al Gruber's house, hoping to draw Dorgan away from her. He looked back ever so briefly to confirm the trajectory of Dorgan's truck. The gambit had worked. Dorgan swerved away from Stella to pursue Barney over the planted border and across Gruber's lawn. But Barney knew he wasn't going to make it to safety before the truck caught him. He wished he could outrun it, but felt he was in a chase dream where his legs were mired in slow motion molasses. Then something clicked in his brain. A realization. And a primal choice.

Dorgan had a monstrous temper, yes, but he wasn't a murderer. Was he? No. He was just a bully. Right? Well, let's hope.

Barney stopped short and spun on his heel to face Dorgan and the oncoming truck. "Enough!" he bellowed, arms outstretched.

Dorgan veered to avoid him, slammed on the brakes and tore a trench into Al's lawn. The rig came to final halt when it dropped a wheel into the koi pond. A pinned fish flapped its tail fin wildly.

Dorgan jumped out of the cab and came after Barney. Barney started to run, then forced himself to turn back and stand his ground. He took a deep breath to calm himself. Oddly enough, wearing Knocker's denim jacket, jeans and boots made him feel brave.

"Stay away from Stella!" Dorgan shouted. "She belongs to my son. She's Joe's woman, not yours!"

"Joe doesn't own her and neither do I and neither do you, you sonofabitch!"

Dorgan's eyes narrowed and reddened, his beefy face flushed.

Dorgan Bailey's gaze remained fixed upon his quarry as he reached backwards into the bed of his truck and with one hand felt around for the latch on his toolbox and hauled out the most enormous spanner wrench Barney had ever seen. It was comically large. But there was nothing comedic about the way Dorgan brandished it. Godzilla-like, the big man took one lumbering step after another toward Barney. With each pendulous swing of Dorgan's brawny arm, his massive chrome tool flashed. Barney was terrified to the core, trembling, wanting desperately to flee, but he did not move. Nor did he allow himself to avert his eyes. Emboldened as he was by his success just a minute ago when he called Dorgan's bluff with the truck, Barney took the offensive and yelled mockingly, "Go ahead, kill me, you damn coward!"

From her lawn, Stella screamed, "Are you crazy, Barney? He'll do it, he'll kill you. Run!"

Barney stared at his attacker who stared back at him. The icy silent stare-off lasted no more than two seconds.

Then Dorgan said, calmly, "OK, Mex, have it your way."

When he saw Dorgan's roundhouse coming at him, the chrome spanner arcing toward his head like a medieval mace, Barney dove to the ground. Flopping down, he felt the wrench fly past his head with a whoosh that fairly parted his hair. In a moment of clarity suspended outside of the normal flow of time, he calmly thought to himself, "Note to self, don't model yourself on Hollywood action movie heroes—they're not real."

Then, inexplicably, he heard Dorgan shriek and saw the man crumple to the ground alongside him, his face twisted in pain and fury. The man grasped at his left butt cheek and raged like a bull.

Barney heard a noise and looked up at Al's bedroom window. The sash window was open and sniper Al took another shot with his BB gun. Pop! This time he got Dorgan in the left arm.

"Get off my lawn, Bailey!" he hollered from the window.

Dorgan rose from the lawn like a giant rock troll and lurched toward Al's front porch, grabbing the wounded arm that owned the hand that clasped his left buttock.

In a volcanic rage, Dorgan yanked free one of the skinny faux Doric columns framing Al's porch and used it as a cudgel, a shillelagh, to smash Al's entry panes. Swinging wildly, he managed to knock the other column away, causing the templed roof of the portico to crash down upon his head. An errant shard gouged his left eye. He fell to his knees, clutching his bleeding face and screaming bloody murder. *Dorgan agonistes!*

Barney's jaw dropped in horror. But when he looked around, he was heartened to see both Stella and Al giving him the thumbs up.

And that wasn't all. Behind him, a small crowd had gathered. "Way to go Barney! You're our hero!"

But he just shook his head in disgust.

~ ~ ~

"Someone call 911," he said to the onlookers. "The rest of you come help me with Dorgan's injuries."

Before he could utter another word, Muphrid, the town's barber-cum-barber surgeon, was at Dorgan's side, tending to the big man's wounds. Stella connected with 911 on her cell phone and someone else brought a towel and bandages. Nancy came across the street with a first aid kit.

Dorgan ceased flailing and reluctantly surrendered to their ministrations.

~ ~ ~

After the ambulance took Dorgan away, Barney took Stella's hand, "Time to go see Fliess."

= CHAPTER 19 =

~ ~ ~

After Barney climbed into his Pinto, he found that he needed to slide the seat backward a notch as Knocker's boots added half an inch to his leg length. But he didn't release the adjustment lever fast enough and the seat slid all the way back to the end of its travel.

"Shit!" He punched the dashboard.

Stella paused at the passenger door. "We can go see Fliess another time, you know. You're kinda worked up right now. You might want to take some time to chill out a little."

"No! We're doing this now! While the iron's hot." He wrangled the seat back into position, muttering curses.

"Are you sure?"

"Yes! Get in. Let's go!"

~ ~ ~

Soon they were barreling down Highway 18, en route to McMinnville. Stella pressed her fingernails into the seat cushion trying not say anything about the excessive speed he was carrying. She kept checking her side view mirror for the approach of red, white and blue flashing lights but there were none. At first, she felt relieved but when the speedometer exceeded 90, she began hoping some law enforcement personage would rein in her reckless boyfriend.

"Babe, you gotta slow down. Seriously."

He barely heard her. But after a time, her words sank in and he obliged, lifting his foot from the gas pedal. The speed bled off for a while, but you could see in his eyes that there was a multi-screen cineplex of violent action movies running inside his skull and gradually the speedometer needle crept back up. Road signs and fence posts flashed by. The tall rectangular rear end of a tractor trailer rig ahead loomed larger and larger at an alarming rate. Soon the big cargo doors filled the view in the windshield.

Stella gasped and dug her fingernails deeper into the edges of the seat. "Barney! Forgodsake!"

Barney swung around the big rig, accelerated past and moved rightward ahead of the truck's gleaming front grille seconds before an oncoming car whooshed by. The truck driver hit his air horn. Barney flipped him the bird. Then he swooped down on a sedan that was ambling along at a mere fifteen miles per hour above the legal speed limit. Barney flashed his brights and swore. The sedan edged halfway onto the shoulder to let Barney's flaming chariot fly by.

Stella blew through her lips, glad to still be alive. "Take it easy, Babe! There's no point in getting us killed. Or thrown in jail, forgodsake."

"Not getting us killed. Not going to jail," he said, through clenched teeth. "What we ARE going to do is nail Jason Fliess."

She slumped down in her seat, resigned to whatever would come next. At least if they were going to die, they would die together. Some consolation.

~ ~ ~

After a time, Barney came to his senses and slowed down. He glanced sidelong at his frightened girlfriend. "Sorry, Stella. You were right. I was getting a little crazy there. Help me find this place, OK?"

Google Maps on Stella's cell phone got them directly to Fliess' storefront law firm on the main drag in McMinnville. The office faced across the side parking lot of a single-story office complex toward a property boundary of trees and bushes. Directly outside the office, the now familiar black Escalade with plates that read "JGF LAW" sat parked under a red sign proclaiming, "Reserved for J.G.Fliess / Violators will be Towed." Cafe curtains hung in the office windows, which gave a welcome feel, but the tinted glass thwarted casual view of the goings-on inside. On the window above the brass curtain rod, these neatly lettered words appeared: Law Offices / Jason Goldman Fliess, Attorney-at-Law / OSB #9283741.

A sign on the (also tinted) glass door read "Open," so the two walked in, Stella conscientiously brushing the mud and blood off Barney's denim jacket, the denim jacket formerly muddied and bloodied by Knocker.

And there he was, the man of the hour, Jason Fliess, sitting resplendent in a large oxblood leather executive swivel chair behind an elegant dark cherry wood desk illuminated by a green shaded casino style desk lamp and surrounded by style-coordinated cherry wood client chairs upholstered in maroon velvet. Despite the plural designation, "offices," on the window, there was in fact just one office comprising little more than a single room whose walls were unadorned save for his framed law degree, various licenses and a few family photos. One wall was lined with legal volumes, a file cabinet and a stack of cardboard boxes. A coffee maker sat on a stand near a kitchenette in the corner. Fliess was on the phone—a trendy retro 1920s candlestick style telephone with separate handheld receiver and transmitter. Fliess looked up to see who'd come in. He was a smaller man than Barney recalled, though perhaps that was due to the contrast with his super-sized executive chair. Nevertheless, he looked young, fit, trim and arrogant in his pin stripe vest, flamboyant red tie and Yves Saint-Laurent dress shirt with gold cuff links. His dark hair was perfectly coiffed.

Fliess looked down at his blotter calendar, looked back up at the duo and seemed surprised. He muffled the transmitter mouthpiece against his vest and said, "Stella? What're you doing here?" Bringing the transmitter back to his lips he said brusquely, "Yeah, listen, I've got to go. Let me call you back in..." He whipped his Rolex wristwatch up into view, "thirty minutes?"

Down went the receiver into its cradle hook and the whole assembly went back onto the desk. Then he sat back with fingers knitted behind his head. "What a surprise! What brings you in today, Stella? Is this guy giving you trouble?"

"Fuck you, you smug little con man!" Barney expelled the words before he knew what happened.

Fliess stifled his shock. "Excuse me?"

"We're here so I can ask you a few questions about your dealings in the Beanie Baby trade."

Fliess' mouth contorted in amusement. "Oh, yes, I'd be happy to answer any and all questions you might have. Let me check my calendar—"

"Can it. We're here now."

"Well I have other clients coming in," he said, running his finger across the blotter. "How about Tuesday at ten next week..."

"I don't think so! You don't have any clients, and cancel 'em if you do. We're here and not leaving till we get some answers. You're not going to squirm out of this."

Fliess, affecting urbanity, remonstrated, "I'm sorry, I think you're being very uncivil. I'm going to have to ask you to leave my office."

Stella jumped forward. "Listen, you worm, you never return our emails, you hang up when we reach you on the phone, we're not about to let you get away this time—"

"Excuse me? Are you accusing me of something?"

Barney shouted, "Yes, you asshole! You've been—"

Stella jumped in. "You've been swindling Muphrid Thatcher ever since your partner in crime PK Sharma died."

Fliess jumped up and slapped his desk with both hands. "Get out of here! I'm talking to you Stella, and your—your—biker thug boyfriend here. Jeez, is that blood on his jacket!!? Boy you pick some real winners, don't you?"

Barney exploded and grabbed Jason across the desk by the designer lapels. The casino lamp flew off the desk and shattered on the floor in a hundred green shards. "You sonofabitch—sit down!"

"Gihh! Tell your psycho boyfriend to get off me!"

She shot back, "Don't you ever say that about Barney—"

"Barney!? Barney Starr?"

She replied triumphantly. "That's right, the reporter from the *Portland Mirror*." She sat back and let that sink in, then concluded. "If you'd been through what he's been through this morning, you'd be a little crazy too."

Still squirming in Barney's grip, Fliess' garbled response came out simply, "Yeah?"

"Yeah! He nearly died saving my life. From that killer ape, Dorgan Bailey. If Barney hadn't ducked, he'd be in the morgue right now with a twenty-pound spanner buried in his skull. So you just cut him some slack, Jack!"

Fliess mumbled as his throat slid down against Barney's gripping fists. He pleaded through clenched teeth, "Okee, okee. Ken yoo ashk'im tuh let go my nack?"

"Barney, stop. Please."

Barney let him down. Fliess brushed himself off, trembling. He didn't realize that Barney was trembling too. "OK, obviously you're both quite overwrought over whatever the hell happened during this morning's—uh—traumatic events. Let's all calm down and talk like reasonable people, OK? Let me cancel my next appointment. Just—let's—all—stay—calm—and—" He pulled open his top right desk drawer.

Barney's technicolor imagination saw the snub-nosed revolver in the drawer before it came into view as a dark form in Fliess' gripping hand. Without thinking, Barney flew across the desk again, sweeping away family photos and knickknacks and grabbed Fliess' wrist. The force of the pre-emptive attack threw the executive chair over backwards. The two men sprawled on the floor, and the dark object flew from Fliess' hand and skittered across the Berber carpet. Fliess and Barney began slapping and hitting at each other like girls. Finally, Barney pinned him down and held a fist high over Fliess' face. "You were going to shoot me weren't you, you treacherous bastard!"

With a stricken expression, Fliess began weeping, shielding his face from Barney's fist. "No! I was going to call my client! That was my cell phone. Please don't hit my face! Pleeeease!"

Barney looked over at the dark object. It was indeed a cell phone. Calling to cancel a client was likely a ruse, Barney thought. Fliess was probably going to call 911. It didn't matter. Seeing Fliess in such a pathetic state, he saw himself as a boy, cowering before his father's rage, promising to be better next time, please don't hit me.

"I'll cooperate. Just don't hit me, please don't—" Fliess pleaded.

Barney began to weep too, then cry, then came gasping sobs. "I'm sorry, Jason. I won't hit you. I won't hurt you. I'm s—sorry! What's wrong with me? I've let everyone down."

He stood up and helped Jason to his feet. He looked at himself, at his—Knocker's actually—muddy, bloody denim biker's jacket and jeans and boots and looked at Stella, who was also weeping. "What have I become? What's happened to me?"

~ ~ ~

Barney turned and walked to the door, arms raised in a gesture of surrender. Stella raced to his side and said over her shoulder as they exited, "I think we need a time-out, Jason. We'll be back in a couple of hours. You'll be here, right?"

Jason nodded weakly. "Sure."

"Good, 'cause if you aren't, I know where you live and I'll come over and personally kick your ass."

~ ~ ~

Outside, Stella said, "You OK, babe? Whaddya wanna do now?"

For the longest time, he just stared past her, down the length of the boulevard in the direction of Linfield College. She looked over her shoulder toward the college and wondered if maybe he was considering applying for a new degree that would take him on a safer career path. Marketing perhaps.

Finally, he yanked off his filthy denim jacket, held it up and declared it to be ill-fitting. "It's time to go clothes shopping."

"Seriously?"

"Is there a Fred Meyer around here?"

"Yeah, just a few blocks from here. Where're you going? The car's over there."

He explained that he needed to walk off his anger; she agreed that that was probably a good idea. So that's what they did.

At the store, Barney first washed up in the restroom and then got down to business, modeling his apparel choices for Stella. Before long, he strode out in the sunlight wearing a fresh ensemble of well-fitting beige Dockers trousers, a rust colored shirt, black corduroy vest and of course a new pair of Keen shoes. The old denims he tossed—with Stella's permission—into a convenient dumpster. "From Knocker's to Dockers!" he announced ebulliently. "I feel more like myself again."

"Where to now, chief?"

He considered a moment. "To the City Center. County Recorder's Office."

She convinced him to go by way of the nearby park that fronted the river. It was a way to decompress for a while, clear his thoughts. They walked along the left bank talking and the stress slowly ebbed away. "Is this the Yamhill River?"

"Yep," she said. "South Fork."

"Is that where your message in a bottle went?"

"If it got outta Rock Creek, yep. Maybe that's it down there."

"Which one?"

There were dozens of bottles littering the riverbank.

"Each one with a message in it," he deadpanned.

She laughed, "Everybody wants out, don't they?"

They walked on for a while along the waterside path, grass on one side, a railing on the other side along the river bank. Suddenly he stopped and leaned on the railing, scuff-kicking at the concrete path. "You know, I'm really embarrassed—about my behavior back there." He rubbed his face. "I don't know what got into me."

"Yeah, you did go a little nutso, dintchya!? You were kinda channeling Knocker there for a while. I saw it coming. Couldn't have stopped you any more than I coulda stopped a freight train." She added, "Maybe you should decide what you're going to say to Jason before we go back? Just sayin'. What do you think you're gonna get out of him?"

"I don't know. An admission of guilt? Ha! That's not going to happen."

"You already have what you need. You've got evidence, you're an eye witness to the body bag business."

"Yeah, but I wanna nail 'im. I want to expose the extent of his larceny. I want to quantify it. How much exactly is he selling those chips for? How much, conversely, is he denying Muphrid?"

Stella ran her hand back and forth along the railing. "Maybe the police should be handling this?"

"Honestly, I don't know that anything strictly illegal is going on. Just immoral. Unethical." He started walking again and looked at her with a boyish grin. "Wanna know the truth, Stella?"

She nodded. "Of course."

"I'm curious. I want to know what PK's 'marvelous scheme' was. In detail I mean."

She stopped short, looked to the heavens and exhaled. "So what is it you—? What exactly are you trying to do here? Are you trying to nail Jason for ripping off Muphrid? Or just write an interesting story about a clever money scheme? Or talk about those whatchyacallit, speculation bubbles?"

Barney squatted down, picked up a broken corner of the concrete slab and tossed it into the water and waited for the "ploop!"

"All of the above, I guess," he said.

"Not gonna work. Too many balls in the air. You're gonna confuse your readers. Hey—you're confusing *me*!" Stella looked around, thinking. "All right, let me ask you this. You're a journalist, right? What do journalists do? Journalists write articles. Stories. What's the theme of your story?" While he considered the answer, she upped the ante. "In one word."

"One word?"

"Yeah, one word."

"Hm. Greed, I guess." He considered his answer and decided to stick with it. "Yeah, that's it. Greed."

She kissed him on the cheek. "Good, Grasshopper. Now you are ready."

~ ~ ~

They proceeded to the Yamhill County buildings, just a mile's walk from the park. Having some basic experience collecting public information and armed with journalist's credentials (no one needed to know about his *contretemps* at the *Portland Mirror*) Barney easily obtained a facsimile of Prashant Kumar Sharma's will and property transactions. Jason Fliess' tax records were however, to Barney's dismay, off limits. But he had enough information now to make inroads. Outside, the pair sat on a bench and pored over the copied documents while Barney intermittently consulted the investigative journalist's pricey friend, the vast LexisNexis database.

Returning his attention to PK's last will and testament, Barney stabbed at one clause in particular. "Bingo! That's what I'm going to ask Jason about."

Stella leaned over to see. She read the paragraph aloud, "'The inventory of plush toys is to be divided equally between the two beneficiaries, Jason Goldman Fliess and Muphrid Elmo Thatcher.' Now, Jason was the executor who was supposed to make sure that happened, right?"

"Yep."

Stella looked at the clause again. "Well Jason did that, sort of, by buying out Muphrid's share of the Beanie Babies."

"For the market value of the toys, not what was hidden inside."

"Hmm."

"That would constitute a breach of fiduciary responsibility. I think. I'm not sure. I'm not a lawyer. It just says plush toys." Then he sat back and said, "We're not allowed to see his tax records, but I'm sure he was doing some funny business, tax-wise."

"Tell me."

"The chip-laden Beanie Babies. Buy low, sell the innards high, write them off for a tax advantage. It's tricky, I'll explain the details later."

"No, explain the details now!"

"OK. First he pays Muphrid for a bag—no, half a bag, because they're splitting the inventory equally—of one hundred Beanie Babies at what he deems the average market value for collectible Beanie Babies. So he gets fifty free and clear, then buys Muphrid's fifty at twenty-five apiece for twelve hundred fifty dollars. Pretty generous, yeah? While he's at it, he gives your friend Nancy Laut—"

Stella gritted her teeth. "Nancy's not my friend."

He chuckled, then continued, "He gives officer Nancy two hundred fifty bucks for her protective services when they exhume the body bags."

"So he's spent fifteen hundred dollars so far."

"Right. Then he goes home, rips the chips out of the Beanie Baby butts, packages 'em up and auctions the chips off for thousands each."

"Wow."

"But that's not all—and here's the rest of the funny business, kind of the deep-fried dessert topping on his sleaze-infused confection. He donates the full set of one hundred Beanie Babies to his favorite McMinnville charity—and takes an income tax write-off, according to their average market value, which is what he paid Muphrid. So he can document the valuation. So the total—"

"Wait, let me figure it out," Stella said. "One hundred times, what did you say, twenty-five dollars each? That's, uh, twenty-five hundred dollars."

"Right! He takes a twenty-five-hundred-dollar income tax deduction for the Beanie Babies."

"And rakes in beau coup thousands, maybe hundreds of thousands, of dollars selling off the chips," she said, shaking her head in disbelief.

"Paying sales tax, presumably, but still..."

Stella frowned. "That little shit! And Muphrid thinks he's getting a good deal."

"Yeah, and the charity thinks Jason's a magnanimous guy," Barney added.

"All right, bottom line," she said. "You gonna throw that in his face?"

"No point. I already have my evidence. I'm not a prosecutor, just want to give him a chance to tell us his side of the story." He smiled slyly. "And maybe ferret out some more juicy details."

"Not gonna beat 'im up this time?" She grabbed his sleeve for emphasis.

"No! I promise."

She bumped his fist approvingly. "Good to know you're back on track, babe!"

They got up and started for Jason's office when Barney jerked Stella aside, told her to look away from the street. There was the black Escalade again, cruising by City Hall. Jason rode as passenger this time, with his big young bald goon Milo at the wheel, driving slowly, scanning.

"Shit! He's set his attack dog on us."

He grabbed her hand and they ducked down a side street. When they were safely out of view, she turned to him, panting. "Your paranoia is infecting me, Barney. Cool your jets!"

He laughed, "You're right, I'm still a little edgy, huh?"

"Uh, yea—ah!"

Meanwhile, Milo and Jason pulled up to a bistro and went in.

Barney and Stella wended their way back toward Fliess' office, but before long, to Barney's amazement, they came upon Jason's favorite charity, Play Haven. "Let's go in!" he said.

Inside, there was nothing but fruit colors everywhere—toys, balls, wood block cars and trains and pint-size extruded plastic chairs. The din of children's banter, electronic games, occasional shrieks and banging of building blocks echoed from every wall. It was a lively, happy place. A young woman greeted them openly. "Welcome to Play Haven! Can I help you with something?"

"Yes, you can!" After the *de rigueur* introductions, Barney asked her if she knew Jason Fliess.

"Oh yes, of course! What a generous man! He's been such a friend to us at Play Haven!"

Yeah, this was going to be tricky.

"Are you friends?" she asked.

"Um. Acquaintances."

She offered them adult-sized chairs, but Barney declined. "We can't stay long, just were curious to see the charity he constantly talks about—and donates to, as I understand it."

"You mean the Beanie Babies? Or the checks?"

"Checks?"

"Yeah. $500 a month," she stated. Well, that was a surprise. "But what matters to the children is the Beanie Babies."

"Did you know those are collector's items? They could have a lot of value."

The woman stepped back. "You're not from the IRS or something?"

"Nooo, no," said Stella, nervously laughing. "We're friends from Sweetbread."

"Sweetbread! Oh, I love that town!"

"And this is my—boyfriend. He's a—"

"I'm a reporter, doing a human-interest story—"

"Oh! About Jason?" The woman's face lit up.

"Well, not exactly, I'm covering Deena Poole—"

"Oh, the dessert lady!"

"Yep."

"So what brings you to McMinnville?"

Stella started to speak but Barney cut her off. "Actually, the more I hear about Jason's generosity, the more I am thinking about writing a human-interest piece about him as well."

"How lovely! He's a good man. Don't know why he's still single!"

"Yeah. Anyway, I was wondering whether you knew he was giving you collector's items?"

"Collector's items? Oh, you mean these Beanie Babies? Huh! That may be, I don't know. But honestly, I don't think these stuffed animals would be very valuable. They're old and their little behinds are torn." She asked the little red-haired girl with big round Harry Potter style glasses leaning against her leg for her Beanie Baby owl. The little girl thrust the owl as high up as she could, like a trophy.

The woman took it and showed it to Barney. "See? Jason says they were defective rejects from the assembly line. Well, that just endears them all the more to these kids who come from abusive homes or were abandoned altogether. They feel like rejects from the assembly line too. So they develop a special bond with these stuffed animals. It's very therapeutic."

"I can well imagine." He snapped his wristwatch into view. "Oh boy, I'm afraid we've got to run along!"

"Oh sure. Would you like a quick tour before you go?"

Stella glanced at her cell phone time display. "Yeah, no, we're running late, but maybe another time?"

"Certainly!"

"Well thank you for your time."

"It was my pleasure folks. Please say hello when you see Jason. Tell him Hope sends her regards."

~ ~ ~

Back at Fliess' law firm, the sign on the door declared the offices

"Closed" so the two looked for a place to wait.

"Let's wait in the Pinto," Stella said.

"Naw, I don't want them to see us and run away."

So they found a blind in the bushes. It was chilly, so they huddled close. And waited. The huddling was so enjoyable, the time passed quickly.

Eventually, inevitably, the shiny black Escalade reappeared, cruising slowly through the parking lot. Lest there be any doubt about its owner, there was the vanity plate again, "JGF LAW." Milo was still at the wheel. Rolling along quietly with the tinted windows rolled down, Milo and Jason scanned the parking lot. The latter pointed his index finger suddenly at the Pinto and clapped Milo on the shoulder. The SUV halted. He noted the Greenpeace bumper sticker. That was the reporter's car, all right. Jason jumped out, ran over to the Pinto, looked inside and, finding it empty, shooed Milo away. The Escalade would be a dead giveaway to those two of his presence at the officially closed office. Milo drove out the back of the parking lot in search of a free space somewhere in the neighborhood.

Once the SUV was out of sight, Fliess trotted toward his office door, looking left and right like a wary fox. He squinted at two people coming around the corner of the building but was relieved that he recognized neither of them. Confident there was no evidence of the Starr-Gervais duo, he unlocked his office door and ducked inside, leaving the "Closed" sign swinging in place. He relocked the door behind him and pulled the blinds so as to shield his lair from view.

Now was the time for the pair to pounce.

When he heard the knock on the door, Fliess went to it said through the blinds, "Milo, you're back already?" He parted the blinds and nearly fainted when he saw Barney and Stella. He pointed demonstratively to the "Closed" sign. Barney pointed to the posted hours. Before unlocking the door, Fliess texted Milo, "Come quick!" After an extended negotiation with the pair that included assurances of non-violence, he reluctantly let them in, assessing Barney's new look and commenting that he'd "cleaned up nicely."

Barney explained that he was primarily interested in writing a story about the chip-mania that PK and Jason had participated in, just needed some background information and he did not have an axe to grind with Fliess. That last part was a lie, of course.

"Well, it was all on the up and up," Fliess said, as he re-opened the blinds and flipped the sign to tell all passersby they were welcome to come in, to please come in. Pleeease come in. Someone, anyone!

Fliess returned to his desk. "It's just trading, auctioning off collector's items. There's nothing more to say about it. Are we done?"

"No, not quite." Barney watched Fliess grimace with exasperation. "PK wrote a note in the margin of a book about speculative bubbles saying he had a marvelous scheme, but the full description was in a safe place."

"Like where?"

"I thought you'd know."

"Why would I know?"

"Because, besides being his partner in this scheme, he left half his inventory to you after his death. There's a clause in his will that says he would bequeath to you—and Muphrid by the way—a full detailed description of the scheme, the instruction manual in other words. Do you have PK's will so we could look at it?"

"Oh, it would take a long time to find it—"

"No problem! I have a copy right here!" Barney slapped it down on the desk. The desk seemed larger than before and then it dawned on him that there was a lot more table-top real estate available since all the knickknacks had been smashed or otherwise cleared away in the earlier fracas. "Here you go!" Barney pushed the legal format sheaf toward Jason. Jason flinched, still gun shy from the aforesaid fracas. "Don't worry, I'm not going to hurt you, man." He never felt so badass in his life.

"I know you're not. I'm not afraid of you!"

"Well good. I was a little overwrought this morning. My apologies." Barney was actually enjoying being feared. That both pleased and worried him, but he let it go. "Now let's get back to the will. It says—"

"I know what it says. PK said he was going to write up the whole scheme and, yes, it was stipulated in the will that it should be shared with Muphrid, but I never found it."

Barney rubbed his soul patch. "Maybe you found it, but didn't want to let the cat out of the bag. I mean Muphrid hasn't a clue what's in those Beanie Babies. You've been profiting handsomely—by stiffing him. By the way, Hope says hi."

"Hope?" Jason's eyes popped wide open like he been zapped by a taser. "You talked to Hope!? What are you, some kinda snoop?"

"I'm a journalist, man. I talk to everybody."

"Well, stay away from her. Look, what do you want out of me, anyway, Mr. Starr?"

"Just Barney. You can call me Barney. Let's dispense with the formalities. We've come such a long way together, you and I."

"The fuck we have. Again, what do you want from me?"

"A story. I want to tell a story. Also...I have a bone to pick with you. You've been ripping off my friend Muphrid."

~ ~ ~

Milo found no parking along the boulevard so he went around to a quiet side street and slid in behind a Mini Cooper. When he got out, he saw that his vehicle's rear end was overlapping the red zone of a fire hydrant, so jumped back in and pulled forward till bumpers touched. But the Escalade was still overlapping the parking citation zone. So he shifted into first gear and slowly shoved the Mini Cooper a couple of feet forward, then backed up a foot. He winked at his image in the rearview mirror.

He felt around behind the driver's seat and gripped Jason's "equalizer," to wit, an aluminum baseball bat.

Walking back to the boulevard, slapping the bat into his open palm, children gave him wide berth and stared at him as he passed.

~ ~ ~

"Ripping off my friend Muphrid Thatcher? Is that what you call handing him thousand two-fifty bucks a month?"

Stella leaned on the desk and narrowed her eyes, "Those bags were worth a hundred times that much."

"I could have given him half of what I gave him and he'd still thank me!"

Barney sat back and said, "And why is that?" He paused. "I think it's because Muphrid hasn't a clue about the value of those collector's edition Beanie Babies. Now why is that? Why doesn't he have a clue?"

"Because he's a simpleton!"

"Wrong! Let me ask you the same question but this time I want an honest answer. Why doesn't Muphrid have a clue about the chips hidden inside those stuffed toys, chips that are far more valuable than the toys?"

Jason did not answer.

"Stella, maybe you can help the man with the answer."

She said, "I'd love to. Because Mr. Fliess did not inform Mr. Thatcher about the scheme, let alone..." She pulled the will toward herself and pointed to a specific clause, "...rewrite the partnership contract to include Mr. Thatcher as replacement for the deceased Mr. Sharma."

Jason squirmed.

~ ~ ~

Milo was getting irritated with the pedestrians who walked three abreast toward him without yielding to him, so he shoved the flanking wingman in the group so hard the three of them stumbled sideways onto a lawn. "Asshole!" is what he heard in triplicate as he marched determinedly ahead. But when he lifted the aluminum bat just a bit from his cupped hand and shot them a threatening backwards glance, they suddenly fell quiet and seemed very willing to put the incident behind them.

It wasn't much farther to the office complex where the Pinto was parked. He ran his hand up and down the shaft of his bat, eager to put it to work. The car would be a good warm-up for the main event, he thought to himself.

He stood for awhile, eyeing the car longingly, then he decided to skip the foreplay and focus on the job at hand.

~ ~ ~

"I'm no expert but that's legal malpractice I think, a dereliction of your fiduciary responsibility as PK's executor, isn't that right?"

Stella said, "Jason, I think you'd better get yerself a lawyer—oops! Silly me! You ARE a lawyer!"

Jason wordlessly assessed his position, glumly realizing that he was cornered; Barney was holding his law license hostage. For what in return? An expose? That wouldn't constitute a deal, offering a rock instead of hard place. What did this reporter want?

"What do you want from me?"

"Look, Jason, I'll tell you what I want. It's not punitive—though I think you are a rat for stiffing Muphrid. I could publish now and get you disbarred or at least have your license suspended. No, I just want you to do your job. With or without PK's write-up, you need to include Muphrid as your partner, share your chip profits—and pay him back for his share of past profits."

"Oh come on, gimme a break! I'm not going to do that! This was me and PK all the way. We worked out the details of the scheme, I did all the legwork. I got the jewel cases made for the chips. See those boxes?" He pointed to the stack of cardboard boxes by the wall. "Hundreds of specially made jewel cases. I packaged the chips in them and mailed them off to buyers. I managed the books, distributed the proceeds. PK played the market like a violin and kept the money rolling in. He was a virtuoso and I was his accompanist. Muphrid doesn't know his ass from a hole in the ground. He doesn't deserve the benefits of the wealth machine that PK and I created."

"But PK must have had a different opinion, otherwise why would he have stipulated that Muphrid take his place in your partnership and share the wealth equally with you?"

"Beats the hell out of me." Jason spit the words out. "This whole scheme—er, business plan—has depended on acumen and discretion and, sorry if this is an unkind thing to say but...it requires a modicum of intelligence. I was afraid Muphrid would bungle the whole thing and kill the goose that lays the golden eggs."

"Or the ram that wears the Goldman Fliess—I mean golden fleece!" Barney couldn't help himself.

Jason rolled his eyes. "Yeah, yeah, yeah, old joke. Just tell me what you want."

"I have told you," Barney said.

"And I'm telling you it's not reasonable to give away the store to a half-wit, regardless of what PK said."

Stella interjected, "Jason, I'm sick of you insulting Muphrid! Muphrid is a fine and decent man. And he's not stupid, regardless of what you think. Anyway, the whole thing about sharing the chips is not your call. PK said to share the business with Muphrid whether you like it or not."

"You're legally bound," Barney added. "And I have a damning story to report unless you make good. You won't have to worry about scheduling any more clients if that story comes out."

"Are you threatening me? This is extortion."

"No sir, it's justice."

Jason sighed. "All right. But how do I know you aren't going to publish the story anyway?"

"What choice do you have? Certain disbarment versus my assurance not to embarrass you."

Jason sighed again. "All right. I'll make good, so—"

"When?" Barney interjected, then answered his own question. "You have one week, buster."

Jason sighed yet again. "All right. One week. Are we done here?"

"Not quite. I want you to tell me where PK's write-up of his marvelous scheme is. You do have it, don't you?"

"No. He was going to mail it to me before he left for India, but never did. Even if I had it, I wouldn't share it with you, it's confidential," Jason said. That much was true.

Something stirred in Barney's brain. Mail. Envelopes. The envelope that PK used to bookmark the story about Tulip Mania. Could that be—?

Barney whispered into Stella's ear, then turned to the attorney.

"Jason, we gotta go."

Just then Stella looked up and screamed, "Holy crap!"

It was Milo. More precisely stated, it was the big balding goateed head of Milo framed in the glass door above the "Open" sign that said "Closed" on their side.

The door swung open and there stood Milo, bat in hand, grinning maniacally. "Heeere's Milo!"

Jason yelled, "No Milo! No! Put that thing down! We're OK here. Jesuschrist, what's the matter with you!?"

"Sorry boss, I thought you needed protection."

"Not any more. We've worked things out." Jason closed his eyes and pinched the bridge of his nose. Then he opened his eyes and said, "Milo, get me the Edgerton file." He turned to the pair and explained, "Sorry, I actually do have a client coming in soon, so if we're done here…"

"Sure." The two stood up. As Milo moved to the file cabinets Barney marveled, *sotto voce*, "You called me a thug earlier—you've got a personal thug that could grind me into dust!"

"He's been a big help with difficult clients."

"Kind of overkill wouldn't you say?"

Jason leveled with his interlocutors. "I might be a bit on the paranoid side. I was bullied in school. Ended up withdrawing into books and the debate club. And then I discovered the power of the law, the idea that if I mastered rules backed by force—" he looked at Milo coming back with a fat manila folder, which he flopped on the desk, "I could defeat the worst bullies."

Barney looked at the towering young man. "Then why do you need a bodyguard?"

"For difficult clients, as I said. Anyway, Milo is more than just that.

213

He's my office manager and general factotum. While he's going to school."

"School?"

Milo spoke, "Yeah, Linfield College."

"What are you studying?"

"Law. I want to be a prosecutor!"

"I figured as much."

"A career in law. Like uncle like nephew!" Jason said.

"Milo's your nephew?" Stella studied the 6'4" maybe 280-pound sleek headed Milo and then examined the diminutive Jason. "Seriously?"

"Yeah, my sister married a U of O linebacker. As I like to say, that union doubled the biomass of my entire family."

There was a pregnant silence, then Barney burst out laughing. Then Stella began chuckling. Jason started giggling. Milo caught the laughter bug too. Soon all four were convulsed with laughter.

When the mirth played itself out, Milo leaned on the desk and offered the others some coffee. "Or I can get you an espresso from next door."

"No thanks," Barney said. "We were just leaving."

"One for the road then?"

"Oh...sure."

"None for me," Stella said. "I'm good."

As Milo poured, he looked up solicitously. "Room for cream?"

Barney shook his head. "Just black, thanks."

Milo handed Barney the lidded cup then ran and held the door for the couple.

"Oh—just one other thing, Barney," Jason said.

"Hm?"

"Not to end on a sour note but I'm sending you a bill for the damage around here."

"Fair enough. But you don't have my address."

"I'll send it to Stella. You're—er—residing there at the moment, yeah?"

"Uh, yeeeeah...how did you know?"

"Oh come on, Barney. Everyone knows about you two. It's a small town, after all."

= CHAPTER 20 =

~ ~ ~

On the way back to town, the peripatetic reporter strayed not far beyond the speed limit—in spite of his eagerness to examine the envelope tucked into PK's book. The farmland rolled by on either side of the highway. Soon there appeared a sign for a turnoff to go see the valley's largest glacial erratic rock. Normally, Barney would have taken the detour but this afternoon he sped past it.

Near Sheridan, the turnoff to Sweetbread appeared. That turnoff he took.

~ ~ ~

Climbing the gentle hill into Sweetbread, Stella's cell phone sounded its ringtone.

"Yeah?"

Barney glanced over at Stella who was listening intently to the voice at the other end.

"Sure. I'll tell him," she said. "Yeah, no, ten a.m.'s fine. Hang on, I'll ask him." She covered the cell phone microphone with her thumb. "Deena's had a change of heart. I thought Deena was gonna have your guts for garters, but she wants you to come to the taping of her show tomorrow morning."

"You've got to be kidding me!"

"Not kidding. She said she's turned over a new leaf because of your article, wants you to cover her show when she announces her new line of healthy desserts."

"Healthy desserts? You can't be serious!"

"Serious as train wreck."

Barney downshifted. "I believe you're serious, I just don't know how serious she is."

"We'll find out, huh?"

"Sure. Why not? But tell her I'm not working for the *Portland Mirror* anymore. You know, 'cause I got fired because of her."

She uncovered the microphone hole. "He says fine. But he doesn't work for the *Portland Mirror* anymore." After a pause, she turned to Barney. "She says she'll talk to them."

He jutted his lower lip and nodded. "OK. If she can sweet talk them into giving me back my job—"

"He says OK...ten o'clock sharp?...Yep, he'll be there...Fine. Bye!"

"Wait—what if they don't hire me back?"

"You'll still get do your article. Sell it to *Willamette Week* or something."

He nodded, "Sounds like a plan. You're the best, Stella."

Here came the town entrance sign. "Welcome to Sweetbread. The place that feels like nowhere—"

~ ~ ~

Barney parked in Stella's driveway and they walked across Main to Muphrid's front door. No one answered. They opened the yard gate but there was no sign of the barber anywhere to be seen among the mounds.

"He must be at the shop," Stella suggested.

"Or with his mother."

They walked up Main, past Jeremy's, over the bridge to Hayes Street where the Yamhill Barber plied his trade.

Inside, Muphrid was just finishing up with a customer, whipping the man's apron off like it was a matador's cape. The customer was a portly man with a thick salt and pepper mustache. He handed Muphrid a twenty, told him to keep the change, then went over to one of the waiting chairs and sat down again. He pulled up a pant leg, produced a syringe, saying to the curious others, "Insulin. Gettin' prepped. My wife has one of Deena's treats waiting for me when I get home!" He proceeded to inject himself in the thigh. "Go on folks, don't mind me, I'll be outta here in no time."

As the man withdrew the needle, Muphrid said, "That's Mr. Rolfson. He's one of my best customers."

Mr. Rolfson gave an "ah shucks" wave with his syringe-bearing hand. "Muphrid's the best barber in Yamhill County."

After a couple more exchanges of pleasantries, the mutual admiration spent itself and Muphrid asked, "What brings you good folks to my shop? Need a shave, Barney?"

"No, no thank you."

"Another hair cut?"

"No."

"How 'bout you, Stella?"

"No thanks, Muphrid. We're here 'cause we didn't find you at home."

Barney explained, "Remember that book we were looking at?"

Muphrid nodded. "Yep."

"Can we see that again?"

Muphrid blinked twice, rocked on his feet and shifted into the weird singsong that he used whenever he was uncomfortable. "Nooooo? I'm afraid not."

"Why not?"

"I don't have it anymore?"

"What!? What do you mean you don't have it anymore?"

The barber hung Mr. Rolfson's apron over the back of the barber chair. "I gave all o' PK's books away this morning."

Stella and Barney froze. Barney's eyes fairly bugged out. He exclaimed, "Why'd you that!?"

"Mrs. Ordonne—Astrid, you know? I told her about the book you was lookin' at and the Tulip Mania thing and she ast me if she could borrow it. I said she could have that an all the others too. Never looked at PK's books muhself. I don't look at books much anyways. An' I needed the space. It's funny, ya know—hm?" The two were already out the door.

Mr. Rolfson looked at Muphrid, "In a big hurry those two!"

"Ever-body's in a hurry these days, it seems."

~ ~ ~

Barney and Stella made a dash for "ANY OLD THING Antiques & Collectibles."

The sign on the door said, "Back in 10 minutes." Stella rattled the handle, but it was locked.

"Hey, there she is!" Through the glass, Barney saw Astrid coming out to unlock the door.

Once Barney and Stella were inside, the gray lady ambled back to her desk with the couple following close behind. There was a box of books on the floor nearby. Barney seized *Popular Delusions* and held it aloft.

"Is the envelope still in there?" Stella asked anxiously.

"Hmmm...yep!"

Astrid looked on with great curiosity. "What's this all about?" she asked.

Stella explained the whole thing while Barney ripped open the unaddressed blank envelope with his car key. He pulled out a neatly folded single sheet of paper, printed on both sides.

~ ~ ~

The watermark indicated that it was a copy of the original.

"Look at this!" Barney pointed to official stamps and signatures. It was notarized...by Jason G. Fliess himself.

"So Fliess lied about not having it!" Stella said.

"That appears to be the case."

Astrid Ordonne stood by, transfixed.

"It's a detailed explanation of PK's money-making scheme. What he was up to while he was living here. And presumably what his attorney has been carrying on ever since PK died." Barney shook out the folds and prepared to read it out loud.

Stella frowned with caution. "Wait a sec' Barney—isn't this supposed to be confidential? I mean are we going to get in trouble if we read it?"

"No, it was left to be found. It's fair game."

The two women shrugged and indicated they were ready for a reading.

Here's what it said:

~ ~ ~

My Most Marvelous Retirement Annuity Scheme
(Revision #4)

My name is Prashant Kumar ("PK") Sharma. If you are reading this, I am probably dead or incapacitated. So I won't care if you come to know about my marvelous money making scheme.

I retired from Intel a few years ago. I was test engineer at one of their semiconductor fabrication plants (which they call "fabs"). When a silicon wafer containing hundreds of chips (which they call "dice") is ready, it undergoes wafer testing. Defective chips are marked with ink for rejection and discarded. The job was tedious and I daydreamed about retirement. I was on the lookout for schemes to retire early with as much money as possible.

One day I came upon a book by Mr. Charles Mackay called Memoirs of

Extraordinary Popular Delusions and the Madness of Crowds. *Some of the stories concerned speculative bubbles. The one especially I liked was about Tulip Mania. In the 1630s, there was a bidding frenzy for prized tulips in Holland. People went mad and spent very, very large sums of money for certain tulip bulbs.*

If I could get in early on a speculative bubble then exit before it collapsed, I could acquire very, very much wealth and live a very comfortable retirement and travel to Delhi to visit my family as often I wanted. That's when I hit upon my marvelous scheme. It occurred to me that I already had all the ingredients I needed to create my own bubble!

When IBM decided in the early 1980s to use the 8088 processor chip in its historic first PC computers, I decided to keep the discards, hoping they would become valuable someday. I sneaked them out of the fab in stuffed animals called Beanie Babies. My colleagues thought I was an odd duck carrying stuffed animals around, but no one suspected I was smuggling defective 8088 computer chips out of the fab. It was a little scary. If I got caught I would not only get fired, but I might get sent to jail for industrial espionage.

When I got close to retirement, my prediction came true. The first IBM PCs and even the 8088 computer chips that powered them could be found in computer museums because they were historic and rare. But what was both historic and most rare of all was defective 8088 chips, the ones marked with ink for disposal. As far as I knew, I was the only one in the world who had these defective 8088 chips. But no one would care to own one unless there was perceived value. How could that come to happen? Somehow, there had to be a spark to light the fire of a bidding frenzy, like in Mr. Mackay's book.

And that's when I came up with a devious two-phase plan to start my bubble!

Phase I was what I called "ownership." Psychologists say that exclusive own-ership of something makes others covetous and increases the thing's perceived value. But there has to be some interest to start with. Thus, the first phase would begin with advertising...

I contacted my attorney and friend, Jason Fliess. I told him all about my scheme. We worked out a partnership deal to share profits. Jason photographed a jewel case with a chip in it on a piece of blue velvet. We used that for an ad in Collector's Digest and he wrote the text of the ad explaining how rare and historical and valuable these chips were.

The two of us started tweeting about these chips and I started a blog extolling the amazing value of such historical artifacts.

At the same time, I opened an account on the auction website HotAuctions.

The Yamhill Barber

My account was Ashram Papakilo. Perhaps you can figure out how I came up with that name! Then I applied for nine credit cards and opened nine more HotAuctions accounts with names like DelhiDude and AntiquesCowboy and so forth. I needed all those accounts to light the fuse. Using Ashram_Papakilo, I auctioned the first chip for $200. Then I used several of my other accounts to bid the price up to $580. (Although it was a bidding competition between DelhiDude and AntiquesCowboy, I was selling to myself, so I could set whatever price I chose and not lose any money.) I did this again and again with different chips. One day, a stranger joined the bidding, someone called CuteCatVideo. I used my accounts to compete with CuteCatVideo, but when he (or she) reached $837, I bailed out. I had sold my first chip! Jason arranged for shipping. We were both very excited.

One day, I came up with an even more devious technique. These were timed auctions, which means there was a time limit that cut off bidding. There is a thing called sniping. At the very last second of a timed auction, a "sniper" will be waiting with a slightly higher bid and will hit the Enter key a split second before the auction closes, thus shutting out the competition. That day, I got CuteCatVideo in a bidding war and waited until the last second to pounce like a Bengal tiger and deprive him/her of their chip. I did this to a few others. I knew it made them mad and even more determined not to lose out next time. But I made them wait. After waiting a week, I auctioned a chip with an early date—1981, which is the year the first PC came out—so it was highly desirable. CuteCatVideo and some of the others I'd sniped out of their prizes were all there. The bidding went crazy, nobody wanted to get sniped out of their prize and the price surpassed $1500. I was very much excited!

I invited Jason to my house and we celebrated with a bottle of champagne. This marked the beginning of Phase II, which I call "speculation." People were now buying chips not to own for their own sake, but to resell at higher prices. They even took out ads to tout the historic value of their 8088 chips. Prices inflated very very fast and I sold my chips at ridiculously high prices. The bubble had formed and I was making more money than ever!

Prices for the defective chips continued to climb over time. When I took early retirement, I moved to the small wine country town of Sweetbread, Oregon where I rented a house from the town barber, a nice man named Muphrid Thatcher. Now I had lots of time to sit back and watch the almost daily bidding that flared like bonfires. Prices were rising quickly, so even Jason got in on the action, using the handle, MiddleMonths. See if you can figure out how he came up with that name! He bought and sold frequently and, since that was not covered in our contract, he kept 100% of those profits. But the marginal increase in price was very less compared to the amount I took in when I sold one of my chips, because I acquired them for nothing. (In accounting terms, my basis was zero.) Jason of course got 20% of my take each time.

Since then, I have become grossly overweight and my health is in serious decline, mostly because of my consumption of Deena Poole's delightful desserts. So I asked Jason to draw up a will for me. My will stipulates that upon my death, half my inventory of Beanie Babies should go to Jason and the other half to my renter Muphrid, who has been a good and kind friend to me.

Meanwhile, the 8088 chip bubble continues to inflate. I am profiting handsomely and without any risk, since I paid nothing for my inventory. If and when the bubble collapses I lose nothing. However—and this is key—the law of supply and demand says that it is important for me to limit the supply to a trickle if I want to keep the demand (and prices) high. There is an art to this and I am learning by trial and error. I hope Jason will stick to this plan after I am dead.

So far, though, so good!

~ ~ ~

Astrid and Stella looked at each other and then both looked at Barney.

"I've got my story!" he said.

"But you promised Jason you wouldn't publish the story."

"That's when I didn't know he was lying to me. All bets are off now."

Upon request, Astrid made a photocopy of PK's "manifesto" and the duo set out for home—Stella's home that is.

~ ~ ~

A breeze sent autumn leaves scuttling across the sidewalk as they passed Deena's manse. Across the street Armand Ordonne was scaling his A-frame ladder into the under-branches of his maple tree, leaf vacuumer in hand.

Near the top of the ladder, he squared his feet securely on the second treadle down and pressed his knees firmly against the upper treadle. He hadn't been up there since that fateful day with the dog and the little hooligans. The memory was fresh in mind and he visually chose which branch he'd cling to if there were another mishap. He took a breath and flipped the power switch.

Alas, the machine was still in blower mode and Armand was instantly propelled sideways, arcing with the toppling ladder like the arm of a metronome. A moment later, he was dangling from the maple branch, cursing a blue streak at the kids who were not present to witness their handiwork.

"Help!"

Running across Main, Stella grabbed the ladder and brought it upright under Armand's flailing feet. Barney braced it while the man found a treadle with his toes and returned his weight to the ladder. He looked down and assured himself that his platform was stable, looked near and far for the presence of children, then released his rescue branches and climbed down.

"Thanks, you two. Those damn kids!"

Stella handed him his blower, "Here ya go. C'mon, Armand, take it. Ya gotta get back in the saddle, ya know."

He took the device charily as if it were an angry ferret or an irritable snake. He looked at the mode switch and flipped it to "vacuum," took another breath and flipped on the power switch. It was sucking not blowing. He exhaled. He looked importunately at Barney who still had the ladder in his grip.

"OK, Armand, I'll hold on."

"Thanks, Barney."

After vacuuming the loose leaves off this tree, Armand came down, thanked them again and said he was going back to something safer—his stamp collection.

~ ~ ~

"Make yourself comfy, Bernardo," Stella said as the couple entered her living room. "And write your story while I rustle up some grub."

Barney opened his laptop, laid the manifesto on the coffee table and prepared to set to work when he abruptly stopped.

"What is it, babe?"

"I gotta let Jason know."

"Why?"

"I don't know, just seems like the right thing to do. Let him know he blew it by lying to me." He pulled out his cell phone and found Fliess' number in his call log.

After niceties, Barney told the mendacious attorney that he was going to submit the story after all.

Fliess remonstrated, "You've no idea the damage you're going to do."

Barney's response: "You don't know that, Jason. My experience is that we humans are terrible at predicting the future, especially when we're scared."

"Look, it's been working to everyone's benefit so far, why screw it up?"

"Because of the law. Remember what you said about mastering the rules? You didn't say manipulating the rules, you said mastering them."

"But this has helped people, not just me."

"Maybe they were helped less than they would have been otherwise." Barney wanted to wrap this up and get to work, so he concluded with a self-protective lie of his own: "Listen, Jason, I've already submitted the story, so my calling you is just a courtesy to let you know that this story will soon be a news item."

"This is going to ruin me! The chip market will collapse."

"Come on, you've already made a bundle and you've still got your lucrative law practice."

Now it was time to bargain. "Look, Barney, if you hold the article, I'll cut Muphrid fifty-fifty, make him an equal partner, share the scheme with him, if he's capable of understanding it."

"Too late, Jason. You lied to me, why should I trust you now? Anyway, I can't recall the article now, it's already out. And now you have no choice but to cut Muphrid in, if you want to keep your license."

Jason Fliess groaned and hung up.

Stella looked her question at Barney.

"It went as well as could be expected. Now I've got to write the story I've supposedly already published!"

Here is what Barney plinked out on his laptop:

~ ~ ~

TULIPS AND COMPUTER CHIPS: A tale of genius and greed
First in a three-part series
By Barnard Starr

Lanky and pale, Muphrid Thatcher surveys the mounds in the yard of his rural Oregon home. The peculiar decision to keep a straight razor tucked into his overalls speaks to his metier: he is a barber—indeed, the sole barber—in the quaint Yamhill County town of Sweetbread. As for the mounds in his yard, they contain not bodies, as one might surmise upon viewing the Beanie Baby plush toy hanging from his belt adjacent to the razor—a pairing that suggests some form of derangement in a grown man. No, Muphrid Thatcher is a kind, gentle soul. And no, the mounds do not contain bodies. Concealed within them, reposing quietly under the lush grass, is gold. Virtual gold, that is.

To understand the nature of the gold hidden in the mounds, one must begin with the story of a brilliant but reclusive Indian computer test engineer from Delhi who rented Thatcher's house in the early 2000s. During his residence in Sweetbread, the man, who went by the name of PK Sharma, put into operation a cunningly clever get-rich scheme modeled on the 1630s speculative bubble in Holland known as Tulip Mania. More on Tulip Mania shortly...

It concluded as follows:

Fliess and Sharma were, in effect, the OPEC of antique computer chips. For a number of years, they kept the heat on by artfully manipulating the supply and demand.

We will explore this intriguing phase in the next installment.

After dinner he read it to Stella, made some corrections and submitted it to *Willamette Week*. They jumped on it.

~ ~ ~

She cooed and moaned and said, "You're gonna win the Pulitzer Prize, Barney, I just know it."

Then she said, "Wanna hear something funny?"

"Sure."

"When I was a little girl, we raised chickens and of course there were always a few pullets."

"Pullets? What are pullets? I'm sorry, I'm just a dumb college boy."

She pinched him. "Can it with the false modesty, Bernardo. Pullets are young chickens. So I thought it was funny how everybody got so excited when someone won the Pullet Surprise!"

A tiny smile crept into the corner of Barney's mouth.

"Get it? Pullet Surprise? You don't think that's funny?"

A big laugh welled up and burst forth. "Ahahahaha! Very funny! Ahahaha!"

"OK, don't overdo it! Let's move on to more important things..."

"Like?"

"Like you and me, my sweet Bernardo!"

= CHAPTER 21 =

~ ~ ~

Barney's cell phone woke him long before he was ready to be awoken. It took a while for his sleep-muddled brain to make sense of the ringtone.

"Hello?"

Beside him, Stella opened one eye.

"Yeah, this is Barney Starr...uh-huh...hmm...uh-huh..."

Stella got up on one elbow.

"You're kidding me, right?" Barney sat up, wide awake. "You want to—? Whoa, give me a minute to process this...uh-huh...yeah...sure, I suppose."

Stella questioned Barney with open hands, mouthing the words, "Who is it?"

He covered the cell phone's microphone hole and said, "It's the *Portland Mirror*. They want me back to cover Deena's show."

"Hooray! I guess Deena's sweet talk did the trick!"

He abruptly uncovered the cell phone and said into it quickly, "Yeah, I'm still here. Sure, but I'm not gonna do a fluff piece...uh-huh...it's entirely my decision?...uh-huh...just attend the taping, no obligation, huh? I can decide after? Sure, I guess that'll work...OK...yeah, you too. Bye!"

Stella nearly jumped on him. "Tell me!"

He explained that his last piece in the *Portland Mirror* pricked Deena's conscience. She didn't want to be famous for making Americans sick. From now on, she would make all her desserts with non-nutritive sweeteners and healthy oil for the deep frying. She wanted Barney to cover the story, since he was the inspiration for her transformation. He should come

225

to the taping at her home at 10 a.m. and be prepared to interview her directly afterward.

All this of course required the *Portland Mirror* to put him back on the payroll. As it turned out, his editor saw last night's article about chip mania and was highly impressed, impressed enough to hire the aspiring investigative reporter back even if Deena had not called for his reinstatement.

Things were looking up!

And yet Barney was ambivalent about the Deena story. He couldn't put his finger on it, but something didn't sit right with him.

Oh well, 10 o'clock he'd be there, rain or shine.

~ ~ ~

As it turned out, the weather gods were smiling the next morning. The air was clear and a bit on the cool side, but the brilliant sun felt warm on the back. Unswept autumn leaves illuminated the sidewalks in yellows and magentas. They colored Deena's front lawn, making her gaudy candy-themed garden even gaudier. Film crews were already on site. At the curb was parked a large windowless truck with its big roof-mounted mast antenna extended full length like a stanchion to the sky, a cable coiled helically around it from top to bottom. A generator inside the truck hummed away, supplying juice through a fat cable that ran up the entrance path, up the porch stairs, through an ajar front door into the living room and thence into the kitchen.

Inside, there were bright lights set up in the living room and kitchen. The makeup artist was dusting Deena's face with a powder puff while the sound engineer adjusted the microphone boom. A nervous balding man ran around with a clipboard and kept checking his watch, chirping out orders in a high voice. At one point he reverted to hand signals, starting with a finger to the lips, for off to the side, the cameraman was filming a short intro segment with the show's host, a smartly dressed middle aged woman with a trim figure and an effulgent smile.

Stella tapped Barney on the shoulder, whispering reverentially, "I think that's Shawna Spiegelman!"

Barney tapped a rigger on the shoulder. "Is that Shawna Spiegelman?"

"Yep."

"Cool!"

Shawna's smile neither flickered nor faltered as she attempted to speak to the camera while fending off the locals. Jeremy Gervais got in on the action, boasting that Sweetbread—the town whose mayor he was!—was not only home to Deena Poole but other attractions such as Vindemiatrix winery and the good food at the Rock Creek Roadhouse and tourist friendly businesses such as the Glassworks up on Buchanan Avenue. Ray and Reggie interposed plugs for their respective hardware and grocery stores. Shawna thanked them all profusely, complimented "the town that feels like nowhere else" and deftly turned the viewers' attention away from the eager boys back to the plush Victorian decor and Deena the Diva who was ready to take center stage.

"Good morning Deena!" Shawna said as she sat down opposite Deena on the big wingback sofa.

Deena nodded graciously. "Thank you for coming, Shawna."

"It is my pleasure, as always. Now let's get down to business, shall we? As I understand it, you have something special in store for us today."

Deena smiled. "Yes, I do indeed!"

"Your loyal viewers and dessert devotees—including myself!—have been anticipating the unveiling of a mystery dessert but evidently that's off the table now in favor of a surprise announcement."

"That's so, Shawna. I am about enjoyment, but I'm all about healthy living, so I am blazing a new trail with this surprise dessert. Barney Starr pricked my conscience with his article in the *Portland Mirror* and I have turned over a new leaf—literally. My friends at AgriCorp have engineered a super-duper Roundup Ready stevia plant whose leaves are twice as sweet as regular stevia! Without the calories! But let's head to the kitchen where I'll show you how it's done!"

The entire film crew tagged after Deena and Shawna as they traversed to the gleaming kitchen.

Once the film crew got set up again, Deena laid out the ingredients while speaking to the camera. "This is velvet cake, which I made last night. You can find the recipe for it on my website. I used my new stevia and punched it up with a half cup of an East Indian delight called jaggery. I learned about this sugar substitute from my late great friend PK Sharma who used to live just down the street from me. No calories, just sweet goodness!"

Barney typed this word into his cell phone. "Yep, just as I thought! Look at this, Stella, jaggery is just basically unrefined sugar."

She peered at his screen and frowned. "Hmm."

Meanwhile, Deena was busy putting the ingredients together.

"This is whole cream peppermint ice cream—whole cream is the rage among health aficionados these days, is what I hear. This I will put on top of the cake...like so ..." She scooped the cheery bright pink ice cream over the deep brown velvet cake. "And now we drizzle aspartame sweetened caramel, which I've kept on a low heat in this saucepan over here...again, no calories...like so..." She ladled the viscous golden liquid over the ice cream, "... with some chocolate sprinkles, just for fun. And now for the batter..." She used a wide spatula to slather her patented tempura batter all over her burgeoning creation. "And now I lower the whole melange into my Deena Poole Dessert Deep Fryer (R)...like...so..." The fryer had a mesh screen suspended above the oil to set the cake on. With the press of a button, the mesh slowly descended, dropping its delicious freight into the hot oil.

As the submerged batter sizzled, she explained that she decided to switch over to coconut oil. "Coconut oil used to be taboo because it's a saturated fat, but health aficionados tell me these days that it's actually a good fat. So...I'm gonna recommend coconut oil to all of you out there!"

Barney scratched his head and frowned. "I can't do this, Stella."

Stella looked concerned, whispering, "Why not?"

"She's either lying, ignorant or deluded."

"Then say that in your article."

He shook his head. "I'm not going to do that."

"So what *are* you going to do?"

He just shook his head.

After a minute or so, Deena pressed a button on her Deena Poole Dessert Deep Fryer (R), and her creation emerged from the oil. She slid it off the mesh onto a serving platter. She cut a piece and tasted it. "Mmmmmm! You're gonna love this!" That was her trademarked catch-line. She proceeded to cut pieces onto small plates and handed them out to the crew and the little audience. You could hear the oohs and aahs and yums.

While people were enjoying her morning dessert, she went to a side table, which had a large bottle of what appeared to be vitamin capsules. She held the bottle up for the camera to zoom in on. The label said "New!" and under that, "Deena Poole Miracle Fat Remover (R)."

She explained that she had already lost ten pounds taking these capsules—one after each meal.

"This Miracle Fat Remover (R) sends fat and toxic waste products out with every breath. Just three capsules a day and you breathe your fat away! If you're in a hurry to lose weight, just breath harder—take a brisk walk, do jumping jacks, jump on a treadmill, take a roll in the hay!" She winked. Then she held the bottle up next to her head and uttered her new catch-line: "You CAN have my cake and eat it too!"

Barney was speechless, shaking his head.

~ ~ ~

After the taping, Deena grabbed her cane and marched toward Barney. "Helll-o there my dear friend!"

She extended a handshake, which he warily accepted.

"You don't seem as enthused as I expected you'd be—what with my turning over a new leaf since your article came out!" She looked puzzled.

"Wellll..."

"I'm all about healthy enjoyment these days! I thought you'd be pleased," she said, sounding hurt.

"Yeah, that's what I wanted to talk to you about..."

She brightened up. "Exactly! Let's do our interview!"

He sighed, "I can't, Deena."

"You can't?"

"I mean, I won't."

"Why not?" There was a look of hurt in her eyes and a pleading in her voice.

He explained that he couldn't, in good conscience, simply shill for her when so much of her "new leaf" was just an updated version of the old leaf, that her surprise dessert was no healthier than her previous fare. She argued to the contrary, growing quite defensive, that the medical science he was basing his objections on was inconclusive and there was disagreement about what was healthy and what was dangerous.

"At the very least, I will tell all sides of the story, Deena."

She leaned in toward him and said in a confidential tone, "You know, Barney, the reason I wanted you to cover my show today was not only for my benefit. I felt bad that you'd lost your job because of me. I like you, in spite of the things you said in your article. You were just doing your job. I was hoping if I asked for you to interview me, that would get them to hire you back."

"Well, that they did. But, like you say, I have to do my job. All I'm saying is this. I like you and I don't want to write another article that will offend you, but that's exactly what I will write if I write anything at all. What I am telling you is this. Ask my editor to send someone else if what you want is a promotional interview. As for me, I'm recusing myself."

Deena leaned on her cane and pondered for a while. "Fair enough Barney. Can you contact your editor for me?"

"Sure. Before they fire me again."

"Oh, I don't think they will. I certainly hope not! Tell you what, I'll contact your editor and put a good word in for you. Hopefully they'll have other stories for you to cover."

"I would appreciate that."

So they parted amicably.

~ ~ ~

Stella hung on Barney's arm on the way out, kissing his cheek. "You're a good man, Barney."

"Thanks."

"A dope for passing up a big opportunity to get back into the news business. But a good man."

They walked back to Stella's house. The sky was bright blue and the air pleasantly cool. The fallen leaves fluttered away from their footsteps.

All at once, Barney's cell phone began vibrating in his pocket. It was his editor at the *Portland Mirror*.

"Heard you declined the interview—"

"Yeah, feel free to fire me again."

"Nothin' doin'. We have other plans for you."

His editor had read the story about PK Sharma's manufactured mania and was quite impressed.

"How did you see it so fast?"

His editor explained that the story had gone viral overnight. He saw it on Facebook and Twitter and WhatsApp. Everyone at the City Desk read it. And the execs. Now the *Portland Mirror* wanted rights to the series.

"It's too late, I am committed to *Willamette Week*."

"Let me handle that, Barney."

~ ~ ~

That afternoon, Stella got a text message from Jason Fliess: "What's your boyfriend's phone number?"

Moments after she responded, Barney answered his phone and the sad tale began as follows: "Nice going Barney, thanks a lot. Your story got around and the chip market has collapsed." He went on to describe how he was now sitting on an inventory of chips, jewel cases and packing materials that would never be used.

"Furthermore, the people at Play Haven are furious at me. I'm a pariah now. My neighbors, the ones who read your article—and that's almost everyone—look at me like a leper. Someone even keyed my car. Thanks a lot, asshole."

At that, Fliess hung up.

"What was that about?" Stella inquired.

Barney smiled ruefully. "My byline is becoming well known."

= CHAPTER 22 =

~ ~ ~

The next day was Friday, normally a quiet day, but today was not a normal day. From morning onward, a stream of cars trickled in, almost all of them disgorging gawkers and people asking for directions to Muphrid Thatcher's house. They wanted to see the mounds, they wanted to see the Beanie Babies and the chips. They wanted to meet The Barber.

After giving numerous tours of his yard, Muphrid finally stopped answering his doorbell.

To his dismay, people found easy access into his garden and he had to chase them out—but they wouldn't leave without an autograph from the famous Yamhill Barber.

As soon as he got the last visitor out of his yard, Muphrid put a lock on his gate.

He leaned backwards against the gate, pulled out his cell phone and called his reporter friend. "Barney, tell them to stop coming here, please!"

~ ~ ~

The weekend was even more intense. It was hard to find parking along Main Street.

Stella had her hands full waitressing at the Roadhouse. There was a line out the door for lunch. Inside, a clutch of tourists gathered around the countertop Beanie Baby.

"This must be one of 'em!" a woman said, grabbing it off the chef's counter.

A man took it from her and felt its buttocks. "Yep, there's a chip in there!" He turned to Stella as she was picking up an order. "How much do you want for the rabbit?"

"It's not for sale, pal," she said.

232

"I'll give you five hundred bucks."

"You'll have to talk to the owner." She turned to the man with the dyed black comb-over, pencil mustache and bolo tie. "Mel, this guy wants to buy our rabbit."

"Five hundred," the man announced.

Mel shook his head.

Another man in the group shouted, "Seven hundred. I'll give you seven hundred dollars for the bunny."

A woman at a nearby table stood up. "Seven fifty!"

Pretty soon, the whole restaurant erupting in chaotic bidding. Utensils and even bread plates got knocked to the floor in the commotion. People jumped up with ever higher bids for one of the storied plush toys with an actual 8088 chip inside (or so they surmised by the bump in its sewn-up sit-upon).

Eventually, a man with a cowboy hat in hand and expensive snake skin boots took the prize for fourteen hundred dollars.

People slammed down payment for their meals and rushed out the door, bound for Muphrid's home. They were dismayed to see a sign that said, "Please leave me alone." It didn't stop the doorbell from getting rung, just on that off chance he'd answer. But he didn't answer. They couldn't open the gate, but they could peek through the cracks between the boards.

Out of exasperation, Muphrid opened the door and dumped a basket full of Beanie Babies onto the porch. "Take 'em, folks, an' leave me in peace, OK?"

Men, women and children swooped down on the pile like vultures and picked the porch clean in moments. Those who were denied and had none bargained with those who had one. "Hundred bucks for your Beanie Baby."

"Forget it."

"Two hundred!"

And so it went.

Soon word got out that the barber was dispensing free Beanie Babies and a crowd formed. At this point, Officer Nancy showed up and dispersed the crowd. She put a yellow police ribbon across Muphrid's front entrance, strung it from a bush to the corner of the fence. Barney and Stella showed up just as Nancy was leaving. "You really started something here, Barney. Not sure I like the invasion, but the tourist business is booming."

~ ~ ~

Down in McMinnville, the people who'd read the first installment of "Tulips and Computer Chips" swarmed into Play Haven, offering to buy the disemboweled Beanie Babies. Even these vandalized specimens were valuable now, as they were part of the story. The money came pouring into the day care center for the piles of plush toys they had to offer. At one point, a middle-aged woman with a bouffant hair-do and Ralph Lauren purse offered the owner a wad of cash for the plush frog she saw on one of the kiddie tables. Before the cash could exchange hands, a little girl took the froggie. The owner—Hope—said to the woman, "How about another one; here's a cute moose."

The woman insisted on the frog or nothing.

The woman took the moose and presented it to her grade school adversary. "Here, little girl, here's a cute little moose instead."

The girl would have none of it, she wanted the frog too.

They were at loggerheads. The woman got into a tussle with the tike over the frog. The dispute had become physical. The matron got hold of the frog's legs and the hapless amphibian got pulled this way and that until the inevitable fate befell it: its legs tore off.

The woman and the girl stared at the pieces of the dismembered Beanie Baby frog. The woman said to Hope, "It's ruined. I don't want it anymore." She tossed the green legs at the girl's feet and walked away in a huff.

Picking up the legs, the girl said to Hope, "I'll take him home and ask my mom to sew his legs back on. Then I'll nurse him back to health. I think I'll name him 'Ow-ee', 'cause he got a big ow-ee!" Then the girl frowned. She opened her little change purse and counted the money. "I have one dollar and fifty-six cents. But my mom has lots more money, she can pay you."

Hope said, "If you can nurse Ow-ee the frog back to health, you can have the little guy for free, OK?"

The girl lit up. "Really!? OK! Thank you, Miss Play Haven!" She gave Hope a little girl hug and then ran off to tell her mom the good news.

~ ~ ~

Over at the business park, Jason Fliess' phone wouldn't stop ringing and emails flooded in. Everyone wanted one of the fabled chips. Milo was packaging chips as fast as he could for delivery and also for the drop-ins who paid on the spot.

It was a very busy weekend!

~ ~ ~

Monday rolled in and Barney got a call from his editor at the crack of dawn.

"I couldn't pry *Willamette Week* loose from the article, but we've had a new development that might interest you..."

Barney disentangled himself from Stella and sat up in bed with his back against the headboard. "Tell me."

For the longest time Stella watched Barney saying nothing. A little voice murmured from the phone, but she couldn't make out the words. He periodically nodded and smiled, "Mmhmm...mmhmm..."

Finally Barney spoke, "OK, deal," and hung up.

For a while he said nothing, just reflected. Finally, Stella could take it no more. "What!!?"

Over at the *Portland Mirror*, they were jealous of *Willamette Week* for scooping them on this big story about the Beanie Babies and chips. But no matter, there were other fish to fry.

"Remember, I told you about the CEO's daughter pilfering and cooking the books at the *Portland Mirror*?"

Stella nodded.

"Well father and daughter have been indicted."

"Really!"

"Yep. For embezzlement, breach of fiduciary responsibility to the shareholders, extortion even."

"Wow. Sounds like they're up shit creek, huh!"

"Without a paddle," he added.

She sat up next to Barney. He looked longingly at her breasts resting on the counterpane. She pulled up the sheet not exactly for modesty but to bring his attention back to what she had to say. "Too bad they wouldn't let you write that exposé."

He tilted his head. "I got to come to this town and meet you instead. I call that a bargain, the best I ever had!" he said, quoting the lyric from the Who song.

She blushed slightly. "I gotta agree with ya there, Bernardo. I'm sure happy with how that bargain worked out!"

"But there's more," he said.

"More?"

"Yep. I get to write the exposé after all! After the fact, but after all."

She blinked, trying to understand.

"They've been kicking themselves over losing out to *Willamette Week* over this chip story. Me doing the embezzlement story is sort of their consolation prize."

"But isn't it too late?"

"Heck no. I've already done all the research. I can get an in-depth story out before any of our competitors."

She chuckled. "Interesting thing."

"What?"

"You said, 'our'. You said, 'our competitors', didn't you?" She stroked his cheek, "You're back on board, arntchya?"

"Yes, I guess I am."

They caressed each other, the sheet fell away from her breasts and the morning was filled with delight.

~ ~ ~

Over the next few days, Barney hardly left Stella's house, furiously plinking away on his laptop, writing three stories simultaneously: The exposé of the newspaper CEO and daughter and parts two and three of the "Tulips and Computer Chips" series.

It was *not* hard to stay indoors, as the weather had turned cold and overcast with a sprinkling now and then. And, weather aside, the wine-and-lovemaking evenings provided the most compelling reason to stay in.

Occasionally though, when he needed a daytime break from his writing, he'd grab an umbrella and wander over to the offices of Jeremy "the Webster" to hang out with Stella then have lunch with her over at the Roadhouse. It was a fun break for her too and she especially enjoyed the experience of being waited *on*, instead of the other way around, for a change.

~ ~ ~

Meanwhile, Jason helped Muphrid get his life back. A sign out front announced:

PRIVATE RESIDENCE
Mound Tours by reservation only
Fri-Sun 10:00 am and 2:00 pm
For reservations or purchases:
jgflaw.com/beaniebabies

So Jason, as usual, handled the sales of chips and, for the first time,

Beanie Babies (with chips or torn tushes).

~ ~ ~

One day, there was a knock at the door. Barney set his laptop on the coffee table and walked to the front door, past the pile of automotive magazines still lying on the carpet. It was Stella's cousin, leaning on his cane. From the porch, the portly man called through the door, "Hey Barnaby, it's me, Jeremy!"

"Hey Jeremy! Come on in."

The mayor cum webster came in and sat on the sofa, laying his cane on the floor. "Hope this is an OK time?"

"Sure, why not?"

Jeremy huffed, swept his hands across his thighs and made ready to speak. "I want to extend, on behalf of the whole community, my sincerest thanks."

"Thanks? For?"

"For bringing new life to this town."

Barney laughed. "All I did was write a couple of articles!"

"Well—say, can I trouble you for a glass of water. Seems I'm thirsty all the time. Diabetes, ya know."

Barney filled two tumblers from the kitchen tap, set them on the coffee table and returned to his chair at the end of the table.

Jeremy resumed, "We've never had so much business before." He laughed, "It's almost more than we can handle!"

"Well, in all fairness and truth in advertising and so on, I've got to say that is a fortuitous by-product of my work. I wasn't trying to drum up business. In fact Jason—you know, Jason Fliess?"

"Yeah, I know Jason."

"Jason was furious at me for ruining his collector's chip business."

"Well, he's rakin' in the dough now like never before—and sharing with Muphrid. Muphrid in turn is sharing with the town. For instance, he gave Nancy the full amount for laser removal of that damn chinstrap tattoo of Kyle's."

"No kidding?"

"Yep. Grandpa Tom is sure happy. Told Kyle that he already saw some peach fuzz coming through so the boy wouldn't need the tattoo anymore."

Barney nodded approvingly.

"That's not all. With projected revenues for our businesses, our tax base is expected to rise. And guess what?"

"What?"

"According to projections that Stella worked out for me, we're going to have enough money in the budget to fix the railing and repaint our entry sign and start an after-school program to keep the kids out of trouble. That's the plan anyway, if business continues like this for a while. Keep writing your articles!"

"I'm just wrapping up Part 2, so that should go out in the next few days."

"Great!"

"No guarantees it's going to boost business."

"Hey good news, bad news, it's all the same. It puts us on the map."

"As Oscar Wilde said, 'The only thing worse than people talking about you—is people not talking about you!'"

Jeremy smiled. "But there's another dimension to this. You've brought people together, got 'em out of the doldrums. It's been pretty exciting around here since you arrived!"

"Well, that's not my doing. I just happened to be on the scene when things happened."

"Perhaps. But there is one thing that you can't deny."

"Hm?"

"I've never seen Stella so happy, at least not for a long time."

"Yeah, well, I don't want to raise expectations too high. I'm not sure where she and I go from here—"

Now Jeremy's expression darkened. "Don't hurt her. She loves you like crazy. I'm afraid you're gonna blow outta town and leave her behind brokenhearted, that you'll forget about her. This may be an enjoyable fling for you, but it's everything to her, you have to understand that. I will find it hard to forgive you if you leave her in tears. Understand?"

"Yes, I understand what you're saying. And no, this isn't just some fling. I feel—I think I love her too. All I know is I love being with her day and night. She's really an amazing woman, very smart and—"

"And a looker, cute as a kitten, hot as a tamale, I know. And that's coming from a cousin that remembers when she was in diapers!"

Barney blushed and his dimples appeared.

"Anyway, I know how these things go and if you two don't go the distance, let down her gently, OK?"

"Sure."

"'Cause she can be a hellcat if she thinks she's gotten the shaft and might rip yer eyes out—and I'll personally beat the shit of you!" Jeremy laughed and clapped an admonitory hand on Barney's shoulder.

Barney gulped. "Message received."

~ ~ ~

Barney pushed his way through the clots of tourists haggling over the chip-bearing Beanie Babies. In front of Vindemiatrix Winery, his pushing started the agitated group to jostling each other, which precipitated a round of fisticuffs. He ducked into the winery for cover. Robert Vandershur greeted him, smiling sardonically. "Looks like you really started something with your articles, Barney-boy!"

"This wasn't in my plan, you know."

"No, it's the Law of Unintended Consequences," the elder man said, adjusting his spectacles thoughtfully. "But you needn't be apologetic. The fiscal benefits to this town are considerable."

"That's what amazes me. I mean, Jason Fliess—"

"PK's attorney, yes?"

"Yes. Jason warned me that if I revealed PK's scheme to create himself a financial bubble, it would collapse the bubble. And that's exactly what happened."

Robert chuckled. "It's the cartoon character running off the edge of the cliff principle."

Barney thought about this for a moment. "Oh, right. Wile E. Coyote is fine running across thin air until he looks down, then—poof! Down he goes!"

"Yep." Vandershur poured a shallow glass of Pinot and offered it to Barney. When Barney accepted it, the patrician vintner poured a second glass for himself and motioned for the both of them to sit down at one of the cafe tables away from the window where you could see the restive crowd outside from a safe distance. "But then something unexpected happened, didn't it?"

"Yeah, everyone is jockeying—" Barney motioned with his eyes to the fracas outside, "—to outspend the next guy or gal for anything and everything I mentioned in my story."

Robert took a sip, then looking straight into Barney's eyes over the rim of the glass, asked socratically, "And why do think that is?"

"Because I made everything here famous."

"That's right. Your story imparted meaning to PK's chips, to the Beanie Babies—both the kinds with chips and those without—and who knows what else? The value of these things and the sky-high prices are based on meaning, not any kind of intrinsic value—except for maybe the plush toys. Anyhow, it was your tale of scheming and skullduggery and sleuthing and misadventures that created a rich lore that people are buying into."

While Robert paused to take a sip, Barney said, "Reminds me of when I visited London as a college student. I absolutely had to make the pilgrimage to 221B Baker Street."

"Sherlock Holmes' address, right?"

"Yep. And you know what I saw there?" He didn't wait for Robert's reply. "A dozen other pilgrims. At the address of a fictional character who never existed!"

"Except in people's imaginations. It's the power of storytelling!"

"Mm."

"So your story—or more precisely the story that you came upon—has fired up people's imaginations and created a demand for anything connected with it. Now, the other side of demand is supply. Supply is what levers the prices up or down. In this case, there are a lot of would-be collectors pouring into town but a limited number of artifacts. That has pushed prices up so fast it's making even my head spin. And even I"—at this Robert looked sheepish—"even I have bought into it. Behold!" He got up and opened a cabinet...full of Beanie Babies. He watched for Barney's reaction which was a pitying shake of the head. "Don't tell anyone, OK?" He laughed. "You may not realize it, but you have recapitulated PK's original scheme, but on a larger scale. This frenzy is feeding on itself, like a firestorm."

"Well it will probably burn itself out pretty soon."

"I don't think so, Barney. I don't see this abating any time soon. Especially if—well, I shouldn't suggest this, but—"

"But what!?"

"But if you were to write a series of articles about the mania itself, it would be like pouring gasoline on a fire." Robert leaned back with an impish grin. "It would make my new collection here ever so valuable. Think about it!"

Just then five people came in the door for a wine tasting.

"Looks like you have customers, Robert."

"I do indeed. Nice chatting with you. Remember my suggestion!" The older man got up and told the younger man to feel free to stay as long as he liked, then turned to greet his newcomers. "Welcome to Vindemiatrix Winery. My name is Robert Vandershur and—oh, look who just came out!—this is my wife Callista. On the red end of the spectrum we have a two-year-old Syrah and three different years of Pinot. As for whites, what whites are we showcasing today, Callie?"

Callista took the ball. "We have a Chardonnay and a Pinot Gris, both very good years."

Barney downed the rest of his Pinot and walked to the door. "Thanks, Robert for the wine...and the food for thought!" The bell over the door tinkled as he pulled it open. The crowd outside had evaporated. In its place was Al Gruber, who greeted Barney cheerily.

"Hey." Al caught Barney by the sleeve. "Guess what?"

"Hm?"

"I—" Gruber looked around furtively and noticed Stella stepping out of Jeremy's office down the street for some fresh air. When she saw Al and Barney, she leaned into the door to tell Jeremy she'd be back and then came walking over the bridge to where the two men stood talking. Al saw her approach so he lowered his voice and spoke quickly and confidentially to Barney. "I've hired your buddy, Jason Fliess, to represent me."

"Really! For what?"

Al glanced up to make sure Stella wasn't within earshot yet. "I'm suing the pants off that son-of-bitch, Bailey."

"I think you have a good case against him."

"Better believe it! Property damage, intimidation—"

"Hi Barney!" Stella called.

Barney waved to her, then said to Al, nearly whispering, "Of course, Dorgan could countersue for the BB you put in his ass—"

"I was defending my property, which he was trespassing on."

"What about his eye injury, he might come after you for that?"

"You gotta be kidding me!"

"No, there are stranger lawsuits, but on the other hand it would be hard to show negligence on your part. After all, he got hurt tearing down your porch."

Stella arrived and both men went silent. She took Barney by the arm and pecked a kiss on his cheek. Al observed this with an embarrassed grin. "What's the secret?" she asked.

"Huh?"

"You both got real quiet all of a sudden."

"Al's hiring Jason to sue Dorgan for damages." Barney looked at Al who was none too pleased to have his story publicized without his permission.

Stella said, "Is that true?"

Al nodded.

"I hope you take that bastard to the cleaners!" She added, "By the way, nice work with the BB gun. You just may've saved Barney's life." She gave Al a hug. He stiffly returned the hug.

"I was just trying to get him off my lawn, that's all."

"Well, I'll be forever grateful to you, Al. In fact, I want to settle up the score with you and make things right."

Al stepped away from the winery door to allow another group of tourists entrance. "What do you have in mind?"

"I want to replace those koi fish I took," she said. "And ate."

He waved her off. "Don't worry about it. Dorgan mashed my last koi with his truck, but I'll say he killed 'em all. I'll make him pay for everything."

Stella would have none of it. "I'm gonna replace the koi I took, I wanna do it. It's my way of thanking you for saving Barney, so don't say no."

Al Gruber shrugged and looked helplessly at Barney. "There's no use arguing with this woman. Guess you know that!"

= CHAPTER 23 =

~ ~ ~

The next day was Saturday. Stella was over at the roadhouse waitressing and that's when the call came in.

Barney's editor was disappointed that he'd declined the interview with Deena, but could understand. Wait—he "could understand"? Why was his editor suddenly so understanding!? Oh, the *Portland Mirror* wanted Barney to stay on for the other story, the real investigative piece, about the Mirror's crooked former CEO and his larcenous daughter. The editor wanted to meet with Barney as soon as possible. *Would this afternoon be all right?*

"Uh, sure, what time?"

The meeting would be at 3:30 at the office. Meanwhile, Barney should review his original, unpublished piece about the high-level malfeasance of the top executives at the *Portland Mirror*. Review and make notes for a possible update.

After the call, he texted Stella:

Gotta go back to Portland this aft.
Why?
Mtg w/editor.
When?
3:30. Lv here by 2 pm @ latest.
Wait 4 me!
How long?
Off work 1:30. Pls wait.
K

Barney rustled up some lunch and settled in with his laptop, reviewing his previously spurned investigative piece, now a hot item.

At 1:30, he packed his bag.

At 1:50 he began wondering what happened to his girlfriend, so he texted her.

R u coming?

Yes. Gimme 5 min

At 2:00 he grabbed his bag and started for the door when the door swung open.

~ ~ ~

Stella poked her head in. "Come outside, someone wants to see you."

Barney knitted his brow. "Who?"

"Just come out, you'll see."

He came out.

The whole town was out there. Maybe not the whole town, but almost everyone he knew was milling around on the front lawn, picking up plastic cups of wine from a card table Callista was manning. When they saw him emerge onto the porch, the people turned toward him like so many compass needles.

Barney blinked with incomprehension.

Mayor Jeremy lifted his cup, "To Barnab—To *Barney*, our star! You came to town with a bang—ha ha!—but proceeded to bring out the best in us. You saved a little girl's life. Your first article inspired Deena to turn over a new leaf. And your article about Chip Mania has brought tourist revenue into Sweetbread that is benefiting businesses here and will enable the town to move forward with long delayed projects, such as fixing that damn bridge railing!"

At this, Nadia muttered aloud, "I'll believe it when I see it."

With a discomfited frown followed by a sunshine smile, Jeremy concluded, "Yeah, well, um, you'll see it soon! Anyway, thank you Barney from all of us!"

Everyone touched cups together and murmured, "Hear hear!"

Stella was standing to the side, grinning from ear to ear.

After a long-bemused silence, Barney finally spoke. "I'm—I'm—overwhelmed. I don't know that I've done anything to deserve this, this, honor. But I am honored. Deeply." He walked to the card table with a few remaining half-filled wine cups and took one.

244

Stepping back a few paces so he could see everyone, he lifted his cup and said, "You're all stars, each and every one of you. This I know from personal experience. At one time or another, each of you rose to the occasion. What I've done wouldn't have been possible without your help and—" he looked at Stella, "—collaboration."

He looked down, collected his thoughts, then said, "Speaking of stars, there's a kind of stellar event that my dad taught me about when I was a boy called a nova. Unlike a supernova that explodes spectacularly once and for all, a nova does repeat performances. A nova happens when a star that simmers quietly most of the time every so often brightens and shines brilliantly when it needs to—then goes back to its normal life until the next time. That's what you folks are like."

One by one, Barney addressed the people there—Astrid and Armand, Ray and Reggie (after sorting out which was which), the members of the Chinstrap gang, Al, Jeremy, Nancy, Callista and Robert and their children, Mel and of course Deena.

Then he turned to the barber. "Muphrid, I really misjudged you at first, was actually afraid of you! But as I've come to know you, I've learned what a caring and decent man you are."

"Well, you're a nice man too, Barney. You're my friend."

Barney smiled warmly. "And I'll never forget how you caught and steadied me after I came out of that damn tree."

"Ohhh...the tree was your friend too, don't be mad at it. It was just being a tree."

Barney puzzled over how to respond, then said simply, "You're a sweet man, my friend."

And now it was Stella's turn. Barney turned to her. "And Stella. Stella, you've been—" but at that instant there came a commotion.

~ ~ ~

It was Dorgan Bailey, on foot, patch over his left eye, lurching ferociously toward Al Gruber. The crowd parted.

"Hey Gruber, you assfuck, I heard you're fixin' to sue me!" The words came slow and slurred.

Al Gruber momentarily went pale, then witnessed the most amazing thing. Rogerdog, with a patch on his left eye, went running toward the big man. Dorgan couldn't see the dog and the dog couldn't see Dorgan. Each was on the other's blind spot, so collision was all but inevitable. With an

"Uff!" Dorgan toppled over the dog and went down, hitting his temple on the curb. The dog ran away, unhurt, but Dorgan was not so fortunate. He lay in the gutter, dazed and bleeding.

At that moment the Bailey's Garage tow truck arrived with Zach at the wheel. The young man leaned out the window. "Mr. Bailey, are you all right? Your wife sent me in case you got in trouble. Are you OK?"

Dorgan looked up with a scowl. "What the fuck does it look like!?"

The big man attempted to get up but crumpled back to the ground. Undeterred, he managed to crawl on hands and knees to the truck. He tried to climb into the cab but kept tumbling back onto the ground. Zach jumped out, came around and sized up the situation. There was no way he could lift the man's 300-pound bulk into the cab, but he had an idea what to do. With a whirring sound, he lowered the T-bar until Dorgan could crawl onto it. Once on it, he rolled over into a seated position facing the rapt crowd. Zach raised the T-bar a couple of feet off the asphalt so Dorgan's feet could swing free, then he hopped into the cab.

"Wait for me!" It was Nadia. She leapt onto the running board, pulled the passenger door open and tumbled in. Zach revved the engine, made a U turn and headed back to the garage. As the truck drove off, Dorgan—sitting on the T-bar with his heels dragging on the asphalt—snarled at the gawking onlookers. "Whaddya all lookin' at!!?"

And then the truck was gone.

~ ~ ~

Barney held up his wine cup. "As I was saying,Stella, you've been so—"

He'd barely gotten the words out when Deena arrived, walking with her cane, a bakery box cradled in her free hand. "Before you go, Barney, I have something for you." Barney took the box from her. "Go ahead, open it." It was a slice of her original mystery dessert, the one she sidelined in favor of her "new leaf" healthy dessert. "There's a scoop of rocky road inside," she said, "that represents the rocky road we've come together, but the good news is we came together as friends after all. I'm on a better trajectory because of you."

Barney thanked her and carried the dessert to his Pinto in the driveway and placed it on the passenger seat. He went inside the house and returned with his laptop and toiletry kit and tossed them into the back seat. He looked at his watch and grimaced. He was running way late. So he waved to the group, "Gotta go!"

He motioned for Stella to come to him. Stella was instantly at his side, in tears.

He drew her close and kissed her, the throng oohed but he paid them no attention. "Come live with me, Stella," he whispered.

"Oh Barney, I—I—just—"

"Cold feet?"

"A little, I guess. I mean I love you and from the moment I met you. I've always wanted to—but it's such a big—I mean, suddenly I'm scared—I mean I need a little time to—"

Barney put his finger to her lips. "It's OK, Stella. Take your time. Think about it. I'll wait for you."

She smiled. "Thank you, Barney. It's just—"

"It's OK, really."

"I'll call you."

He nodded, started to say something more, thought the better of it and said softly, "OK."

Then he waved again to the townspeople, got into the car and pulled out onto Fillmore.

= CHAPTER 24 =

~ ~ ~

As he turned right onto Main and headed south out of town to Sheridan—the way he'd come in—Barney looked into his rear view mirror and saw that his Sweetbread friends had migrated to Main and were raising a toast to him. He waved and smiled and shook his head in wonderment.

Driving under a bright afternoon sun, he thought back on the false alarm concerning Muphrid and laughed, *I worry too much!*

With one hand he opened the box on the passenger seat and lifted a dessert slice to his mouth. "Mmm..." It was sweet, really sweet. Really, *really* sweet. The super-crystalline sugar continued exploding sweetness onto his tongue.

"Goodgod that's sweet!"

He decided to leave the rest for later.

While he was licking the sticky residue off his fingers, back at the pink Victorian mansion, Deena went into her kitchen, clapped her hand over her mouth and gasped.

The rest of the mystery dessert was on the floor, half-eaten. Nearby her little dog was lying on his back, paws in the air.

"Oh dear."

~ ~ ~

In front of Stella's house, the crowd wandered off until it was just her and Al Gruber.

Wiping away her tears, she said, "Before you go, Al? I have something for you. Wait here."

Stella ran inside and came back out with a large Ziploc bag full of

248

water—and a half dozen little orange fish.

"Just to show you that all is forgiven, I went to the pet store and got these baby koi to replace the one I skewered and served to my guests." She thought for a moment, then added, "And the ones Dorgan smashed with his truck."

She brought the bag to the edge of the koi pond and prepared to dump the fish in.

Al laughed. "You didn't need to do that. Anyway, those aren't koi."

"Sure they are, they're babies—koi babies!"

"No, Stella, those are guppies."

"No, Al, they're koi fry. Just wait, they'll grow up to be adult kois someday, just like the ones you had."

"Ohh-kay!" What else could he say? "Thank you."

Stella went back into her house and sat down, thinking. After a time, she sat up resolutely and marched over to her computer and began typing an email to Knocker:

Dear Joe,

I have decided that I'm done with you. I met this wonderful man, Barney Starr. He's a top reporter for the Portland Mirror. *And I have decided to move in with him at his place on Hamilton Street in Portland. So don't bother looking for me, because I will not be living at my old house any more. But I will rent it out, so you can live here after they release you next month. Don't worry, I'll give you a good rate. But you and me, we're over. You'll have to find someone else to be your punching bag. I'm not going to be that for you anymore. Barney's a good man, ten times the man you'll ever be! Even the street he lives on was a better president than any of those stupid president streets in Sweetbread! That's why that guy is on our money—got it? So it's me and Barney from now on—got it? And I'm not looking back. Goodbye Joe. It's over, Rover.*

Have a nice day,
Stella

~ ~ ~

Barney's cell phone played its "Stella message" tone. Keeping one eye on the road, he picked it up.

"Hi Stella!"

"Wait for me in Portland, I'm coming to live with you!"

Well, that was the super-crystalline icing on the cake!

Barney was smiling, smiling in spite of himself.

In light of circumstances, Barney Starr was smiling. Smiling broadly and unselfconsciously.

On this sparkling autumn day.

<<<<>>>

About the Author

Bruce Toien lives with his wife in Sherwood, Oregon. He has written stories and poetry since adolescence and has published two prior pieces: an analysis of T.S. Eliot's poetry in the *DeKalb Literary Journal* in the late 1970s and, more recently, a novel, *The Yamhill Barber*, which he illustrated. He has bachelors degrees from the University of California in English Literature and Physics. Like his wife, Gail, Bruce is an avid outdoorsman, enjoying running, cycling and nordic skiing. In 2004 he joined a Norwegian ski trek across Spitsbergen Island near the North Pole. In the process of learning Norwegian, he wrote two poems in that language, which he later translated into English and those appear in this volume. He is currently working on a new science fiction novel based on his Spitsbergen adventure called *Signatures in the Ice*. Bruce works in IT, currently at Kaiser Permanente, as a database architect and developer.

Made in the USA
Las Vegas, NV
04 February 2023

66854636R00152